FOR LAUREN G. AND LAUREN F.,
WHO GAVE ME THE CONFIDENCE
TO WRITE THIS BOOK

The Secret Bridesmaid

You are cordially invited to the wedding of

Harrison Oliver Hodges and Michelle Emily Ace

18 September 2021

IMP. BRIDESMAID NOTES

* VERY IMPORTANT: Harrison only allowed ONE beer before the service and ONE whiskey for courage before his speech. When drunk, has a tendency to
  - (a) ramble
  - (b) do the robot dance
  - (c) take off his shoes and swing them round his head by the laces

* VERY IMPORTANT: Michelle only allowed ONE glass of champagne before the service and ONE gin and tonic for courage before her speech. When drunk, has a tendency to
  - (a) slur
  - (b) burst into a spontaneous rap
  - (c) prank-call her boss pretending to be Kermit the Frog

* DON'T FORGET: To write down the bride's and groom's names for the vicar. During the rehearsal, he announced he was delighted to be joining the hands of Harriet and Michael

* DON'T FORGET: To politely remind the grandmother of the groom it's best not to loudly comment on the best man's "flat toosh" whenever he walks past
* DON'T FORGET: Keep Uncle Adrian away from Aunt Sacha AT ALL COSTS. Things haven't been the same since the last family wedding when she hit him over the head with the table plan
* DON'T FORGET: To check the alpacas are now wearing PINK bows for their photo shoot with the bride and groom, NOT APRICOT bows

"What's he doing?" Michelle wails, grabbing my hands. "He's ruining everything!"

I glance at the dance floor. Harrison is currently pouring the third bottle of whiskey all over it with one hand, while waving a plastic lighter in the other. His shoes have already been lassoed round his head and tossed to the side during Queen's "Don't Stop Me Now."

"I'M GONNA SET THIS DANCE FLOOR ALIGHT, BABY!" he declared through the DJ's microphone just moments ago.

Normally that would signal a series of fairly out-there dance moves—for example, the Worm. In this case, though, it would seem that Harrison intends *literally* to set the floor alight.

The crowd is delighted with this bizarre turn of events. The bride is not. Perhaps most surprisingly, the groom's eighty-four-year-old grandmother is in the front row, cheering him on with calls of "Light that dance floor up, Harrison! You light it up!"

I need to act fast.

I turn back to Michelle and look determinedly into her watery eyes. "Everything is going to be fine, Michelle. Now, I need you to do two things. First, I want you to remember that one of the things you love most about Harrison is his spontaneity, his adventurous spirit, and his willingness to take risks."

Her eyes dart wildly to her new husband, who is now leading a chant of "LIGHT IT UP! LIGHT IT UP!" as he continues to add to the growing pool of whiskey.

"Second, I need you to go over to the bar and order ten flaming sambuca shots. They need to be lined up on the bar but not lit until I say. Got it? Now go! Go!"

Lifting the skirt of her ivory lace wedding dress, she runs full pelt in the direction of the bar, weaving through the tables and almost knocking over her great-aunt, who is still tucking into the exquisite crème brûlée dessert, oblivious to the groom's antics.

I turn on my heel and hurry to join the DJ, snatching the microphone from him and bringing his repeated cries of "BRING ON THOSE DANCE-FLOOR FLAMES!" to a swift halt. He looks deeply offended until I shoot him my finely tuned disapproving stare.

"Sorry," he whispers. "I got carried away."

"I can see that, DJ Arnold." I seethe. "*I can see that.*"

He recoils and retreats behind me.

The groom has now finished pouring the whiskey. Holding the lighter aloft, he clicks it. Nothing happens. He's too drunk and it's too slippery. He keeps trying, his forehead furrowed in concentration. This is the moment I've been waiting for.

"Ladies and gentlemen," I say into the microphone, causing all heads to swivel in my direction, "please give it up for the bride, who is waiting at the bar for her new husband and the bridal party to join her!"

I point to the back of the room. The crowd turns to Michelle, who is waving happily.

"Time to light them, Michelle!" I instruct, beaming at her.

The guests erupt into excited cheers.

As they make their way to her, Harrison remains standing on the dance floor.

"Wait! What was I about to do?" he asks himself, peering in confusion at the pool of whiskey at his feet. "Oh, yeah!"

"Don't forget the groom, ushers!" I prompt hurriedly, causing them to interrupt his train of thought and lead him to his new wife.

I lower the microphone and turn to DJ Arnold. "Put on Ricky Martin, 'Livin' la Vida Loca.' And you're on your last warning."

After a polite request to the catering staff that they mop up the whiskey, I lean on the back of a chair and watch from afar as Michelle and Harrison clink glasses and down their drinks, then encourage their mothers to follow suit.

As the mother of the bride slams her shot glass onto the bar, the guests go wild.

"Well done," a voice says, from the table next to me. "That situation was escalating. I'm impressed with how you handled it."

I smile at the bride's great-aunt, who has now finished her pudding, and is watching me curiously. Turns out, she was perfectly aware of the situation.

"It was nothing," I assure her.

"Michelle is lucky to have such a fantastic bridesmaid. You seem very close. How do you know each other again?"

"Primary school—we've been friends for twenty-six years. I wouldn't miss this for the world," I say, grinning as Harrison lifts Michelle and twirls her around. I nod to the empty dessert plates. "Wasn't the crème brûlée delicious?"

Only one of those three statements is true.

I have known Michelle for seven months, two weeks, and three days. And she's paying me to be here.

The crème brûlée was delicious, though.

CHAPTER ONE

My name is Sophie Breeze and I'm a professional bridesmaid.

Yeah, it's a thing. Let me explain.

The idea started brewing just over two years ago, when I was a bridesmaid in my cousin Cara's wedding. Cara is a commercial lawyer at a firm in London. She's very intelligent, hardworking, and an expert at handling stress with a cutting sense of humor. But, it turned out, she was secretly having a meltdown that she couldn't find time to organize her wedding. Three months before the big day I woke up to a phone call from her at 3:00 A.M.

"Sophie? Sophie, are you there?"

"I'm here." I yawned loudly. "What time is it? What's happened? Are you OK?"

"No, I'm not OK," she whimpered. It sounded like she was crying.

I sat up immediately. I'd never heard her like that before. We'd practically grown up together and I hadn't once seen her cry. Not as kids, when she fell off her bike into a bunch of brambles and stinging nettles. Not as teenagers, when she didn't get into Cambridge like she'd always dreamed. Not as adults, when she found out that her loser ex-boyfriend Geoff had been cheating on her. Not even when she ate that *super*-hot jalapeño by accident and had to play it cool because she was in front of her boss.

"Cara, what's wrong?" I was trying not to panic as I turned on the lights. "Is it Mike? Has something happened?"

"No, he's fine." She sniffed. "He's upstairs, sleeping perfectly soundly. The bastard."

"Cara, what's going on? Have you guys had a fight?"

"No, no. Oh, Sophie. It's the *weddiiiiing*!"

"The wedding?"

"*Yes!* The wedding! It's in *three months*! And I haven't done anything! It's going to be a disaster! *What am I going to do?* I'm so sorry to call you at such a ridiculous hour but I haven't been sleeping and you were the only person I could think of to make me feel better about all this!"

I breathed a sigh of relief and slumped back on my pillows, rubbing the sleep out of my eyes with a smile. It wasn't the first time I'd received a call like that from a bride or groom. I'd been a bridesmaid many times before and there is always a moment of panic when nothing feels like it's coming together and suddenly that looming date seems much closer than it was the day before.

And who wouldn't experience it? Hello, you're organizing a celebration for the people you care about most on the planet! Anyone would be seized by fear. I completely get it. Luckily, by then, I also happened to be well practiced in handling it.

So, first things first: *calm the bride or groom.* "Cara, I need you to take deep breaths for me."

"But my brain is just so frazzled with work and I haven't even looked at the caterer's menu and I think I may have told the florist I was happy with lilies but you know how Mike's mum feels about lilies and I don't know what I was thinking and we still need to book a DJ and no one is going to be available at this—"

"Deep, deep breaths," I interrupted gently. "Breathe with me here. Deep breath in and deep breath out. Deep breath in and deep breath out. That's it. And again. Very good, you're doing really well."

Next step: *make them feel better about their panic.* "Keep doing those deep breaths for me. Great. Now, Cara, this is completely normal—everyone has these moments in the lead-up to a wedding. It can feel very overwhelming and like you don't have the time to get everything sorted."

Followed by: *a reality check.* "I completely understand that three months doesn't sound very long but most of the issues you're worrying about right now can be sorted in a matter of minutes, at most hours, and you have about ninety days to get it done. Plenty of time!"

Then it's all about: *practicality and making them feel in control.* "This is what we'll do. We'll make a neat list of everything that still needs to be done so it feels a little more ordered—I'm sure it's a bit of a jumble in your brain and that's making you worry. Once you have everything listed, you'll feel much calmer."

"I do have a spreadsheet," she said. "None of it's done, but it's listed."

"Perfect! You pop that across to me now if you like, or in the morning."

Move into: *their support network.* "You're not in this alone, Cara. Why do you think bridesmaid and usher roles exist? We're here to help you, whatever you need. Don't be afraid to ask or delegate. How about I come over for a cup of coffee tomorrow and we can go through everything that needs to be done and work out who can be in charge of it? I can come to the office."

"You—you'd do that?"

"Yeah! Can you spare your lunch hour?"

"I guess."

"I'll be there. I know a couple of DJs from some weddings I've been at who are local to your venue, so we can check them out. Plus there's loads of time to talk to the florist and change things, no problem. I'll call her, if you like, and report back if she has any questions."

Nicely setting you up for: *reminding them what this is all about.* "Honestly, Cara, it's going to be the best day, no matter what happens, because everyone is there to celebrate you and Mike getting married. Nothing else matters."

"I suppose. There's just so much pressure for it to be perfect."

And crucially concluding with: *laughter.* "It will be. Even if the DJ is shit because no one's available and we end up having to hire Uncle Fred to play the first dance on that bloody tin whistle."

She burst into giggles. "Oh, my God, do you remember the Christmas he got that?"

"How could I forget? I'll never forgive my mum. She thought it would be a lovely token from her trip to Dublin."

"It was just the worst. I don't think my ears have ever recovered."

"Yeah, well, it was also around then that Granny went deaf. Coincidence? I don't think so. Dad may have hidden the tin whistle after the second Christmas he tried to play it for us all. Poor Uncle Fred never found it."

"And here I was panicking about insignificant details like lilies when I should have been working out how we can track down a new tin whistle in time for Uncle Fred to perform a solo during the signing of the register!" She chuckled and let out a long sigh. "Sophie, *thank you.* I needed a laugh. And you're right about everything, as usual. It'll be fine. I think I just got a bit overwhelmed."

"Anyone would! There's nothing to thank me for. Tomorrow we'll get this show on the road. It'll be perfect, you'll see. Go and get some sleep."

"You really are the best. Hey, you know what, Sophie?" she said, yawning. "You should do this as a job."

"Take late-night phone calls? That seems . . . creepy."

"No! Being a bridesmaid. You've been to, like, a billion weddings and you know your stuff. And you love them, so you'd be doing something you're passionate about. Seriously, I feel sorry for the people who don't have you in their bridal party. It could be a full-time career. You could be a professional bridesmaid."

"What? That's not a thing."

"It could be."

I snorted. "OK, sure, Cara. I'll just become a professional bridesmaid."

"Why not? It's like what you're doing now, but instead of having corporate bosses, you become, like, a PA to brides."

"Your lack of sleep's caused you to become delirious. That already exists! Ever heard of wedding planners?"

"Yeah, but people don't always want to hire a planner because they like to put together their own weddings. I wouldn't hire a wedding planner, even though I desperately need the help! A professional bridesmaid, however, would be there to support the bride and help her plan without losing her mind along the way. Much cooler. Anyway, you should think about it."

"OK, crazy lady. Get some sleep, please."

"Night, Sophie. And *thank you*."

I hung up and nestled back into my pillows, ready to get a few more hours' sleep before I had to be up for work. But the next day I was unable to get the idea out of my head. *A professional bridesmaid?* It was ridiculous. Completely absurd.

Wasn't it?

The Monday morning after Michelle and Harrison's wedding, I stroll into my office (OK, it's not really an office, it's a tiny cupboard room in my South London flat with a desk in it, but whatever) and turn on my laptop to find 534 unread emails waiting for me since I checked last night.

This isn't unusual. I'm not just in touch with the bride and groom for each wedding, but also various family members, suppliers, and venues.

Still. I'm going to need another coffee.

I wander back from my office (OK, *fine*, cupboard) into the kitchen and put the kettle on. While I wait for it to boil, I smooth the pink blouse I'm wearing for work today. Even though I'm self-employed, I always prepare for work just as I did when I worked as a personal assistant in the City. I get up at six, shower, do my makeup, and pick an office-appropriate outfit.

Cara always makes fun of me for doing this—"Just work from home in your pajamas like a normal person"—but I never know when I'll have to rush out for emergency meetings. For example, the other day I was in the middle of trying to book a quaint cottage in the countryside for a client's hen do when I got an urgent call from a bride asking if I could come straight-away to speak to her father, who had fallen out with her over the guest list. I had to rush out of the flat and get there before all hell broke loose. I've witnessed *huge* family fallouts over the guest list, and it was crucial I arrived before anyone said something they regretted.

Luckily, I got there just in time to calm the situation and encourage a compromise: the guest list *would* include Nick and Sarah, the father of the bride's neighbors, whom the bride had never met, but we *couldn't* extend the invitation to his entire Friday Wine Club. The members would, however, be invited to the Sunday BBQ.

Father and bride are, happily, still talking to each other.

But they might not have been if I'd arrived a few minutes later, having had to change out of my pajamas before leaving.

Cara is the only person who knows my real job, aside from my parents and, of course, the clients. To everyone else, I'm a PA for some finance office in the City. I can't risk anyone else finding out because it would ruin one of my biggest selling points: no one needs to know I've been hired to be there. This is strangely appealing to a lot of brides and their families—they don't want anyone thinking they can't handle organizing their big day.

A large part of my job is learning everything I need to know about the bride to convince the guests and, more often than not, the bridal party that we're the best of friends and there's a very good reason they've never heard of me before—I've been living in the rain forests of Guatemala for the past five years or I'm in the Witness Protection Program.

Yeah, I know. I've gotten creative.

The kettle clicks and I make my coffee, thinking about everything I need to do today, which includes calling the string quartet performing at the wedding next weekend and asking them to please remove Kanye West's "Gold Digger" from the proposed set list they sent me (really, guys? *really?*). As I stir in the milk, I hear the post arrive, and, taking my mug, I go to pick it up and bring it into my office, plonking it on my desk and myself in my chair, ready to tackle those emails.

But something in the pile of letters catches my eye: an expensive-looking, thick cream envelope with my name written across it in elegant calligraphy.

If anyone can recognize a wedding invitation, it's me.

The thing is, I already have the wedding invitations I'm expecting from my personal life. I don't know anyone else getting married. Intrigued, I pick it up, admiring the style of the envelope and the neat wax seal on the back. My heart does a little flutter at how gorgeous it is.

Uh-oh. *Am I potentially turned on by this exquisite stationery?*

"I need to go on a date with a human," I say aloud to no one.

Opening the envelope, I pull out the gilt-edged invitation. As I read the names of the happy couple, any good feelings I woke up with vanish in an instant.

From: info@allaboardpartytours.co.uk

To: Sophie.Breeze@zapmail.co.uk

Subject: HEN DO JUNE 2022

Hi Sophie,

Thanks for your query about the ALL ABOARD PARTY
TOUR: HEN DO SPECIAL on 4 June 2022 for 20 people.
It is a fun-filled excursion down the canal on your very own
party boat, with a bottle of prosecco for every hen . . . *two*
bottles for the bride!

Would you like to upgrade to the stripper package?

Best wishes,

Tina

From: Sophie.Breeze@zapmail.co.uk

To: info@allaboardpartytours.co.uk

Subject: Re: HEN DO JUNE 2022

Hi Tina,

Great, thank you for getting back to me.

What exactly is the stripper package?

Best wishes,

Sophie

From: info@allaboardpartytours.co.uk

To: Sophie.Breeze@zapmail.co.uk

Subject: Re: re: HEN DO JUNE 2022

Hi Sophie,

You, the bride and your hens will just love the ALL ABOARD
PARTY TOUR: HEN DO SPECIAL STRIPPER PACKAGE!
For a small extra fee, it is a fun-filled excursion down
the canal on your very own party boat, with a bottle of
prosecco for every hen . . . *two* bottles for the bride!
And a stripper!

Would you like to upgrade?

Best wishes,

Tina

From: Sophie.Breeze@zapmail.co.uk

To: info@allaboardpartytours.co.uk

Subject: Re: re: re: HEN DO JUNE 2022

Hi Tina,

Wow. Thank you for that further information.

Do we get to choose the stripper?

Best wishes,

Sophie

From: info@allaboardpartytours.co.uk

To: Sophie.Breeze@zapmail.co.uk

Subject: Re: re: re: re: HEN DO JUNE 2022

Hi Sophie,

Of course!

Nearer the time I will send you photos of the strippers available and you can choose* the HOTTEST HUNK for your ALL ABOARD PARTY TOUR: HEN DO SPECIAL STRIPPER PACKAGE!

*We cannot guarantee the stripper you choose will be the one performing on your cruise on the day.

Best wishes,

Tina

From: Sophie.Breeze@zapmail.co.uk

To: info@allaboardpartytours.co.uk

Subject: Re: re: re: re: re: HEN DO JUNE 2022

Hi Tina,

I'll consult the bride and get back to you on this.

Best wishes,

Sophie

From: info@allaboardpartytours.co.uk

To: Sophie.Breeze@zapmail.co.uk

Subject: Re: re: re: re: re: re: HEN DO JUNE 2022

Hi Sophie,

Don't forget we also offer the ALL ABOARD PARTY TOUR:
HEN DO SPECIAL STRIPPER PREMIUM PACKAGE!
For a small extra fee, it is a fun-filled excursion down
the canal on your very own party boat, with a bottle of
prosecco for every hen . . . *two* bottles for the bride!
And a stripper . . . performing CIRCUS SKILLS!*
*We cannot guarantee the circus skills your stripper will
choose to perform on the day.

Best wishes,
Tina

D aniel invited you to his wedding?" Cara shrieks, staring at the invitation I've just handed her. "Is he *insane*?"

I shrug and take a gulp of wine. "Maybe it's a gesture."

"A gesture of *what*?"

"A gesture of . . . I don't know. Goodwill?"

"He is *such* a wanker."

I swallow more of my wine. Cara takes a deep breath, watching me closely, and slides the invitation back across the table. We're in a fancy near-empty bar a few doors down from her office. We tend to end up here whenever something big happens to one of us, like the day after Cara had her wedding meltdown, or the time when I landed my first professional-bridesmaid job, or today, when my ex-boyfriend sends me his wedding invitation.

"What are you going to do?" Cara says, folding her arms.

"What do you mean?"

"Are you going to reply?"

"Of course." I frown, shoving the invitation into my bag and out of sight. "It's a wedding. It would be unacceptable not to reply."

She snorts. "But it's totally acceptable for him to send the invitation in the first place."

I shrug and pour myself another glass.

Her expression softens. "Are you OK?" she asks gently.

"I'm fine," I say, as confidently as I can. "I'm fine."

"But it wasn't that long ago you broke up and . . ." She trails off.

I know what she was going to say. Everyone knows. Daniel was the love of my life. He broke my heart. I haven't met anyone since. I haven't even been on a date since. And he's getting married. To Francesca, the girl he met in June last year, two months after breaking up with me.

Oh, God. I'm going to need tequila.

"We're going to need tequila," Cara says, getting up to go to the bar.

I met Daniel in my first year of university. We were in the same halls and became close friends, along with everyone else in our block. He was the one who admitted it first, on a drunken fancy-dress night during the second term. I was dressed as a grasshopper. He was dressed as a ham and cheese sandwich. We were outside chatting with some of our friends, and they slowly drifted away until it was just me and him. We were in the middle of talking about *High School Musical 2* when he blurted out his feelings for me. I was so stunned, I didn't say anything. I just stared at him. Then one of our friends came out of the bar and threw up into the plant pot by the door, and I had to take her home.

After that, nothing happened for ages. Our friends always talked about it. They kept telling me he really did like me, but I wasn't convinced. We were so different. He was popular, fun, and outgoing, the life of the party, always doing hilarious, crazy things. I, on the other hand, was so sensible and reliable that at junior school my headmistress asked if I would mind being head girl *and* head boy. I proudly became the first head person the school had ever had.

Not only were Daniel and I very different, but I was also terrified. I felt so lucky to be friends with him. I wanted to protect that friendship. I didn't want our group to change.

One night, after a few too many vodka shots, I admitted to my friends that, OK, I did quite like him. And that same night he kissed another girl in our friendship group.

"You see?" I wailed, when we got home and I climbed into the empty bath for a deep, meaningful conversation with two of my housemates. "He doesn't *actually* like me. Not seriously."

The confusing do-we-really-like-each-other saga continued until third year, when, in Cara's phrasing, we decided to "get over ourselves" and started going out properly. And it was perfect. We knew each other so well, we'd been such good friends, that the relationship was easy. Daniel and Sophie. Sophie and Daniel. Everyone had known it was going to happen. It was meant to be. Nothing about our friendship group changed, except nights out were much more fun because Daniel and I weren't getting irrationally jealous or pretending that we didn't want to be around each other all the time. When we all moved to London after graduating, we didn't want to move in together straightaway as that wasn't sensible, but we spent so much time together that soon it wasn't sensible to live apart.

I couldn't believe I'd been so lucky as to find someone like him. He was The One. He made me laugh all the time. I felt guilty when my single friends complained about dating and the difficulty of finding someone. I felt I didn't deserve to be so happy.

Then eight years after we got over ourselves and got together, he got over me.

I didn't see it coming. That was the most humiliating thing about it. I had no idea. Not one clue, right up until the evening he sat me down on the sofa to chat. I was completely ignorant. A true idiot to be so smug in a relationship I thought was a happy one.

He didn't love me anymore, he said. He was so sorry.

"Here we go," Cara says, placing a shot with a lemon slice in front of me and holding up hers to clink.

We down our shots and I grimace at the burning sensation in my throat followed by the sourness of the lemon.

"Did you know about the engagement?" I ask, as she takes her seat. "Did Jen or anyone tell you?"

As we're so close, Cara has become an honorary member of my friendship group, having visited me several times at university, then being dragged along to most parties I've ever gone to as my support crew. Already a key figure in the circle, she became indispensable after Daniel broke up with me and I had to see him at the occasional pub gathering with all our mutual friends. While others, like Jen, had to be neutral, Cara was firmly on my side.

"Sophie, of course I didn't know," she says gently. "I would have told you."

"They must have been engaged awhile. Or they're getting married super quickly. I can't believe they managed to secure Belmond Manor at short notice—it's one of the most sought-after venues. Although I suppose they are getting married in February, so it's not peak season. You should google Belmond Manor when you have a moment. It really is the most beautiful place. . . ." I trail off.

"But, really, why did he invite you?" Cara asks, still confused. "It doesn't make any sense."

"Maybe he felt it would be unfair to invite the whole group from university and not me. He wouldn't want me to feel left out. He was always quite thoughtful like that."

"Oh, come on! You're thirty-one! This isn't the school playground."

"Well, that's the only reason I can think of. We always got on well. And things haven't been the same with our uni group since we broke up. It's been so awkward for everyone. Maybe he wants to change that and make it better between us. Maybe he wants us to be, you know, friends."

"By inviting you to his *wedding*? Sophie, if he'd wanted to be pals, he would have invited you to bloody dinner at Pizza Express or something. And maybe if he'd wanted to stay friends, he wouldn't have shacked up with someone only *two months* after ending an eight-year relationship, and wouldn't have proposed to her after a *year*." Cara shakes her head, her lips pursed. "I hope I bump into him soon so I can punch him in the face."

I laugh. "Well, then, I hope you don't bump into him. He never did anything wrong."

"*Ha!*"

"Technically, he didn't! Yes, it was fast, but he didn't cheat on me. Look, Cara, I know you're worried but I'll be fine. I know I will be. It's just . . . opening that envelope, it was like all the pain I thought I'd finally got over came flooding back. Eight years of my life wasted on someone who's proposed to someone else after just one. Meanwhile, I'm sitting at home alone, attracted to premium thick matte envelopes with an eggshell finish. Ugh." I rest my forehead on the table. "I'm a disaster."

"You're not," Cara says, patting the top of my head. "Although we should maybe talk about the envelope thing another time."

"What's wrong with *me*?"

I lift my head from the table to look at her. A beer mat is stuck to my face. Brilliant.

"*For God's sake!*" I cry, as Cara reaches over to peel it off sympathetically. "See? I'm a mess. Someone who downs shots of tequila on a Monday night and walks around with beer mats stuck to their face!"

"That's a slight exaggeration and you don't normally do tequila on a Monday night. You're the most sensible, in-control-of-everything person I know. No one would ever describe you as a mess," she assures me, signaling for the barman to bring us two more shots. "Look, that invitation was a cruel shock. Reply and forget it. Focus on your career. You have so much going for you right now! Daniel was never supportive of you! Do you remember how he used to tease you about your love of weddings? And not in a nice way but in a really snobby way? And now look! Without him, you've made a career out of your passion."

I nod slowly. "You're right."

"Of course I am. Eugh, don't let Daniel's wedding invitation throw you off course. You're much happier now than you ever were with him."

The barman brings over the shots and lemon slices. We clink glasses, down them, and slam them back on the table.

"Yes, I need to remain focused on work instead of my disastrous personal life. I need the brides and the brides need me."

"They certainly do. Any fun weddings you're working on at the moment?"

"All of them are wonderful in their own way," I declare, prompting her to roll her eyes. "But I could do with the next big project coming my way."

"I thought you were crazy busy."

"It's coming to the end of wedding season. I have some over the next few months but not many. I need to drive all thoughts of Daniel and his posh one out of my brain. I could do with having absolutely no time to think," I say determinedly.

"You could try . . . oh, I don't know . . . dating?" Cara says, with a sly smile. "You haven't done that in a while. It might take up some time and it would be an excellent distraction."

"I'd rather spend my time guiding people in choosing the perfect napkin color that reflects them as a couple."

"When was the last time you had sex?"

I pretend to be distracted by the drinks menu.

"Sophie?" she presses. "Have you had sex since you broke up with Daniel?"

"I've been very busy with—"

"So it's been over a year, huh."

"Hey! That's not too bad," I say, throwing the beer mat at her. "I'm busy. And we were together for eight years! It's not been easy to move on, then jump into bed with someone else. Obviously, *he* didn't find it all that difficult."

"Mike has a colleague I think you'd click with," she says, throwing the beer mat back across the table at me. "He's good-looking and loves dogs."

"What more could a gal want? I'll consider it but, honestly, I'm all right for now."

"Fair enough." She holds up her glass. "To us! Being all right for now."

I clink mine with hers. "Cheers to that."

"And you know what else?" she says, a little too loudly. "Fuck Daniel and his eggshell invitation, or whatever you said it is. His voice was so booming and his hair was always stupid."

I burst out laughing. We spend another hour in the bar, drinking wine and talking about Daniel's flaws, until we remember it's a Monday night and we should probably get home. I give Cara a huge hug before I get on the tube to Balham, thanking her for being there in my moment of need.

"Not a problem, favorite cousin," she slurs, heading toward the Central line. "And remember, let yourself have a moment to be down, then RSVP, say no, and forget about it. You're all right for now, remember."

It's sound advice. I need to let myself be down about it tonight, and tomorrow I'll move forward. I'll reply and forget this ever happened.

I get home and slump onto the sofa. I scroll through various playlists on my phone until I find the song I'm looking for and press play. Katy Perry's "The One That Got Away" begins blaring through my Bluetooth speakers. I let out a "Ha." Cara will find it so funny when I tell her I picked this song to listen to, over all the great songs about love and loss out there.

Then I pull the invitation out of my bag and clutch it to my chest, closing my eyes as tears roll down my cheeks.

~~~

TUESDAY, 8:00 A.M. PHONE RINGS.

ME: Hello?

TIMMY: Sophie? It's Timmy. Why is your voice so croaky?

ME: Sorry, late night.

TIMMY: Working?

ME: Sure.

TIMMY: Is now a good time to chat? I need some advice.

ME: It's always a good time. I'm your bridesmaid! That's what I'm here for. How can I help?

TIMMY: I've been thinking about the chairs.

ME: Which chairs? Ceremony or reception?

TIMMY: Ceremony. I have a vision.

ME: Go on.

TIMMY: Picture it . . . Gray. Chiffon. Sashes.

(*Pause*)

TIMMY: So, what do you think?

ME: Brilliant.

TIMMY: Really?

ME: Yes. Perfect. What sort of chair do you picture it on?

TIMMY: There are different types?

ME: Yes, and you can have whatever you like. The venue offers a selection. I can make a suggestion?

TIMMY: Tell me.

ME: Chiavari. Traditional, elegant, a bit rustic, and it will look classy with the gray sash.

TIMMY: Let me google it, hang on. . . .

(*Pause*)

TIMMY: OMG. Love it.

ME: It suits you and the vibe you're going for, I think.

TIMMY: You're a genius.

ME: Nah, just doing my job.

TIMMY: Chiavari, eh? Who knew chairs were so important? You're the best. I'll be in touch soon about the wedding favors too.

ME: I look forward to it. Have a good day!

TIMMY: You too. Oh, and, Sophie?

ME: Yes?

TIMMY: Strong coffee, ibuprofen, and Hula Hoops, sweetheart. The hangover will be gone by midday.

ME: I'm not—

BEEEEEEEEEP

CHAPTER THREE

Just as Timmy hangs up, my doorbell goes.

I groan, pulling the duvet over my head. It will be the postman with some kind of delivery and, hopefully, he'll leave it with another flat in the building for me to pick up later. *Why* did I decide to drink so heavily on a Monday night? What was I thinking? And *tequila.* I'm going to kill Cara. Does she think we're still twenty? Were those shots really necessary? Why did we even . . .

Oh, yeah. Daniel's wedding invitation. That's why.

I think I'm going to throw up.

Seconds later the buzzer goes again, and when I still don't respond, it goes off a few more times. Realizing now that it can only be a frantic bride in a state of panic, I slide my legs out of bed and sit up, pushing my tangled hair back from my forehead. I grab my dressing gown from the back of the door and throw it on, quickly forming in my head an I-look-like-this-because-I'm-super-sick line to give whichever bride I'm faced with, hoping they won't think I'm horribly unprofessional.

"Hello?" I say into the intercom.

"Sophie? My God, is that you? You sound *awful*! What's happened to your voice? Are you hungover? On a Tuesday? Is that why you were so slow in coming to the door? I thought you might be dead!"

I close my eyes, the pain in my head suddenly much sharper than it was before. "Mum. Hi."

"Are you going to buzz me in?"

"Do I have a choice?" I mutter under my breath, pressing the button and leaving my front door off the latch in preparation.

I shuffle into the kitchen and start filling the kettle. I hear her talking as she comes up the stairs, before she's even in the flat, her voice echoing around the walls of the building. I put the kettle aside, realizing that painkillers are a lot more necessary right now.

"Why are the walls so scruffy? And this carpet could do with a proper vacuum. Is a dog living in this building? Hairs everywhere! And what's that smell? It's like seaweed."

She bustles into the flat, spying me in the kitchen holding the paracetamol. "What happened?" she asks, her eyes widening as she hangs her coat and handbag on a coat hook. "Did you get robbed?"

"What?" I take the paracetamol and a gulp of water. "Why would you think I'd been robbed? The flat isn't messy."

"No, but you look dreadful!"

"And you naturally jump to the conclusion that I've been robbed."

"Well, something's happened, Sophie. It's a Tuesday and you're popping pills like there's no tomorrow! I hope you're not doing this on a daily basis?"

I rub my temples. "I just have a headache, Mum. I'm not a drug addict."

She makes her way into the kitchen and takes over kettle duty, switching it on, then reaching for two mugs from the cupboard. "You're hungover, then?"

"I'm sick."

She raises her eyebrows and gives me the look that only parents can, even when you're in your thirties. "Are you really sick?"

"Technically, yes."

"From alcohol?"

"Do the details matter? I'm sick, and that's all there is to it."

"Was it a date?" she asks, neatly placing two teabags in the mugs. My mum does everything very delicately, even when it comes to everyday things like making tea.

"In a manner of speaking. It was a date with Cara."

"Why were you out with Cara on a Monday night?"

"Wait a second. Why are you here?"

"How nice of you!"

"You know what I mean," I say, rolling my eyes—it hurts. "It's lovely to see you, Mum, but what are you doing at my flat on a Tuesday morning?"

"You forgot about our brunch."

I frown and plod past her, heading into the bedroom to find my phone and check my calendar. She's right, of course. We have a catch-up brunch scheduled for today. I go to stand in the kitchen doorway. "Mum, it's eight thirty A.M."

"Yes?" she says, as she pours boiling water.

"Do you understand the meaning of brunch? It's breakfast and *lunch* pushed together."

"That's right."

I stare at her. "So why are you here now?" I ask, hoping the paracetamol kicks in soon.

She gets the milk from the fridge, her forehead creased. "You said to meet you for brunch. So, here I am."

If my head didn't hurt already, I'd be banging it against the wall.

"Yes! But brunch isn't at eight thirty! That would be breakfast!"

"It's all very confusing," she says, with an exaggerated sigh, handing me my tea. "Anyway, I'm here now."

There's no point in continuing this battle. I've already lost. This situation is so Mum that I really should have been better prepared. There's no doubt that my organization skills come from her side of the family. Dad is the complete opposite, head in the clouds, loses everything, never quite sure where he's meant to be but having a jolly time along the way. Mum, on the other hand, has several color-coded diaries and takes great pains never to be on time for anything. She is, instead, always early. In this case, several hours.

Before she retired, a year ago, Mum worked in public relations for TV personalities and was so used to dealing efficiently with the consequences of bad press that she's the master of finding solutions and opportunities in any life hiccup that comes her way. She's smart, busy, and practical, and has a resting pensive expression as though she's already trying to work out how best to deal with the next problem before it's even happened. Having such a sensible mum is mostly a good thing, especially when things go wrong and she can set you on the right path, but it can also be quite intense.

I always feel exhausted after a conversation with her.

"So, are you going to answer my question?" she says, moving into the lounge and perching on the sofa.

Thank goodness I hoovered in here yesterday or there would have been a comment. Her house in Putney is always tidy, everything where it should be. Dad likes to move coasters on purpose just to see her reaction: "Here you go, a nice cup of t—Hang on! Where's the coaster that should be on this table? I don't know how this—Oh, there it is! On the table over there! How did that happen? I must have moved it. Anyway, here you are, darling, a nice cup of tea on the correct coaster."

He does this at least twice a week and she still has no idea how things move.

"Which question was that?" I ask.

"Why were you and Cara out drinking heavily on a Monday night? It's not like you."

I'll have to tell her eventually. I scan the room for the invitation and see it poking out from the side of the sofa behind Mum. Oh, yeah. I held it last night while I listened to sad pop songs. God, I'm tragic.

"This is why." I hold it out to her. "I'm going to get into the shower. I have a hundred things to do this morning."

"Oh, Sophie," she says sadly, reading the invitation.

"I'm fine. Honestly," I say, as chirpily as I can, heading into the bathroom. "I just needed to have a rant last night to Cara and now I'm ready to forget about it."

I lock the door and catch a glimpse of myself in the bathroom mirror. I look *awful* and feel instantly ashamed of myself. Ashamed and annoyed that I've let Daniel have this effect on me when I'm over him—make me sleep in past my alarm, cause me to be irresponsibly hungover when I've got lots to do, and leave me feeling like I'm somehow failing at life when I know I'm not.

Having said that, I do notice from my reflection that I removed the makeup from one eye last night, clearly forgetting I have two.

"Pull yourself together," I say, turning the shower on. "You're better than this."

I'm going to reply to that invitation, forget about it, and continue with my life. Yes. That's right. In your face, Daniel. I will *not* be attending your stupid wedding with its stupid perfect invitations and stupid dream venue with a stupid four-course fine-dining menu. Instead I'm going to do something *awesome*. Something Daniel would never expect me to do. Something outrageous. Something daring and different. Something completely out there. Something impressive that makes people go, "Wow!"

Something like . . . skydiving! Why not? Throw myself out of a plane. I can do that. I'll book it for Daniel's wedding day.

Then if he happens to ask one of our mutual friends what I'm doing that means I can't go to his wedding, they'll be like "Oh, Sophie? Yeah, she's skydiving."

BOOM. Take that, Daniel.

Then he'll be like "What? Sophie's skydiving? That's so brave and crazy and amazing! I got her so wrong. I never deserved her. She'd never want me back."

And whoever he's talking to will go, "Nah, mate, she wouldn't."

I step into the shower feeling empowered. By the time I finish, I'm ready to get to work and stop feeling sorry for myself.

"Do you want to talk about it?" Mum says carefully, when I emerge from my room dressed and scrolling through emails.

"Talk about what?"

"The invitation."

"Thanks, Mum, but I've done too much talking about it already. Where is it? I'll put it on my desk and RSVP later today."

"Uh-huh." She nods slowly, handing it over.

I take it, smiling. "It's OK, Mum. I'm going to say no."

"Ah." Her shoulders relax. "Well, that's the right decision. He shouldn't have invited you. A cruel thing to do."

"I don't think he was going for cruel." I laugh. "I think he was trying to be nice."

"Don't let it get you down. You're better off without him."

"I think so."

"You've got plenty going on in your life. No time to worry about the past."

"Exactly."

"He was always sponging off you. Depending on you. Dad and I never liked him."

"Sure."

"Do you know what you need?"

"A Bloody Mary?"

"Someone to spoil you! Someone to get excited about. You

work so hard! And although I'm fully supportive of the fantastic career path you've chosen," she emphasizes, "I am slightly aware that it might not be too healthy to be around weddings all the time when you've got Daniel's to deal with."

"It's OK, Mum," I assure her. "I don't see it that way. These weddings are my job."

"I read about a new company the other day, which organizes dates for groups, rather than one-on-one. That way you can go with some friends and have a good time even if you don't meet someone in the group you're matched with."

"Mum," I groan, "please, no dating advice."

"I would never *dream* of it," she says, looking shocked. "I'm simply saying you deserve a fun night out being spoiled by a dashing young man."

As far as parents go when it comes to dating, mine really aren't pushy. Mum's always been much more interested in my career and my financial stability, and I haven't given her the easiest of rides, announcing after several years of being a PA that I was moving into a career of being a bridesmaid. That I suddenly became single again at thirty didn't faze them at all in comparison with that.

"Daniel's actions are beyond me," she continues. "But perhaps we can put a positive spin on it. Maybe it's the motivation you need to get back out there. When you're ready, of course. You know, see who's who."

I can't help but smile. "Thanks, Mum. I'll consider it. And now that this awkward conversation has come to a natural end, I've got some phone calls to make and emails to sort before we grab brunch."

She holds up her hands. "I won't get in your way. I can just . . ." She glances around the room, her eyes coming to rest on the stack of bridal magazines on the coffee table. ". . . do some reading. Maybe I can help with one of your weddings."

I leave her happily flicking through the latest copy of *Bridal* and head into my office (cupboard). I'm in the middle of answering an email about fabrics when Mum appears.

"Don't tell me you're bored already. Seriously, Mum, you can't order brunch before ten o'clock at the earliest."

"Look!" she exclaims, shoving the magazine in my face. It's open on the page of engagement announcements.

"What?"

"The daughter of the Marchioness of Meade is engaged!"

"Yeah, Lady Cordelia," I say, looking at the picture of her standing next to her fiancé at some posh London event, a huge diamond sparkling on her left hand. "I saw that last week."

"I can't believe I didn't know about this!"

As much as I don't really appreciate my mum interrupting my work to tell me a celebrity is engaged, I understand why she's so excited.

Lady Cordelia Swann is one of those household names that every generation knows, from parents to teenagers. The only daughter in one of the oldest, most aristocratic families in Britain, not to mention one of the wealthiest, she's been in the society pages from the age of two. Girls at my school were obsessed with her and her best friend, Lady Annabel Porthouse—they were our age and always went to the coolest parties, had famous boyfriends, wore the best designers. Lady Cordelia's mum had been a model in the sixties and a socialite before she married the marquess. Lady Cordelia has kind of faded from the public eye over the past few years, becoming more private as she got older, but the Swann family are still very well known.

They even made a TV movie about Lady Cordelia's life, focusing on the period she lived in her Chelsea town house during her twenties with a famous rock star. It was called *Lady Cordelia Swann: The Wild Years*. It was about as good as it sounds.

"This will be the wedding of the century," Mum continues,

looking at me hopefully. "That's why I thought you'd be interested. You should write to Lady Cordelia Swann and offer your services."

"What? Don't be ridiculous. She'll be hiring the most expensive wedding planner in the country."

"Well, she's a fool. You're the best person for the job."

"A typical thing for a mum to say." I smile at her. "But thanks all the same."

She takes the magazine back and gives a drawn-out sigh. "Shame. Imagine working on a wedding like that."

"Yeah," I say, getting back to my email. "Imagine."

WhatsApp Group "Clare's Hen"

Hi everyone! Super excited to celebrate Clare's hen with you all in a couple of weeks! When you have a moment, please can you click on this link and fill in your menu choices and any dietary requirements for the Saturday night meal. Thanks! And a reminder that Clare has asked for the theme to be RAVE so please bring bright colorful outfits and I'll supply glow sticks and plenty of neon face paint! Thanks so much xxx
http://marcosrestaurantbrighton.co.uk/

Jessica
Excitingggg! I'm gluten-free, hope that's OK!

No problem at all!
Just fill that in on that link ☺

Corinne

OMG CAN'T WAIT! Is there a vegan option?

> Absolutely! If you follow that link it
> shows all the options

Rachel

EEEEEEEE!! Woop woop! So excited for this!
Can I just ask what the dress code is? Do we need
to wear specific clothes?

> So excited too! Yes, the theme is RAVE so
> please wear bright clothing! ☺

Fran

Amazing!! OMG shall I bring neon face paint?

> That's so lovely of you to offer, but don't
> worry, I've got the neon face paint ready
> to go!!

Rachel

We should SO buy those glow sticks!!

> Great idea!! I've got those at the ready

Sarah

YES, so excited for this.
I don't eat seafood if that's OK!

> Of course, no problem! Make sure you
> pop that in the dietary requirements when
> you follow the link

Sarah

I'm not allergic or anything, I just don't like it ☺

> Ah, no problem! There's lots of other tasty
> options on the menu and only one sea-

food choice I think, so have a look when
you click the link and see what you think

Mandy

This is going to be AMAZING!
Please can I get the steak frites?

Of course! If you select that option
once you've clicked through on the
link that's all sorted for you ☺

Naomi

I've filled in my choice, thanks so much
for organizing! What should we wear for
the meal? Is it black tie or anything?

Thanks for filling it in! The theme for
Saturday night is RAVE, so please don
some colorful clothes

Holly

Can't wait for this, work is the worst at the moment,
so need to get away! Excellent theme, do you need me
to pick up some neon face paint or anything?
Or is it not that vibe?

Thanks so much but no need to worry,
I've got neon face paint ready to go!

Jenna

I'm so sorry to be difficult but I'm now a
vegetarian and I also can't have dairy!! SORRY!!

That's not a problem at all! You can
select one of the vegetarian options
on the link and then just put no dairy in
the dietary requirements

Anna
CAN'T WAIT for this!! When you say colorful
clothes, would a yellow dress be OK? Sorry, it's all I
have!

> That sounds great!
> A yellow dress would be perfect!

Carey
Sorry to be late to the party, I see
I've missed a few messages!
So, is there a theme?

CHAPTER FOUR

You are cordially invited to the wedding of

Nisha Sharma and Luke Forde

25 September 2021

"Damn it," Nisha whispers, examining the intricate henna on her hands and forearms. "I can't find them anywhere."

"Find what?" I ask, checking my sari is suitably placed over my shoulder and not about to come undone any time soon.

"Luke's initials," she tells me, turning her hands over to inspect the other side. "They're supposed to be hidden in the design."

"If they're supposed to be hidden, isn't it a good thing that you can't find them?" I smile, admiring the ornate patterns adorning her skin.

"Sort of." She sighs, lifting her arms to check around her elbows. "The groom has to find the initials on the wedding night. If he can't, tradition says I'll have the upper hand through our marriage." She grins mischievously at me. "I want to know where they are so I can do my best to hide that part of me from him. I don't want to start our married life with him thinking Destiny is choosing him to have the upper hand."

I laugh, shaking my head at her. "Maybe they're hidden in the henna on your feet."

"No, they're definitely somewhere on my hands or arms," she says firmly, letting her arms fall to her side, her many bangles jangling down to her wrists. "He'd better not find them before I do. I'll be pissed off if he does."

Working with Nisha has been one of the best wedding experiences of my life. She's having an Anglo-Indian fusion wedding, with a traditional Hindu ceremony at a grand hotel in Kent. She came across my website when she was in full panic mode a few months ago, overwhelmed with the pressures of combining the most important traditions from both cultures, but eager to have control and not let either family take over. Luke, her fiancé, is lovely but shy and disorganized, and wasn't bringing much to the table, so Nisha, an already very busy doctor, was coping with most of the planning.

She'd explained to me before that she had a small group of close friends from when she was studying medicine, but two lived abroad and the other was a GP and mother of two so Nisha wasn't keen to lump her with wedding errands. She hired me to play the role of Louise, a good friend and colleague. As far as everyone else knows, I'm a hospital administrator. Together we stormed her to-do list in time for today.

The celebrations kicked off at Nisha's home yesterday with the *mehndi* party: all of the women gathered together and a henna artist created the designs for the bride and her guests. I'd spent hours helping Nisha and her family decorate the house with twinkling lights and bright flower arrangements across mantelpieces and other surfaces already covered with colorful tablecloths. Neon cushions were scattered across the patterned rugs in the sitting room, and I'd helped her mum hang drapes of bright pink, purple, and blue along the walls and windows. I'd got pins and needles in my arms hanging dream catchers and jars of tea lights from the trees in the garden, but it had looked spectacular when everyone arrived.

There was music, entertainment, and a copious amount of food, and everything went perfectly, except for Nisha irritating the henna artist by fidgeting. The bride has to sit very still for a long time while she has the elaborate and symbolic designs inked onto her skin, but Nisha kept wanting to get up and greet everyone as they arrived.

"Sit still!" the artist bellowed every time Nisha saw someone come through the door, his face so scrunched up with fury that his features almost disappeared. "You must be *still*!"

That evening it was the *sangeet*, which was like a mini wedding, with dancing and singing and, at one point, a flash mob—everyone in Nisha's family had learned the same dance and even her grandmother was swinging her hips and arms with everyone else.

Today, Nisha looks more beautiful than ever in her heavy red and gold embroidered bridal *lehenga* and adorned from head to toe in shimmering gold jewelry. She had known from the beginning that she wanted to stick to a traditional red and gold bridal outfit, but it had taken visits to seven shops before we found her dream look.

At six o'clock this morning, she took me aside and presented me with a pair of beautiful gold dangling earrings. I told her she wasn't supposed to give me anything as it was my job to be there, but she looked me in the eyes, clasped my hands, and said, "Sophie, I'm going to need you at every moment today and I'm so grateful in advance. And that is because I'm more hungover than I've ever been in my life."

I laughed but stopped when she looked as though she was about to throw up, leading her speedily to the bathroom.

I'm truly amazed that she survived the *haldi* ceremony this morning, which began at seven, when turmeric paste was applied to her and Luke by family and friends.

"She looks very solemn," one of her aunts commented affectionately, as someone wiped turmeric across Nisha's cheekbones. "Still and thoughtful as she prepares herself for her marriage."

I agreed, deciding it best not to explain that Nisha was so still and tense because she was concentrating on not throwing up the wine she'd consumed the night before.

Luke, meanwhile, looked terrified as the paste was slathered all over his face and torso. "Is it meant to burn?" he whispered to me, as more was applied to his chest and stomach.

Looking at Nisha now as she checks her striking eye makeup in the mirror one last time before we set off for her wedding ceremony, you would never have known that a few hours ago she was begging me to postpone it and let her curl up under her duvet with a cup of tea, watching old episodes of *Grey's Anatomy*.

Nisha's brother appears in the doorway. "The buggy's here!" He gestures for us to follow him. "Come on!"

Nisha shoots me a look and I can't help but laugh.

Throughout the wedding preparations, she has made so many hilarious side comments to me about being driven to her wedding on a golf buggy—"Not a Bentley, Sophie, not a Rolls-Royce. Not even a *car*. I'm arriving at my wedding in a *buggy*. Its top speed is fifteen miles per bloody hour!"—that it has, bizarrely, turned out to be one of the parts of the day I am most excited about.

When we finally get out of the door, we're greeted with the sight of the decorated buggy. She grabs my hand, a huge smile across her face. "Why would I want to arrive in anything else?"

I couldn't agree more. It's the coolest mode of transport I've ever seen. I want one.

As we reach the hotel where the ceremony will take place, I wonder how Luke is getting on with the white horse he's supposed to be arriving on. He's never been on a horse before and was genuinely terrified when we discussed it.

"Don't worry, you'll be fine," Nisha's father told him, clapping him on the back. "I arrived for my wedding on an elephant, and let me tell you, elephants are very big. Much bigger than a horse."

"Shame we couldn't get the tiger to accompany the groom," Nisha's mum said to her husband. "That would have been something."

"I told you," he replied, irritated, "there were no tigers available!"

"The horse is good." Luke gulped, his eyes widening. "I'm fine with just the horse."

In fact, as the noisy parade of singing family members and banging drums alerts us that the groom is approaching, it seems as though Luke is very much at ease on his handsome white horse, loving every moment of his grand entrance. In the end it takes a while to coax him down but eventually he hops off with aplomb and gives his noble steed a pat on the neck. "Thank you, old friend."

I make a mental note to suggest that Nisha give Luke riding lessons for his next birthday.

I laugh as I watch him make his way toward us, grinning from ear to ear, his future mother-in-law proudly leading the parade ahead of him.

A few hours later, my feet are aching from dancing and my jaw hurts from all the smiling. I have never laughed so much as when Luke's Irish cousin Hugh, who has flown over from Dublin, tasked Nisha's dad with a dance-off, a challenge swiftly accepted, to the three-hundred-strong crowd's delight. The chaos that ensued in the middle of the buzzing dance floor was a wonderful spectacle to witness, as Hugh attempted an Irish jig to the rhythm of Indian music and Nisha's dad launched into a traditional dance performance with such gusto that his wife shouted,

"Don't you dare break your hip on your daughter's wedding day! Don't you dare!"

Taking a break from the dance floor, I check my phone to see a missed call from Leslie Thompson, the mother of one of my clients who got married over the summer. She's left a voicemail asking me to call her back when I can, so I head outside. I'm too curious and worried to wait until the morning to find out why she's phoned.

Bella Thompson's wedding was one of the most lavish I've helped with so far, with the biggest budget. Leslie is a hugely successful entrepreneur and absolutely terrifying. Bella hired me to get her mum off her back—Leslie had repeatedly asked Bella to hire a wedding planner but Bella didn't want to feel like she wasn't in control. I was a happy compromise.

Why would her mother be calling months after the wedding? Did I forget to do something that they've only just noticed? Has she called to complain? My brain whirs through all the possibilities but I can't think of anything. The wedding was perfect, even if I do say so myself.

"Sophie, hello," Leslie says, answering on the second ring. "Thank you for calling back."

"Hi, Leslie, lovely to hear from you. I'm sorry I missed your call."

"How have you been?" she asks.

I try to work out from her tone whether she's angry or fine, but it's annoyingly neutral. "Good, thank you. All well with you and the family?"

"Yes, thank you. As it's a Saturday, I assume you're busy working, so I won't keep you long, but I wondered whether you'd be available on Monday. I'd like you to meet a friend of mine. She's planning a wedding and is looking for some help. I think you might be the person for the job. I've told her it was down to you that Bella's wedding was so beautiful and stress-free."

"Wow!" I'm relieved and extremely flattered. "That's very kind of you. What time on Monday?"

"Would three o'clock suit?"

"Sounds great. Where shall I be?"

"You can come to our house to meet her. She's coming for tea that day."

"Perfect. I look forward to it."

She chuckles softly, as though I've said something funny. "Yes, well . . . We'll see you then. Thank you, Sophie."

She hangs up and I feel elated. A referral is the best compliment I can receive and Leslie was hard to read at the time. My priority is always the bride and I knew that Bella was happy with how everything went, but it's an extra bonus to know the rest of the family is pleased, too. I click on my calendar and add the meeting to my Monday schedule.

"There you are!" Nisha says to me, poking her head round the door. "Dance with me!"

"Coming," I say, following her back into the reception. "Are you having a good time?"

"The *best*, thank you," she cries gleefully, stopping to point out her new husband, who is shimmying across the dance floor. "And I'm not the only one."

I grab her hand. "Shall we join him up there?"

"Yeah," she says, smiling. "Let's."

CHAPTER FIVE

O W!" I rub my forehead after an object has been lobbed in my direction. I pick it up from the floor and narrow my eyes at Cara. "Did you just throw a breast pump at my head?" I glance around the shop to make sure no one has seen.

"Yes, I did," she says. "I have excellent aim, too. Right in the face."

"You can't just throw breast pumps at people. You might have broken it and then we'd have to pay for it," I tell her grumpily, putting it back on the shelf.

"Well, maybe I wouldn't feel the need to throw breast pumps at people's faces if they'd listen to what I was saying instead of being on their phone."

I roll my eyes and put my phone into my bag. "Sorry. I'm trying to organize a last-minute brass band to play at a wedding coming up and a group sent me a quote."

"We're supposed to be picking out a gift for the baby shower we're going to in about ten minutes," Cara points out, gesturing in exasperation at the shelves lined with products. "I need your help."

"You're right, I'll focus," I say determinedly. "How about a snugglerug for the baby and some nice oils for Jen?"

Cara blinks at me. "What the fuck is a snugglerug?"

"I bought one for another baby shower I went to last year—it's super cute. It's like a cushion thing that you can lay the baby on. It's meant to be good for tummy-time exercises."

"It's like you're speaking another language." Cara sighs, running a hand through her hair. "Tummy-time exercises?"

"They help the baby get moving. But it's also nice and cozy for them."

"Do they make snugglerugs for adults? Sounds like something I need."

I laugh, ushering her to the right shelf. "Here you go." I proudly hand her an elephant one with a little rattle attached to it. "Adorable, right?"

"When did we get so old that we spend our weekends either at weddings or baby showers?" Cara asks, picking up a bottle of nipple cream and wincing. "Remember when we didn't have anything on at weekends and we'd just hang out? That sounds mental now. I can't even imagine what that's like."

"It'll be nice to see Jen properly with the girls before the baby comes along," I remind her.

"The baby isn't due until December."

"I encouraged Jen to host a baby shower earlier rather than later. She'll be exhausted when it gets nearer the time and won't want a load of women barging into her house," I explain, then notice what she's doing. "Cara! You can't open the nipple cream unless you're going to buy it."

She reluctantly puts it down. "I just wanted to see what it's like. You're such a spoilsport."

Once we've chosen a few more gifts for Jen, we head out of the shop and toward the tube, Cara ranting the whole way about how it's unfair that, when a baby comes along, women's nipples get ruined and men's aren't affected. We attract a few strange looks, but you get used to that when you're with Cara. Her voice carries.

"By the way, how was the wedding yesterday?" Cara asks, losing her footing slightly as the train hurtles through the tunnel.

"Amazing." I smile. "So colorful and vibrant."

"I bet the food was delicious," she says enviously.

"Unbelievable. I ate so much, I couldn't move for a good ten minutes after they cleared the plates."

"Any juicy stories? Come on, there must be something. Crazy things always happen at weddings. It's like everyone loses their heads."

"There was an argument between one couple that got a bit rowdy after the banquet—she threw a Bellini into his face—but I made sure they took it outside so the bride and groom didn't notice. And one of the bride's uncles was so drunk, he was chatting to a garden statue for ages before I told him it wasn't a real person. I got him into a taxi home, sharpish. Oh, and there were about fifteen speeches, because people kept grabbing the microphone to say a few words." I shrug. "But not much else happened."

Cara throws back her head and laughs, making the carriage glance irritably in our direction. "You see? People always go crazy at weddings. It's like they forget who they are and how to behave. I don't know how you have the patience to put up with it."

"It's nice," I say, as the doors open and we step onto the platform. "For one night, everyone can forget all the problems they have to sort and the work that's getting on top of them. They're just there to have fun and celebrate people they love."

"Yeah, which is why all rules are thrown out of the window and suddenly it's acceptable to start twerking with your mate's uncle on a dance floor," she says, getting onto the escalator behind me.

"What? You twerked with someone's uncle?"

"Course not! That was just an example of something someone *might* do at a wedding. Completely random."

"Oh, really?"

"Speaking of weddings, have you replied to Daniel yet?"

"Classic change of subject to avoid answering the question.

I want to hear about this twerking incident." I fish for my bank card before we get to the barriers.

"You haven't RSVP'd to him yet, have you?"

"I haven't had time."

"Sophie!"

"What?" I check my phone to work out how to get to Jen's house. "I really haven't had time. I'll do it when I get home this evening."

"Please don't tell me you're thinking of going to your ex-boyfriend's wedding," she says, falling into step with me.

"Of course not! Why would you say that?"

She shoots me a look. "Because I know you. You'd say yes because you'd think it was the right thing to do. And you hate turning down wedding invitations. You can't say no."

Cara is wrong. I haven't been thinking about saying yes to Daniel's. I've actually been trying not to think about it.

"You need to be more . . . sassy," Cara continues.

"I can be sassy!" I argue. "Just this morning I said no when someone messaged asking if I could pick up the cheddar today for their five-tiered cheesecake. I told them I was at my friend's baby shower and it would have to be tomorrow. They got a bit shirty but I stood my ground."

"Wow." She purses her lips, trying not to laugh. "You're right. You *are* sassy."

"Hey, you don't understand. It's quite hard to track down a cheddar encased in the color of wax they're after. I hope it's still in stock tomorrow." I bite my lip. "Maybe I should try to pick it up today, on my way home."

"As long as afterward you reply to Daniel's invitation, telling him no. Otherwise, I'm going to come over and tick that RSVP box for you."

I let out a sigh as we reach Jen's house. "Fine. I promise I'll do it tonight, OK?"

"Good." She marches up to Jen's door and rings the bell. "Oh, and by the way, if Jen makes us play that baby shower game where you have to lick melted chocolate out of a nappy, I'm going to kill myself."

The door swings open and Jen squeals when she sees us.

"Hey, Mumma-to-be!" Cara gives her a big hug, then heads in. "Grab your nipple cream, girls! Let's get this party started!"

The next day I feel nervous heading to Leslie Thompson's house. The first time I met her it went well but it wasn't the most pleasant experience. I consider myself a bit of an expert when it comes to handling parents in the run-up to a wedding, having been in a variety of high-stress situations, but Leslie Thompson was on another level. She fired questions at me, and was so intense, she made my palms all sweaty.

"Geez, Mum," Bella said, interrupting her when she'd been grilling me on budget. "This isn't one of your board meetings. Would you take it down a notch?"

I guess that Bella isn't going to be at this meeting, considering it's about someone else's wedding, and I hope Leslie's friend will be a little more relaxed. Then again, Leslie had laughed when I said I was looking forward to this meeting.

Which doesn't seem like a good sign.

"I knew you'd be a few minutes early," Leslie says, opening the door before I've had a chance to ring the bell. "Come on in, Sophie."

I take great care to wipe my feet on the doormat before I walk into Leslie's pristine house. I've been here several times, but it doesn't get less impressive. The hallway is very modern in its simplicity. Everything is white and clean, with shiny marble floors, huge mirrors that line one wall, and a black stone table with gold legs that has one item on it: a tall, elegant crystal vase that's always bursting with fresh flowers. Her house is all sharp angles and unique architecture.

"Beautiful flowers," I say. "I love delphiniums."

"They're one of my favorites." She gestures for me to go into the sitting room. "My friend isn't here yet, so let's go on through while we wait."

"Wow!" I exclaim, seeing an amazing spread of tea cakes, macaroons, and finger sandwiches laid out on the stone coffee table in the middle of the sparse room.

"It's a bit much," Leslie says, with an apologetic smile, revealing a softer side that originally took me months to find. "But you'll understand when you meet my friend."

"Is she a big macaroon fan or something?"

"She's . . . particular. She likes tradition."

"Noted." I perch on the edge of the sofa, terrified to move anything out of place. "Thanks so much for recommending me to her. I'm honored."

"I wouldn't thank me quite yet." She sits on the sofa opposite me. "Have you had a nice weekend? Did you have a wedding?"

"On Saturday. It went really well."

"Where was it?"

"Kent." I shift slightly. "Is there anything I should know about your friend before she arrives?"

"She's quite self-explanatory and, to be honest, I've only got to know her recently so I'm not sure I can be of much help," Leslie replies, brushing off my question with a wave of her hand. "Tell me, whereabouts in Kent was the wedding?"

A few minutes after three, the doorbell rings and our small talk comes to an abrupt end. We stand up and I wait while Leslie goes to answer the door. As they warmly greet each other, I check my outfit nervously, examining my blouse for any creases and patting my hair.

I put on a big smile as Leslie appears in the doorway.

"Come on through, Victoria. Let me introduce you to Sophie Breeze, the secret bridesmaid."

Leslie steps aside and a tall, elegant woman enters the room. My smile freezes.

"Sophie, I'd like you to meet my friend," Leslie announces, "the Marchioness of Meade."

CHAPTER SIX

ere's the thing: I have no idea how to greet a marchioness. Seriously, I've never had to greet one before. Is it a curtsy? Or a handshake? Or both? *No one teaches you how to greet a marchioness.*

I'm frozen to the spot, overwhelmed by this turn of events, as Lady Meade stands before me in a pale blue dress, with a matching jacket, and a designer handbag looped delicately over her wrist. Her thick dark hair is neatly twisted back into an elegant updo, showing off her pearl-drop earrings, and she's one of those women who seem never to age, her skin impossibly glowing with barely a wrinkle. Her striking chestnut-brown eyes are framed by expertly penciled bold eyebrows, complemented by an understated nude lipstick.

"Uh . . . hi. Hi, Lady Meade, it's lovely to meet you," I blurt out, my brain kicking into gear.

I stumble toward her and she smiles graciously at me, putting out her hand. I shake it while instinctively attempting a small, awkward curtsy.

"Are you all right?" she asks, her grip tightening on my hand, pulling me up. "What's the matter?"

My curtsy is so clumsy, she doesn't even realize what I'm trying to do. This is a bad start.

"Yes!" I say hurriedly, letting go of her hand. "Yes, great! I . . .

um . . . I just . . . Foot cramp! I got a bit of a foot cramp there. Sorry."

"I did wonder," she says, gliding across the floor toward one of the sofas.

"I'll fetch the tea," Leslie says, with a bemused smile, and disappears to the kitchen.

I go back to my seat, placing myself opposite the marchioness, and sit in silence, embarrassed by my introduction. I am *livid* with Leslie Thompson for not giving me a heads-up. The Marchioness of Meade? After the royal family, this is the most famous, most aristocratic family *on the planet.* She didn't think to mention that?

This is like a weird dream. A crazy, weird dream. Because if Leslie thinks that Lady Meade might want to hire me, that means she'd be hiring me for her daughter, Lady Cordelia. Lady Cordelia Swann.

"Do you often get foot cramps?" Lady Meade asks, breaking the silence.

Well, this is mortifying.

"No," I say, trying to look calm and collected. "Just . . . sometimes."

"Strange. Perhaps your shoes are too tight."

"Yes." I nod. "Perhaps."

Oh, *God,* this is the weirdest conversation *ever.* Quick, Sophie, change the subject. Think. I glance around the room for inspiration. "Do you like macaroons?"

She blinks at me. "I beg your pardon?"

"Macaroons," I repeat, gesturing to the cake stands. "Do you like them?"

She hesitates. "Yes."

"Me too. Macaroons are great."

Macaroons are great? Do you even know what you're saying?

Please, please, kill me now.

"Would you like a macaroon, Sophie?" she asks politely, seemingly unperturbed by the strange turn the conversation has taken.

"Oh, no. I'm fine, thank you. Would you like one?"

"Not for the moment, thank you."

"Here's the tea," Leslie announces, coming into the room with a smart black and gold teapot, matching teacups, and matching saucers on a tray. "Does everyone take milk?"

I breathe a sigh of relief that she's back. I clearly cannot be trusted to speak any sense around the marchioness on my own. As I take a cup of tea from Leslie, I give myself an internal pep talk.

I can handle anything. I have always been able to handle anything. There is no need to lose my head just because I'm in front of someone famous. I need to treat her like I would any other prospective client. I can do this. I can absolutely do this.

I think.

"So, here we are," Leslie begins, sitting down next to her friend. "We may as well get started. As I mentioned to you, Victoria, Sophie offers a very discreet and efficient professional-bridesmaid service. She guided Bella with all her decisions, helped her with any issues that arose throughout the process, and was able to oversee everything. She was a great support to her." She turns her attention to me. "I'm very grateful to you, Sophie."

"Oh! It was a pleasure," I say enthusiastically, blushing.

"When you mentioned your . . . *situation*, Victoria, I thought Sophie might be able to help." Leslie pauses, picking up her teacup and taking a sip. "No one who came to the wedding was aware that Sophie was a professional bridesmaid. They all think she's a real friend of Bella's."

"How intriguing," Lady Meade says. "I've never heard of someone being a professional bridesmaid before."

"Neither had I before I became one." I laugh nervously. "But here I am!"

"Why don't you fill Sophie in on everything and we can see if she fits the bill?" Leslie suggests.

"Good idea." The marchioness clears her throat, her expression turning serious. "It is of the utmost importance that this meeting and all future meetings are completely confidential. You may be aware, Miss Breeze, that there has been some press interest in my daughter's engagement, and should it get out that I have consulted a professional bridesmaid . . . Well, I'd like to keep everything as private as possible."

I swallow the lump in my throat.

"Should I feel you're up to the task," she continues, "and should you be inclined to accept the challenge of guiding my daughter in organizing her wedding, you'll be asked to sign a nondisclosure agreement. Awful, I know, but sadly necessary. Are you comfortable with that?"

"No problem," I squeak.

"Good. Right, then." She takes a deep breath. "My daughter, Cordelia, is engaged to be married to Jonathan Farlow. The wedding will be in May."

"May," I repeat. "As in May 2022?"

"Yes. Would that be difficult?"

"No! No, of course not. That's totally doable. Eight months. *Pleeeeeeenty* of time. How many guests are you thinking?"

"Roughly four hundred. Maximum four hundred and fifty." She gives Leslie a knowing look. "There are a few cousins I'm hoping to miss off the list."

Leslie nods in understanding.

"Four hundred and fifty guests," I croak, a smile fixed on my face. "Lovely."

God, my palms are even clammier than they were when I was watching Andy Murray play the Wimbledon final. Eight months to plan a wedding this big? Is she *nuts*?

Play it cool, Sophie. Play. It. Cool.

"The wedding will be at our house in Derbyshire and, to be honest with you, Sophie, most of the logistics I will be overseeing myself. I've never considered hiring a wedding planner for Cordelia. They tend to take over and I don't like the idea of being told what will happen in my own home. But I'm hoping to find someone to help with the small details, the personal touches that make a wedding unique and special." She hesitates. "And then there's the matter of Cordelia."

"Like Bella, she wants to be in charge of her own wedding," Leslie jumps in.

"That's understandable, and exactly why I started my business," I assure them. "As a professional bridesmaid, I'm merely there to aid the bride in producing her vision for the day and be a helping hand to her. I'm not there to take control, but rather help the bride *feel* in control."

Lady Meade looks pleased.

Well done, Sophie. MUCH better than the macaroon chat.

"I'll be there for Cordelia every step of the way," I continue, feeling like I'm on a roll. "I'll attend any appointments she wants me there for, do any odd jobs she doesn't have time for, help her with any decisions, and be at her side on the big day. And I can play the part of whoever you and Cordelia wish. An old friend, a new friend, a distant cousin. I learn everything about Cordelia there is to know, ready for any questions that come my way. So you can rest assured that no one will ever discover who I really am."

She frowns. "You learn everything about Cordelia?"

"Only what I need to know to pass as a friend," I say brightly.

She nods, and the room falls into silence as she considers my pitch.

"Well, this sounds like just the arrangement I was after," Lady Meade says eventually. "Thank you, Leslie."

"Hiring Sophie was Bella's idea and, I must say, one of her

better ones," Leslie says, then adds wearily, "Let's not forget the time she thought it would be a good idea to get a tattoo in Thailand."

"If you're happy with all of this, Sophie, I'd like you to meet Cordelia."

"Sounds great! I'd love to."

Lady Meade holds up a hand. "I must warn you, my daughter isn't easy. Getting her onside will be a challenge."

"Don't worry," I say confidently. "I understand that hiring a bridesmaid is a strange concept. I've come up against some . . . reluctant brides before and they always come round in the end."

"You haven't met Cordelia," her mother says, her eyes locking with mine. "Trust me when I say this is not going to be a smooth operation. Cordelia has a habit of pushing everyone away from her, including her own family. That's why I'm in desperate need of someone to . . . manage her in the lead-up to the wedding. Without her realizing she's being managed, of course. Anyway, now you know the basics, we can cover the details with Cordelia. Would you be available to meet her this week?"

"Let me know a time and date that would work for you both, and I'll be there." I fish one of my cards out of my bag and hand it to her. "All my details are on there."

"Wonderful. I'll be in touch." She stands up, and I realize she's waiting for me to leave, I assume so she can talk through our meeting with Leslie once I've gone. I pick up my bag and she reaches out to shake my hand. "Goodbye, Sophie."

"Goodbye, Lady Meade."

"I'll show you to the door," Leslie says, guiding me out into the hallway.

I'm still in a bit of a daze as she passes me my jacket.

"Well done," Leslie says quietly, opening the front door. "I think that went very well."

"Thank you so much. I don't know how I'm ever going to thank you for such an opportunity."

"Oh, Sophie, as I said, I really wouldn't thank me quite yet," she says, glancing behind her, then lowering her voice to a whisper: "You haven't met Cordelia."

CAFÉ, LONDON BRIDGE, TUESDAY, 1:00 P.M.

CAROLYN: Thanks so much for meeting me here. I have such a busy week that seeing you in a lunch break felt like the only option.

ME: It's no problem! It's great to see you. You mentioned you had something to run past me?

CAROLYN: So, as you know, Darren and I have been thinking about the theme of our wedding.

ME: Yes, how exciting!

CAROLYN: I know! And we've finally come to a decision.

ME: Amazing. Tell me all.

CAROLYN: OK, are you ready?

ME: I'm ready.

CAROLYN: The theme is . . . *Star Wars*! What do you think?

ME: I think it's *brilliant*!

CAROLYN: You do?

ME: I do! I really do. It's so . . . *you two*.

CAROLYN: That's what we think! My parents aren't thrilled but, as you know, Darren and I are the biggest *Star Wars* nerds *ever* . . .

ME: You met at a *Star Wars* convention, you own every piece of *Star Wars* memorabilia you can think of, and didn't you have a *Star Wars*–themed twenty-first birthday party?

CAROLYN: *Yes!* And for my eighteenth and thirtieth too! So, I've told my parents this is what I want and I hope they'll support me.

ME: Good, you have to do what makes you happy. This is your day. And if you need any help with talking to your parents, let me know.

CAROLYN: Thanks, Sophie. You're the best.

ME: This is so exciting. We can do so much with this theme. So many ideas already!

CAROLYN: I know, right? Actually, the main reason I wanted to see you today is to discuss your outfit.

ME: How intriguing.

CAROLYN: So, for the wedding I'm going to be dressed as Princess Leia and Darren is going to be Han Solo.

ME: Perfect.

CAROLYN: And all the ushers are going to be Stormtroopers.

ME: Inspired!

CAROLYN: And my little niece, the flower girl, is going to be R2-D2.

ME: Could this get any cuter?

CAROLYN: And then there's you . . .

ME: Go on.

CAROLYN: You're such a big part of our wedding, we couldn't have done anything without you.

ME: That's so sweet of you.

CAROLYN: You *have* to be a main part. You *have* to be a main character from the franchise.

ME: That's really lovely.

CAROLYN: Sophie, it is my honor to ask you to be . . . *Chewbacca*!

(*Pause*)

ME: Chewbacca? The big furry one?

CAROLYN: Yes! The Wookiee! What do you think?

ME: I think . . . that's . . . great! Really great! I would *love* to be Chewbacca on your wedding day.

CAROLYN: I knew you'd love it! We can hire you an amazing realistic Chewbacca costume, and we thought maybe you could learn how to do that sound he makes, you know the *RWWWAG-GGGHHHHH* sound!

ME: Of course. I'll learn it so perfectly, it'll feel like Chewbacca's there with you as you say your vows.

CAROLYN: Oh, my God. I'm welling up. You're going to be the *best Chewbacca ever*! I'm so happy!

ME: Me too, Carolyn. Me too.

CHAPTER SEVEN

The London town house belonging to the Marquess and Marchioness of Meade looks exactly like the house in *Mary Poppins*. Walking along Grosvenor Crescent, I half expect Mary herself to emerge from one of the shiny doors with the Banks children in tow, wearing boaters and singing something jolly about flying kites.

"Bloody hell," I whisper, gulping as I look up at the white columns framing the doorway.

I'd already had to give myself a pep talk when I was in the shower, telling myself that, in case I had forgotten, this was *the* most important moment of my career. With the Swann family endorsement, I would surely gain a huge list of future clients with stratospheric budgets. I have to win over Lady Cordelia and make this whole process a success. I spent last night poring over every article I could find about the Swanns, making sure I'd be as prepared as possible.

The problem is, there's not much out there recently about Lady Cordelia Swann. I know all about her teenage lifestyle, but people can change a lot in their twenties, and the last articles that said anything interesting about her were from at least seven or eight years ago. Since then she'd cropped up at a few parties or been photographed at exclusive events, but it would seem that she'd withdrawn from the public eye a while ago. She has a successful jewelry business, Swann & Co., that was launched a few years back when anything she put her name to sold out in minutes. It's still a bestselling line and, from the little information I could find on the company's website about its founder, she remains in charge of the business side of things as well as the collection designs.

There's even less online about Jonathan Farlow, her fiancé. He only became of interest to the press on their engagement, but if tabloid reporters were hoping for something juicy, they must have been gravely disappointed. Jonathan grew up in the Norfolk countryside and works in finance. He's not on social media and there's barely any information about him online, only one article of interest, one of those "out and about" society columns written by a journalist describing an art gallery opening at which Lady Cordelia and he were present:

> I spent a large part of the evening speaking to a cheerful, modest man named Freddie. We got chatting after I stepped on his foot and he apologized to me. It was only later, after I'd left, that I realized the very kind gentleman in question had in fact been Jonathan Farlow, the fiancé of Lady Cordelia Swann. I now understand why he'd been blushing so much during our conversation—nothing to do with my charm and wit as I'd first suspected, but the fact I'd been calling him Freddie all evening! He'd been much too courteous to correct me.

Jonathan didn't sound like Lady Cordelia's type at all. She had always been linked to trendy musicians or actors who looked like they hadn't washed in a while. At one point, she dated an up-and-coming artist, but the relationship ended a couple of weeks later when he was arrested for fraud. Jonathan, on the other hand, sounds normal.

Just as I'm about to press the doorbell, my phone starts vibrating. I check the caller. It's a portaloo company I was trying to reach all day yesterday and for the majority of this morning. I'm a few minutes early, so I go back down the front steps and take the call on the pavement.

"Hi, Russell, thanks for calling," I say, trying not to stare as a Maserati casually drives past and parks up the road. "What's going on? You left a message saying it was urgent."

"We've got a big problem, Sophie. We're double-booked for next weekend."

"What do you mean?"

"We can't do the Delgado wedding."

"You're kidding."

"I'm not. My twit of an employce got the weekends mixed up. We're providing the loos for a big corporate event next weekend, but we had it down for this weekend. The thing is, we can't miss out on this business as they're taking the whole lot of our luxury cubicles."

"Russell, please tell me this is a joke. The Delgado wedding is under two weeks away!" I exclaim, panicking.

Normally I'm quite calm about last-minute wedding complications, but toilets are absolutely cssential and the right sort of portaloos that match the vibe of a wedding can be hard to find. Rosemary Delgado is an extremely elegant, sophisticated, high-maintenance bride, and her wedding reflects that. As did the luxury portaloos we'd booked.

"You know this never happens, Sophie," Russell says nervously. "I really am sorry."

"I promised them you were a family-run business with the best luxury portaloos in Essex! Now what are we going to do?"

"I'll help you to find another company—"

"What luxury-loo company is going to have availability next weekend?" I practically yell into the phone.

"It might be OK, being October! I promise I'll do all I can to help and we'll of course pay back the deposit."

"I can't believe this is happening."

"I'm so sorry. I really am. I hope you can sort something out and it won't be too tricky tracking down some other toilets."

"Too tricky? This is a total disaster, Russell!" I throw my free hand up in the air. "A *total toilet disaster!*"

Just as I yell into the phone, the door of the Meades' house swings open and a man steps out, jumping slightly at my outburst. I recognize him immediately. It's Lady Cordelia's brother, Thomas, or to give him his full courtesy title, Viscount Dashwell. A lot of last night's research went into working out the various peerage titles of this family.

It is VERY confusing.

He stops on the steps, a bemused expression on his face.

Bollocks.

"Russell," I squeak into the phone, the heat rising to my cheeks. "I have to call you back."

I hang up and shove my phone into my bag, attempting an apologetic smile.

"You can use our loo, if you like," he says, gesturing into the house.

"No, that wasn't . . . uh . . . That sounded weird, but it's not me, it's someone else," I say hurriedly. "Someone else's toilet disaster. Ha."

"Right."

This is not the best introduction. Potentially worse than the macaroons-are-great comment I led with when I met his mother. I feel the need to explain myself.

"It's a portaloo thing. A portaloo disaster. My friend is freaking out. She booked some for an event next weekend, but the company has double-booked because one of their employees got a weekend mixed up for this big event and . . . and . . . Why am I telling you all this? Sorry!" I laugh nervously. "You really don't need to hear about the portaloo situation."

"Actually, it sounds tense," he says, the corners of his mouth twitching as he tries not to laugh. "You'll have to let me know how it all ends." He gestures up to the house. "Were you about to come in?"

"Yes! Yes, I was. I'm here to see Cordelia. My friend. Cordelia's my friend."

God, Sophie.

I honestly don't know what's wrong with me. Why am I speaking like I'm completely insane? I don't know if it's the nerves or what, but I'll need to up my game if I'm going to pull this job off.

"Ah. Yes, Mum mentioned that Cordelia had a friend coming round." He looks at me suspiciously. "Which is weird. I didn't realize Cordelia had any friends."

I laugh. He doesn't.

"Oh. You—you weren't joking."

He shakes his head, then smiles, his hand outstretched. "I'm Tom, Cordelia's brother."

It's quite odd meeting someone you've spent the night researching and thus have a bullet-point list on in the file in your handbag.

Thomas, *Lord Dashwell*

* Thirty-five
* Cordelia's elder brother and only sibling
* As the eldest son and heir, granted the courtesy title of Viscount Dashwell
* Educated at Eton and Bristol University, studied English literature
* Works in a small publishing house as a commissioning editor of nonfiction
* Has a house in Chelsea
* Resides alone—his housemate and friend from university, Leo, moved out a year ago

* Notorious playboy in his early twenties; has had a spattering of high-profile relationships
* Currently single; last long-term relationship—he dated a fashion designer for sixteen months—was more than three years ago
* Like his sister, he seems to have taken a bit of a step back from the press and social scene in the last few years
* Once revealed that his favorite drink is a caipirinha
* Hates cooking but wants to improve

Meeting him in person, I can now add the following points to my list:

* Has gentle brown eyes, around which crinkles form when he smiles as he's doing right now
* Has tousled dark hair that looks like it doesn't often get brushed
* Has much more stubble than in the pictures online

"Hi, I'm Emily," I lie, shaking his hand and trying to be cool and collected, like I'm not a crazy person who rants about toilet disasters all the time. "Nice to meet you . . . uh . . . Lord Dashwell."

"Tom, please," he corrects. "Nice to meet you too, Emily."

Lady Meade had emailed me following our first meeting with a time and date to come to their house to meet her daughter, and had also asked if I could let her know what name I'd be going under for the operation. She highlighted again the importance of the secrecy element in my employment and mentioned she wouldn't even be telling her husband, who, she assured me, would be horrified at the idea. The only people in on it would be Leslie Thompson, Lady Meade, Lady Cordelia, and me.

Together, we'd decided my name would be Emily Taylor. If

we went with anything unusual, people would be more surprised that they hadn't heard of me. Surely, at some point, Cordelia had met an Emily and potentially talked about her—guests, therefore, might think "Emily" rings a bell.

As discussed with Lady Meade, my story goes like this: I met Cordelia just a few years ago at an art gallery, when we were both admiring the same painting. We then stayed in touch, becoming close friends. My parents have retired to Australia, I don't have any siblings, and, after a variety of temporary jobs working out what I wanted to do, I'm now an in-house corporate-events planner. I'm not much of a going-out person.

Simple, believable, and, most important, not that interesting. People ask fewer questions about you when everything you give up willingly is boring.

"So, Emily, you're here for wedding chat, then?" Tom asks, his dark brown eyes watching me intently.

"Yes. It's very exciting!"

"Don't let my sister boss you around," he says, with a knowing smile. "And remind her that a wedding is supposed to be *fun*. For some reason she's in a very bad mood this morning, despite the lovely family dinner we had last night. So I'm going in to the office, even though I was thinking of working from home today and hanging around here."

"You've been told to make yourself scarce, have you?" I chuckle.

"I believe her exact words were 'Fuck off.' "

"Oh! Right."

"I hope she didn't force you to take the day off work just to come here to chat about her wedding," he says. "Not that I'd put it past her."

"I'm working from home today. As long as I log on, it's fine."

"Well, I won't get in your way. I'm sure she's looking forward to seeing you." He steps aside, letting me come up the steps to the door. "I'll see you at the engagement party. If Jonathan still wants to go ahead with the wedding that is, poor guy."

He shoots me a grin, then heads off down the road, shoving his hands into his pockets as he goes. I watch him for a moment. He's not what I expected at all. He seems so easygoing and warm, the opposite of his intimidating, restrained mother. Even the photos of him that I've seen in magazines and online seem completely at odds with the guy I've just met—he's usually pictured at posh events, in smart suits, wearing a serious expression. But just then, he was so smiley and relaxed, in jeans and a loose shirt.

I guess just being the son of a marquess doesn't mean he goes around wearing a three-piece suit and a monocle all the time.

"Emily?"

Spinning round, I see Lady Meade waiting in the doorway.

"Lady Meade, hi!" I say hurriedly, praying she doesn't think I was perving on her son, considering I was staring at his back as he walked away.

"Come in," she says, holding the door open. "Now that Tom's gone, it's just Cordelia and me in the house, but I thought I should get used to calling you Emily."

"It's a good idea," I reply, my eyes widening as I take in the beautiful hallway of her house.

I'd dressed up for the occasion, wearing the smartest black dress I own and taking way too much time to do my makeup, but I still feel too scruffy to be in a place like this. The polished wooden floor is impossibly shiny, glinting in the light from the strikingly large crystal chandelier hanging above our heads from the high ceiling. Heavy gold-framed portraits of important-looking people from the past, in wigs and ball gowns, line the wall of the red-carpeted staircase straight ahead, and on the antique table by the door there are a vase of white roses, an elaborate gold table lamp, and a black leather guest book. It feels like I've walked onto a London set for *Downton Abbey*.

"Cordelia is in the kitchen," Lady Meade says, her voice a little strained. "Please do come through."

I follow her along the hall, the clacking sound of her heels echoing through the silence of the house, and enter into a huge, shiny kitchen with French windows opening onto a tasteful, landscaped garden. Sitting at the island in the middle, Lady Cordelia is flicking through a magazine. She looks up as I come in, and our eyes meet.

If looks could kill, I'd have died on the spot.

Like the rest of her family, she's dark-haired, blessed with long, thick curls, a stark contrast to my limp, mouse-brown hair. She's got the model frame and sharp cheekbones of her mother, the bold eyebrows also being a noticeable family trait. She's wearing navy silk pajamas and her hair is tied half up, with a loose, messy bun lopsided on the top of her head. I wish I looked this good when I'd just woken up.

It's so strange to meet *the* Lady Cordelia Swann, the person whose picture I used to have on my wall because I was desperate to be like her, to have her perfect life of going to glamorous events wearing designer clothes and big bug sunglasses. Here she is, right in front of me. An actual human being. I feel embarrassed that I know so much about her life yet I'm only just meeting her in person.

I *wish* I could tell Cara about this.

"Cordelia," her mother says tentatively, "this is Sophie, whom I told you about. Or Emily, as we shall be calling her. I'm sorry about Cordelia's appearance, Emily. I did tell her we had company this morning but she seems to have selective hearing."

"Hi," I say, leaving my bag on the floor and going over confidently with my hand outstretched. "It's really nice to meet you."

She does not shake my hand. She looks irritated that I've approached her, recoiling on her chair.

I drop my hand and, having been prepared for an icy greeting, steel myself, refusing to be thrown by her glaring rudeness.

"Congratulations on your engagement," I begin cheerily. "I thought we could start by you telling me a little bit about your wedding and I can tell you what I do, answer any questions you have. Then we can—"

"I won't be telling *you* anything," Cordelia interrupts, looking me up and down. "Your services won't be needed. You can show yourself out."

"Cordelia!" Lady Meade snaps. "Please!"

"This," she says, pointing her finger at me, "is ridiculous. I can't believe you've tried to hire someone to be my friend. It's humiliating and stupid."

"I'm not being hired as your friend," I jump in. "I'm being hired as your bridesmaid."

"I don't need a bridesmaid."

"In which case, you can see me as someone simply here to help you with the wedding."

"I don't need *help*." She folds her arms, leans right back in her chair, and smirks at me. "And if I was going to ask for some, I'd hardly come to you."

I've handled reluctant brides before and I can already tell that dealing with Cordelia is going to be a bit like dealing with a child in a strop. I just have to be calm and indifferent to her cutting comments. She wants a reaction.

"You may find organizing such a big wedding overwhelming at times. There's a lot to do and May isn't that far away," I point out calmly. "You can send me on errands, anything you don't have time for or can't be bothered to do. You can ring me if you're worried about something, or want a good rant. If anything isn't quite right or something goes wrong, I can help you to find a solution. The most important thing for you to know is that I'm here for you."

When I finish, there's a moment of silence before she throws her head back dramatically and laughs. "Are you *for real?*" she says. She closes the magazine, slides off her chair, then slinks round the other side of the island toward the door.

"Cordelia, where do you think you're going?" Lady Meade asks sternly.

"Away from here." She snorts, giving me a look of disgust. "This whole professional-bridesmaid thing is such an embarrassment—I can't even bear to be in the same room as her."

"Cordelia—"

"Mum, it's a big fat NO from me, got it? Good. I'm going to head back to mine and let you fire her in peace."

"You're going to leave in your pajamas?" Lady Meade asks, horrified. "At least, shower and change here, Cordelia."

"Fine, Mum." She sighs. "Wouldn't want to embarrass you with my lack of propriety."

She disappears into the hallway and we hear her stomping up the stairs. I can't believe the girl I worshiped when I was a teenager is so horrible. How strange that when she was sixteen she seemed like she was already a sophisticated thirty, and now at thirty, she's back to being a spoiled, snobby adolescent who hasn't got her way. I pick up my bag as the disappointment starts to sink in. This would have been the wedding of a lifetime, and I so badly wanted to be a part of it.

"I'm sorry, Lady Meade. Thank you anyway for your time."

She frowns. "You're quitting? I told you it wasn't going to be easy. I thought you said you were up to the challenge."

"I am!" I reply, confused. "But it sounded like Lady Cordelia fired me."

"She has no right to fire you. She didn't hire you. I did."

"I know, but my job is to help the bride and if she's really against—"

"Cordelia has always been stubborn," Lady Meade cuts in. "She'll come round to the idea eventually. She needs you,

Sophie . . . sorry, Emily. She needs you, *Emily*. Of that I am certain. I can't let her do this alone. I won't let her do this alone."

She seems different suddenly. Determined, but distracted. The moment is gone as quickly as it came. When she looks up at me, her eyes are stony, her manner calm and in control. "So, now that's decided and the first meeting is over with, we'll see you at the engagement party tomorrow night," she states, moving to show me to the door. "I'll send you the details. It's black tie, so I hope you have something appropriate to wear. If not, let me know. I can give you some recommendations and will, of course, foot the bill. Please don't be late."

"But I—"

"I'll pay your deposit now so we have it all set in stone." She ushers me out of the front door. "The engagement party is your perfect opportunity, Emily."

"The perfect opportunity for what?" I ask, standing on the front step.

"To persuade Cordelia that every bride needs a bridesmaid," she says. "Don't they?"

And before I can answer, she slams the door.

From: Sophie.Breeze@zapmail.co.uk

To: customerservice@wizztshirts.co.uk

Subject: Problem with order L5782

Hello,

I have tried phoning the customer service number regarding my order L5782, but have been unable to reach anyone.

The 20 personalized T-shirts I ordered have arrived but there is a mistake with the wording.

I can return them, but please could a new batch of 20, with the correct wording, detailed in my original order, be produced and sent out as soon as possible. The hen do that they're for is soon. I have attached a copy of the original order.

Best wishes,

Sophie

From: customerservice@wizztshirts.co.uk

To: Sophie.Breeze@zapmail.co.uk

Subject: Re: Problem with order L5782

Hi Sophie,

Thanks so much for getting in touch and huge apologies that you have had trouble reaching us. I'm sorry to hear that you are displeased with our product and we will do everything we can to rectify the problem.

Please can you let me know what is wrong with the T-shirts you received?

Kind regards,

Meg

From: Sophie.Breeze@zapmail.co.uk

To: customerservice@wizztshirts.co.uk

Subject: Re: re: Problem with order L5782

Hi Meg,

Thank you for getting back to me.

The T-shirts I was sent have printed on the back: COOK PATROL.

As you'll see from my original order, it should be: COCK PATROL.

The bride has specifically requested these! Excuse the crudeness.

Best wishes,

Sophie

From: customerservice@wizztshirts.co.uk

To: Sophie.Breeze@zapmail.co.uk

Subject: Re: re: re: Problem with order L5782

Hi Sophie,

Thank you for your email. I will put through your order once again now and make sure that the correct wording is in place.

Please can you confirm that you would like the following?

20 x T-shirts in pink

Printed on back of T-shirts: COOK PATROL

> Kind regards,
>
> Meg

From: Sophie.Breeze@zapmail.co.uk

To: customerservice@wizztshirts.co.uk

Subject: Re: re: re: re: Problem with order L5782

Hi Meg,

No, that is incorrect. I would like the following:

20 x T-shirts in pink

Printed on back of T-shirts: COCK PATROL

> Best wishes,
>
> Sophie

From: customerservice@wizztshirts.co.uk

To: Sophie.Breeze@zapmail.co.uk

Subject: Re: re: re: re: re: Problem with order L5782

Hi Sophie,

I'm so sorry, I can't see the difference?

> Kind regards,
>
> Meg

From: Sophie.Breeze@zapmail.co.uk

To: customerservice@wizztshirts.co.uk

Subject: Re: re: re: re: re: re: Problem with order L5782

Hi Meg,

I would like COCK. Not COOK.

> Best wishes,
>
> Sophie

From: customerservice@wizztshirts.co.uk

To: Sophie.Breeze@zapmail.co.uk

Subject: Re: re: re: re: re: re: re: Problem with order L5782

Hi Sophie,

Please forgive my stupidity. I was reading your previous emails too fast. Hectic day in the office! Sounds like a fun hen do!

I confirm that I have put through an order for the following:

20 x T-shirts in pink

Printed on back of T-shirts: I WOULD LIKE COCK

Thank you so much for using our service and we look forward to printing more personalized items for you in the future!

Kind regards,

Meg

CHAPTER EIGHT

I have a feeling I'm not going to enjoy this engagement party. For one thing, the bride hates me, and for another, I can barely breathe in these Spanx. They're so *clingy*. But they also help me feel good in this ridiculously expensive dress that I bought earlier today. Lady Meade had emailed me with the details of the engagement party, apologizing for the lack of a formal paper invitation: it was at 7:00 P.M. in the Grand Ballroom of the five-star luxury hotel the Rosewood, London, dress code black tie.

I've attended black-tie events before, including black-tie weddings, so I had options in my wardrobe, but I felt that for *this* occasion I had to go all out. As soon as I'd got through all my emails this morning, I called Cara and asked her to come shopping with me on her lunch break.

"So, why exactly do you need to buy a new dress for this engagement party?" she asked, waiting for me in the changing room of a gorgeous, much-too-expensive boutique she had suggested. "You've been to a hundred before."

"Not like this one," I replied, stepping into a sparkly sequin dress and fiddling with the zipper. "The client is going big."

I wish I could tell Cara that the client is Lady Cordelia Swann, but I've signed the NDA. Cara would go crazy if she found out—when she was sixteen, she tried to copy Cordelia and Lady Annabel, who were photographed together at Ascot with matching newly dyed bright red hair. Cara bought a cheap bottle of dye and turned her hair a bizarre neon orange. "It said 'red' on the bottle!" she wailed.

"It also cost ninety-five pence," her mum pointed out.

I smile to myself, thinking back on that, and how Cara would react if I told her that I have now met Lady Cordelia Swann and I can confirm that she is the absolute *worst* and last person in the world anyone should copy.

"What do you think?" I asked, stepping out in the dress.

Cara jumped. "Bloody hell. You almost blinded me."

"With my beauty?"

"With the fuckload of sequins. Get that thing off before my retinas are burned beyond repair. Put on the black one I picked out, the one with the high neck," she instructed.

"I suppose it's a bit too attention-grabbing," I agreed, ducking back behind the curtain.

"You'd blind the guests and your new client would sue."

A few minutes later, I emerged in Cara's pick and her face lit up. We both agreed it was perfect. Classy, elegant, and simple enough to blend in. I paired it with heels I already owned (the dress was floor-length, so they couldn't really be seen anyway), a black and gold clutch bag, and the gold dangling earrings Nisha had given me. I booked a last-minute blow-dry and spent about an hour getting my eyeliner just right.

Just as I'd been about to leave, my phone started ringing.

"Hi, Mum," I said, looking at the back of my dress in the mirror to double-check that the Spanx line—so high it was just below my boobs—wasn't visible.

"Hi, darling, just checking in! How are you?"

"I'm heading out the door to a party. Can I call tomorrow?"

"Oh, wonderful! A party! I'm glad you're keeping busy. You deserve some fun!"

"What's that supposed to mean?" I said, picking up my clutch.

"You know, after Daniel's wedding invitation."

"Oh. That." I glanced into my office (cupboard) and saw it on the desk, still unanswered. "Yeah, I'm fine."

"Your dad is furious. He says it was cruel of him to invite you and that you're much better off without him."

"Tell Dad thanks. Anyway, I think my taxi's here, so I'd better go."

"Have fun!" she trilled. "You never know who you'll meet!"

As the taxi pulls up to the Rosewood, I check my dress and take some deep breaths, glancing out of the window at the beautiful hotel ahead. That's when I see them: a horde of reporters clambering over one another to get closer to the iron gates of the archway entrance to the hotel courtyard. Word must have got out about the party.

"Wait!" I cry to the taxi driver as he gets closer. "Don't stop, you need to go round the back or something. Keep going."

I absolutely can*not* have my picture taken in the lead-up to this wedding. If I was photographed with Lady Cordelia or going into her party and that was online somewhere, there was a chance that someone who knows me might spot it and be a tad confused when I was captioned as Emily Taylor.

"Round the back?" He frowns into the rearview mirror.

"Yes."

"But the entrance to the hotel is here."

"I can't be seen by those photographers, so I'll have to find another way in."

He raises his eyebrows as we drive past the hotel and turn left to go round it. "Are you famous or something?"

"No! I'm nobody."

"Sure." He taps his nose. "Don't worry, love, you can trust me. Are you that actress from the film with the dog?"

"No," I reply, distracted by trying to spot another door into the hotel.

"I know! It's the one set on the farm with What's-his-name!" His eyes widen in excitement. "Hey, your accent was really good."

"Thank you. I'll hop out here," I say, noticing an open loading-bay door with a van pulling into it.

"Sorry your marriage to that old guy didn't work out," the taxi driver says, as I attempt to slide out as elegantly as possible in my dress. "Next time, eh?"

I smile graciously at him and shut the door, making a note to check out all films set on a farm tomorrow to work out who the hell he thought I was, before I totter down the pavement toward the loading bay, holding up my dress carefully.

"Good evening! Don't mind me!" I say cheerily, waving my clutch, when I receive a strange look from the man waiting to unload crates from the van. "Ah, hold the door!"

A hotel porter pushing a large trolley comes barreling through and looks startled at my cry, before he moves the trolley aside to open the door for me. I dodge the random bits of litter and lettuce leaves scattered across the sloped concrete and reach him without falling flat on my face.

"You know there's a main entrance round the other side, right?" he says, after I thank him.

"Is there? Oh, well, I'm here now! Thanks again."

I hear him chuckling as the door closes behind me and I make my way along the corridor. It's dimly lit by strip lights and has several doors leading off it to what I assume must be mostly storage and laundry rooms. I reach the end and have the option of branching off to the left or the right, or through a set of double doors straight ahead. I stand and deliberate for a moment, then decide to go straight.

"Watch yourself!"

I slam myself back against the doors I've just come through, narrowly dodging someone carrying a tray of full gravy boats. I've walked into the kitchen.

I put a hand against my heart and exhale, imagining what might have been. Showing up to Lady Cordelia Swann's engagement party covered with gravy stains wouldn't have been a good look.

"Excuse me, are you lost?"

A young chef chopping herbs is watching me in amusement. I smile apologetically at her.

"Yes! I'm supposed to be upstairs in the hotel."

"Yeah, you haven't exactly dressed for the kitchen." She nods to a door on the other side of the room, wiping her hands on her apron. "Come on, I'll show you the way."

"Thank you!"

"Which waiter brought you down for the tour and left you?"

"Excuse me?"

"The waiter who, after your meal, invited you to see the kitchen. They shouldn't abandon you here. Who was it? I'll have a word."

"Oh, it was no one. I came here myself," I say, trying not to get distracted by the goings-on in the kitchen. It takes all of my willpower to follow her and not the pastry chef, who marches by with a tray full of freshly baked custard tarts.

She glances back at me over her shoulder. "If you say so. I hope you enjoy the rest of your evening. Through these doors and straight up those stairs. You'll find yourself back in the dining room."

I thank her and head to the top of the stairs, the atmosphere shifting as I go from the loud, stressful, busy kitchen to the calm, serene dining area, piano keys tinkling in the background. I walk round the tables and along the bar, trying to look as though I know where I'm going. If I don't find my way to the Grand Ballroom sharpish, I'm going to be late. Lady Meade asked me specifically to be on time.

With a fresh sense of urgency, I burst out of the restaurant and run straight into the back of someone, sending him stumbling forward.

"I'm so sorry!" I gasp, before he turns round to see who barged into him and almost knocked the champagne glass out of his hand. He does a double take.

"Emily?"

"Lord Dashwell! Oh, my God, hi!"

Of course I *had* to knock into him. It *had* to be the hot brother, who is heir to half the country or whatever. It couldn't have been a random stranger staying in the hotel whom I'd never see again.

"I'm so sorry," I say, my cheeks burning. "Are you OK?"

"I'll survive," he replies. "Please don't call me Lord Dashwell—it makes me sound two hundred years old. It's Tom."

"Right, sorry. Tom."

"It's nice to see you again. You look great."

"Thanks. You too!"

Which, of course, he does. His hair is still tousled, but in a styled way this time, and every man looks good in a tux.

(Actually, apart from that guy, Kem, in my sixth form, who wore a tux that was much too small for him to our prom. One of the buttons of his shirt popped off on the dance floor midway through "Summer Lovin'" and hit a girl in the eye.)

"Did you eat here before the party?" he asks, looking over my shoulder and into the restaurant. "Or come here for a drink at the bar before it all begins? The calm before the storm, as it were."

"A drink," I reply hurriedly, thanking him for a perfect answer. "I had some work stuff to tie up, and I didn't want to be on my phone in the party."

He laughs. "Right. I suppose you know about the time Cordelia threw that guy's phone out the window when he wasn't listening. She's lucky it missed that goose. Would have taken it out."

"Oh, yeah." I'm laughing along. "That is a hilarious story. She's so funny!"

Must keep phone hidden at all times. Cordelia is a PSYCHO.

"Anyway, we should probably get to the party. Do you know where the Grand Ballroom is by any chance?" I ask. "Or were you waiting here for someone?"

"I was just trying to phone a friend of mine to see where she was," he explains, holding up his phone. "She likes to be fashionably late."

"Oh, right." I smile, leaving him to it. "I'll see you in there."

"I can come with you and show you the way," he says, putting his phone away and falling into step with me.

"No, please don't worry! You should wait here for your date. I'm sure I can find it myself."

"It's all right." He shrugs, opening a set of doors as we turn the corner onto another corridor. "I don't want Cordelia to think I've gone missing from her party. And she's not my date. By the way, how's your loo situation?"

"Excuse me?" I reply, horrified.

"The portaloo disaster." He laughs. "Remember? You were on the phone outside my parents' house and there was a toilet disaster."

"Oh, right!" I say, blushing. "I think my friend's sorted it now."

This is half true. I haven't confirmed with the new company, as I want to see the loos before I let Rosemary make any commitment, but it's a strong lead.

"I'm pleased to hear it. Ah, here we are. The Grand Ballroom."

A tall woman with a neat bob and bright red lipstick, wearing a smart black trouser suit and a headphone set, is standing at the door with two hotel porters and security officers. She acknowledges Tom, then asks my name, checking it against the list on her iPad screen before offering me a warm smile. "Welcome, Miss Taylor, do go on through."

The doors are opened and the first person I see is Lady Cordelia, standing just inside with Jonathan, waiting to greet her guests as they enter.

"Look who I found, Cordelia," Tom says, taking a glass of champagne offered by a waiter and handing it to me, oblivious to her thunderous expression. "Now you might enjoy your party, considering there's someone here that you actually like."

As her eyes narrow to slits, I smile at her before taking a large gulp from my glass.

I don't normally drink on the job, but I think I'm going to need it.

CHAPTER NINE

"All right, what the fuck are you doing here?"

At the sound of Cordelia's voice echoing around the loo, I genuinely stop mid-pee.

Mid-pee. That's how terrifying she is.

I'm in a cubicle, and had been enjoying a brief moment of peace and quiet away from the party, where I've had to smile like the Cheshire Cat all evening. I was particularly nervous to meet the Marquess of Meade, Cordelia and Tom's father. As you'd expect a marquess to be, he's tall and imposing, with thick dark hair, graying at the sides, and a stern, square jawline. He also has the same kind, dark eyes as his son. I met him briefly, introduced by Lady Meade. He was very polite, but the hotel manager had appeared swiftly after we met to ask a question about the canapés, so I'd left him to it.

After that, I'd done my best to mingle with various guests, who had stepped straight out of the society pages of *Tatler*, before escaping to the ladies'.

Cordelia must have spotted me slipping away.

"I know you're in there," she yells, knocking on my cubicle door. "*Emily.*"

"I'll be out in a second!" I squeak back.

The bathroom falls into silence. I try to continue but she's given me such a fright, I swear she's scared all my pee away. Eventually, I manage to finish and try to yank the Spanx up quickly and shimmy my dress down, before taking a deep breath and opening the door with a calm and kind expression.

"Are you enjoying your party?"

She purses her lips in irritation. She looks intimidatingly striking. She's wearing a fitted red dress with matching lipstick, her hair swept over one shoulder, falling in loosely styled waves. She has on gold drop earrings and a matching bracelet, both of which I recognize from studying her recent collection online. She wouldn't look out of place in a James Bond casino scene. I go to the sink to wash my hands, her raging eyes fixed on me.

"Don't ignore me, I asked you a question," she seethes. "Why are you *here*? I told you, you're fired."

"Look, I really don't want you missing out on your party because you're in here chatting with me, so why don't we—"

"Why don't we what? Go back out there and pretend to be BFFs?" She scoffs. "I honestly thought my mother couldn't embarrass me any more than when she did the cha-cha at my sixteenth, but then she goes and hires *you*."

She's speaking with such venom, it's difficult to keep a level head. But I remind myself that Cordelia doesn't know me at all. This isn't personal.

"Why are you embarrassed?" I ask simply, throwing a hand towel into the wicker basket next to the sink and helping myself to the posh hand cream. "My job is to help you with your wedding preparations, that's all. I work for brides all over the country. There's nothing embarrassing about it. Organizing a wedding is a wonderful but stressful time in anyone's life, and considering the number of people you're having, it's really—"

"BLEUGH!" She mimics sticking two fingers down her throat. "Save me the sound bites. I've told you, I don't need any help."

"How do you know? You might do nearer the time."

"I have the best contacts in the world," she sneers, folding her arms. "Why would I need someone like *you*?"

"Because the best contacts in the world might not be around when you need someone to talk to."

"Fucking hell, could you give the nice-girl act a break?" She throws up her hands in exasperation. "I don't need 'someone to talk to.' I'm not eight years old. Do all your clients fall for this crap?"

I take a deep breath. *It's not personal, it's not personal, it's not—*"Cordelia—"

"I want you to leave," she interrupts. "I know the sort of person you are and what you're doing here. You may have fooled my mum, but you're not fooling me."

"I'm not fooling anyone!"

"Says the girl who lies for a living." She tilts her head, smiling triumphantly as my eyes drop to the floor. "As I was saying, you're done here. Please leave. And make sure you don't get photographed by the press. I don't want anyone thinking I associate with people like you."

"Who exactly do you think I am?" I ask, clenching my fists and trying hard not to raise my voice. "You keep saying 'people like you.' What does that even mean?"

"People who will do anything to climb to the top," she says plainly. "It's obvious and repulsive. You spotted a moneymaking opportunity and you went for it. Trust me, I've seen it all before."

"Lady Meade approached me," I point out as calmly as I can. "She wants me to help you. I didn't ask for this."

"Do you really think Jonathan believed you're actually my friend? Do you think anybody will? No one has ever heard of you, and in our circles everyone knows everyone."

"Jonathan looked convinced to me," I say truthfully.

He'd been surprised at first when I introduced myself as Cordelia's friend and bridesmaid, adding that it was an honor to be a part of his wedding.

"You didn't tell me you'd picked a bridesmaid!" he exclaimed happily to his fiancée, after giving me a kiss on each cheek. Cordelia did not deign to greet me. "I thought you didn't want any!"

"So did I," Cordelia muttered, under her breath.

Luckily, neither Tom nor Jonathan heard her, and Jonathan appeared so happy to meet me he seemed oblivious to the fact he'd never heard of me before.

"You met at an art gallery? Cordelia, I can't believe you haven't told me any of this! She's been very secretive about you, Emily." He chuckled, then looked at me with suspicion. "Hang on. Did I meet you at the Easter ball? I think I remember! You'll have to forgive me, I'd had a few that night and it's all a bit of a blur." He spotted someone over my shoulder and his face lit up. "Ah! There's my cousin! I'd better go and say hi. Really nice to meet you, Emily. I'm glad Cordelia has someone looking after her."

I moved away so he could greet those coming in after me but felt elated at such a successful meeting. The fiancé is always a big hurdle. The idea they might not know one of their partner's friends, let alone a friend close enough to be part of the bridal party, is always a tricky one to navigate.

Thankfully, a lot of the time they're so embarrassed they don't remember your name cropping up or potentially having met you, they're willing to let it go.

As I'd thought when I'd first researched the couple, it seemed odd to me that Jonathan was with Cordelia. He was warm, welcoming, cheerful, with adorable dimples when he smiled and bright, interested eyes. Where she was closed off, he was open, the sort of person you'd want to play poker against. She, on the other hand, is impossible to read, and once you're in, I can guess you immediately want to get out.

"Jonathan may be convinced for now but there's no chance

you can keep up this façade," Cordelia says. "People will look into you."

"They won't find anything. They will only ever know Emily Taylor. This secret is safe. People are more trusting than you think."

"You won't last a second. Anyone can see through you."

"Look, I appreciate that this wasn't your idea," I say, refusing to take the bait and argue with her. "I get that you don't need any help or any new friends, that's fine. But I promise you, I can pull this off, if you let me. I do it all the time. It's my job and I intend to do it properly. I've been hired to help you with your wedding and then that's it—you never have to see me again. Lady Meade is adamant that I stick around. I'm your employee, here to do whatever you want. I don't have to be your *real* friend. Just give it a chance. If it doesn't work out, then it doesn't work out, but we should at least try."

"And if it doesn't work out, you'll quit," she says, looking thoughtful.

"It always works out," I reply confidently.

"But if it doesn't," she says, taking a few steps forward, closing in on me, "then you'll quit."

It's an order, not a suggestion. A lump begins to form in my throat as she towers over me, her expression fierce and determined. But I can't let her see my fear. She's definitely the sort of person to thrive on it. I can't understand how someone as cold and calculating as her once launched a hugely successful range of unicorn and rainbow hair scrunchies. "I'll do whatever is best for you and your wedding," I say, holding her gaze. "If my employment ends up obstructing your plans and your happiness, then I will, of course, step away. But that's not going to happen. I've never quit a job before, and I don't intend to do so now."

She takes a step back and flicks her hair over her shoulder. "Fine, then. I'll give it a try."

"Great," I say, with a warm smile.

"And we agree, when it doesn't work out, you'll quit."

"I won't quit."

"Oh, yes, you will." She turns on her heel and marches to the door, then looks over her shoulder at me. "You can be sure of that."

I wait a few minutes before I go back to the party, collecting myself and checking my reflection in the mirror. I'm a little disappointed that such a posh toilet doesn't have deodorant lurking in a basket somewhere—it would come in handy for all the society fallouts that must happen in bathrooms like this all the time. After my "chat" with Lady Cordelia, I feel a bit clammy.

I've had difficult brides before, who aren't naturally open to me, and it's definitely unusual for a parent to hire me—it's only happened a few times before. And I can understand why some might be a bit thrown or confused by the idea: it's not your average job.

But for her to be so rude isn't something I've come across previously. I'll have to steel myself for this wedding process, because I doubt she'll make it easy.

"I have to think of the long game," I tell my reflection. "This is a big step for my career. I can do this."

I pop open my clutch and reapply my lipstick, then march out of the door with my shoulders back and my head held high. *I can do this.*

"There you are," Lady Meade says, appearing next to me. "Where's Cordelia? Have you seen her?"

"Yes, we had a very pleasant chat. She should be around here somewhere. Would you like me to find her?"

"If you could keep an eye on her," she says, smiling graciously at a passing guest. "She's never been fond of big events."

"Lucky she's not having a big wedding," I joke.

Lady Meade does not share my sense of humor, shooting me a concerned look. "I suggest you mingle and introduce yourself to people, before Cordelia gets the opportunity," she says.

"Why do you say that?"

"I overheard her telling my friend Clarissa that you were a gate-crashing mime artist," she informs me wearily. "She's clearly hoping to embarrass you out of the job."

"Thanks for the warning."

"I'd better get back to the guests," she says, placing a cold hand delicately on my shoulder. "Good luck."

I wait until she's gone to down the rest of my champagne, popping the empty glass on a waiter's tray, then waltz into the crowd and join in with the first conversation I reach. A blond woman is telling the group about a disastrous date she's just been on and I slot in happily next to a tall, mustached young man in his twenties. He politely shuffles round to make room.

"He took me to a bar that had all this neon lighting and I thought it was a bit tacky, considering the first date was in a really lovely, cozy pub," she's saying, everyone nodding along. "But then the background music stopped and it turned out to be a karaoke bar."

The mustached man gasps. "Not my scene."

"Mine neither, but I understand that some people enjoy it and it can be quite fun with your friends," she points out, the mustached man looking unconvinced. "So I sort of laughed along with it and tried to listen to his conversation over the dire noise of a woman attempting a Leona Lewis hit."

"A very challenging vocal range," someone comments, to murmured agreements.

"Then he suddenly got up and left me at the bar. Said he was going to the loo." She closes her eyes in dread at having to recall what happened next. "But he appears onstage, declaring the next song is for me."

"Oh, no," I gasp, completely engrossed. "What was it?"

" 'Truly Madly Deeply' by Savage Garden."

The crowd's reaction is unanimous: a grave mistake.

"So, he's not getting a third date, then?" the mustached man asks, with a grin.

"It's a no," she confirms, then sips her champagne and looks at me curiously. "Did I see you arriving with Tom earlier?"

"I thought he was here with that actress, Savannah Reed," the mustached man says, before I can answer. "He told me earlier that he was going to find out where she was."

"Oh, they're *old friends*," someone else comments, with a knowing smile. "That was all yonks ago now. I heard she's after Christopher, these days. You know, Dashwell's friend from school who always tells the same joke about the brown trout."

There's a murmur of recognition around the group.

"Sorry, it's so hard to keep up with who's with who in these circles. It's like musical chairs," the blonde says to me, with a wave of her hand.

"I'm not with anyone," I assure her. "I'm Cordelia's friend."

She almost drops her drink. The mustached man and the rest of the group look me up and down with great interest, as though I've just said something highly unusual.

"*Cordelia's* friend?" the blond woman repeats in astonishment. "Really?"

"Yes."

"Hang on," the mustached man says excitedly. "Are you the bridesmaid?"

"That's right." I smile.

"The bridesmaid! Yes. We've heard about you," someone says, with a smirk.

"Is it true?" the mustached man asks, his eyebrows waggling. "About your job? You can tell us."

Oh, no. Fear jolts through me. Secrecy was the most important thing to Lady Meade. If they know, everything's ruined.

"My job?" I squeak.

"Yes." The woman nods eagerly, lowering her voice. "Is it true you're an escort?"

WHAT? I choke on my spit in shock. Mustached man gives me a delicate pat on the back.

"Cordelia let it slip to our friend Lex over there," she says, jabbing a nail to a cluster of guests nearby. "She said it was a big secret, but you don't mind telling us, do you? We won't judge."

"What's it like?" someone asks. "Is it like that book, *Secret Diary of a Call Girl?*"

"I *loved* that TV series! You should write a book about your experiences," someone else advises me. "It would sell like hotcakes."

"Yes, so true!" The blond woman nods, grinning mischievously at me. "You must have some *hilarious* secrets."

"I . . . I'm not . . . ," I begin, my face burning with embarrassment.

"Don't worry, only a few people here know," the mustached man says, winking at me. "And we promise we won't tell a *soul.*"

~·~

WhatsApp Group "Clare's Hen"

Carey, where are you? You
went to the bar about an hour ago!

Just checking you're OK?
We're still all in the VIP booth, upstairs
Hey Carey, we're heading onto the
dance floor, let me know you're OK!
Has anyone seen Carey?

Jessica
Hey, we're in the smoking area!
LET'S GET SHOTS!

Is Carey in the smoking area
with you, Jess?

Jessica
Yes!

Naomi
No, Jess, I'm in the smoking
area with you. My name is Naomi.
Sorry, she's not here with us!

Jessica
Whoops!! Soz Naomi
NAOMI IS A LEGEND BTW GUYS
LOVE ALL YOUR PALS, CLARE
CLARE's HEN GROUP 4EVA!!

Has anyone seen Carey?
I haven't seen her in a while

Rachel
Is she with Clare?

Fran
Nope fho I'ma wit Clare

Rachel

You with Clare, Fran??

Tell her to get on the DANCE-FLOOR!

We need the bride, bitches!

Fran

Caot come becuws in cat

Rachel

???

Fran and Clare are in a
taxi heading back to the hotel ☺

Rachel

Noooooooooo COME BACK!!

It's only 3 a.m.!! BITCHES ON TOUR
Y'ALL!!

Fran

I been sick

Itst car

Rachel

Oh no!

Fran

Driveerrr cross

He meaanh

Mandy

OMG GUYS GUESS WHERE WE
ARE?!?!

IN THE DJ BOOTH!

Anna

Ahhhhhhhhhhh it's AWESOME!!

Jenna

HAHA!! I can see you!!

Mandy

LIVING MA BEST LYFEEEEE!

Amazing!! Is Carey with you?

Holly

I remember now!! Carey left a while ago
with the stripper!!

Mandy

WHAT? WE MISSED THE STRIPPER?
AHHHHH!! WTF

Jenna

Where's the stripper???????

Rachel

I thought Clare didn't want a stripper!
LOVE THIS TURN OF EVENTS!!

Jenna

I WANNA BE WITH THE STRIPPER!
WHERE IS HE?

Fran

OMtGp STRIPPERRRRRRRRR
Taxi turn bck!!
Comin bk to club
STRIPPERRR
Where u? need tll driver

There isn't a stripper!
We didn't hire a stripper!
Fran, no need to come back!
You get back safe with Clare, OK?

Fran
I Ive strippers
strippersssssssss

Jenna
I can't believe Carey is with the stripper!!

> There really is no stripper
> Do you think she's OK??

Holly
Wait, maybe she said she was
leaving with A stripper.
Not THE stripper

Jessica
GO CAREY!! HILARIOUS!

Anna
Yesssssssss Carey!!!! Can't wait to
hear all the details!!

Jenna
Ahhhhhhh you LEGEND Carey!!!

Carey
Wait, what's going on? Hi, I'm here!!
Whoa so many messages

Mandy
TELL US ABOUT THE STRIPPER!!

Naomi
Is he super hot??

Carey
Is who hot??

Naomi

THE STRIPPER

Carey

There's a stripper??? WHERE??

Holly

You're with the stripper!!

Carey

Who's a stripper??

Holly

You said you were off with the stripper!!

Carey

I said I was getting strippers!!

Anna

Huh?

Mandy

You're getting strippers?! HOW MANY?!

Carey

Six

Jenna

Bloody hell Carey!! Six men?!
You FOX

Fran

STRIPPERSSSSSS

Naomi

Always the quiet ones!!

Carey

Huh? What men?

Naomi

Six strippers!!

Carey

FFS

I'm getting CHICKEN STRIPPERS

I'm in Domino's!

Anyone want some?

Fran

Bride nd me BCK AT CLUUUUUUB!

Where's stripper?

CHAPTER TEN

G ood morning, Cordelia! How was your weekend?"

She does a double take and then, rolling her eyes dramatically, returns to looking straight ahead without slowing down on the cross-trainer. Gyms already make me nervous, what with everyone being very sporty and the intense trance music they always play, but with Cordelia there, it's much more intimidating than usual. I'm trying to act as nonchalantly as possible, like I go to the gym all the time and I'm totally at ease around all this spaceship-style equipment.

"Are you stalking me now?"

"Your mum mentioned you'd be here after your early business meeting this morning, so I thought I'd pop by to see if you wanted to go for a coffee afterward," I explain, as she continues her workout. "We can discuss dress ideas. Lady Meade tells me you're deciding on which designer to go with. We can brainstorm together."

"Don't you have another bride you can annoy?" she grumbles, beads of sweat forming on her forehead.

"You are my priority today," I reply.

"I thought the deal was that if I need you you're there for me. And I don't need you. So you can leave now." She presses some buttons on the screen in front of her to make the workout harder, her eyes focused on her reflection in the mirrors lining the wall.

"And I'll be speaking to whoever's on the front desk about them letting just anyone walk into this supposedly exclusive gym."

"Your mum put in a word for me. And, technically, you're right, but I got the feeling you might not think to call me when you need help. Sometimes it's hard to ask," I say brightly, determined to keep putting a positive spin on everything. "I thought it best to be here, just in case."

"I don't want you here."

"I can understand that—you seem very focused, which is great. Keep those knees up! Ha-ha. Do you want me to wait outside until you're done?"

She looks at me strangely, then slows down until she's stopped altogether. She steps down from the cross-trainer and I hand her the towel hanging over the handlebar.

"Don't you ever give up?" she asks, patting the towel across her face.

"Why would I want to?"

"For one thing," she says, raising her voice so everyone else in the gym can hear, "all the wedding guests now think you're either a high-class hooker, an uninvited mime artist, or a pan-flute teacher who was trying to pitch your services for the wedding."

"I didn't hear the pan-flute one. That's kind of cool."

"And for another thing," she continues, ignoring me, "I plan on making your life hell until you're forced to quit. It'll be much easier for both of us if you give up now."

A tiny part of my brain thinks, *She has a point.* We're only at the beginning of the process and, so far, this has been the worst wedding experience of my life. I've had to deal with demanding brides and even more demanding grooms, disorganized bridesmaids, crude best men, last-minute rips in dresses, hair disasters, and bored children running riot through church services and fancy receptions, not to mention animals.

Don't get me started on the time the goats got loose and

we discovered them on the tables before the wedding breakfast, munching on the centerpieces.

But I've never been in a situation where the bride is so determined to attack me personally every chance she gets.

I will not let her defeat me, though.

Lady Cordelia Swann is my biggest challenge yet, and I'm going to face it head-on. If I can win her over, I can win *anyone* over, and before I know it, I'll be organizing high-society weddings left, right, and center, with the best contacts and suppliers the UK has to offer.

That's what's keeping me going. That's what I have to keep telling myself.

"I don't think I'll give up quite yet," I say, shrugging.

"I'm not joking when I say I'm going to make your life hell," she threatens.

"And I'm not joking when I say I'll be waiting outside for you when you're ready. I'll get you some fresh water. Enjoy the rest of your workout."

I turn on my heel and march out, my smooth exit marginally ruined by tripping over the corner of one of those stupid gym mats on which a woman is stretching. I exhale once I'm through the door to Reception, then stroll over to speak to the man behind the front desk.

"How many exits are there from the ladies' changing room?"

"Um . . . one."

"Are you sure? Just the one? No fire escapes or anything?"

"Oh, well, there's a fire door at the back, but that's only to be used in an emergency."

"And that exit leads into which street?"

"Ixworth Place," he replies, clearly curious.

"Perfect, thank you."

I get a bottle of water from the vending machine, then head out of the building, wandering round the corner and down

Ixworth Place and stopping at the side door there. I lean against the wall and get my phone out, answering some emails that have come through this morning.

The new portaloo company I found passed my inspection test with flying colors and has confirmed for the Delgado wedding this weekend. I happily forward the confirmation on to the bride.

After about twenty minutes, the fire door swings open and Cordelia comes out, having showered and changed. She's in a blue and white striped shirt tucked into skinny black jeans, and heeled black boots, wearing big sunglasses that take up most of her face, her designer gym bag slung over one shoulder.

I wait for her to shut the door behind her before I step forward into sight.

"Great timing!" I exclaim, making her jump and nearly causing her sunglasses to fly off. "I was just finishing up my emails."

Her jaw clenches and she pushes her sunglasses up her nose. "You almost gave me a heart attack!"

"Really? I did tell you I'd wait outside for when you were done. So," I say brightly, "do you have any recommendations for places to go around here?"

"I'm not going anywhere with you," she grumbles, getting her car keys out. "If you keep following me, I'll call the police."

"Lady Meade said you're having trouble finding inspiration for your dress. I have a mood board at the ready, filled with ideas for a bespoke couture wedding dress. It includes all your favorite designers, and some others you may not have thought to consider. Give me five minutes of your time. I'll buy you a kiwi and lime smoothie."

She sighs. "Right. You just happen to know my favorite drink. Tell me, did my mother also let you have a good read of my diary while she filled you in on all my preferences, daily schedule, and gory details of my life?"

"Kiwi and lime smoothies are your favorite, too?" I feign surprise. "That's so weird!"

"A match made in heaven."

"It's only five minutes. Then I'll leave you alone."

"Forever?"

"For today."

She winces, then lets out a sigh. "Fine. Five minutes."

I mentally punch the air and walk alongside her to the smoothie bar down the road. I keep an eye on her while I order the drinks, terrified she's going to run away when my back is turned, but, thankfully, she doesn't. She chooses a small round table by the window, plonking her bag on the floor. While the blender whirs loudly and I pay, she speaks to someone on the phone—Jonathan, I think, as she looks a little less miserable for the duration of the call—then hangs up, taking off her sunglasses and placing them carefully on the table.

"Here you go." I put the green smoothie in front of her and take a sip of mine as I sit down opposite. "This is really good."

I get out my phone and log into a private board on Pinterest, spinning my phone so that it's facing her on the table. She doesn't look at the screen. Her eyes are fixed on me.

"These are some ideas I thought you'd like based on what I've gathered from your style, which may be helpful or may not. Have you had any thoughts or seen anything you like?"

She doesn't answer, continuing to frown at me in confusion, so I decide to keep going until she stops me.

"If there's anyone you'd like to speak to or showrooms you'd like to visit, you can let me know and I can help you book in those appointments. And I can come with you to—"

"This is seriously what you do for a job?" she interrupts, her eyebrows raised. "You follow brides round, like a sheep, doing whatever they say?"

"Well, I don't really see it that way. It's a little more . . . involved than that," I reason. "I wouldn't call myself a *sheep*. More like a sidekick, here to help. Robin to your Batman, if you like."

She scoffs. "Why would anyone want to be Robin?"

"Because . . . uh . . . Well, we're going off subject. This isn't about me, it's about *you* and what *you* would like for your wedding. Is there anything at all I can help you with?"

"You'll help me with *anything*? Anything I want."

I nod. "Yes. As I said, see me as your helpful sidekick. I won't get in your way. I'm just here for whatever you need."

There's a long pause as she watches me. Then she leans forward across the table, clasping her hands together. "All right then. I've been thinking about the band I want."

"Great!" I say enthusiastically, pen at the ready. "Was there a specific group that you had in mind? I can check their availability."

"Yes. Oasis."

I look up from my notepad. "Oasis. As in, the rock band Oasis?"

"Yes."

"The rock band with the Gallagher brothers? That Oasis?"

"Yes."

"The famous band that split up a few years ago. And have vowed never to get back together. You want that band to play at your wedding."

"Wouldn't that be so cool?" She twirls the straw in her smoothie. "They're the perfect vibe for the champagne reception, I think. Don't you?"

"Cordelia, I—"

"Speaking of the champagne reception, the flooring in the main hall will need to be completely redone. I won't have my guests walking in on those horrible ancient tiles. You need to talk to Daddy about that."

"You want me to ask the Marquess of Meade to refloor the

hallway of your grade-one-listed stately home?" I ask, hardly able to breathe. "That's a joke, right?"

She looks stunned. "Why would I be joking? Oh, and then I need to talk to you about the swans. A very important job for your list."

"The swans."

"I've always dreamed of having swans lead me down the aisle."

"You want swans at your wedding. In the church."

"No offense, Sophie, but are you sure you've done this brides-maid thing before?" she asks innocently. "You've been repeating everything I say, but I've noticed you haven't written many notes. I don't mean to belittle you, but isn't it your job to do whatever I want, no questions asked?"

I clear my throat and focus back on my notepad, jotting down "re-form Oasis, redo flooring, gather swans." She's giving me im-possible tasks so that I'll quit.

"As I was saying, a bevy of swans must go down the aisle ahead of me. Isn't that gorgeous? It may be tricky to train swans, but I'm sure there's nothing you wouldn't do for your dear friend." She reaches over and pats my hand. "Which leads me to the tiara. It's important to wear a very special piece of jewelry on your wed-ding day, I think. I've decided on Queen Alexandra's Kokoshnik Tiara. You must know it, of course?"

I shake my head.

"How strange," she says, tutting at me. "You're a little behind in your research. It's a very famous tiara, given to Queen Alexan-dra on her twenty-fifth wedding anniversary. I think it will suit me very well. Could you get that out on loan for me, please? It's spelled K-o-k-o-s-h-n-i-k."

"Where exactly would I be loaning that tiara from?" I ask nervously, writing it down.

"The Queen, silly!" She laughs. "Who else would have it?

It's one of her favorites. Oh, and one last thing off the top of my head, before I have to dash, what do you think of suspending peacocks from the ceiling over guests as we dine? I think we'd need a hundred or so to make an impact. And you'll need to work out how to keep the poor darlings up in the air while we eat but so that we can see them when we look up—glass platforms or something hanging from the chandeliers? Oh, I don't know, I'm awful at this sort of thing, but I know it's right up your street."

"Cordelia," I say, lowering the pen. "You can't be—"

"I also need you to get me ten photographers for the day. One is simply not enough. But they all need to be famous photographers, not just anyone. And I read somewhere that a bride had two thousand candles at her wedding? How sparse! I'm going to need at least four thousand. Make sure you write that down."

She stands up, swinging her gym bag over her shoulder, smiling down at me.

"Thank you *so* much, Sophie. Oops, Emily, I mean. You really are a lifesaver. And I know I've only given you a few of the small things to work on for now, but don't worry, I'll be sending you more ideas soon."

As she swivels to leave, her gym bag flings round and hits her still-full green smoothie glass. It knocks over and splatters all over me. I yelp, jumping up from the table, my precious notebook, phone, and clothes covered with green sludge. I quickly pick my phone off the table, desperately trying to save it with napkins.

"Whoops!" She giggles before waggling her fingers at me. "See you."

As I wipe the rest of the smoothie off my phone, gratefully taking the fresh batch of napkins offered to me by the girl behind the bar, I watch Cordelia walk to her car through the window.

She grins the whole way.

TUESDAY, 6:00 P.M., PHONE RINGS.

ROSEMARY: Hi, Sophie, is this a good time?

ME: Absolutely! How are you? Almost the big day!

ROSEMARY: I know! I can't believe it's this weekend!!

ME: Are you feeling OK? Anything you need me to do last minute?

ROSEMARY: I'm great, mostly down to you. Thanks so much for everything, especially sorting the portaloos. What a nightmare! Thank you.

ME: It's what I'm here for.

ROSEMARY: I do have a favor to ask you, but I'm scared you'll hate me!

ME: Don't be silly, ask away!

ROSEMARY: I was thinking—you know my other two bridesmaids . . .

ME: Your gorgeous cousins, Ava and Jo.

ROSEMARY: Well, it's so nice that they're both redheads.

ME: They really are stunning.

ROSEMARY: And I was looking at pictures of us all together and I thought how amazing and neat it looks, them redheads and me dark-haired, you know?

ME: Sure.

ROSEMARY: It makes me . . . stand out, if you know what I mean.

ME: Naturally.

ROSEMARY: And on my wedding day, I want to stand out. Especially in pictures.

ME: Of course!

ROSEMARY: I feel nuts asking you this but . . . do you think you'd consider dyeing your hair for the wedding?

ME: Sorry?

ROSEMARY: It sounds crazy, I know, but I've been thinking about it and now I can't get the idea out of my head! If you were all redheads, I think it would look so gorgeous! Matching! What do you think?

ME: Right! Yes! It would look lovely!

ROSEMARY: The photos will be incredible. So, are you OK to sort that?

ME: Absolutely.

ROSEMARY: Are you sure you don't mind?

ME: Of course not! I'll book a hairdresser now so it's done for the weekend.

ROSEMARY: I'll pay for it! Thank you so much, Sophie. You're the best ever! And I just know you're going to look stunning!

CHAPTER ELEVEN

O h, my God," Cara gasps, when I walk into the pub. "Your hair!"

"I know." I pull out the empty chair at the table and take off my jacket. "What do you think?"

I was wondering about canceling on the pub quiz night that Jen has organized, but it's so rare I can go to group things that I thought I should make an effort. I'd have much rather sat at home on my own, figuring out how I was going to deal with Cordelia's list of demands, but I thought it would be good for me to allow myself a bit of fun.

I'm also aware that everyone in our friendship group will know about Daniel's wedding, and I want them to see I'm absolutely fine.

"It's very different," Jen says enthusiastically. "Good different."

"Really?"

"Yeah." She nods, grinning at me. "You look cool."

"I agree," Mike says, giving Cara a look. "It's very trendy. Very cool."

"Yeah, trendy," Cara repeats, acknowledging his signal. "But it's so . . . different."

"I fancied a change. Thank you, Mike," I say, as he fills one of the spare glasses on the table from their bottle. I move round the table to greet everyone. As well as Jen and her husband, Ollie, there's Becca, Aiden, and Ryan, all of us friends since first year of university.

"Whoa, whoa, whoa." Cara holds up her hands, staring me down. "You're going to leave it at that? You walk in here with this huge change of lifestyle and you expect us to accept your explanation of 'I fancied a change'? We need answers!"

"It's only my hair, Cara." I smile, picking up my glass. "It's hardly a lifestyle change."

"Is this because of Taylor Swift?"

"What? Why would I change my hair because of Taylor Swift?"

"You did last time."

"No, I didn't," I protest, even though she's right.

I wanted to look young and carefree like Taylor does in her music video for "22," so I attempted a fringe like hers. It lasted two days. Fringes are *very* hard to maintain and I don't have the time or energy with such a fast-paced career.

(And it looked awful.)

"I know the inspiration behind this!" Cara suddenly says, her face lighting up as I sip my wine. "Lady Cordelia Swann!"

I spit my wine out, coughing and spluttering. Mike hands me a tissue to dab my chin.

"Do you remember Lady Cordelia?" Cara continues, oblivious. "When she dyed her hair red back in our teens, I tried to do the same, but it went . . . er . . . wrong."

"Wasn't she on one of those reality TV shows?" Jen asks, Ollie nodding along.

"No, she was much too classy for that," Cara says defensively.

"Yeah," I mutter into my wine, attempting a more successful sip, "she's *really* classy."

"I remember her," Becca says, stirring her gin and tonic with her straw.

"She was a socialite a while ago, we were obsessed with her, weren't we, Sophie? Anyway," Cara shrugs, "I thought you might be harking back to our youth with this redhead vibe."

"I like it," I say defiantly. "I think it suits me."

"I think so too," Ollie agrees, before noticing something at the bar. "Ah, I think they're giving out quiz sheets."

"I'll fetch one," I offer, getting to my feet. "I need the loo anyway."

"Me too," Cara says, her chair screeching across the floor as she pushes it back.

I notice she gives Mike a meaningful look and I have a fleeting worry that somehow they know about the Lady Cordelia thing. But surely she wouldn't have joked about her if she knew. Mike doesn't know about my real job anyway.

"Seriously, what's with the hair?" Cara asks, once we've passed a quiz sheet to our team and set off for the loo. "You didn't tell me you were going for such a drastic change."

"It was requested by a bride," I inform her quietly, making sure Jen hasn't tagged along without us noticing.

"She asked you to dye your hair ginger?"

"Yes."

"Because?"

"Her other bridesmaids are redheads and she's brunette and she thought it would be good in the photos if all the bridesmaids were matching and she stood out." I push open the door to the toilets. "Yay, no queue!"

"Hang on." Cara laughs, going into the cubicle next to me. "She asked you to dye your hair ginger to blend in more with the other bridesmaids so she could stand out. Because it isn't enough that she will be in, oh, I don't know, a *white wedding dress*?"

"I don't think it looks that bad."

"That is *madness*."

"Trust me, it's not the craziest demand I've had this week."

"Your job is nuts," Cara says, when we're washing our hands.

"But I have to say, it's truly entertaining. I feel sorry for all our friends who have no idea about these crazy tales. Was I as out of control as these brides when I was getting married?"

"No, you were perfect."

She grins. "Do you say that to all your brides?"

"Only my favorites," I say, going to open the door.

"Sophie, wait," she says, lurking near the hand dryer. "Before we go back out there, I need to tell you something."

"Is everything OK?" I ask.

"I'm just going to say it." She takes a deep breath, looking pained, then blurts out, "Daniel's coming here tonight. Aiden invited him."

"What?" I lean on the basin, feeling a bit light-headed. "He's coming here? Tonight?"

"Yeah."

I stare at her in horror. "Is Francesca coming?"

"No, she's staying home with the puppy."

"The *puppy*?" I whimper, mortified to find my eyes filling with tears. "They have a *puppy*?"

"I bet it's ugly."

"No puppy is ugly."

"I bet Daniel's is."

"Oh, God."

She watches me, her expression tense, full of sympathy. "Are you OK?"

Pull yourself together, Sophie. Don't be pathetic.

"Yeah. I'm . . . I should have . . . I mean, it's all the university group so of course he's coming. Why didn't I consider this?"

"Jen didn't invite him," Cara assures me. "They all think it's really messed up that he sent you a wedding invitation. She purposely didn't invite him because she wanted you to have a fun night out and then, well, just before you arrived Aiden dropped it into conversation. He didn't realize it would be such a big deal."

She gives me a small smile. "If it makes you feel any better, Jen laid into him big-time. You do not want to mess with a pregnant woman."

I run a hand through my hair. "Argh, I wasn't prepared for this. I don't know how to act around him."

"You've been around him before and you've always played it so well." She rolls her eyes. "If I was forced to hang around my exes, I'd be livid and probably end up throwing a drink or something, but you've always been so calm and civil. I'd go so far as to say you've been *nice* to the knobhead."

"Yeah, but those times he wasn't engaged to someone else. He hadn't sent me a wedding invitation. I'm not sure I'm ready to handle this."

"Sophie, you are one hundred percent ready to handle Daniel and his stupid marriage," Cara says firmly, grabbing my hands. "Look at you! You're a gorgeous, fiery redhead with a high-flying career and pregnant friends who will fight to the death for you— literally. I was genuinely worried that Jen was going to smash Aiden's face into the table."

Cara looks me dead in the eye, then continues, in a gentler tone, "If you want to go, we can go. But, personally, I don't think you should miss out on an evening with friends simply because an ex-boyfriend is taking a step forward in his life. He's out of yours anyway. You're on different paths now. Who cares what happens on his? Let's only focus on yours."

I let her words sink in, then look at her suspiciously. "That was really wise."

"Yeah. It was."

"Did you write that down earlier?"

"I actually messaged your mum as soon as Aiden said Daniel was coming. She told me what to say. I memorized it."

I laugh, shaking my head at her.

"Come on," she says, "let's get back out there. The first quiz round is geography and Mike, albeit a clever man, has no concept of where anything is in the world. The other day he got Munich and Milan mixed up. I should be there before he says anything stupid and gets us kicked off the team."

I nod and, together, we walk out of the ladies', Cara leading the way with one hand holding mine. Butterflies are going crazy in my stomach and my fingers are tingling with the nerves.

Daniel is there, sitting at the table. He looks good. He's wearing a light blue shirt and beige chinos, an outfit that actually matches unlike many of his questionable choices when we were together. His hair is much shorter and he's lost some weight but has also apparently toned up. He looks really healthy and happy.

DAMN IT.

He sees me and immediately looks astounded, his eyes widening in surprise. I start panicking about how bad I must look to cause such a reaction, then remember my hair.

"Hi!" he says, standing up awkwardly to greet Cara and me with a wave.

Others at the table are sitting tensely. Jen throws a dirty look at Aiden, who shrinks back into his chair.

Cara smiles indifferently at him, taking her seat. "Oh, hi, Daniel. Hey, Mike, can you pass me the wine? When does the quiz start?"

"Hi, Daniel," I say confidently, swallowing the lump in my throat and going over to kiss him on each cheek, as though I'm greeting an old friend, which I suppose, technically, he is. "How are you?"

He's wearing the same cologne he always used to. Gucci. The smell of him hits me much harder than seeing him. Funny how a scent can bring back a hundred memories.

"Hey, Sophie, I'm good."

The elephant in the room is stomping around so heavily, I have to comment on it.

"Congratulations on your engagement," I blurt out.

"Thanks! It's all very exciting."

"Yeah. So exciting. Wonderful news." I'm making sure I say all the right things. "And you have a puppy!"

"That's right. Simba. He's a dachshund. Want to see a picture?"

"Yes!"

"Here."

He gets his phone out of his pocket. His screensaver is a picture of him and Francesca, obviously taken just after he proposed. They're beaming at the camera, her eyes slightly red from crying, and she's holding up her left hand, the emerald sparkling in the sunshine.

And I haven't even been on a date since we broke up.

Not. One. Date.

I can feel the anxious gaze of our friends watching our interaction while trying their best to pretend they're talking about something else. I wait for him to scroll through his photos, stealing a glimpse at the snapshots of his new life. It looks happy and fun and perfect.

"Here he is," Daniel says, clicking on a photo of the cutest dachshund puppy in the world.

"He's adorable. I like his eyebrows."

"They make him look intelligent, I think."

"Yes, very authoritative."

"He's thick, though. Adorable, but an idiot. Guys," he says, addressing the table and interrupting their conversations, "I have to tell you this story about my dumb dog yesterday. It's hilarious. He basically got stuck in one of Francesca's jumper sleeves. So, he was on the sofa next to me, right . . ."

As Daniel takes center stage and launches into his humorous story, I quietly move away from him to take my seat next to Cara. She smiles at me proudly. The others burst out laughing at a point in Daniel's story and I laugh along, but I'm not listening to a word he says. I'm too busy dealing with the bucketload of emotions I'm currently feeling—relief that we managed a perfectly normal discussion, irritation at him showing up and ruining what was supposed to be a relaxed, happy evening for me, and sadness that out of everyone around this table, I used to know most about him and now I know least.

Daniel's entertaining story comes to an end and a man at the bar announces the quiz is about to begin. I sip my wine as a team name is decided on and we launch into the first round. I've never been brilliant at quizzes, and with Daniel here I'm even more reluctant to pipe up with an answer in case I get it wrong and everyone laughs at me, offering Daniel validation for breaking up with such a loser.

I confidently know one answer during the second round—the "Name That Film" round—when the only clue provided is a quote about the dangers of giving your heart away to something wild.

"Oh, I know," Daniel says, tapping the quiz sheet excitedly, "it's that cheesy musical. What's it called? *Moulin Rouge!* That's it."

Ollie starts to write it out and I have to stop him. "No, it's not. Sorry, it's *Breakfast at Tiffany's*."

Daniel frowns at me. "Are you sure?"

"Yeah, I'm sure. Sorry."

"Don't apologize for getting an answer right." Becca smiles, as Ollie crosses out what he's written so far.

"Hmm," Daniel says, shrugging. "I still think Nicole Kidman said it, but if you're sure."

I waver. "I . . . uh . . ."

"I think it is *Breakfast at Tiffany's*," Jen says, nodding thoughtfully. "Now that you've said it, it definitely sounds right."

"OK." Daniel shrugs, as Ollie writes down my answer. "You

were always good on films, Sophie. That is," he adds, with a smile, "only rom-coms."

"What?" I laugh, as though his throwaway comment is not affecting me to the core. "I don't just watch rom-coms. I like lots of films."

"Only the ones when you know there's a happy ending," he notes, taking a sip of his drink. "Any hint that things might not turn out as they should and you'd scarper." He sees my expression and grins. "It's not a bad thing!"

It is a bad thing, though, I think, smiling perfectly so no one will notice it's bothering me. *That was a dig. You think I only like happy films, the ones that bored you. That's what you're implying, isn't it? Francesca probably likes watching Oscar-winning gritty films where everyone dies at the end.*

"Can we have some focus, please?" Ollie cuts in, shooting Daniel a look. "Did you hear that last question? In which 1997 romance film did actor Rupert Everett sing Dionne Warwick's 'I Say a Little Prayer,' catapulting the song back into the top forty almost thirty years after the original was released?"

Daniel smiles at me. "Sophie?"

"It's—it's *My Best Friend's Wedding*," I say, admitting defeat.

While Cara shakes her head at an oblivious Daniel, everyone else on the team congratulates me for getting another answer. Unbelievable how Daniel has managed to make me feel ashamed of getting quiz questions correct.

I twist my wineglass round, wondering how I became so predictable.

"We'll get the next round," Cara announces during the break in the quiz, standing up and patting Mike's back to encourage him onto his feet. "Same again?"

There's a murmur of agreement and Cara and Mike head to the bar.

"You know, Sophie, I think you should keep your hair that color," Jen says, rubbing her bump. "It suits you."

"I agree." Becca nods. "It looks great."

"Thanks." I laugh, embarrassed. "Maybe I will keep it."

"Really?" Daniel says, unable to hide his disapproval.

I raise my eyebrows at him. "Is it that bad?"

"No, no, it's not *bad*," he emphasizes, as the rest of the table falls into a tense silence. "It's just not very you. It's . . . out there."

He accompanies his description with jazz hands. As I work out what I should say, Becca comes to my rescue, launching into a story about when she cut her own hair as a kid. Daniel listens to her, enraptured, while I look down at my hands, thinking about what he meant.

Red hair, according to Daniel, is *out there*, and therefore doesn't suit me. Am I not cool enough for this color? Is that what he meant?

"No, course not," Cara tells me, when we're waiting together outside the pub for our Ubers to arrive. "He's just being a prick."

Daniel left with Aiden as soon as the quiz finished, saying he'd better get back to the puppy, which was no doubt being spoiled rotten and having all of its basic training ruined by Francesca. I waved him a cheery goodbye as he exited the pub to return to his perfect life.

"Don't torture yourself with a throwaway comment that he probably didn't mean anything by," Cara continues, Mike nodding next to her. "Who cares what Daniel thinks anyway?"

"I wish I knew what he meant by 'out there.' Is it a good or a bad thing? And what was with him going on about me only liking happy endings? Does that make me boring? Does everyone think I'm boring?"

"Sophie, stop," Cara pleads, grabbing my arm. "No one thinks you're boring. Daniel is not in your life anymore. What does it matter what he thinks? All that matters is what *you* think."

"Yeah, but it was the way he said it. Like, this hair color was too daring for me or something. Too out there for someone who hides in the shadows, trailing after everyone else," I add, thinking about Cordelia's sheep comment.

"I don't think that's what he meant," Mike says.

"Me neither," Cara agrees.

"He'd be right, though, wouldn't he?" I reason. "He knows I don't have the guts to do something crazy like dye my hair red. I'm boring and safe, like the movies I watch."

"But you have dyed your hair red," Mike points out, his brow furrowed in confusion.

"I know, but . . . Never mind."

"Go home, get cozy, and stop thinking about it," Cara recommends, as my Uber draws up. "You were amazing tonight. Handled a horrible awkward situation like a pro."

"No reason for it to be awkward," I say, giving her a hug goodbye. "I'm happy for him."

"You've said no to his invitation, though, right?" Cara prompts.

"Yes. Course," I lie, opening the car door and jumping in. "Get home safe!"

I sit back, wracked with guilt for lying to Cara. She's right. I have to say no and put this whole thing behind me. I've put it off long enough.

I get home, walk straight into my office, and pick up Daniel's wedding invitation.

I run my finger over the embossed letters.

I've been pretending I didn't have to say goodbye to him quite yet.

When I found out he was dating someone else just two months after we broke up, I wondered whether I was crazy and had dreamed up our entire relationship. I was still in that horrible agony of a breakup, when you wake up and have an actual ache in your heart because that person is gone. And he was already dating someone else and putting pictures of them together up on social media. Him and Francesca in the Lake District. Him and Francesca sipping cocktails in a rooftop bar. Francesca rock-climbing, looking down at the camera from the top, sticking her tongue out and making a stupid face.

I blocked him eventually, so I wouldn't be subjected to the torture.

"I wish you hadn't sent me this invitation," I say out loud.

I pick up a pen and tick the box next to "I will not be attending," slide the RSVP into the return envelope, and put it into my bag.

I'll post it tomorrow.

From: Carla@marissamedleycakes.co.uk

To: Sophie.Breeze@zapmail.co.uk

Subject: Clare Walsh wedding cake

Dear Sophie,

Hope you're well. We met when you came with Clare Walsh for her cake tasting recently and you very kindly gave me your details, as well as Clare's.

I'm sorry to bother you, but I wanted to run something past you as one of Clare's bridesmaids and most trusted friends. Clare's fiancé, Dominic, called and left a message, asking me to change the wedding cake as a big surprise for Clare on the day.

As you may recall, Clare ordered a three-tiered ivory fondant-iced cake with climbing sugar flowers up each tier. Dominic has requested that we change the order and produce a wedding cake in the shape of a camel. He

informed me that he proposed after a camel ride on a
holiday in Marrakech.

I'm not sure how to proceed in this circumstance. The last
thing I would like is for the bride to be upset on her wedding
day because, when the cake is revealed, it is not in fact the
classic ivory design she ordered, but instead a camel.

I would hate to ruin the surprise but I'm a little
uncomfortable to go ahead with such a drastic change
without permission from the bride.

I thought I would ask your thoughts on the matter before
contacting Dominic.

Should I go ahead and make the camel? Do let me know
your thoughts.

Best wishes,

Carla

From: Carla@marissamedleycakes.co.uk

To: Sophie.Breeze@zapmail.co.uk

Subject: Clare Walsh wedding cake FOLLOW UP

Hi Sophie,

Lovely to speak to you this morning, thanks for giving me a
call.

I have just got off the phone with Dominic and, as you
advised, I suggested that we stick to the cake Clare
ordered for the wedding day, as it's her dream cake, BUT
in addition I could still create a surprise camel cake for the
bridal party dinner the night before.

Just like you suggested, I carefully explained that the camel
was a thoughtful, wonderful surprise but we wouldn't want
to risk causing Clare a pang of disappointment if she didn't
get the wedding cake she'd imagined.

He began to agree with me and by the end of the call,
I think he thought it was all his idea in the first place!

I'm thrilled to now be making two cakes for the happy

couple—a camel cake *and* a traditional three-tiered. Thank you for all your help. And don't worry, as promised, I didn't mention you at all.

Out of interest, do you know if the camel Clare rode had one hump or two?

Best wishes,

Carla

From: Sophie.Breeze@zapmail.co.uk

To: Carla@marissamedleycakes.co.uk

Subject: Re: Clare Walsh wedding cake FOLLOW UP

Dear Carla,

I'm so pleased it all got worked out.

Regarding the camel humps, I have managed to stealthily get it out of Clare that the one she rode had one hump.

Best wishes,

Sophie

From: Carla@marissamedleycakes.co.uk

To: Sophie.Breeze@zapmail.co.uk

Subject: Re: re: Clare Walsh wedding cake FOLLOW UP

Dear Sophie,

How did you manage to get that information from Clare about the camel humps "stealthily"?

My colleagues and I are dying to know!

Best wishes,

Carla

From: Sophie.Breeze@zapmail.co.uk

To: Carla@marissamedleycakes.co.uk

Subject: Re: re: re: Clare Walsh wedding cake FOLLOW UP

Dear Carla,

Clare is currently under the impression that I am doing an evening course in zoology.

She's already messaged me twice, the first time asking if tortoises make good pets, and the second time wanting to know if it's possible she just saw a toucan fly over her head in Covent Garden.

It's going to be an interesting lie to keep up, but all worth it for the camel cake surprise!

Best wishes,

Sophie

CHAPTER TWELVE

The Monday after the Delgado wedding, I get a phone call that makes my heart soar.

It's the PA of world-famous photographer Clio Vaughn. They received my message and Clio would be happy to schedule a meeting. I agree on a date, time, and place with the PA and then, when he hangs up, I punch the air in victory, dancing on the spot around my office (cupboard) and almost banging my head on the corner of the bookshelf.

After extensive research, I discovered that Cordelia had bought some original work by Clio and been recently photographed at an exhibition of hers. I deduced she must be a fan. I sent an email to Clio's PA on the off chance that she might consider photographing the wedding of Lady Cordelia Swann. I said that I appreciated that Clio might not be interested in a wedding, but that of course this wasn't just any wedding and Lady Cordelia was a huge admirer of her work.

I didn't think I'd get a reply, but the Swann family name carries weight and it's caught Clio's interest, especially since she's currently working in London. Emily Taylor will be meeting Clio Vaughn at the Dorchester at 11:00 A.M. next Friday.

The confirmation comes through on email and I quickly reply thanking the PA, careful to sign off as Emily. Because of the magnitude of this wedding and the importance of keeping up Emily's identity, I'd created a separate email account. Emily

Taylor definitely needs her own for all these strange requests she's sending out. The meeting with the photographer is a win, but so far Emily's emails to Liam Gallagher's manager have gone unanswered.

When I've finished responding to Clio's PA, I close my laptop and pick out what to wear for when I see Cordelia, Jonathan, and Lady Meade today. They have an appointment with a London florist, and Lady Meade thinks it's best I accompany them.

"Cordelia was thinking a lily-of-the-valley bouquet, which is beautiful, but I think has been overdone since Catherine's wedding," she told me yesterday over the phone. "I suggested we consider a few ideas, perhaps something a bit more unique and unusual, before making a final decision and she snapped my head off. We could do with a voice of reason."

Feeling puffed up that Lady Meade thinks I'm a voice of reason, I told her I'd be delighted to attend. It took me a while to realize that the Catherine she'd mentioned was the Duchess of Cambridge.

"Thank you, Emily." She sighed. "Cordelia says that a white bouquet will match the swans, but I'm not sure what she's talking about. I hope she's not planning on bringing swans anywhere near my house."

"No, I'm sure she's not," I assured her, laughing nervously.

It wasn't a lie. Cordelia had only talked about swans going down the aisle in the church. I thought it best to stay quiet about the peacocks.

I left the flat feeling positive and in control. If I could land a meeting with a top photographer, maybe I had a chance of ticking off some of the other outrageous demands on Cordelia's list. I get a coffee on the way and sit on the tube, looking at my fellow Londoners cheerily. *Today is a good day,* I think.

The florist's studio is a ten-minute walk from the station, and when I arrive, I'm not sure I'm in the right place. I check the address again. I'm definitely at the right one, but it looks like a normal house on a residential road. I ring the bell.

"Yes?" a voice crackles through the intercom.

"Oh, hi! I'm Emily Taylor. I'm here to see—"

The door buzzes and I push it open. I'm stunned by the interiors, which are all very modern, in stark contrast to the pretty Victorian style of the outside, and I'm slightly freaked out when I'm greeted by a young man in his twenties, dressed from head to toe in black and wearing a pair of white gloves. Although he's clean-shaven, the pronounced stubble above his top lip reveals he is currently attempting to grow a mustache.

"Welcome, Miss Taylor," he says in a clipped accent, gesturing up the stairs. "Please follow me."

Concerned as to why he's wearing a pair of gloves, I head up the stairs, taking in the photographs lining the bright white walls, all arty shots of various flowers on a black background. As we near the top, I hear muffled voices. It sounds like an argument and I notice the gloved man shudder as he stops before a door on the landing. He opens it to reveal a large studio space, brightly lit by the sun shining through the huge windows. In the middle of the room is a long table with bright yellow stools.

A small middle-aged woman with curly platinum hair, purple lipstick, and statement gold hoop earrings is sitting with a weary expression on one of the stools at the end of the table in front of what looks like sheets and sheets of bouquet designs. Lady Meade is sitting near her, rubbing her temples, with Jonathan perched next to his future mother-in-law. Cordelia is pacing by the windows.

"Hello, Emily," Jonathan says brightly, appearing grateful for a distraction from the conversation they were having before I walked in.

Cordelia scowls when she sees me. I'm getting used to it.

"What have you done to your hair?" she asks, wrinkling her nose.

"Dyed it. Temporarily," I add.

She tilts her head. "Why?"

"Emily, hi," Lady Meade jumps in, looking as though she's only just keeping it together. "This is Nicole Percy."

The purple-lipsticked woman stands up to shake my hand. "You're the bridesmaid."

"Yes. Sorry, I hope I'm not late."

"Cordelia insisted on being early," Lady Meade explains. "I wanted to call you to let you know, but she didn't give me much notice."

"I didn't want to bother you," Cordelia says to me, in a sickeningly sweet tone, walking over to her handbag, which is resting on the table. She pulls out a packet of cigarettes. "You've got so much to be getting on with already."

"Yes, and I've made good progress actually. I'm looking forward to discussing it with you."

I can see she's taken aback, but hides it by concentrating instead on getting a lighter out of her pocket.

"You cannot smoke in here," Nicole says suddenly, as Cordelia puts a cigarette between her lips. "You're welcome to go outside, but please do not light that in my studio."

"Fine," she says, as Nicole glares at her. "I'll save it for later."

"I didn't realize I was meeting you today, Nicole," I say, trying to break the tension in the room. "I'm a big fan. I saw the arrangements you did for Melissa Fuller's wedding last Christmas. Absolutely beautiful."

Nicole's expression softens. "You were at that wedding?"

"I saw it on Instagram. I follow her. She's one of my favorite actors."

This is a lie. I saw Nicole Percy's flower arrangements for Melissa Fuller's wedding on the #weddinginspo feed that I check many times a day. Before then, I didn't have a clue who Melissa Fuller was.

"Thank you. Melissa and I shared a magical vision. Most brides I work with appreciate that they are working with an *artist*, not just a florist."

Cordelia ignores her pointed comment, going back to staring out of the window.

"Yes," I say, hopping up onto one of the stools. "Your space is lovely. It feels like a painter's studio."

The man who led me to the room—I discover he's Nicole's assistant, Francis—steps forward and inhales dramatically, commanding our attention. For a terrifying moment, I think he's about to launch into some kind of performance piece but, thankfully, I'm wrong. He's merely taking the stage for a speech it sounds like he has made many times.

"Nicole is a leading artist of the floral London scene with a unique, impassioned, and ardent approach to floral design. Inspired by the world around her, the soil on which she steps, the air she breathes, and her untamed connection to nature, she produces floristry the like of which has never been seen before. Her tools are but flowers, her brushes are the petals parading the planet's organic colors, and her canvas is all we see before us. It is her duty and honor to connect with you, to interpret your desires and create a concept of sensational harmony."

He finishes with a great flourish of his hands and Nicole bows her head in gratitude as the room falls into silence. Jonathan looks at a loss as to the politest way to react to this unexpected speech, and lifts his hands to clap, then seems to think better of it, settling for an enthusiastic double thumbs-up instead.

I purse my lips, my eyes watering as I attempt not to laugh.

Then something extraordinary happens. I glance at Cordelia and she happens to look at me at the same time. Our eyes meet and the corner of her mouth twitches as she tries very hard not to burst out laughing either. We're thinking the same thing and we share a smile, which prompts Cordelia to let out a giggle that she attempts to cover with a coughing fit.

"Sorry," she says, clearing her throat. "Tickle in my throat."

"Very interesting words, Francis," Lady Meade says, shooting her daughter a warning look.

I have never been more grateful for such absurdity. Thanks to Francis and his Shakespearean turn, Cordelia and I had a *connection*. A fleeting one, but a connection all the same.

There's hope yet. I *knew* today would be a good one.

"Perhaps we should begin to discuss ideas," Lady Meade prompts, as Francis glides to the stool next to me and takes his place. "I know Cordelia—"

"Please." Nicole raises her hand.

Lady Meade is not used to being interrupted and a flash of irritation crosses her expression, but it's gone as quickly as it came.

"First, we need to rid the studio of the negative vibes," Nicole says sternly. "I cannot work in this atmosphere."

"I don't feel any negative vibes," I say, with a look of approval from Lady Meade. "I feel extremely grateful to be here and uplifted by the prospect of working with such a renowned florist. I mean, *artist*."

"Before you arrived, Miss Taylor, there was a feud," Francis informs me, in an audible whisper. "Nicole cannot create a vision of harmony when such tension exists. She needs to begin with peace. That's why she starts the process here in this vast, empty studio and not in her shop, among the flowers."

"Flowers aren't . . . peaceful?" I ask innocently.

Cordelia has another tickle in her throat, sharing a bemused look with Jonathan and moving away from the window to sit down next to him.

"Not before they are placed within the art form," Francis explains.

"Oh, I see. Yeah, I know what you mean," I say, nodding. "When they're all in those pots, they can look a bit messy."

"I do not like mess," Nicole informs me. "I do not like a messy studio and I do not like a messy ambience. A feud creates a mess."

"There's no feud, I assure you," Lady Meade tells Nicole, with a touch of impatience. "Cordelia and I merely had a small difference of opinion, but we will come to an agreement, won't we, Cordelia?"

"I doubt it. But I don't really care." Cordelia shrugs. "It's my wedding and if I want the theme to be gold and black, that's what we'll be doing."

"*Our* wedding," Jonathan corrects, with a knowing smile.

"Sorry," Cordelia says, rolling her eyes and grinning. "*Our* wedding."

It sounds like he's had to make that correction a few times.

"I thought you wanted a lily-of-the-valley bouquet," I say, confused.

"She did," Lady Meade says. "But apparently she's changed her mind."

"We'll need to change the swans to black ones," Cordelia barks at me, whatever connection we had forgotten.

"Cordelia, *please*, stop this nonsense," Lady Meade pleads. "You're only being difficult with the flowers because you're trying to get back at me over the guest list."

"I don't know what you're talking about," Cordelia says innocently.

"We can't remove them from the guest list, you know that! It would be unimaginable. It would be a scandal, talked about among our friends for the rest of time. Your father won't let it happen."

Jonathan shifts in his seat, glancing at Cordelia nervously.

"Remove who from the guest list?" I ask.

"I don't care about the scandal it would cause," Cordelia snaps at her mother, ignoring me. "They're not coming to my wedding."

"Yes, they are," Lady Meade says, with such authority I get a shiver down my spine.

Cordelia's jaw clenches as she glares at her mother, who holds her gaze with steely determination.

"We can talk about this later," Jonathan says, as brightly as he can, attempting to defuse the tension. "Let's focus on the flowers. Cordelia?"

He places a hand over hers and she breaks away from the staring contest with her mother to look at him impatiently. He smiles encouragingly.

Cordelia's anger seems to dissipate a bit. She sighs, standing up and grabbing her handbag. "I don't have time for this," she says, under her breath, marching across the room toward the door.

"Where do you think you're going?" Lady Meade asks sharply. "We haven't finished."

"I have. I'm done," Cordelia replies, and slams the door behind her.

We hear her stomping down the stairs. Jonathan looks down at his hands in his lap.

"Shall I?" I gesture to the door.

"No, don't follow her," Lady Meade instructs. "Let her have her moment."

"I'll go," Jonathan says, pushing his stool back, the legs screeching across the floor. "Thank you so much for your time, Nicole. I look forward to working with you."

"I'm sorry, Lady Meade," Nicole begins, once Jonathan has left, "but I cannot accept your request for me to undertake the floral design of this wedding."

"Nicole, do be reasonable," Lady Meade says, stunned.

"I will not work with your daughter," Nicole says firmly, Francis nodding vigorously next to me in agreement. "She clouds the clarity of my vision. The answer is no. But thank you for coming today. It is an honor to meet you."

"I see." Lady Meade stands up and I nervously follow suit. "I must say I'm disappointed, but I respect your wishes. Thank you for your time."

They shake hands, and Francis leaps to his feet to usher us out. Lady Meade doesn't speak until we've left the house and have walked a good few meters down the road. She stops and lets out a long sigh, beside an empty parking space.

"I'm guessing they took the car," I say, biting my lip. "Do you want me to call you a taxi?"

"That's quite all right. I'll call our driver. Would you like a lift?" she asks, getting her phone from her handbag. "Ah, a text from Jonathan. He apologizes for taking the car and has called my driver, Joe, who is already on his way. We can drop you anywhere you'd like."

"No, thank you. That's really kind but I can walk to the tube. It's not far."

"Very well. What a pity to have lost Nicole Percy," she says wistfully. "I thought she would be the perfect choice. She's the best."

"We'll find another florist," I say confidently, deciding I should wait with her until her car arrives. It would be rude to leave the Marchioness of Meade stranded on her own.

"Anyone who's *anyone* has Nicole Percy as their florist," Lady Meade informs me, with a hint of tongue-in-cheek. "Maybe that's why Cordelia was against her from the start."

"A florist who is less well known would be more interesting. Cordelia isn't one to follow the crowd," I point out. "She likes to be different."

"I suppose. Nicole knows what she's doing, though. We can't have just anyone."

"Of course not. They have to be the best of the best."

"Yes, but that's not what I meant. We need someone who can handle my daughter. I'm not sure if you've noticed," she says, staring into the distance, "but she has a bit of a temper."

OK. Here goes.

DRAFT ONE

Her Majesty The Queen
Buckingham Palace
London
SW1A 1AA
Madam,
With my humble duty, I am writing to you to ask whether
you would consider loaning Queen Alexandra's Kokoshnik
Tiara for my friend who . . . fhjdslfnlskBFEUpr
Ugh. Start again.

DRAFT TWO

Her Majesty The Queen
Buckingham Palace
London
SW1A 1AA
Madam,
I hope this letter finds you and the family well. We have
never met, however I believe you may know the Swann
family and I was wondering . . . !!!!!!!
Oh, my God, this is impossible.

DRAFT THREE

Her Majesty The Queen
Buckingham Palace
London
SW1A 1AA
Madam,
This is a somewhat bizarre request. Bear with me.
As you are aware, you own the beautiful Kokoshnik Tiara
and . . .

FFS, you can't say "Bear with me" to the Queen, Sophie! Have you lost your mind? I actually hate this.

DRAFT FOUR

Her Majesty The Queen
Buckingham Palace
London
SW1A 1AA
Madam,
How are you? I . . .

Sure. Go casual. The Queen will love that.
GET YOUR HEAD IN THE GAME!!!! Start. Again.

DRAFT FIVE

Her Majesty The Queen
Buckingham Palace
London
SW1A 1AA

Madam,
I am writing to you today with a request that I hope Your
Majesty will consider. Would you possibly . . .

AAAAH!
I hate my life.

CHAPTER THIRTEEN

C ordelia has somehow got worse.

There I was, thinking we had a new connection, a simple shared smile where we were both on the same page, joining in the comedy of a ridiculous florist/artist. It had given me so much hope because when something silly happens you look at your friend as you laugh, right? Your *friend*. She didn't make eye contact with her mum, she didn't look at Jonathan, she looked at *me*.

It had to mean something. Or so I thought.

Instead of the beginning of a beautiful friendship, though, it seems to have gone in the opposite direction. The "connection" I thought had been there must have been a figment of my imagination. When my phone first vibrated with a message from her after the disastrous meeting with Nicole, my reaction was an excited gasp.

This is it! I thought, opening my WhatsApp. *Maybe she'll be messaging asking to go for a drink and chat about fun wedding stuff!*

I could not have been more naïve: *Pick up dry cleaning. Tomorrow, 2 p.m.*

I thought maybe she'd made a mistake: she'd meant to put it in her diary as a reminder but had accidentally sent it to me. But a slew of instructions has since come through, without a word of gratitude or acknowledgment that I'm not really her PA. I'm her bridesmaid.

It's been getting worse all week. I've been asked—no, not asked, *told*—to respond to emails that she's forwarded me with no explanation, book hair and beauty appointments on her behalf, and at one point fetch a coffee randomly for her therapist, whom she wasn't even seeing that day. The therapist looked stunned to see me standing on her doorstep, saying, "Your skinny almond-milk extra-hot latte," and slammed the door in my face, clearly thinking I was a total loon.

"Who is this new bride of yours?" Cara asks in disgust.

She had just asked me where I am and I'd told her the truth—on the train to go to a farm shop in Hertfordshire to get a specific truffle oil that Cordelia insisted she needed for cooking that evening. Apparently it's not sold anywhere else in the country and she doesn't trust a courier to pick it up. She only trusts her "favorite bridesmaid."

"She's a bit high-maintenance, but it's fine," I insist, lying through my teeth. "I can do other work on the train."

"A bit high-maintenance? She sounds like the boss from *The Devil Wears Prada*. What's her name? You know, Meryl Streep's character."

"Miranda Priestly," I inform her.

"That's the one. She's like a real-life Miranda Priestly, except she's getting married, not running a high-fashion magazine empire. Why are you putting up with her?"

"Because she's an important client."

"Well, in my opinion, she can shove her truffle oil up her—"

"All right, calm down." I chuckle, looking out of the window at the fields sweeping by. "How's everything with you?"

"Fine. Work's stressful. Mike's obsessed with a new video game, so that's annoying." She sighs heavily. "Do you think he'll ever grow out of video games?"

"If he hasn't grown out of them at the age of thirty-five, I don't think it's likely."

"I'm going to break it accidentally on purpose. Don't tell him."

"My lips are sealed."

"What are you up to this weekend?"

"Working, I imagine."

"You don't have a wedding?"

"No, but I have a lot of wedding stuff to do."

"Any chance of meeting for a drink?"

"Yeah! I'd love to see you and catch up."

"Ah," she says, "not with me. With someone else. Mike's friend Scott is really nice and he's super keen to meet you."

"Cara," I sigh, "no. I'm not going on a date."

"Why not? You said you could meet for a drink!"

"Yes, with *you*. Not with someone I don't know. It's hard enough making time for my friends and family, let alone some random guy."

"He's not a random guy, he's Mike's friend. It would be fun! You might enjoy it."

"Sorry, I've got too much work to do."

"Come on, Sophie, live a little. In that *Devil Wears Prada* movie, she realizes running errands for that bitch isn't worth giving up her social life."

"This is completely different from that film," I argue.

"I don't know, Sophie. It's early Thursday morning and, instead of doing anything you really care about, you're currently on a train all the way to Hertfordshire to get a bottle of truffle oil. It sounds very similar to me."

There's a beeping in my ear as a call comes through. I check the ID. "Cara, I've got to go. I have another call."

"Is it Miranda?"

"I'll speak to you later."

She hangs up reluctantly and I pick up Lady Meade's call, catching her just before she rings off.

"Emily, good morning."

Her voice is sharp and stern, and I straighten in my seat as though I'm in trouble with the headmistress.

"Lady Meade, how are you?"

"Where are you?"

"On the train to Hertfordshire. If this is about Cordelia's truffle oil, I'm on my way to the shop and will be back with it as soon as possible."

"I'm not sure what you mean by truffle oil, but that can wait. I need you to come to our house," she says urgently. "When can you be here?"

"Uh, well, I guess I could see what stop I can get off to come back into London."

"If you would, thank you."

"Is everything OK?" I ask, gripping the phone. "Has something happened?"

"Yes, something has happened. Please send me a message to let me know your timing. I can send a car to pick you up from whichever London station you return to."

"Oh! Thanks so much, I'll let you know as soon as possible."

"Thank you, Emily. Goodbye." She hangs up.

I quickly search the fastest way to get back into London and, thankfully, check just in time. The next stop has a train going to King's Cross in ten minutes, and we'll be at that stop in five. As I pack away my laptop and gather my things, I wonder what on earth requires such urgent attention.

By the time I get into the shiny black car that collects me from King's Cross, my mind is whirring through possibilities, ranging from something silly, like Cordelia refusing to wear a priceless family necklace, throwing it into a pond, and they need someone to fish it out, to Jonathan having realized it might be a good idea to marry someone who can be kind occasionally and threatening to call off the wedding.

"Oh, good, they've gone," Joe, the driver, says, as we approach the house.

"Who've gone?" I ask, peering out of the window.

"The photographers. They were lurking outside this morning, flicking their cigarette butts all over the pavement." He tuts. "They must have got bored."

"There were press here earlier?" I breathe a sigh of relief that they're gone. "Why?"

"Lord Dashwell was out last night and they photographed him with an American pop star. Now they've assumed something's going on. Happens all the time. One of the family says hello to someone, and the next day it's all over the papers that they're romantically involved. Exhausting. Anyway, he's having his Chelsea house renovated, so he's staying here at the moment and the press was swarming around the door all morning."

"Wow. Which pop star? Have I heard of her? What's she like?"

I don't know why this annoys me. For goodness' sake, I've only met him twice. It's completely unreasonable for me to be irritated by this news. Just because he was nice to me at the engagement party. He's single and good-looking and a *viscount*. He's one of *Tatler*'s most eligible bachelors. He must date all the time. And even if he didn't, he's hardly going to look twice at me.

Not that I'd want him to. I'm too busy to date.

Ugh, why am I even thinking about it?

"I'm not sure who the pop star is." Joe chuckles. "She's got brown hair."

"Ah. Her."

"Sorry, I've never been good with that sort of thing." He laughs, parking outside the house. "I get confused."

"Right. Yeah, someone like him, he must have a new famous girlfriend every week."

"You'd think," Joe says, catching my eye in the rearview mirror. "But not so much, these days. I'd say he's grown out of that scene. They both have. You should have seen some of the types Lady Cordelia dated! One lad used to stick gum to the roof of the car every time he rode in it."

"That's awful!" I say, undoing my seat belt. "Thank goodness she found Jonathan."

"Exactly. Someone who might finally be good enough for her. Not that I'm sure anyone is, as you'd agree! She's much too good for all of them, in my opinion."

"Uh. Sure, yeah. Well, thanks so much, Joe," I say, climbing out of the car, wondering if we're talking about the same Cordelia. "So kind of you to come and get me."

"Any time, Emily!"

Before I'm at the top of the steps, the door opens and Lady Meade ushers me in. She waves at Joe, then shuts the door behind me, saying everyone's in the kitchen.

The atmosphere is clearly tense. Cordelia isn't there when I walk in, but the marquess is, with Jonathan and Tom. Jonathan is pacing, looking frazzled. The marquess is staring out of the window, his hands behind his back. Tom is leaning against the kitchen counter, clasping a mug of tea and yawning. His hair has definitely not been brushed this morning—in fact, I'm almost certain he's just got out of bed. He sees me in the doorway and smiles.

He's got such a nice smile. It makes me smile in response. It must be the crinkles round his eyes . . .

Wait. Stop this. *Focus*, Sophie. You can't go round with a dopey grin on your face when there's been some kind of emergency! And you just heard he was with some pop star last night.

Back to serious face. Serious, professional face.

"Hey," he says sleepily, to me. "What are you doing here?"

"Hi, Emily," Lord Meade says, acknowledging me with a nod. "Did Cordelia call you?"

He's wearing a smart tailored suit and his brow is furrowed

in deep concern. Interestingly, his tie is at odds with the rest of him, a bright jolly red with swordfish dotted about on it. I wonder if this shows a splash of humor beneath his serious façade, but from the look on his face, I'm guessing he's not in a mood for fun at the moment.

"What's happened?" I ask, as Lady Meade floats in behind me. "Where's Cordelia?"

"She's upstairs," the marquess responds, glancing upward. "She won't leave her room."

"Drama queen," Tom mutters into his tea.

"This isn't the time to joke," Lady Meade scolds.

"I get that it's a big deal, but was it necessary for her to barge into the house this morning and go raging about waking everyone up and making my hangover a lot worse?" he says, taking a sip of tea and wincing. "And now she's dragged her friend here for emotional support and I'm sure Emily has better things to do."

"You can surely understand why Cordelia's upset," Jonathan says.

"Besides, you shouldn't be hungover. You should be at work," Lord Meade reminds Tom.

"I'm working from home today," he retorts. "I have a meeting this afternoon and it was decided it made sense that I don't bother going into the office."

His father raises his eyebrows. "Yes, I can see you're hard at work."

"I would be if Cordelia hadn't been shouting the house down."

"What's going on?" I ask, unable to take the suspense any longer. "Is Cordelia OK?"

"This morning we received this." Lady Meade places a long, perfectly manicured finger on a thick envelope lying on the island in front of her and pushes it across the surface. "Have a look."

From the style, I know straightaway it's a wedding invitation. Curious to see whose wedding has caused this much of an upset among them, I pull it out and begin to read. It's an expensive and traditional invitation, thick cream card with swirly black embossed lettering.

The invitation is from the Earl and Countess of Derrington requesting the pleasure of their company at the marriage of their daughter, Annabel, to Mr. Aubyn Ludlow on 21 May.

I stop. I read it again, just to be sure.

Oh, God.

"It's the same date as your wedding," I say, staring at it in disbelief. "It can't be. Is this Lady Annabel Porthouse?"

"I'm afraid so." Jonathan sighs, biting his lip nervously. "Such bad luck."

"It has nothing to do with luck," Lady Meade says. "It's sabotage."

"Mum, come on." Tom groans, rubbing his forehead. "Don't be ridiculous."

"Why else would they send out a wedding invitation seven months in advance?" she asks bitterly. "They knew that's the date we'd settled on."

"We should have sent out save-the-dates," Jonathan remarks.

"Nonsense. We don't do that sort of thing," Lady Meade says plainly, looking disappointed he'd even suggest it.

"Cordelia is very upset," Jonathan comments, unbothered by Lady Meade's scolding. "She says Annabel's done this on purpose."

"I'm disappointed in Ned," the marquess says, and I realize he's referring to Annabel's father, the Earl of Derrington. "This isn't like him."

"What are we going to do about it?" Lady Meade asks.

"Why do we need to do anything?" Tom says, yawning again.

"Have the wedding on the same day. Cordelia didn't want to invite them in the first place, remember? Which I couldn't agree with more. She went mad when you said she had to invite them and now you've got a great excuse for them not to come."

Ah. That solves that mystery. I thought Annabel and Cordelia were best friends, though. I can't remember reading anything about a fallout, but there must have been one.

"Don't be absurd," Lady Meade says. "We have near-identical guest lists."

"Right, so you'd see who your real friends are." Tom shrugs, looking pleased with himself. "Anyone who goes to their wedding and not Cordelia's you can cross off the Christmas card list."

"Do take this seriously, Thomas," his father says wearily.

"Poor Cordelia," I say, staring down at the invitation. "What a nightmare."

"I know." Jonathan sighs. "She so wanted a spring wedding."

"Is moving the date an option?" I ask the room.

"I suggested a late-summer wedding instead," Jonathan answers, his eyes falling to the floor. "But Cordelia was quite adamant that her wedding come before Annabel's."

I lift my eyebrows. "Before?"

"Cordelia may have mentioned this to you, but there's always been some . . . competition between Annabel and Cordelia," Lady Meade explains. "They were at school together. They used to be good friends, ran in the same circles. But then . . ." She pauses, searching for the words. ". . . they grew apart."

"Maybe when Cordelia's had time to calm down, she'll be more reasonable about dates," Jonathan says, trying to persuade himself as much as everyone else in the room. "It's just come as a shock. That's all."

"Yes, it has," says a voice behind me. "But I have a solution."

I spin round to see Cordelia entering the room, dressed in a smart emerald-green minidress with tights and high-heeled boots, her sunglasses swinging from her fingers as though she hasn't a care in the world. Smiling broadly, she breezes past me to go into the welcome arms of her fiancé and I'm hit by a wave of expensive perfume.

"Look, Cordelia," Jonathan says, his face brightening as she approaches him. "Emily came to cheer you up."

"How thoughtful," she says, not looking at me.

"Cordelia," her mother says, bewildered, "you're feeling better?"

"Much. I apologize for my behavior this morning, but I've had time to put things in perspective. If Annabel wants that date for her wedding, it's hers."

Jonathan kisses her. Lord and Lady Meade look shocked. Tom simply nods in approval before taking another gulp of tea. "Great. I can go back to bed, then," he announces. "I mean, back to work."

"It hit me as soon as I heard Emily arriving," Cordelia continues, ignoring him and beaming at me. "Just the sound of your footsteps inspired me."

Uh-oh. This can't be good.

"Really? Great," I say, a lump forming in my throat. "Well, a late-summer wedding will be absolutely lovely—"

"Oh, no, silly billy, the solution is not to have a summer wedding." She laughs loudly, as though I've said something simply *hilarious*. "The solution is to have a winter wedding."

"Splendid," Jonathan enthuses. "Sounds good to me."

"I suppose it gives us more time," Lady Meade admits, sharing a look of confusion with her husband.

"More time? Don't you mean less?" Cordelia chuckles. "You are funny."

"Have you banged your head? It goes spring, summer, autumn, winter," Tom says, frowning at her.

"Oh, I'm sorry, you think I mean next winter!"

"Which winter do you mean?" I ask tentatively, already know-ing the answer.

"*This* winter," she confirms cheerily.

"Cordelia," Lady Meade says, aghast, "you can't possibly—"

"A New Year's Eve wedding," she states. "Perfect, don't you think? Friday, the thirty-first of December, 2021. Isn't that a lovely date? Something about it. Anyway, I've already spoken to the vicar just now on the phone and he says that date is free. So I've booked it in! Didn't want to miss out."

There's a stunned silence in the room.

"Why are you all looking so surprised?" Cordelia continues, laughing at our horrified expressions.

"Because you're suggesting you get married in December," Tom says. "And it's October."

"So? It's not like it's going to be hard. I have the best family and the best bridesmaid in the world. Emily can help me with ev-erything." A smile slowly spreads across her face. "Right, Emily?"

"She has a life, Cordelia." Tom scowls. "The world doesn't revolve around you and your wedding."

"I disagree," she says curtly.

"It's going to be a lot of hard work . . . ," Lady Meade says, trailing off deep in thought.

"Fun work, though," Cordelia corrects. "So, what do you think, Emily? I know helping Mum and me organize such a big wedding in two months is rather a lot to ask, so I completely un-derstand if you simply can't take on the responsibility of brides-maid. No one will think any less of you. Perhaps it's better if I have no bridesmaids." She tilts her head at me. "You're such an amazing friend and I'd hate you to feel pressured into doing something you don't want to do."

I see what she's doing. I *won't* let her win. I lift my eyes to meet hers, holding her gaze. God, I hate the way she's looking at me. So superior. As though she's got me. As though she *knows* she's got me. *Quit,* her eyes are saying. *Just like I said you would. Go on, quit.*

Well, sod that. "Don't be silly. Being your bridesmaid is an honor," I say calmly, smiling back at her. "Two months for us to organize the wedding of the century? No problem. Let's get to work! What can I do to help?"

Jonathan squeezes Cordelia's shoulders excitedly, thrilled that all tension seems resolved. Lady Meade shifts uncomfortably, her eyebrows knitted together as she looks from me to Cordelia and back again. She's the only one in the room who can translate our exchange as being a standoff.

Challenge accepted, Cordelia.

Challenge. Fucking. Accepted.

CHAPTER FOURTEEN

WHAT AM I THINKING?

This is stupid. A wedding in two months? *Two months?* I've been egged on by Cordelia's superior attitude and now I've landed myself in a huge mess. It's *impossible* to organize such a grand wedding in two months. Organizing an intimate wedding within two months would be stressful, but a society wedding for a few hundred people? Maybe with a super-experienced wedding planner, with the perfect suppliers on speed dial, all of whom happen to be available, but when we have to do everything ourselves? It can't be done.

IT. CAN'T. BE. DONE.

"It can be done, I suppose. We have the venue and the church sorted," Lady Meade says, once I've encouraged the foolish notion. "Dashwell Hall looks beautiful at Christmas. And the suppliers we've already booked will no doubt do their best to accommodate the new date. But we need to make quick decisions and send out the invitations immediately. I'll call the stationers."

"Am I the only one in the room who thinks Cordelia has lost her mind?" Tom says, prompting her to make a face at him. "Seriously, why don't you just have the wedding next year?"

"Because I want to be married to the love of my life as soon as possible," Cordelia replies, beaming up at Jonathan, then muttering, "and I won't let Annabel win."

Tom appeals to his father. "You must agree this is nonsense."

"If your mother thinks it's possible . . ." Lord Meade replies.

"Do you think everyone is going to be free on New Year's Eve?" Tom adds. "What if the caterers and florists or whatever are already booked? Emily, you do events and stuff, right? Suppliers have dates booked in way in advance, don't they?"

"Then they can change their schedules," Cordelia says simply.

"Hmm, now that I think about it, Tom may have a point," I say, pensive. "You may have to make some sacrifices."

"Like what?" Cordelia asks, irritated. "I don't want to make any sacrifices and I don't see why I should."

"Like what *band* you were thinking of booking, for example," I stress, still smiling like a robot as though everything is under control. "It might be tricky for you to book them at such late notice."

"What band did you want?" Tom asks.

"It's a surprise," she says, her eyes glinting at me, daring me to tell.

"Maybe you should have a think about a backup," I suggest, reminding myself that I wasn't letting her down. A good bridesmaid will go the extra mile but will also manage expectations. Especially ridiculous ones. "And," I continue, remembering how she wanted to change the flooring at Dashwell Hall, "I'm not sure you'd have time for those *interior* changes you wanted."

"Interior changes?" The marquess looks horrified. "Whatever do you mean?"

"My friend is in a band!" Jonathan blurts out, clicking his fingers. "We can ask them to play! They're good, too. Very punk-rock style. Cool, right?"

Cordelia and her parents can't hide their horror at the idea, and I seize upon the opportunity to do my job. This sort of thing, I can handle in my sleep.

"Such a cool idea," I say enthusiastically, before letting my face drop, "although, if it was me, I probably wouldn't want to play at your wedding."

"Why do you say that?"

"Because then I'd miss out on all the fun! You know," I say casually, as though I haven't thought about this before, "if you're performing you'd have to set up and you couldn't join in with any of the dancing. Your friend wouldn't get to enjoy all the best bits. But I'm sure he wouldn't mind—he'd probably love to play for you."

"Hmm." Jonathan looks thoughtful. "Maybe we shouldn't ask him. I don't want him to miss out on the actual wedding."

"What a shame," Lady Meade cuts in, giving me a grateful smile, while Tom smirks behind his mug. "I'm sure we'll find another appropriate act to fill his shoes."

"So we've decided, then?" the marquess says, glancing at his watch. "Two months it is?"

"We've decided," Cordelia states. "What could be more glamorous than a New Year's Eve wedding?"

"In that case, I think it's appropriate we make our way to Dashwell," he says. "Makes sense to be in the venue and work out how everything will go. Everyone able to come along this weekend?"

"Good idea," Lady Meade agrees. "And, Emily, you must join us. You've never been to Dashwell, have you? You'd be very welcome."

Everyone looks at me, so no one notices Cordelia's shocked expression in reaction to the invitation. An invitation to the Meade stately home is like a dream, a position I never imagined I'd ever be in. Dashwell Hall is one of the most famous estates in the country and I've been offered a personal invitation to stay there.

But it also means being in the middle of nowhere, shut away in a big scary house with Lady Cordelia Swann.

There is no guarantee I'd get out alive.

"I'd love to come," I hear myself say. "Thank you."

"That's decided, then," the marquess says, clapping his hands together. "Tom, will you be joining us?"

"I can come Friday evening after work," he says, then turns

to me. "If you want, I can give you a lift. Jonathan and Cordelia have a two-seater."

"That would be . . . oh, wait! I've just remembered it's . . . uh . . . my friend's birthday dinner on Friday evening. I can try to get out of it."

It is actually my dad's birthday dinner, but Emily's parents are supposed to be in Australia. I can already hear the disappointment in my mum's tone when I'll have to call her to say I won't be able to come. Even though it's just me coming over for dinner with them, I know they're both really looking forward to an evening together.

"No, you can't miss your friend's birthday celebration," Lady Meade insists. "Why don't you come on Saturday morning first thing, if that suits?"

"I can organize a taxi to pick you up from the station," Cordelia says, watching Tom.

Before I know it, it's all arranged. I'll be joining the Swann family for a weekend in the country and, together, we'll work out how to throw this wedding in two months.

What am I doing?

As soon as I get home, I schedule everything into my diary so that I won't be neglecting any of my other clients, typing out everything I need to do and when. Thank goodness I don't have another wedding on New Year's Eve.

There's an email waiting for me from a potential new client who's getting married next year. I never like to say no to any bride, but I can't imagine taking on anyone new at the moment. Even though her wedding is next autumn, I wouldn't be able to fit in any introductions until after Cordelia's wedding and that may not sit comfortably with her. I reply, explaining that unfortunately I'm not taking on any new clients as my schedule is full, and as I press send, I know that Cara would be proud of me saying no to someone.

You see? I can be sassy.

With my brain so busy, I know I'll never sleep and I need sleep to get things done. I run myself a bath and force myself to leave my phone in the study. (FINE. Cupboard.) I need to have some time to myself, to close my eyes and relax, soaking in the hot, lavender-scented water.

After just a few minutes, I'm too hot and bored. I get out, guiltily letting out the water—such a waste, next time I'll shower—and pull on an old T-shirt, brush my teeth, grab my phone, and get into bed. I try to sleep, but keep remembering things I need to do, sitting up and writing them down so I don't forget them in the morning.

At around 1:00 A.M., my phone starts vibrating. I still haven't managed to sleep. I reach over to grab it. When I see the messages are from Cordelia, I sit bolt upright and turn on the light.

Are you awake?
Hello?
Sophie, wake up!
I'm going to call if you don't reply
Don't make me call
I hate calling

Hi! I'm awake. All OK?

Hi, I need your help
Can you come meet me?

Now?

Yes
I'm serious

Is everything OK?

Everything is FINE
But I need your help with something

It's bridesmaid stuff
It needs to be sorted now
Can you come?

> Of course!

Thanks. I'll send you the address
I'll meet you there in half an hour
Wear dark clothing
Something you can run in

> Why?

She doesn't reply to my question, but a few seconds later sends an address in Kensington, then goes offline. I swing my legs out of bed and turn on the light, then search for a pair of black leggings and a black hoodie. I put on my trainers, grab my keys and my phone, and order an Uber.

Alarm bells are ringing. Why does she need me at one o'clock in the morning? Why do I need to wear dark clothing and why would I need to run? It sounds weird. Some kind of bridal exercise regime? But, then, why would I need to wear dark clothing?

I can't say no, though. If I said no, she'd insist I'm fired. She'd be able to report to her mother that I had flatly refused to be there for her. And I wouldn't be able to lie and say otherwise.

So here I am, hopping into an Uber in the early hours of the morning and speeding toward West London with no idea of what I'm getting myself into.

I arrive at the address and see her waiting for me, kitted out in dark clothes and scrolling through her phone. At least she's here. I'd thought this might be some game in which she'd have been cackling away while sending those messages to me, then going back to sleep while I waited all night in the cold. But so far, so good.

"You're late," she says, as I thank the driver and climb out of the car. "I said half an hour."

"It takes longer than that to get here from my place."

"I don't like it when people are late."

"Won't happen again."

"Good." She looks me up and down approvingly. "Let's go, then."

We walk along the quiet, elegant road, dimly lit by fancy streetlamps, the ones they have in old movies. A fox potters along ahead of us, ducking through the railings into the park next to the pavement. There are no lights on in the windows of any of the houses or boutiques. This is all very weird.

"What exactly are we doing here?" I ask tentatively, shoving my hands into my hoodie pocket.

"I'll tell you in a minute," comes the irritated reply.

We walk round the corner until she comes to a sudden stop. "Here we are," she announces, turning to face the wall that's lining the pavement.

"Where?"

She nods at the brick wall. "*Here.*"

I look from her to the wall and back to her again, wondering if the stress of the wedding has caused her to lose her mind. "Um. OK?"

"Do you know the dress designer Melanie Kendall?"

"I've heard of her. Up-and-coming British designer. The Duchess of Sussex wore one of her gowns recently."

"That's the one. She's designing Annabel's dress."

"Lady Annabel Porthouse?"

"Yes." Cordelia nods bitterly. "*That* Annabel. Anyway, Melanie Kendall's studio is the house just here, on the corner of the road we walked down. Number fifty-four."

"OK?"

"Look, I don't have long to find someone to design and create the perfect wedding dress."

"I agree."

"So, it's of the utmost importance that I see Annabel's dress designs. I need to know what style she's going to be in. I want to make sure mine's different from and much better than hers. I have to see the drawings."

"Cordelia," I say, a fear creeping into my mind, "why did we need to dress in dark clothing?"

"We're going to break into Melanie Kendall's studio and take pictures of the designs," she says, her eyes wide with excitement. "We need to hop over this wall into the back garden."

"You're joking, right?" I laugh nervously, my throat closing. "This is a big joke. A big, mad joke."

"It's not like I can ask! No one's going to let me or anyone else see them," she says defensively. "Her dress will be eagerly anticipated by the press. Just like mine."

"Cordelia, we can't break into someone's studio."

"Imagine if my dress is shit compared to hers!" she cries, throwing her arms up in the air. "*Imagine.*"

"OK, I think the wedding stress has got a little bit on top of you," I say gently. "You're feeling overwhelmed with everything. We need to go home and have a little downtime."

"Sophie, I'm perfectly calm," she says, in, admittedly, a soft, collected manner. "You don't understand. Annabel is my nemesis. Isn't there someone who bullied you? Someone who made you feel really small?"

Yes, I can think of someone, Cordelia.

"Yes, of course, but I'm not going to—"

"Who made you feel like that?"

I can't say it's her, so I consider the next best person to fit the bill.

"Someone at school," I admit, shifting my weight from one leg to the other. "That was ages ago. And, Cordelia, your wedding is about you and Jonathan! No one else. You can't compare—"

"Tell me who the person was. Come on," she says impatiently. "See this as bride-bridesmaid bonding or whatever."

"It was a guy. Graham Slater." I shrug, pretending his name doesn't affect me still. "He laughed at me a lot. He wasn't very nice."

"He made you feel bad about yourself?"

"He made fun of me all the time in front of the rest of the class."

She nods. "Was it your hair?"

"What? No!" My hand automatically flies up to my head. "Why would you assume it's my hair?"

"No reason."

There's an awkward silence. I glare at her. "For your information, he took the piss out of me being a goody-goody," I explain.

"Yeah, that makes sense."

"Cordelia!"

"Look, we don't have time to go into all these details, but Annabel is essentially my Graham Slater," she tells me, exasperated. "Imagine if Graham's parents were friends with your parents. Imagine if everything you ever did, Graham did better, then laughed in your face for being useless. Imagine if Graham pretended to be your friend and then betrayed and humiliated you. Imagine if Graham stole your wedding date."

"What did Graham—I mean Annabel do to betray you?"

"The point is, take a moment to think about everything I've just said," she says, brushing aside my question. "Do you understand why I need to make sure that my dress is nothing like hers?"

I sigh heavily. I still hate Graham Slater. "Yeah, I guess."

"Then all I'm asking is that we sneak in, take a couple of

pictures, and sneak out. No one will know we've been there. No harm done!"

"I said I get it. That doesn't mean I'm going to help you break in. That's a crime," I say. "Cordelia, this is ridiculous. You're talking about breaking the law!"

"Her studio isn't alarmed," she insists, turning to face the wall. "She doesn't keep any materials there, none of the dresses."

"How do you know the designs will be there?"

"Because Annabel had a meeting with her today. She posted it on her Instagram." Cordelia rolls her eyes and puts on a posh, high-pitched drawl, I assume attempting to mimic Lady Annabel: " 'An amazing meeting drafting wedding-dress designs with my talented, inspirational friend Melanie! Can't wait for you guys to see it! #blessed! #omg #weddingdress.' Trust me, the designs are in there. I've worked with Melanie before and she's not very tidy. Her drawings are all over her desk. The one for Annabel will be there." She adds under her breath, "Traitor."

"If you've worked with Melanie before, just ask her for a rough idea of Annabel's dress."

"No. First, she'll have signed an NDA so won't be able to discuss it. Second, she may tell Annabel I've asked and that would be *mortifying*." Cordelia points at the wall. "This is the only way."

"This is nuts. We can't!"

"Why are you so afraid to take risks?"

"I'm not afraid to take risks!" I argue. "I'm afraid to go to prison!"

"Graham Slater might have been right about you, Sophie," she says, looking disappointed. "Look at your life."

"Why are you turning this on me? Don't call me a sheep again, because I'm not," I huff. "If I was, I'd follow you blindly over this wall, but here I am, standing my ground."

"Your life revolves around you being a goody-goody."

"This is stupid! I'm not burgling someone's studio!"

"Always doing the right thing. Never breaking any rules. Playing it safe." She narrows her eyes at me. "Something tells me you're afraid."

I brush a lock of hair behind my ear impatiently. Suddenly Daniel flashes into my brain, his stinging comments about my love of happy endings and lack of brazenness to pull off red hair echoing in my mind. Ugh.

"You're afraid to get out there and take chances." She sighs, tilting her head at me sympathetically as she twists the knife in further. "So you hide behind your brides, no eyes on you."

"That's not true," I protest, glaring at her.

It's a bit true, though. Isn't it?

"Look, Sophie, I get that this is a big ask but it's an important one." She exhales, looking at me with such a sincere expression it makes me feel uncomfortable. "*I need you.* And you know how much it pains me to say that. I can't do this alone. Help me. Please. Come on, prove Graham Slater wrong!"

Oh, my God, I can't believe I'm considering this. She knows, too. She can see in my face that she's wearing me down.

"Over this wall, we're into her garden. And the wall isn't very high," she continues. "We pick the lock on her back door and that's it! Her studio looks out onto the patio because she needs the light. I promise we'll be in and out in a flash. We won't touch anything."

"What about cameras?" I ask, biting my lip. "What about alarms?"

"I told you, no alarms and no cameras. I've been here before."

"And you scouted out the place in case you ever needed to *break in?*" I hiss.

"I've also checked and there are no cameras on this road either. Now, would you stop being such a wimp and help me work out how to get over this wall?" she barks. "We already know you're going to do it, so let's not delay the inevitable."

She starts examining the bricks and I bury my head in my hands. "I can't believe this is happening. I'm going to be a criminal."

"Hey, look!" She points to a dip in the wall. "Perfect foothold. Put one foot in there and use it to push yourself up."

"Why do I have to go first?"

"Because I'm guessing you might be the one who needs someone to push them over," she says, folding her arms. "Come on. I promise I'll come after you. I doubt you can pick locks."

"*And you can?*"

"Bloody hell, Sophie, we don't have all night. I have a yoga class at five A.M.!"

"Oh, yes, wouldn't want to ruin your zen," I mutter bitterly, stepping toward the wall. "Nothing like a bit of breaking and entering to strengthen your spiritual core."

I examine the bricks. Does everyone see me as this big, boring wimp? Was Graham Slater *seriously* right about me? Was he flaunting my flaws right from the start?

Daniel broke up with me because I'm not the sort of person to go rock-climbing. He broke up with me because I only like happy endings. I have no sense of adventure. I'm not spontaneous. An all-round goody-goody.

"Stop overthinking it," Cordelia says, watching me curiously. "Just do it."

Placing my left foot in the dip, I reach up to the top of the wall and attempt to haul myself up.

Fuck Graham Slater. Fuck Daniel. And fuck rock-climbing and its lame harnesses. I'm doing this all by myself. No ropes needed. *In your stupid, smug, adventurous face, Daniel.*

"Knew you had it in you!" Cordelia encourages. "Swing your leg over!"

"I'm trying!" I wheeze, my right leg flimsily stretching up as high as possible, my trainer scraping down the wall.

"Here you go," Cordelia says, crouching and shoving her shoulder under my bum, then giving me a push.

My leg hooks over the top and I heave myself up until I'm lying flat, like a worm, along the wall.

"Great! Now, hop down," she says, getting ready to follow me. "It's not that big a drop."

"This is so stupid," I grumble, dropping my legs down the other side of the wall and attempting to lower myself gently toward the ground.

Unfortunately, my upper-arm strength is nonexistent and my fingers don't have enough grip. They slip and I yelp as I fall, landing in some kind of bush before rolling off it onto the ground, landing with a thud.

"Ow!" I whimper.

A few moments later, Cordelia jumps from the wall, landing easily on her feet next to me, like Catwoman. She wipes her hands and puts them on her hips. "Are you OK?"

"No," I whisper grumpily, getting to my feet and wiping the mud and leaves off my leggings. "Let's get this over with."

She gives me a salute and rushes to the back door, pulls hairpins out of her pocket, and slides them into the keyhole. There's a gentle click and she opens the door. "Easy," she says, grinning. "Right, in you go. I'll wait here. By the way, you've still got leaves in your hair."

"Wait, what? You're not going in?"

"Course not," she whispers, looking stunned. "That's why I needed you here in the first place. I can't be seen and I can't have the photos on my phone. That's evidence. You also have mud on your face. Seriously, how did you land so badly?"

"You said there were no cameras!"

"And there aren't." She sighs. "I don't think. Also, we don't know if someone's working late or whatever. You never know. I can't risk being seen inside. Imagine the scandal! Nobody cares about you, though. No offense, but you're anonymous. You go in, get the pictures, then come back out. If anything happens, I can escape before anyone sees."

"Are you *joking*?"

"That won't happen! But just in case." She gestures into the studio. "You've come this far, haven't you? Look, if you do this, I'll drop the Oasis thing, OK?"

I hesitate. "What about the tiara?"

"Fine! Forget the tiara."

"And the peacocks? And swans?"

"Don't push it," she hisses. "Now get in there!"

Steeling myself, I grip my phone, ready on camera mode, then tiptoe into the room, heading toward the wide desk in front of me. Just as Cordelia said, there's paper everywhere and there are scribbles all over it. Using the light on my phone, I scan the designs until I get to the one in the middle at the top of the pile. "Lady Annabel Porthouse" is written in swirly, arty letters at the top and there's a rough sketch of a striking strapless, A-line satin dress with a long, dramatic train. I smile at the design. She's going to look beautiful.

I lift my phone, check that the flash is on, and take the picture. It's done.

I creep out of the studio and Cordelia shuts the door carefully behind me. I give her the thumbs-up and she beams at me. Then we hurry across to the wall. She gives me a push up and this time I wait on top for her to climb up and jump back onto the road first. I don't want to risk falling onto the pavement and breaking something. She supports me as I lower myself, then gestures for me to run, following her along the road and around the corner to where Joe is waiting with the car.

We jump in and he sighs. "I'm not going to ask any questions," he says, and sets off.

"I can't believe we did that!" I squeal, adrenaline pumping through my veins. I feel like I've got off a roller coaster.

"Can I see the picture?" Cordelia asks.

I bring it up and pass her the phone, my hands shaking.

"Ah," she says happily, scrutinizing the design. "My dress won't be like that at all. This is brilliant. I can relax."

"I seriously cannot believe what I just did!" I exclaim, unable to sit still. "I've never done anything like that before!"

"You see?" Cordelia says, amused and irritated at how pumped I am. "Sometimes it's fun to break the rules."

From: Theodore@wecareaboutvintage.com

To: Sophie.Breeze@zapmail.co.uk

Subject: Re: Vintage wedding suitcases

Hi Sophie,

Thank you for your inquiry about our beautiful vintage suitcases.

We have several available for rent. How many was the bride after? And is she planning on putting anything in them?

Many thanks,

Theodore

We Care About Vintage! The Only Retailer
That Really Cares About Vintage

From: Sophie.Breeze@zapmail.co.uk

To: Theodore@wecareaboutvintage.com

Subject: Re: re: Vintage wedding suitcases

Hi Theodore,

Thanks so much for getting back to me. Great news!

The bride was hoping for four or five in different sizes, if that's available?

No, she's not planning on actually using them—the theme of the wedding is "The Roaring 20s" and she's having a vintage travel display, so I think she wants to stack them up next to the table plan with an old globe balanced on the top.

They would be purely for decorative purposes. Is that OK?

Best wishes,

Sophie

From: Theodore@wecareaboutvintage.com

To: Sophie.Breeze@zapmail.co.uk

Subject: Re: re: re: Vintage wedding suitcases

Hi Sophie,

We can provide those suitcases, no problem.

Please let us know which ones you would like from our website.

Many thanks,

Theodore

We Care About Vintage!

The Only Retailer That Really Cares About Vintage

From: Sophie.Breeze@zapmail.co.uk

To: Theodore@wecareaboutvintage.com

Subject: Re: re: re: re: Vintage wedding suitcases

Hi Theodore,

I'm a bit confused by your website as it doesn't actually list the date that any of the suitcases are from?

I'm specifically after ones from the 1920s.

Best wishes,

Sophie

From: Theodore@wecareaboutvintage.com

To: Sophie.Breeze@zapmail.co.uk

Subject: Re: re: re: re: re: Vintage wedding suitcases

Hi Sophie,

Please find attached suitcases in the style of those from the 1920s.

Many thanks,

Theodore

We Care About Vintage!

The Only Retailer That Really Cares About Vintage

From: Sophie.Breeze@zapmail.co.uk

To: Theodore@wecareaboutvintage.com

Subject: Re: re: re: re: re: re: Vintage wedding suitcases

Hi Theodore,

Thank you for sending me those pictures.

I'm a little confused when you say "in the style of"? Just to confirm your vintage suitcases are genuinely from the 1920s?

Best wishes,

Sophie

From: Theodore@wecareaboutvintage.com

To: Sophie.Breeze@zapmail.co.uk

Subject: Re: re: re: re: re: re: re: Vintage wedding suitcases

Hi Sophie,

The vintage suitcases we provide are not from the 1920s, but in the style of 1920s suitcases.

Our customers tend to prefer a reliable vintage product. Real vintage items tend to be old and shabby. Not ideal.

To sum up, our suitcases are vintage in that they're new, but they're vintage, if that makes sense.

Many thanks,

Theodore

We Care About Vintage!

The Only Retailer That Really Cares About Vintage

CHAPTER FIFTEEN

The next day, on my way to a dress fitting for another of my brides, Catherine, I get a phone call from an unknown number and immediately panic.

I stop in my tracks, staring at the screen. It could be Melanie Kendall. It could be the *police*. I could be about to go to *prison*. Although . . . do the police call before they arrest you? Surely they don't give criminals any warning. That makes no sense at all. Unless they're calling to get my alibi? *Are they calling to get my alibi?*

Think, Sophie, think! I NEED AN ALIBI. OK, I was . . . I was . . . home alone! I was home all alone, asleep. No one can verify that. But no one can deny it either.

Unless they check my Uber records.

Why did I get an Uber? Oh, my God, I've left a paper trail! My mouth is so dry.

Maybe I don't answer. No. Wait. I need to answer. I have to know if I'm being investigated. It's better than not knowing. But I don't need to answer any questions. *I have rights.*

"Hello?" I say timidly, answering just before it rings out.

"Emily, hello! It's Jonathan. Jonathan Farlow? Cordelia's fiancé. Ugh, I'm not sure about that word 'fiancé'! It sounds a bit pretentious. Hate using it. Anyway, hi! Sorry! Rambling."

I'm so relieved, I lean against a wall, smiling into the phone. "Jonathan! It's you. Thank God!"

"Is everything all right?" he asks, sounding very concerned.

"Yes! Everything's fine," I hurriedly assure him, pulling myself together. "I was . . . uh . . . I messed up something at work and I thought you might be my boss calling to yell at me. But it's all OK!"

"Oh, I see." He chuckles. "Well, we've all been there! I'm sure you'll get it sorted."

"Absolutely."

There's an awkward pause as I wait for him to tell me why he's calling.

"I hope you don't mind, I got your number from Victoria. Are you busy or can we chat?"

"We can chat!" I say, finding it unnerving to hear Lady Meade referred to by her first name. I suppose she is his future mother-in-law. "I've got a few minutes. I'm on my way to a meeting."

"Great! I wasn't sure who else to ask. Now that the wedding is just two months away, I realized I'd better get thinking about a wedding present for Cordelia. I thought I had plenty of time! Now I don't. I wondered if you could help me find her something on the sly? I'm useless at shopping. Will you help me?"

"I'd love to," I say, trying not to laugh at his panicked tone. "Don't worry, we'll find her the perfect gift."

"Ah, wonderful, thank you," he says, sounding relieved. "You're not free this evening, are you? I can meet you after work? I appreciate it's last minute, so if you're busy . . ."

"I can do this evening," I assure him. "Tell me where to be and when."

"Great! I'll text you."

I say goodbye and hang up, thrilled that Jonathan has selected me to help him with such an important task. I'm determined not to let him down, and it will be nice to have some time with him away from the family. Though I'm slightly surprised when the text comes through with where he wants to meet: Ye Olde Mitre, a pub in Holborn. I was expecting somewhere like the Savoy or the Artesian, fancy cocktail bars in social hot spots.

It takes me a while to find the pub. It's tucked away down a very narrow passageway that I walk past twice, but when I finally get there, I couldn't love it more. It's *tiny*, cozy and unassuming.

"Emily!" Jonathan waves from where he's leaning at the bar waiting for me. "What can I get you to drink?"

"I'll have a white wine, thanks," I say, as he gives me a warm greeting with a kiss on each cheek. "I can get this, though."

"No, I insist," he says, pulling a credit card out of his wallet. "You're helping me big-time, and the least I can do is get you a drink before we start."

"How did you find this place?" I ask, taking off my coat and admiring the homeliness of the surroundings. "I've never been here before."

"Oh, I used to come here a lot when I first moved to London," he tells me, shoving his wallet back into his pocket. "One of my colleagues at my old company introduced it to me. It's one of those rare places in London where I feel relaxed, if I'm honest. A little haven. It's also got some very interesting history. Queen Elizabeth the First apparently danced around the tree outside."

"Really?"

"Wonderful, isn't it? I like to escape here when I need to have a think over a proper pint. Not many of my friends come here—unless you're introduced to it, you might not notice it. It feels a little . . ."

"Hidden?" I suggest, as he searches for the word.

"Yes! Hidden. The perfect place to do some stealthy gift brainstorming."

"Cordelia won't happen upon us?"

"Unlikely. I brought her here once and she loved it, but it's hardly convenient for her. Besides, she thinks I've got meetings running late." He passes me my glass of wine and holds up his pint. "Cheers."

"Cheers!" I take a sip of my drink, trying to imagine Cordelia in this homey pub—the same woman who is glamorous, snobby, and usually quite rude. Although our criminal activity last night has shown me a new side to her: I'm not so sure she completely belongs in the high-society world—not now I've seen her scale a wall and pick a lock with ease.

I haven't heard from her today. I admit I was expecting *something*. A message to say how much she appreciated me helping her out, how much she owes me after I *broke the law* for her, how maybe she was wrong to be so dismissive of me up until now.

But not a peep.

"Thanks again for meeting me," Jonathan says. "I have no idea where to begin."

"She hasn't dropped any hints?"

"Nothing. I even asked her outright, because I was worried I'd missed any signs. I'm not very good at stuff like that," he admits apologetically. "But she said the usual sort of things she always says when I ask her about birthday and Christmas gifts."

"What are the usual things she says?"

"Oh, you know"—he blushes, twisting his pint round on the coaster—"that she doesn't want anything, that I'm all she could ever want"—he waves a hand, his cheeks flushing pink—"that sort of thing."

"Cordelia says things like that? That's so . . . sweet."

"Yes, well"—he grins—"she doesn't say them very often. But, as you know, she's a lot softer than people think. It's all a front."

I nod, pretending I know what he's talking about. I guess last night she showed *some* vulnerability. Her paranoia about Annabel's wedding has to come from insecurity. And Jonathan is so nice, so warm and friendly and open. Surely he wouldn't be with someone completely evil.

"So, any ideas?" he asks me hopefully. "It has to be personal somehow. It can't be any old thing."

"I agree. Let's get a brainstorm going. I can ask you some questions and maybe it will give us some helpful ideas."

"Good plan."

"So, let's start with how you two met. Cordelia has told me the general story, but no details."

This is, of course, a lie. Cordelia has told me absolutely nothing about how she met Jonathan. After having no luck finding any details online about the happy couple and how it all began, I had to ask Lady Meade to fill me in a bit, so I could play my bridesmaid role to the best of my ability. What kind of bridesmaid doesn't know how the bride and groom met?

"You met at a dinner," I prompt, which is as much as I got out of Lady Meade.

"It was a charity auction, to raise funds for a ballet school. We were seated next to each other."

"Cordelia never mentioned it was for a ballet school!"

"That doesn't surprise me, she doesn't like to talk about her charity work," he says, chuckling. "She thinks boasting about it takes away from what it's meant to be. You know she hates any kind of fuss. One of the many reasons I love her. But, over the years, she's donated a lot to the arts and created many scholarships, especially for the ballet, and this school was desperately underfunded. I think she's always regretted not learning to dance when she was growing up." He smiles, adding, "You won't be surprised to hear she was kicked out of ballet class as a child."

"Why?"

"Too disruptive, according to the teachers. Victoria says Cordelia was disruptive because she was bored, and she was bored because she was so much better than the other children. I'm not sure how true that is, but I wouldn't want to argue with the in-laws."

"Cordelia is very elegant," I admit. "I can imagine her being quite good at ballet. So, did you hit it off straightaway at this dinner?"

"Yes, we did," he says, smiling at the memory. "As soon as I sat down, I told her that I'd never been to the ballet before, but I'd been asked to be at the dinner by my company, who needed a representative. They were one of the supporters. Anyway, when I said I thought ballet was boring, she was horrified and started listing the reasons I was an idiot."

"That I can very much believe."

"We didn't stop talking the entire dinner. Completely ignored the rest of the table. I thought she was hilarious—she kept making me laugh. I'm not even sure she meant to. She told me about being kicked out of ballet class and, in return, I told her my most embarrassing moment—when I was a teenager and I went to a fancy-dress party back home in Norfolk but had misunderstood the theme. Well, turned out there wasn't a theme at all, because it wasn't a fancy-dress party. It was a posh sixteenth and I turned up dressed as a Power Ranger."

I burst out laughing.

"Not my finest moment," he says, grimacing. "Anyway, when the ballet dinner was coming to a close, I asked for her number. I had no idea that she was meant to be scary until everyone told me so after I'd met her."

"Something about you made her lower her barriers."

He smiles shyly. "I guess so. But she was different on our first date. It was as though she'd forgotten herself at the ballet dinner. Suddenly a wall came up. She was a bit chilly. Apprehensive and much less at ease. I wasn't about to give up, though. I'd never met anyone who made me feel so . . ." He pauses. ". . . interesting. And interested."

"You are interesting!"

"Not really," he says, shrugging. "I've never been the life of the party, never really stood out in a crowd. But Cordelia made me feel that way. She really listens to me. And I never want to stop talking to her. It's a nice feeling, that. Anyway, enough about me! Sorry, didn't mean to go on."

"Don't be sorry. It's nice to hear your side of the story," I say, beaming at him. "How did you propose?"

"Surely you're bored to death of that one!"

"I've heard the story from Cordelia, of course," I lie. "But, as I said, it's nice to hear it from the groom's point of view. How long did you have the ring before you popped the question?"

"Four months. I'd spoken to Lord and Lady Meade, who were all for it. And my parents, who couldn't have been happier. I was waiting for the perfect moment. At first, I thought I'd do it on holiday, in an amazing restaurant with hundreds of candles and red roses and all that"—he chuckles—"but the more I thought about it, the more I realized that wasn't us at all. I decided I'd have to think of something more intimate, a bit more casual. Then, one afternoon we were at her parents' house, out riding."

"I didn't know you were into horse riding too," I say, surprised.

"Trust me, I wasn't." He laughs. "Not until I started dating Cordelia. I was frightened of horses. Never been on one in my life. Cordelia kept telling me to give it a go, and it got to the stage where I couldn't put it off much longer. Now I enjoy it. I don't like going too fast and I swear the horse I ride, Marjorie, openly laughs at me whenever I attempt my rising trot—as soon as I start, she does that snort thing horses do—but it's fun. Have you ever gone riding with Cordelia?"

I shake my head.

"You'll have to at Dashwell," he says excitedly. "You get to see the countryside best that way. It's very peaceful."

"Sorry, I interrupted your proposal story—please continue!"

"Oh, yes. So, we were out and about, and we'd stopped to

admire the view of the fields. When we were ready to continue, Marjorie refused to move. No matter what I did, she just stood there. I was huffing and puffing, giving her a nudge with my heels, demanding that she move, getting quite cross, if I'm honest with you. But Marjorie wasn't having any of it. It was incredibly frustrating. Cordelia found it so funny that she came trotting back, crying she was laughing so hard. Then I started laughing and I couldn't stop. The two of us idiots were just sitting there on our stubborn horses, laughing away. If anyone had seen us, they'd have thought we were mad. Anyway, that was when I said it. I didn't even think about it. I didn't have the ring on me. I was watching her laughing and I just . . . asked her to marry me."

"That sounds perfect," I say, enraptured.

"Not very noteworthy," he claims. "But she said yes, so there you go. My mum still can't get over that story. She told me off for not planning something more romantic. Not exactly the grand proposal Lady Cordelia Swann deserved!"

"I think it sounds wonderfully romantic! You proposed in a place she loves, and in a moment when you were both truly happy. What could be *more* romantic?"

"When you put it like that, it sounds rather good. Maybe you could have a word with my mother at the wedding."

"I'm sorry I didn't meet your parents at the engagement party. Do they still live in Norfolk?"

He nods. "Right in the middle of nowhere. The first time I took Cordelia there, they made a huge fuss about it. I've never seen them so nervous or the house so clean. They weren't sure what food she'd like, so I'm pretty sure they bought absolutely everything. But as soon as she walked through the door, one of our dogs, Gus, went bounding over to her and she sat down on the floor to give him a good belly rub. I could see Mum's shoulders physically relax. It's the title. It can be misleading."

I try to imagine the alternative version of Cordelia Jonathan is telling me about—one who loves hanging out in tiny old pubs, who happily sits on a country kitchen floor, fussing over a dog.

"What about your parents?" Jonathan asks brightly, jolting me out of my thoughts. "Where do they live?"

"Australia. They retired there," I say, brushing aside this line of questioning with a wave of my hand. "You said one of your dogs, how many do you have?"

"My parents have four. Three springer spaniels and then Gus, a black Labrador. I imagine Cordelia's told you all about him. She and Gus have a special bond. He adores her, follows her around everywhere when we're at my parents'."

"That's so lovely. You must miss them here in London."

"My parents or the dogs?"

"Both." I laugh.

"Certainly, but we see them as much as we can. I don't think Cordelia can be away from Gus too long." He finishes his pint. "So, are you looking forward to this weekend?"

"Yes, although I'm a bit nervous. I've seen so many pictures of Dashwell Hall—it seems a bit surreal to be going there."

"I know what you mean. I was the same when I first went," he says, nodding vigorously. "But Nicholas and Victoria are so welcoming, you sort of forget where you are. They'll put you at ease, don't worry."

"I'm sure," I say, taking the last sip of my wine and putting the empty glass down.

"Right! Shall we go shopping?" He runs a hand through his hair. "Where on earth do you think we should start?"

"Actually, I think I may have an idea. You've given me some inspiration."

His face lights up. "Really? What is it?"

"Well, it's something personal," I begin, "and it doesn't involve any shopping whatsoever."

"In that case, I'm in," he says, without hesitation. "Let's get another round in to celebrate a good job well done!"

"Don't you want to hear the idea first?" I ask. "You might not like it!"

"Nonsense. I bet it's perfect. I knew you'd be the person to ask, Emily." He grins at me, waving over the barman. "I just knew it."

CHAPTER SIXTEEN

Mum can tell I'm nervous about something. Ever since I arrived for Dad's birthday with a wheelie case and a vague story about visiting a friend for the weekend, she's been asking me hundreds of questions about the "friend" and why I haven't mentioned the trip in advance. I'd love to tell her I'm spending the weekend with the Marquess and Marchioness of Meade at their stately home, Dashwell Hall, but I can't.

"You seem on edge," she says to me, filling Dad's wineglass.

"I'm not. Why would I be?"

"I'm not sure. But you are. You're doing that thing you do when you get nervous."

"What thing?"

"Playing with your earlobe."

"What?" I drop my hand into my lap from where I was twisting the butterfly of my earring round and round. "No, I'm not."

Mum gasps, her eyes widening. "You've met someone!"

"Mum—"

"You have, I can tell!" she says excitedly, as Dad rolls his eyes. "Are you going for a long weekend away together? That's got to be it! Why else would you be so nervous and not tell me any details?"

"Mum, I told you, I'm going away with a friend. Someone you don't know. Her name is Emily. Anyway, it's not important."

"Sure, sure," she says, taking her place at the table. "I hope you have a lovely time with your *friend*. Don't worry, I won't ask any more personal questions."

She mimes zipping up her lips. I guess there's no harm in letting her think I'm away with a guy this weekend. Better than her knowing the truth. Ignoring her, I raise my glass.

"Happy birthday, Dad," I say cheerily, clinking my glass with his.

"Thank you, Soph," he says, and starts tucking into the Indian takeaway he specifically requested for his special dinner.

Mum's pretending not to be annoyed by it. She wanted to make a big fuss over him and take him out somewhere, but he was adamant that all he wanted was a "takeaway and a night in with my girls." Dad's never been one for a lot of fuss. He's the sort of person who would rather stay in than go out, sitting cozily on the sofa, reading glasses on, enraptured by the latest thriller. Since he retired from his teaching job at the local comprehensive, he's got into walking and attempted to learn golf, but his favorite pastimes are still reading and writing.

I can tell he misses his job. He was a brilliant teacher, fascinated by history and desperate for all his students to be just as passionate. He's naturally warm, gentle and enthusiastic. The kids and the staff loved him. He was never tempted to go to another school or move into a more senior position. Money wasn't a motivation—Mum has always been the breadwinner—and he didn't like the idea of getting involved in school politics. He's much too disorganized and laid-back for any of that. He simply wanted to teach.

When it was time for him to retire, it was difficult for everyone—we were all unsure of what he was going to do with himself. On his last day at school, he gave a wonderful farewell speech at the prize-giving, which moved everyone in the audience to tears. You could tell his heart was breaking a little.

But, as it turns out, he's settled into retirement nicely. He doesn't miss the marking side of things, he always says, and even though he misses the kids, he's focusing most of his energy on writing his book, a historical murder mystery. He won't tell us any more about it, though. When I ask about the plot, he says, "Now, that would be spoiling the mystery," and taps the side of his nose. The few times I've been at home and he's done some writing, I've found plenty of entertainment in his "writing process." He goes into the study and does some stretching, then sits at the computer, inhaling deeply, saying, "Here we go," and tapping slowly at the keyboard, pausing now and then to read back the sentence and exclaim "Good!" or "Needs work!" as though he's speaking to his class.

"Now," he says, spooning mango chutney onto his plate, "tell me about work, Sophie. How's it all going?"

"It's fine," I lie, taking a sip of wine and avoiding eye contact with Mum.

"I hope now the summer's over, things have calmed down," she says, cracking a popadum and offering me a piece. "You were much too busy the past few months. You need to make sure you give yourself some time off so you're well rested."

"It's good to be busy in my line of work," I remind them. "If things ever calm down, I'll be worried."

"Any Bride- or Groomzillas?" Dad asks, chuckling. "I hope so. Always makes for an interesting story."

"I do have one particularly demanding bride at the moment. In fact—" I pause, planning my words carefully so I don't give anything away. "—I'm not entirely sure how to handle her."

I thought that breaking into the studio was the bonding moment Cordelia and I needed. But it's as though it never happened.

I got a message from her on my way home from seeing Jonathan, but instead of a thank-you for putting my neck on the line, it was instructions to pick up her dry cleaning. Again. Hadn't I proved that I was worth having around by *committing a crime on her behalf*? How had that not won her over? How were we not going for drinks, laughing about the success of our daring mission?! I'd even just come up with the *perfect* gift for her— Jonathan couldn't have been happier—and, yes, fine, she didn't know anything about that, but *still*.

I picked up her dry cleaning as requested and the only other message I got from her was a reply of "OK" when I told her the time my train would be getting in on Saturday so she could arrange a local taxi as she'd offered.

I wonder if she'll ever get over the fact that I've been hired to help her. It's as though she's purposely putting on all these airs and graces, pretending to be the demanding diva socialite the world has painted. But Jonathan has convinced me that's not who she really is at all. How do I get her to drop the act?

"Perhaps we can help with this bride," Mum says, sitting up, already set to find a solution to the problem, whatever it may be.

"She's difficult. She hates me."

"No one could hate you," Dad says.

"She does. She thinks I'm weird."

"You're not weird!" Mum declares, insulted.

"Define weird," Dad says, with a smile, then yelps when Mum kicks him under the table. "I'm only joking! You're not weird, Sophie. You're very normal."

"Maybe that's part of the problem. I'm too 'normal.'" I move my food around my plate. "I thought we'd started to bond, but I'm pretty sure I was wrong. Her mum was the one who got in touch in the first place and she really wants me to help. She's under the impression her daughter needs me. But this client makes it very clear that she doesn't want me around at all."

"Working with a reluctant client is never easy." Mum nods. "I remember when I had to work with—well, I won't name him, so let's just say a *very* demanding presenter. There had been some headlines about his past relations with a married model. He'd just landed a prominent job on a family-friendly show. Of course, he was fired as soon as the story broke. Could have been the end of his career. I was hired by his agent to sort it all out. Did he want me around? No. Did he thank me when I transformed his image and set him out on a path much more suited to his personality? No. He thought he could do it better his way, as though I had no experience whatsoever. I saved his bacon and he couldn't have cared less. It wasn't the most fulfilling of jobs."

"How did you cope with being made to feel you weren't wanted, and not letting it get in the way?" I ask, putting my fork down.

"I suppose I simply reminded myself that I was doing a job. You can't let personal feelings intrude. Would a doctor say no to treating a patient because they weren't very nice to them? Of course they wouldn't. They're there to do a job and that's what they're going to do."

"That's a good way of looking at it, I guess. I can't understand how anyone can be so unpleasant. So determined to dislike me. I swear, the other day we were on the same page. But it's like she won't let herself be friendly. And I know she can be. It's so infuriating."

"Maybe you're not seeing the whole story," Dad suggests, leaning back in his chair. "She sounds like a complicated person. An interesting character. There might be more to her than you think."

"I don't know. I've yet to see one redeeming quality shine through the layers and layers of meanness."

Dad chuckles. "She's that bad, eh?"

"Worse. I don't know how long I can pretend I'm happy to be working for her. Every time she does or says something outrageous, I have to keep smiling. It's maddening."

"The important thing to keep in mind is to get the job done to the best of your ability," Mum says. "If your mask slips a little every now and then, you can't beat yourself up about it. You just keep doing your thing. You help her create the most magical wedding she can imagine."

"It's so tempting to give up and be there for brides who

actually want me. And what if our hatred for each other ruins everything, anyway? What's the point?"

"If you really felt that way, you'd have backed out already," Mum says. "You go above and beyond your job outline. Like all your brides, she's lucky to have you and you know it. That's why you haven't given up on her."

"I agree," Dad says firmly. "You always were a planner. Do you remember the wonderful Christmas party you organized for us?"

"That was hardly a big event, Dad." I laugh. "I was eight!"

"The whole thing was your idea. You went round every house on the street and put an invitation through their letter box," he recalls fondly. "You were so excited, you got up early on Christmas Eve and tried to put the party lights up round the room before I was there to supervise."

"And remember how she went around with the trays of nibbles?" Mum smiles.

"I remember she went round topping up everyone's champagne," he says. "And how cross she was when I didn't seamlessly change the background music from one Christmas album to another."

"Oh, yes, she kept saying, 'It's the *ambience*, Daddy! The ambience!' " Mum giggles, reaching over and taking his hand, which is resting on the table. "You must have learned that word recently, because you were very proud of yourself for using it."

"So, if you can handle a big Christmas party packed with our nutty neighbors at the age of eight, trust me, you can handle this bride," Dad concludes, his eyes bright with amusement.

"Thanks, Dad," I say, appreciative of their confidence and hoping some of it will rub off on me when I face Cordelia this weekend. "I'll do my best."

"Then that will be more than enough." He claps his hands together, grabs his fork, and scans the dishes on the table. "Now, as it's my birthday, I'm guessing I'm allowed seconds?"

Please leave a voicemail after the tone.
BEEEEEEEEEEEEP

Hi, Sophie, it's Candice. Could you give me a call when you get this? I've got myself in a bit of an awkward situation. A really awful situation. I'm so embarrassed. My soon-to-be sister-in-law asked if she can play her accordion at the wedding, an instrument she's only just taken up. She asked if we'd like her to play for the ceremony. She asked this at a family dinner last night, in front of everyone. And guess what I did? I said yes. I SAID YES. They were all looking at me! I couldn't say no! *What am I going to do?* How am I going to get out of it? Help me. Help me, *please.*

Please leave a voicemail after the tone.
BEEEEEEEEEEEEP

Hi, Sophie, it's Candice again. I know I just left you a message, but I've just remembered something else. She said she could only play one song fully and it's "My Heart Will Go On" by Céline Dion. The *Titanic* song, Sophie. She wants me to walk down the aisle to the theme tune of a tragic film about a doomed love. Please call me back ASAP. I actually think I just threw up a bit in my mouth.

Please leave a voicemail after the tone.
BEEEEEEEEEEEEP

Oh, and she's currently learning how to play "Don't Cha" by the Pussycat Dolls. She said, if we like, that can be our first dance. Kill me. Kill me now.

CHAPTER SEVENTEEN

There's no taxi waiting for me when I get off the train in Derbyshire.

I sit down on the lone bench and check my phone to see if Cordelia's messaged to tell me the taxi she ordered is running late. There are no messages and no signal. I can understand why you don't get a bar of reception out here. It really is the middle of nowhere. The station is tiny, a little bigger than a hut, and there's a notice up reminding travelers that it's closed at weekends and to get their tickets from the machine on the platform.

I was the only passenger to get off at this stop and, even though I don't want to be late turning up at Dashwell Hall, it's quite nice to feel as though I'm the only person for miles. It's so peaceful out here. I wrap my coat around me and take in the vast surrounding countryside. In the distance I can see horses grazing and sheep dotted about the fields. It looks like a scene out of a Jane Austen novel. Except for the train tracks and me plonked in the middle in my polka-dot dress, long black coat, and ankle boots.

A few minutes into the wait, I wonder why the taxi is held up—maybe stuck behind some cows trying to cross the road or something equally lovely. I don't get much time in London to just sit and do nothing, and if I do, I'm usually on my phone, but without any signal there's not much I can do. I'm forced to sit and appreciate the world around me. The birdsong. The peace. The fresh air. The gray clouds worry me a tad, considering there's no shelter with the station closed, but the taxi will no doubt be here any minute.

About fifteen minutes in, I'm a little fidgety. I don't want to be too late showing up this weekend, not just because of manners but also because there's a lot to do. I'm desperate to see the house and start working out how we can make Cordelia's vision come to life. The evening with my parents has given me the boost I needed to feel excited about this wedding again. Yes, it feels like an impossible and daunting task, but ultimately it's Cordelia's decision, not mine, and all I can do is be there for her when she needs me.

Half an hour later, I stand up on the bench, holding my phone as high as possible to see if I can get some signal. But there's nothing.

Forty-five minutes in, I'm in full-on panic. I pace around, trying desperately to see what's down the winding, narrow road leading to the station. Did I get off at the wrong stop? I recheck the sign and it's definitely the right place. Maybe I gave Cordelia the wrong time? I scroll through my messages and confirm I told her the correct one. The taxi is either held up or isn't coming and has decided it's not worth letting me know. How infuriating! I'm stuck in the middle of nowhere with no signal. They would surely know that anyone stranded here is in a tight spot and the idea of letting down the Marquess and Marchioness of Meade can't be good for business around here . . .

Another reason for the taxi's no-show pops into my head. It seems by far the likeliest scenario.

Cordelia never booked one in the first place.

ARGH! How could I have been so *stupid*? She's been trying to sabotage me from the beginning. Why would she happily book a taxi for me so I could join the weekend? I can't believe how naïve I am to have believed her.

"What a BITCH," I say out loud, to no one. A cow moos in the distance.

A raindrop lands on the side of my nose.

Brilliant.

I grab the handle on my wheelie case and grumpily walk down the road away from the station, holding my phone in front of me as I go, checking the screen every few seconds. There *must* be a signal somewhere along this road, and as soon as I manage to get a bar, I can google a local taxi company. It starts to rain lightly and I hate myself for not bringing a coat with a hood. Did I pack an umbrella? I must have done. But, if so, it will be in my wheelie case and I can't be bothered to unzip it on the road and fish it out.

The road goes on forever. Not one bar of signal makes an appearance and no cars pass. The rain gets heavier, water trickling down my face, as I continue, praying that a taxi miraculously appears and I'm wrong about Cordelia. I stop to tie up my hair, which is damp and scraggly, now plastered unpleasantly to my forehead and neck. I'm watched by the curious sheep in the field next to the lane. Most are lying in the shelter of a tree, snuggled together. I'm so jealous, I can't look at them anymore.

"This is ridiculous!" I cry, deciding it's time to search for that umbrella.

Crouching, I try to unzip the wheelie case just a little so that the rain doesn't ruin all the clothes I've brought for the weekend, stick my arm in and scrabble about inside. I can't find it blindly, so I open the case fully and have a good rummage.

"Fuck's sake," I grumble. It's in the zipped pocket on the front. "That's perfect. I'll turn up to Dashwell looking like a drowned rat, all my clothes for the weekend ruined."

A sheep bleats sympathetically. The animals are feeling my pain.

The station road eventually comes to a crossroads where

there is a sign pointing me in the direction of Dashwell Hall and an actual pavement on both sides. Encouraged by this sign of civilization, I check my phone again just in case. Raindrops splatter over the screen despite my attempts to shield it with the umbrella. Still no signal. And nothing else for miles. Looks like I'm walking all the way there.

"Please don't be too far, please don't be too far," I whimper, setting off, knowing full well that it is quite a long way because I looked at it on a map and I remember it being a good drive from the station.

After a while, my wheelie case goes over a stray stone, causing me to stumble and stub my toe. Yelping, I stop to give myself a moment. I feel like I might burst into tears. I do not deserve this! I hate Cordelia. I. HATE. HER. And why is there no signal? How is there anywhere in this country still with no signal? This is the twenty-first century! *What is wrong with this place?*

"ARRRRRGH!" I scream in frustration, closing my eyes, clenching my fists, and stomping on the ground to let all my anger out.

A car horn beeps behind me and I jump out of my skin. I spin around to see a mucky old Land Rover crawling slowly toward me. I'm saved!

I drag my wheelie case over and the window rolls down so I can speak to the driver.

Oh. Fuck.

"Emily!" Tom takes in my appearance, his eyes wide with shock. "What are you doing?"

The joy at being saved from my current predicament makes way for an overwhelming wave of humiliation. I can't imagine what I look like but it can't be anything good. My makeup is surely running over my face and my hair is scraped back into a wet bun. I also have mud splattered over my legs, splashed up from the wheels of my case.

"Oh, hi." I smile, trying to appear nonchalant. "How are you, Tom?"

"Were you planning on *walking* to Dashwell?" he asks, ignoring my question. "I thought Cordelia had booked you a taxi."

"My train got in a bit earlier," I lie, wiping my forehead. "I forgot there was no signal out here. I thought the walk would do me good."

As tempting as it is to tell everyone how much of a bitch Cordelia really is, I also know that ratting her out to her brother is not the way forward. The only way this might work is if she starts to trust me. Until then, I have to play along with her game.

Her horrible, crazy game, which includes me breaking into houses in the middle of the night. And being stranded in the middle of the countryside.

Think of the money, think of your career, think of the future clients . . .

"You thought you'd walk in the rain?"

"It's very . . . refreshing."

"It's quite a long way to Dashwell on foot," he says, looking at me as though I'm insane. "Let me give you a lift."

"Oh!" I pretend I've only just thought of this. "Are you sure? I'm happy to walk if you're off out somewhere."

"Get in," he says bossily, climbing out and picking up my case. "I'll put this in the boot."

I follow his instructions and, pulling myself up into the passenger seat, I feel a huge sense of relief. Ideally, Tom would not have seen me looking such a mess, but at least I've managed to get a lift. I get a mirror out of my bag and quickly check my reflection, groaning at the mascara I'd carefully applied this morning smudged around my eyes, my foundation splodging around my nose, my lipstick nonexistent. I start reapplying as Tom gets back into the driver's seat and shuts the door.

"You're a big walker, then," he asks, setting off.

"Sometimes," I say, trying discreetly to wipe away the mascara under my eyes with my finger. "It's nice to be in the fresh air, out of London."

"Sure." He grins. "And, as you say, the rain is very refreshing."

I feel flustered, watching him drive. His arms are all tanned and freckly and kind of flexed with his hands on the wheel. I drag my gaze away from him to look straight ahead. Who knew arms could be so sexy?

"You're lucky I found you," he says, interrupting my thoughts about his arms and making me blush, as though he might have been able to read my mind. "This road is quiet. Most tourists in the area don't come through this station as it's not part of Paxton, the village where the B and Bs and shops are. This station is closer to the hall but very isolated."

"Yeah, I noticed," I say, putting foundation on my nose and blending it in. "How come you're not at Dashwell this morning?"

"Cordelia wanted some fresh fruit for smoothies," he explains, jerking his head at the bags in the back seat. "There's a farmer's market on Saturdays nearby and I volunteered to pick it up."

"That's nice of you."

"It's not completely selfless," he admits. "Have you ever had one of her smoothies?"

I shake my head.

"You're missing out. They're delicious. She said she'd make one for me if I got the ingredients. I'll get her to make enough for both of us. Although you're probably after something a bit more warming."

"A cup of tea would be good."

"How was your friend's birthday dinner?"

"It was lovely, thanks but I'm sorry that I wasn't able to come up here last night."

"You didn't miss much. During dinner, Cordelia and Mum had an ugly fight over the menu choices for the wedding." He sighs, carefully turning a tight corner. "It was very boring and loud for the rest of us."

"Did they come to an agreement?"

He laughs at such a ludicrous thought. "I'm not sure they've ever agreed on anything."

Out of the corner of my eye, I notice him looking at me curiously before he speaks again.

"It's really nice having someone who gets my sister. It sounds strange, but she makes it difficult for people to like her. I don't understand her most of the time, but she's a good person. One of the best, really. It's nice to know I'm not the only one who sees that."

"Hmm." I keep my mouth shut and wonder for the first time whether he's as nuts as she is.

"I'm surprised you forgave her so quickly over that stupid escort rumor she started." He grimaces.

"I'm not an escort," I say, mortified he'd heard about it.

"I know!" He laughs. "Bloody hell, Emily, of course you're not. She just has the weirdest sense of humor. I told her she was lucky to have you as a mate after that strange prank."

"Yeah, well, you know what she's like," I say, clearing my throat and desperate to change the subject. "Was it weird growing up in a house that's filled with tourists all the time?"

"It was a bit. Still is. But we have a private section they don't come into."

"When you say section, do you mean wing?" I ask, making him shift in his seat.

"I guess you could call it a wing." He glances over at me. "Why are you grinning? What?"

"Sorry, it's just so mad," I say, unable to stop myself laughing. "It's like *Beauty and the Beast* or something. You have your own *wing*."

"It isn't my own private wing, it's for the whole family," he explains, a smile spreading across his face, the familiar crinkles appearing around his eyes. "And it's way cooler than that castle in *Beauty and the Beast*."

"That's a big claim. The Beast's castle is awesome. It has turrets and everything." I gesture out of the window. "Brilliant. Now, when I'm in a car, it stops raining. But when I was walking, it had to pour down."

"I thought you were enjoying your refreshing walk in the rain?"

"I was," I say defensively.

"Whatever you say." He grins, pulling up to a set of black iron gates.

A man behind the glass window of a booth looks up, sees Tom, and smiles, immediately pressing something to let us in. The car bumps over a cattle grid and the driveway stretches in front of us, lined with dramatic towering trees. As Tom dodges potholes, I lean forward in anticipation, waiting for my first glimpse of the great house. Eventually, it looms into view. I gasp.

"There it is," Tom says warmly. "Welcome to Dashwell Hall."

CHAPTER EIGHTEEN

Dashwell Hall is magnificent. Rising from the rolling parkland, the large old stone house looks warmly golden and welcoming even under the gray sky, the hundreds of grand windows glinting. With wings stretching off at either side, there's no wonder that the Swanns are able to find peace and privacy here while tourists mill about their extensive, palatial grounds.

A man wearing a high-visibility vest, his hands stuck firmly in his pockets, stands at the point the driveway transitions from clay to gravel and forks, one side leading straight ahead toward the house, the other veering up to a field. A sign reveals that to the left is parking and straight on is private. Nodding to the steward, Tom continues ahead, circling the striking stone fountain in front of the house and parking next to a silver Aston Martin.

"What do you think?" he asks, turning off the engine and unclipping his seat belt.

"I think . . ." I lean back in my seat to take it all in. ". . . your house may be better than the Beast's."

He laughs, watching me. "Except for the lack of turrets."

"I can't believe I'm staying here." I peer up at the house through the windscreen. "It's beautiful."

"Let's go in. Cordelia will be happy to see you."

I climb out of the car and realize that the beauty of the house has distracted me from my current state. I crouch to wipe as much mud off my legs as I can, then straighten and reach up to my hair, yanking out my hair band and combing my hair with my fingers. I turn round to see Tom holding my wheelie case and the shopping, waiting for me.

"Sorry." I hurry toward him, smoothing my damp coat. "Are your family all in at the moment? Right now, I mean?"

"They were in when I left, but there's a chance they're out," he says, his feet crunching over the gravel toward the front door. "Why? Everything OK?"

"Yeah, everything's fine. I wondered whether I might be able to shower and sort myself out before seeing everyone," I explain, smiling up at him apologetically. "I'm not exactly looking my best."

"You don't need to worry about stuff like that. You look great," Tom says matter-of-factly, brushing aside my concern with a wave of his hand. "But if you're worried about it, I can show you to your room before anyone spots us coming in."

As I thank him, the sound of tires on the gravel distracts us and we turn to watch a sleek blue sports car pull up to park behind the Land Rover. The doors swing open and two women emerge. One I recognize immediately.

Lady Annabel Porthouse.

The other girl must be related: they're both tall and slender, with the same delicate facial features, pronounced lips, and honey-blond highlighted hair. Lady Annabel is wearing a long red skirt with a black polo neck, while her friend is in black skinny jeans, a billowing blue shirt, the top buttons undone, and high wedges. An odd choice of footwear for this weather. She hobbles over the gravel behind Lady Annabel, who is striding toward us with boundless energy.

"Tom, hi!" she shrieks, enveloping him in a hug. "We heard you were here for the weekend."

"So lovely to see you!" the other in the wedges exclaims, when she finally catches up, giving him two air kisses and gripping his free hand. "It's been too long."

They turn to me, waiting for Tom's introduction.

"It's great to see you," he says, sounding less enthusiastic. "This is Emily. She's a friend of Cordelia's. Emily, this is Annabel and her sister, Georgia."

"Ah, yes," Annabel says, lifting her chin defiantly. "Cordelia's bridesmaid. So nice to meet you, Emily."

"And you," I say, noticing the gigantic diamond sitting on her ring finger.

"Oh, yes, that's right." Georgia giggles, her eyes drifting up from my muddy boots to my tangled wet bird's-nest hair. "How fascinating. Are you really an escort?"

"Only at weekends," I quip.

Tom snorts with laughter. The girls remain unimpressed.

"You're here for the weekend, too, then? Or are you on your way home?" Annabel asks, noting the wheelie case and folding her arms.

"I've just arrived, actually," I say, taking great pleasure in their barely concealed disappointment. "I came up on the train from London."

"How nice," Annabel says, with a thin smile. "Since we're all out here in the sticks for the weekend, we must do dinner this evening! Don't you think so, Tom?"

"I—"

"We must!" Georgia squeals, nodding vigorously. "*Such* a fun idea, Annabel."

"Unless you have other plans tonight?" Annabel asks Tom, giggling. "Although I don't suppose you do. Come on, Tom, we never hang out anymore."

"Never," Georgia repeats.

"When will we get this chance again? It'll be so fun," Annabel insists. "And don't worry, our parents are here too, so we can bring them along to entertain yours, Tom. We can all talk weddings!"

"I'm so excited already," Georgia says, clapping her hands. "What do you think, Tom?"

"Shall we say seven o'clock?" Annabel smiles.

"Um . . . uh . . ." He looks to me for help but I just stare back. ". . . that sounds great."

"Perfect," Annabel says, placing a hand gently on his arm. "You're so sweet to have us."

"We haven't had a good catch-up in ages, Tom," Georgia claims, somewhat accusingly. "It's such a shame we couldn't go to the engagement party, and since then you've been so busy."

"Yeah, it's been crazy," he agrees. "We shouldn't loiter here on the doorstep. Shall we go in?"

"Actually, we won't keep you," Annabel cuts in, as Georgia opens her mouth to speak. "We were only dropping by to say hello. We must get back home in time for my meeting with Nicole Percy, our florist. She's come all this way specially, so I don't want to keep her waiting. We'll catch up at dinner tonight."

"Wait," I say, before I can stop myself. "Your wedding florist is Nicole Percy?"

"You know her?" Annabel asks, tilting her head in surprise.

"No, not really," I say quietly, wishing I hadn't said anything at all. "I hear she's great."

"She's the best. Such a spiritual, talented woman," she states, flipping her hair behind her shoulders. "There's no one better. The wedding's in May, so we don't have long, but I feel safe in her hands. Anyway, bye, darlings."

"So nice to meet you."

I know what your wedding dress looks like.

I broke into a studio to look at the designs.

I'm so sorry.

PS You'll look so good in an A-line.

After they've given Tom and me kisses on each cheek, they saunter back to their car and beep the horn loudly, speeding back down the drive. Waving goodbye, Tom ushers me into the house, shuts the door behind us, and leans back against it in despair.

"Sorry about that. They're old friends." He winces. "Cordelia's going to kill me when she finds out they're coming for dinner."

"I witnessed the conversation and I'm not sure you had any choice."

"Still. She's going to *kill* me."

While he mutters something inaudible, I stare in wonder at the breathtaking entrance hall before me. A patterned floor stretches beneath a soaring domed ceiling, framed by towering columns. Marble busts sit to either side of the vast set of stairs ahead.

"Wow," I whisper into the silence, a shiver running down my spine. "It's incredible."

"Yeah," Tom says, coming to stand next to me. "It's not bad."

"That's an understatement," I murmur, gazing up at the ceiling. In such a grand place, I automatically feel as though I should keep my voice down in respect. "It's so beautiful. I can't imagine what it's like to live somewhere like this."

"Hasn't Cordelia told you anything about the house?" He smiles knowingly when I shake my head. "Makes sense. She's embarrassed by it."

"Embarrassed?" I stare at him in disbelief. "By *this*? If I lived here, I wouldn't shut up about it. And I've only seen the hallway. How many rooms are there?"

He laughs. "A few."

"A few hundred?"

"Something like that." He breathes in deeply, glancing around us. "It is beautiful, but it's a different world. Parts of it are like a museum. The best bits are the smaller, homely rooms."

"Oh, yes, your private wing."

"Not just *mine*," he corrects, with a sly smile.

"Did you ever knock over a priceless bust or anything when you were little and running around?" I ask. "My mum was furious when I was playing in the house and knocked over a vase. Here, it must be even worse when something like that happens."

"I never knocked over a bust," he says, before lowering his voice, "but I did once scribble with biro on the corner of a portrait by Thomas Gainsborough. I wanted to see if biro worked on an old canvas."

"And did it?"

He grimaces. "I feel very guilty about that one."

"Did you get caught?"

"Actually, no." He hesitates, looking at me strangely. "I've never told anyone that story, except Cordelia. I swore her to secrecy."

"My lips are sealed." I lean in toward him. "Can you still see the biro on the painting?"

He closes his eyes, then nods slowly and shamefully.

"Tom? Is that you?" A voice echoes around the walls, making us both jump. Lady Meade appears at the top of the stairs. "Emily!"

Tom gestures for me to go up while he grabs the bags. Disappointed that the plan to sneak in and sort out my appearance before seeing the rest of the family has gone downhill, I tuck my hair behind my ears and step lightly up the stairs, terrified of leaving dirt on the plush red carpet running down the center.

"Cordelia didn't tell me you'd arrived," she says, greeting me at the top of the steps.

She's in a more relaxed outfit than I'm used to seeing her in—navy trousers and a white shirt with a cashmere cardigan and a long blue bead necklace draped round her neck—and her hair is loose, falling neatly to her shoulders. Something about her air is a little more at ease, too. She's much more at home here than she is in London.

"I found her wandering from the train station," Tom reveals.

"I see."

"I got an earlier train. I should have let someone know but I wasn't thinking and then there was no phone signal." I gesture around the hall. "Dashwell is absolutely beautiful, Lady Meade."

"Thank you. We must give you a tour and, at the same time, run through all the points of the wedding. But," she says, with a polite smile, "it's been a long journey, I imagine. I'll show you to your room and you can freshen up before you get stuck in. Tom, your father is looking for you. He needs some help with the Wi-Fi. It's not working. He would ask Bill to help him, but he's down by the stables. One of the donkeys broke through a fence and he's fixing it."

Tom lifts his eyes to the ceiling. "The Wi-Fi is working perfectly, Mum."

"Apparently not. It does in the state drawing room, but not the family drawing room, and only one of the dining rooms. It doesn't reach the library or the billiard room, either."

This is one of the most bizarre conversations I've ever been part of. Half of it is completely everyday—what parent doesn't need help with the Wi-Fi every now and then? But the other half, the part regarding stables and billiard rooms and more than one drawing and dining room, is so insane, I can hardly believe it's serious.

"I'll find him in a minute," Tom says, with a long drawn-out sigh. "Oh, and, Mum, about tonight. There's been a . . . development."

"Yes?"

"Some sort of misunderstanding, really," he begins uneasily, as I hide my smile, looking down at my feet. "We bumped into Annabel and Georgia."

"At the market?"

"No, here. Outside."

"They were here?" She looks surprised. "Why didn't you invite them in?"

"They were only dropping by so they couldn't stay long, but instead they're going to come and say hello properly this evening. Over dinner."

Lady Meade purses her lips. "You invited them for dinner."

"In all honesty, I'm not really sure what happened," Tom admits. "It was very fast and suddenly it was decided. Right, Emily?"

"Right," I say in solidarity. "It was a whirlwind."

"A whirlwind," Tom repeats, nodding.

We fall silent, waiting for Lady Meade's reaction. She smooths a nonexistent crinkle on her shirt, then lifts her chin, smiling graciously.

"How lovely," she says. "I shall ask Nicholas to give Ned a call and confirm timings. In the meantime, I'd better make sure we have food to serve them." She turns to me. "Come, let me show you your room and get you settled in."

"I'll go and sort the Wi-Fi," Tom suggests.

"Yes, and, Thomas," she says, "I'll leave it up to you to let Cordelia know that the Earl and Countess of Derrington, as well as their daughters, are joining us this evening for dinner." The color in Tom's face drains. "This way, Emily."

"Thanks again for the lift," I say to Tom, taking my bag from him. "I'll see you in a bit."

As I follow Lady Meade, I can't help but smile as I hear Tom mutter bitterly in reply, "If Cordelia hasn't murdered me by then."

CHAPTER NINETEEN

There she is." Lady Meade leans on the fence.

Her daughter is riding a striking gray horse in the distance, galloping across the field.

"Cordelia!" she yells, waving at her. "Cordelia! Over here!"

She hears the cry and spots us, turning the horse in our direction. As she gets closer, I'm surprised to see a smile on her face, not sickly or forced, a real one. She looks genuinely happy. Jonathan's proposal story makes a lot of sense.

"She's always loved horses," Lady Meade explains, as though reading my mind. "She's much more comfortable around animals than people. I think she got that from me."

Cordelia slows and trots over, slightly breathless, strands of hair loosely falling from under her riding hat, her skin glowing from the exercise.

"We've been looking for you," her mother says, stepping up onto the lower rung of the fence to lean over and pat the neck of the horse, her expression softening, crinkles appearing around her eyes as she smiles broadly. "Hello, darling."

She's speaking in a much more affectionate tone to the horse than I've heard her use with anyone else, including her children.

"I told you I was going out," Cordelia says, swinging her leg over and jumping down from the saddle with elegance and ease. "I see you made it, Emily." She sounds impressed.

"She got an earlier train."

"Is that right?" The horse nudges her but is ignored, so pushes past her to get a stroke on the nose from Lady Meade.

"Lady Meade has given me a wonderful tour of Dashwell," I say, looking back past the stables at the house. "Your wedding is going to be magical here."

It's a cheesy comment and the sort of thing I probably shouldn't say in front of someone as cynical and miserable as Lady Cordelia Swann, but it's the truth. I spent the last forty-five minutes trailing after Lady Meade in complete awe as she took me round the maze of grand rooms, each as fascinating as the last, and each with its own treasures and history.

The guest room in which I'm staying—one of many—is practically bigger than my flat, with a giant four-poster bed in the middle of the room and windows framed by red velvet curtains, tied with golden-tasseled cords. When I walked in earlier with my old wheelie case and looked out at the view over the private walled garden, the lake and hills beyond, I was lost for words.

After showering, changing into a fresh dress, and reapplying my makeup, I wandered down the corridor outside my room, lost until Lady Meade appeared, ready to give me a tour. I was shown the rooms that tourists enjoy: the state dining room; the banquet hall, its walls covered with priceless works of art; the grand ballroom with a sparkling chandelier hanging from the ceiling to light the mosaic tiled floor; and the various libraries filled with row upon row of first editions lined up on shelves protected by glass.

We then moved outside, as the marchioness was keen for us to find Cordelia sooner rather than later, but she promised I'd see the rest of the house and the private quarters before dinner. She informed me that we'd need to change our shoes before going outside, as it was a bit of a walk and, thanks to the earlier rain, a little muddy. She led me through a door marked PRIVATE and down some plain back stairs into an old boot room in the part of the house shut off from visitors.

This quickly became my favorite place in the house, because it was the first that felt like it belonged in a family home. Old wax coats hung from hooks lined up along the wall, and there were so many pairs of boots lying around, I had quite a selection to choose from. She found me a pair in my size, and as I shook off the cobwebs lining the top, she threw me a rolled-up pair of socks from a basket by the door, before donning some old boots herself.

Strolling past the walled garden, she explained that she didn't want to disturb the visitors in there at the moment and she'd make sure I saw it later, as she was rather proud of the planting she'd done over the summer.

Her face lit up as we approached the stables, so it was no surprise when she made the comment about Cordelia getting the love of animals from her.

"Oh, and I must show you my chickens," she said earlier, as I was introduced to the naughty donkey that had knocked down the fence that morning. "They're delightful creatures. Wait until you meet Lord Cluck! You'll be very taken with him."

Whether or not this weekend would be a success, I was grateful to have seen a different side to the marchioness. If only the same would happen with Cordelia. Perhaps in this different setting, she'd reveal her softer side, too.

Although she looks physically repulsed at my use of "magical" to describe her wedding, so perhaps not.

"Are you coming back to the house now?" Lady Meade asks her daughter, letting the horse nibble the palm of her hand. "We have a lot to discuss and your father is a little anxious. Your brother also needs to have a word about dinner."

"I'll come up once I've put Tony away."

"The horse is called *Tony*?" I blurt out, unable to hide my amusement.

Cordelia shoots me a cold, hard stare. "Yes. Why? Do you have a problem with that?"

"No! It's an . . . unusual name for a horse, that's all."

"What would be a usual name for a horse? Let me guess," she says, rolling her eyes. "You'd name your horse something like Sparkle or Rainbow or *Magic*."

I know she's mocking me but she's probably right, so I shrug.

"Tony is named after Tony McCoy," she says, and when I stare at her blankly, she looks at me as though I'm the stupidest person to walk the planet. "Tony McCoy? One of the greatest jockeys of all time?"

"He sounds very talented," I say, stroking Tony on the nose as he comes to snuffle at my jacket for any hidden carrots. "He must be very happy to have such a beautiful horse named after him."

Cordelia tugs the reins so that Tony is pulled away from me, then addresses her mother. "I'll be up in a minute."

She walks away with Tony in tow, leading him to the gate to the stables. Lady Meade turns to me. "You're getting to her, you know."

I frown, worried. "What do you mean? Am I doing something wrong?"

"You won't let her push you away," she says, gesturing for me to follow her back to the house. "So, as far as I'm concerned, you're doing everything right."

⌐───⌐

"What a shame Nicole Percy didn't take to you!" Annabel cries, the champagne almost splashing out of her glass. "She really is the best in the business and Dashwell Hall deserves the best. This really couldn't be worse! You're going to be stuck finding anyone by December, Cordy! It'll have to be a rush job! How ghastly. *What ever* are you going to do?"

Cordelia looks as though what she might do is punch Annabel's face.

"What sort of flowers are you thinking for your wedding, Annabel?" I ask quickly, hoping to move the focus away from Cordelia. People like Annabel love talking about themselves, so if you continually ask questions about their life, they think you're absolutely marvelous without knowing anything about you.

"Oh, I would tell you, but it's very secretive," she says, patting my hand. "Everyone wants to know. What I can tell you is it's going to be simply spectacular. Nicole is a genius."

Cordelia is gripping her glass so tightly, her knuckles have gone white and I'm worried it'll shatter at any moment.

"The thing is, Nicole is an artist, not a florist," she says, her voice inflecting up at the end of the sentence, as if it's a question. "That's why the events she does are so different. Everyone can tell that it's not just anyone who does the flowers, if you know what I mean. It shouldn't be done in a rush, with money thrown at it. It really is an art form." She looks at Cordelia sympathetically. "Sorry, *Cordy*, don't mean to rub salt in the wound."

"Nicole is certainly different," I say, glancing nervously at Cordelia, whose jaw is clenched.

Quite frankly, I'm coming round to understanding why Cordelia told Tom to fuck off when he filled her in on the news of who was coming to dinner. She had a meltdown, insisting that her mum call the evening off. She was on the verge of tears as she ranted about it. I wondered how I would feel if Mum and Dad had Graham Slater over for dinner, and knew immediately: sick. I kind of got it.

Annabel is particularly unpleasant and I'm not sure her sister is much better.

The Earl and Countess of Derrington seem nice but they're a

little pompous and self-important, and meeting them has allowed me to appreciate just how impeccably mannered Lord and Lady Meade are. They may be a little closed off, but having spent a day at Dashwell Hall, I can understand why you might have some walls up. It would be difficult to know who to trust when you live in a place like this. But they're so welcoming that I've started to relax and feel at home, despite being in a stately home so grand that earlier I got lost on the way to dinner and ended up in a random courtyard I didn't know existed. Luckily, a man who introduced himself as one of the chefs discovered me and pointed me in the right direction.

This afternoon, I told the marquess his house was really something, and he launched into a wonderful explanation of its history and heritage that continued until Jonathan strolled in with a book and asked me if we'd got to the bit in the story when Nicholas's great-great-grandmother famously danced at a ball with her Irish wolfhound, causing plenty of society gossip about the state of her mind. I was drinking tea at the time and laughed so hard it went up my nose.

By the time Cordelia joined us after putting Tony away, everyone was in a lively mood and seemed excited to start discussing wedding plans. Lord and Lady Meade had put together a list of everything they thought we needed to do and had set things in motion by booking in tastings with available caterers next week.

"Now, we need to start thinking about a photographer," Lord Meade said. "I've had a few recommendations and, Cordelia, you might want to contact them next week, too."

"I was talking about your wedding with someone at work the other day," I said, playing the role of enthusiastic friend, "and they mentioned we should see if Clio Vaughn is available! Aren't you a fan, Cordelia? I think I remember you talking about her."

"Clio Vaughn?" Cordelia repeated, unable to keep the excitement out of her voice. "Yes, I like her work."

"Anyway, ignore this if it's stupid, but I thought I might as well pop her an email to see if she'd do wedding photography and she was really keen! Sorry, I didn't mean to jump the gun and email her behind your back. In the moment, I thought I might as well," I said apologetically. "I was emailing some other photographers about a work event and I suppose I was in event-planning mode!"

"Don't apologize. That's wonderful, Emily," Lady Meade gushed.

Cordelia hadn't said anything, her eyebrows furrowed in concentration.

"Isn't she one of your favorite photographers?" Jonathan said excitedly, nudging Cordelia. "We might feature in one of her future exhibitions!"

"Shall I get back to her and say you'd like to meet up?" I asked casually, pretending I hadn't already booked in a meeting.

"If you wouldn't mind, thank you," Lady Meade said.

"Very thoughtful of you, Emily!" Lord Meade enthused, smiling gratefully at me. "Now, Cordelia, on to the car you want for the wedding . . ."

As the conversation moved on, Cordelia kept her eyes fixed on the table in front of her, determined not to give me a hint of gratitude. But after that she did seem to be in a slightly better mood, a little more positive and involved with the wedding chat.

Of course, that was all destroyed the moment Tom came to join the group and divulged our earlier meeting with Annabel and Georgia. When Cordelia was done telling him where to go, she told her parents she no longer intended to join us for dinner.

I assume Jonathan reasoned with her after she stormed off, because she was there with him, dressed and ready to greet the guests as they arrived. I also noticed Lady Meade go over to her as she came downstairs and gently plead with her to be on her "best behavior." "Don't let them get to you," she said quietly. "Rise above it, darling."

Now I know why that advice was necessary.

"I'm sure the flowers at your wedding will be stunning," I say to Annabel, hoping to conclude the conversation on Nicole Percy.

"It's so much fun planning a wedding, isn't it, Cordy?" she continues, Cordelia flinching every time she shortens her name. "Although now that yours is going to be a bit of a rush you may miss out on some of the fun. What a pity you can't enjoy it."

The cattiness is so blatant, I'm tempted to look for cameras to check we're not on an episode of *Made in Chelsea*, with producers encouraging Annabel to provoke Cordelia as openly as possible. I consider escaping this toxic conversation and glance round the room for an excuse. Georgia is laughing loudly over something Tom has said and is touching his arm. He catches my eye and I look away, heat rising to my cheeks.

"What does your fiancé do, Annabel?" I ask, hoping to seem deep in conversation and not distracted by Tom at all.

"He's in property," she informs me. "It's a shame he couldn't be here this weekend, but he's so busy at the moment. We're off on holiday next week, though, thank goodness."

"Ah, that will be nice," I say, wondering if she's noticed that Cordelia has yet to utter a word. "Are you in property, too?"

"No, I'm an artist," she reveals, put out by my having to ask.

"Wow! What sort of art do you do?"

"I work with charcoal," she informs me, flicking her hair behind her shoulder. "I specialize in portraits."

"That's amazing. Have you drawn anyone interesting?"

"I've mostly done self-portraits."

"Oh. Right."

"What a shame your wedding has to be inside, Cordy!" Annabel exclaims, before I can pester her any further. "The grounds of Dashwell are so beautiful but a Christmas wedding means all your guests will be holed up inside like sardines! What a pity. A spring wedding would have been delightful on the lawns. I must say, I'm pleased I can have a champagne reception outside and people can enjoy our grounds. How sad you won't have that yourself."

"Mmm," Cordelia says, and downs her entire glass of champagne.

"Goodness!" Annabel laughs, her eyes wide with surprise as Cordelia lowers her glass. "Still into that scene, are you? I would have thought you'd be off it after what happened."

A strangled sound issues from Cordelia's throat. Annabel looks at her calmly, no hint of remorse.

"Excuse me," Cordelia manages, and leaves the room.

Annabel watches her go, taking a delicate sip of her drink, then turning to me to say, "How strange." She goes to stand next to her sister and join in with her conversation. With no idea as to what just happened, I place my glass on the side and quietly head out of the room under the watchful gaze of Lady Meade.

I hear a door shutting and follow the corridor to one of the smaller, empty drawing rooms, which has a set of doors opening into the garden. Cordelia is standing outside, smoking. "Are you OK?" I ask carefully, coming to join her.

She looks irritated that I've disturbed her. "I'm fine. I needed a smoke."

"I can understand why," I say. "Annabel's a bit of an interesting character."

"You could say that," she says, taking a long drag.

"She's jealous."

"I don't need you to protect me," she says, exhaling.

"I know."

"And I don't need you to come out here to comfort me."

"I know."

We stand in silence together as she takes another drag. In between, she chews her thumbnail. I want to ask her what Annabel meant by saying "after what happened." It had struck a nerve with Cordelia, whatever she was referring to, and I wonder whether she wants to talk about it. But I can't get the words out to ask.

Instead, I decide to keep things light and try to cheer her up. "Ugh," I say. "Can you imagine her and Nicole Percy in a room together? Seriously, imagine the bullshit you'd have to put up with, listening to those two in conversation."

Cordelia tries her best not to smile, but the corners of her mouth twitch.

"They'd be competing with each other," I continue. "Who could say the most rubbish in the most pretentious words?"

"I'm genuinely not sure who would win," Cordelia says, and flourishes the hand holding the cigarette. "They're both so *artistic.*"

"Both inspired by the world and soil around them."

"Inspired by the *self.*"

"The world is but their canvas."

"Dedicated to creating a concept of sensational harmony."

She catches my eye and we share a conspiratorial smile. The door opens behind us and Tom sticks his head round.

"Dinner is served," he informs us, then lowers his voice. "Shotgun not sitting next to either of them. I've done my time while you two have been having fun out here."

He disappears and Cordelia rolls her eyes, taking one last drag on her cigarette and putting it out beneath her shoe, picking up the butt and sticking it into her pocket. I open the door for her as she goes inside. "Thank you," she says.

There's something different about her voice and it takes me a moment or two to put my finger on it. It's because she actually means it.

Progress.

CHAPTER TWENTY

The following morning, I wake up to my alarm after the best night's sleep I can ever remember having. The mattress is so comfortable and I feel buried in the mountain of pillows, which are all so squishy. It takes a lot of willpower not to roll over and go back to sleep. But I force myself to sit up, stretching and yawning widely. I look around the room and scrunch up my face in excitement. I can't believe I'm waking up at Dashwell Hall.

I swing my legs out of bed, skip across the room, and try to throw open the curtains elegantly, like a Regency heroine might have done when she woke up in a beautiful house after an eventful ball the night before.

But the curtains are actually quite heavy, so when I fling my arms outward, the rings at the top only nudge along a little and I sort of stumble off balance. OK, so not that elegant, but never mind. Pushing the curtains apart with a little more force, I let the sunlight pour into the room.

"Agh!" I yelp, shielding my eyes. Again, not so elegant.

I squint through the window, getting used to the brightness. It's a remarkably sunny day, one of those crisp, cold mornings, blue skies stretching over the countryside. I smile, hugging myself as I enjoy the view. I spot some movement and see a figure jogging down the lawn, waving up at me. I press my forehead to the glass. It's Tom getting back from an early-morning run.

Oh, God. I've just been staring at him, smiling to myself like a total CREEP! In my old McFly 2005 tour T-shirt!

"I wasn't smiling at you!" I say, waving back at him and trying to explain myself even though the window is closed. "I was smiling at the view. Which you happened to be in."

He looks puzzled, slowing down.

"I said, I wasn't smiling at you," I repeat, exaggerating my lip movements so he can see what I'm saying. "I was smiling at the view!"

"What?" he mouths, stopping now and putting his hands on his hips as he catches his breath.

Oh, no. What have I done?

"Never mind!"

He laughs, looking more confused than ever. Panicking, I duck under the windowsill, and hope he'll be so tired from his run he'll forget what just happened. I'm flooded with more embarrassment when I consider that ducking under the window is quite an odd thing to do, and it would have been better if I'd strolled away nonchalantly.

Worried he might still be outside looking up at the window, I crawl along the floor to the bathroom, closing the door and turning on the shower. What is it about this guy that turns me into such a clown? I've been around good-looking men I fancy before and I've been able to act like a socially capable person.

I'm relieved I didn't sit next to him at dinner last night. As suspected, Georgia made sure she had that privilege.

Tom glanced at me, with "Help!" in his eyes, and I'd hidden my smile as she took her place beside him.

As much as I'd have liked to pay attention to Tom and his strangely attractive arms all evening, my main concern was Cordelia and how she would cope with Annabel. After our conversation outside, I felt instinctively protective of her. I couldn't explain it. Cordelia had been horrible to me. She'd gone out of her way to make me quit my job and leave her alone. I should have been rejoicing that she was getting a taste of her own medicine. But something got to me about the Annabel situation. Maybe it was seeing Cordelia not in control of a situation for once, revealing her vulnerability as this former friend took constant shots at her. The odd thing is that Cordelia lets her do it. It's as though Annabel has some strange power over her.

More than once I noticed Lady Meade watching her daughter with concern, distracted while the Earl of Derrington warbled on about his landscaper redoing the grounds for Annabel's wedding. Cordelia barely spoke during dinner and Jonathan took the reins, asking Annabel questions and showing genuine interest, charming as ever. I managed to remain out of focus for most of the meal, and there was only one moment when Annabel showed interest in Cordelia's and my friendship.

"It's odd," she said, picking at her dauphinoise potatoes. "I've never heard of you before now and here you are, a bridesmaid. How long have you and Cordelia been close?"

"A couple of years," I replied vaguely.

"And this is your first visit to Dashwell?"

"Yes. Do your family spend a lot of time here?"

"We used to," she replied, putting down her fork and swirling the red wine in her glass. "Our estate isn't too far. But we're in the country so rarely—our lives revolve around London."

"Hmm," I replied, sipping my wine.

"It's fascinating that I haven't heard of you," she added, watching me curiously. "I had no idea you existed. You're quite the mystery."

"Not at all." I shrugged. "I don't go out much."

"What do you do?"

"I'm an event planner."

"Oh?" She raised her eyebrows. "Which events have you done that I'd have heard of?"

"None. I'm an in-house event planner."

"Oh, dear." She took a sip of wine, deciding not to comment on my career choice any further. "It's peculiar that I've never seen you before at parties and events in London since you and Cordelia are so close."

"I work most weekends."

"And strange that Cordelia's never talked about you."

"Do you two hang out and chat a lot? I didn't think you did."

Touché, said her look. "We're not really in the same circles, these days. Cordelia's not so—how do I put it?—sociable, I suppose. You must be very patient. It's a shame when people can't connect with others." She glanced at Cordelia sympathetically, lowering her voice so only I could hear. "They hide away in the shadows with their self-destructive habits, terrified to step into the limelight."

I shifted in my seat uncomfortably. "The limelight isn't for everyone."

She looked me up and down. "Clearly."

Georgia interrupted our conversation to ask Annabel to tell the entertaining story about when she'd saved a hedgehog, and I was left more confused than ever. I wondered what on earth had gone down between Cordelia and Annabel, and only realized I'd been staring at Cordelia when she caught my eye. I quickly looked down at my plate and spent the rest of the evening trying to blend into the background and dodge any more personal questions that came my way.

It was a very odd evening.

Once I've showered and dressed, I emerge from my bedroom and try to remember how to get downstairs to the breakfast room. After a couple of wrong turnings, one of which leads me into a broom cupboard, I get to a kitchen and catch Tom still in his running gear, rummaging in the fridge.

"Hi," I say brightly.

"Hey," he replies, a warm smile spreading across his face. "Sorry, I couldn't work out what you were saying through the window."

"It was nothing."

"How did you sleep?"

"Really well, thanks. You?"

"Yeah, I was exhausted after an evening listening to Georgia tell me how wonderful she is." He grins, grabbing some orange juice and closing the fridge door.

He unscrews the lid and drinks from the carton, causing me to wrinkle my nose in disgust. "What?" He lowers the juice.

"You shouldn't drink directly from the carton," I tell him sternly. "I hope you're not planning on putting that back."

"Oh, you're precious about that kind of thing, are you?"

"That's not being precious! It's just not being gross."

"Cordelia always yells at me for doing it, too," he informs me, amused. "Which is why I continue to do it. Nothing better than winding her up."

"So mature."

Something about the way he's looking at me makes my heart beat really fast, thudding in my chest so boldly I can hear it. I look away, pretending to be interested in the kitchen surface.

"Have you had breakfast?"

"I was going to grab some," I say. "Is there any toast or anything?"

"It's all laid out in the dining room. You can help yourself."

"Of course it is," I say, trying not to laugh so he doesn't think I'm being rude. "I forgot I was in Dashwell Hall."

"Fresh orange juice in there, too, so you don't need to worry about drinking from this," he assures me, shaking the carton. "I always have to hunt out the cheap sugary stuff."

"Thank goodness."

"What are you up to today?" he asks suddenly.

"I'm not sure. Whatever Cordelia wants to do."

"She and Jonathan have gone riding together. They'll be a while—they only just set off for the stables." He pauses. "If you like, we could go into the local village. I can show you the sights."

"The sights?"

"Oh, yes," he says, his eyes sparkling with humor. "There's the pub with a landlord who's about a hundred and fifty years old and yells at everyone all the time. Then there's the tea shop with such low beams that you'll definitely bang your head at least once. And if you're really lucky, I'll show you the green where I once played the role of 'piece of straw' in an outdoor theater performance."

"Wow." I nod slowly.

"It was a taxing part actually," he continues. "I wore all yellow and had to lie still on the ground for an entire scene. I received rave reviews."

"Hollywood yet to come calling?"

"Any day now." He chortles. "So, what do you think?"

"Um." I hesitate. "I don't know if Cordelia might need me for wedding ideas . . ."

"She may think she does, but Cordelia doesn't control your every move," he says, a flash of irritation crossing his expression. "She's going to be out all morning. Come on, it'll be fun."

"OK," I say casually. "Thanks."

"Great. I'll be down in a bit."

I stand in a daze when he's gone upstairs, my stomach a knot of nerves and excitement. I know it's nothing more than him being nice to one of his sister's friends and he's probably bored, with nothing to do today, but *still*. I shouldn't get excited and let myself be carried away. This is a job and I'm here to help Cordelia with her wedding, not flirt outrageously with her hot brother. Her hot *playboy* brother. Getting involved with someone like Lord Dashwell would not be a sensible move.

I find Lady Meade in the dining room, having breakfast and reading the newspaper.

"He wants to give you a tour of *Paxton*?" she says in surprise, once I've explained Tom's day-out proposal.

"Only if I'm not needed here."

"No, not at all. I think that's a lovely idea. You should make the most of being here before going back to London this evening, and without Cordelia around, there's not much point in talking through the wedding." She folds the paper neatly, placing it on the table next to her plate. "I've been meaning to thank you for last night. I very much appreciated you looking after Cordelia when she left the party."

"I really did nothing," I insist, buttering a piece of toast. "I was just checking she was OK."

"Trust me," she says, with a weary smile, "that's not nothing."

<hr>

From: Gerry@lovelifeandconfetti.co.uk

To: Sophie.Breeze@zapmail.co.uk

Subject: Re: Doughnut Wall

Hi Sophie,

Thank you for your recent query about our FABULOUS HANDCARVED doughnut walls.

Our sizes are small (6 doughnut hooks), medium (24 doughnut hooks) or large (42 doughnut hooks).

Price quotes are as follows:

Small: £20

Medium: £35

Large: £50

We can also provide personalized doughnut walls, should you want your name or any message of your choosing painted across the top (an extra £3 per letter).

Just to reiterate that, unlike other companies, our doughnut walls are HANDCARVED.

We take great care in producing beautiful bespoke doughnut walls that make any event that bit more special. We hope you will agree.

With very best wishes,

Gerry

From: Sophie.Breeze@zapmail.co.uk

To: Gerry@lovelifeandconfetti.co.uk

Subject: Re: re: Doughnut Wall

Hi Gerry,

Thank you very much for this information.

I will be in touch soon to let you know if we'd like to put in an order.

Best wishes,

Sophie

From: Gerry@lovelifeandconfetti.co.uk

To: Sophie.Breeze@zapmail.co.uk

Subject: Re: re: re: Doughnut Wall

Hi Sophie,

We look forward to hearing from you.

Just to check, have you seen ALL our HANDCARVED product walls? We have the following available:

- Doughnut Walls
- Bagel Walls

Do not hesitate to contact us for any further information on our beautiful product walls.

With very best wishes,

Gerry

From: Sophie.Breeze@zapmail.co.uk

To: Gerry@lovelifeandconfetti.co.uk

Subject: Re: re: re: re: Doughnut Wall

Hi Gerry,

Thanks so much for this information.

Can you explain the difference between your two product walls?

> Best wishes,
> Sophie

From: Gerry@lovelifeandconfetti.co.uk

To: Sophie.Breeze@zapmail.co.uk

Subject: Re: re: re: re: re: Doughnut Wall

Hi Sophie,

Of course.

It's exactly how the names suggest—the doughnut walls have hooks on which to hang doughnuts and the bagel walls have hooks on which to place bagels.

I hope this helps!

> With very best wishes,
> Gerry

CHAPTER TWENTY-ONE

"It's like a scene from a postcard," I say dreamily.

Tom raises his eyebrows as he locks the car and comes to stand next to me, shoving his hands into his wax-coat pockets. "A very boring postcard."

"An idyllic, sleepy-English-village postcard," I correct. "It's stunning. Exactly how somewhere in the middle of nowhere should look."

Paxton is made up of a small, picturesque church at one end of the high street, its graceful spire perfectly framing the village skyline, and an ancient pub called the George at the other, with a row of shop fronts set into wonky houses in between. The shops are everything you'd expect, from the secondhand bookstore with stacks of mismatched books in the window to the quaint tearoom that proudly has a sign on the door announcing that dogs are very welcome inside. There are some charming B and Bs, several cottages with colorful hanging baskets and doors that are much too small, and a little supermarket with boxes of fresh fruit and veg stacked outside between a family-run butcher and the post office.

"It is a pretty village," Tom admits, as we meander down the street. "And it's much nicer to see it on a day like today than in the summer when it's buzzing with tourists. You should see the queues in the tearoom. Tempers fly, punches are thrown. The stories I could tell you."

I laugh. "All right, then, when's this tour I was promised going to start? So far, I have to admit, I'm not that impressed with the level of information provided by the guide."

"What are you on about? I told you that interesting stuff about the cockerel ghost on the way here."

"Yes, it was fascinating to hear all about the local rumors that the spirit of a cockerel roams the hills at night, waking everyone up," I say sarcastically. "It sounds to me like it is, in fact, an actual cockerel, alive and well, and the owner of said cockerel doesn't want to own up to having a bird that keeps the village awake all night."

"Excuse you, but cockerels do not live for twenty years. Ah, here we have the infamous florist," Tom says, leaning toward me to whisper in my ear. His breath on my neck makes me shudder. "Cordelia ever tell you about that summer she worked here?"

I stop outside the shop to admire the buckets of fresh flowers. "I think she may have mentioned it, but I can't remember much."

"As tour guide, I feel it's my duty to fill you in. She was fifteen and a total nightmare, as you can imagine," he informs me, keeping his voice down. "She was such a diva, thinking she was a really big star." He chuckles at the memory. "She was always in trouble, and the cherry on the cake was when one night she got drunk with some friends and didn't come home. Didn't tell Mum or Dad where she was. They got the police involved and found her the next afternoon at some actor's house."

"That's not good." I wince.

"It was definitely not good," he agrees. "Dad was furious. He grounded her for the whole summer. She wasn't allowed to be in London. She was sent back here to Dashwell."

"If only my teenage punishments were to have been sent to stay in a beautiful country mansion all summer."

He gives me an apologetic smile and I feel bad for embarrassing him, so I quickly add, "It must have been lonely for her."

"Part of the deal was that she had to get a job. So she ended up working here," he concludes.

"One of my favorite workers," a voice says, from inside the shop, making both of us jump.

A woman appears in the doorway, bustling through with a bouquet made up of autumn colors that she places carefully on one of the stands, then wipes her hands and comes over to us, wearing a warm smile. At a guess, she's in her late fifties, quite short and with a round, open-book face, framed by frizzy curls, and bright green eyes. Her woolly jumper under the apron is bright purple, a perfect clash with the pink trousers she's wearing.

"Hello, Beth." Tom's expression lights up. "How are you?"

"Not as busy as I'd like, I'm afraid, Thomas," she says, her eyes flickering to me with interest.

"This is Emily, Cordelia's friend. She's her bridesmaid for the wedding."

"How lovely." She beams, putting her hands on her hips. "Is Cordelia with you?"

"She's out on the horse."

"Course she is." She notices something in one of the nearby bouquets on the stand next to us and reaches over to rearrange a couple of the stems. "It's a pity she doesn't get out more. She does love it and she's got a good seat. Very elegant."

"I was telling Emily about the summer Cordelia worked here."

"So I heard. A long time ago now. Makes me feel old. I can't believe she's getting married. In my head, she'll always be a bright-eyed teenager, always talking back or biting her nails. Nice chap, isn't he?"

"Doesn't know what he's getting himself into."

She reaches up and gives Tom a good thwack over the head. "Stop it, you. You're very lucky to have such a caring sister."

"Was she a good employee?" I ask, between giggles at Tom's expense. "I admit that I can't imagine her working here."

"As I said, she was one of my favorites. She was so creative. She had a wonderful imagination, which you need with flowers. She was reluctant at first because she was still in such a strop with her parents for sending her back here while all her friends were partying in London. You can imagine, Paxton isn't much fun for a teenager. But she got into the swing of it and started showing up for work early, leaving late. We had some wonderful chats." ·

"You're painting a very sweet image of my dear sister, Beth," Tom teases, "but you're leaving out some key details."

"Her customer-service skills needed a bit of work," she admits, giving him a knowing smile. "She wasn't particularly patient with our more indecisive clients. And then there was the incident with Matt . . ."

"He went to her school," Tom jumps in when Beth trails off. "He was supposed to be going out with one of Cordelia's friends but came here one day and ordered a bunch of roses for another girl in the year above."

"That sounds stupid of him."

"Cordelia chased him out of the shop and threw a bucket at him."

"She missed, mind you, and it was an empty bucket so no flowers were harmed," Beth adds defensively. "The lad deserved it, if you ask me." She tuts, then sighs, placing a hand on Tom's arm. "I'd better get back to work. Do send Cordelia my love. I know she rarely comes into Paxton but tell her to pop by if she has time. I'm open until three today."

"I will," he promises.

"Nice to meet you, Emily," she says, disappearing into the doorway.

"She's wonderful," I say, falling into step with Tom as we head toward the green.

"She is. And she's been here forever, grew up in Paxton and

took over the family business. If you think she's funny, you should have met her mum. Scathingly witty, but you did not want to get on her bad side."

"I'm not sure I'd want to get on Beth's bad side. How's the head?"

"I think a bump is forming," he says, feeling the top of it. "She's ruthless."

"Obviously very fond of your family."

"Who isn't?" He grins, turning the corner and coming to an abrupt halt. He inhales deeply, pointing across to the green outside the pub. "There it is. That's where I lay. Even now, my performance brings a tear to my eye."

"I feel as though I missed an important event in British theatrical history. Perhaps you could re-create the moment."

"What's that?"

"Let's see if you've still got it in you," I tease, strolling toward the grass. "Unless your acting prowess isn't what it once was. You did say it was a taxing role, lying down and becoming the piece of straw."

"Please." He catches up with me. "Natural talent doesn't fade with time. But it was a summer performance and the grass was dry. The stage is looking a bit muddy."

"You're such a townie."

"Whoa," he says indignantly, grabbing my arm. "I'm a country boy at heart, I'll have you know."

He strides into the middle of the village green and, glancing quickly around, I assume to make sure no one he knows is nearby, he dramatically flops onto the grass, straightening out and closing his eyes.

"I don't know," I say, grinning broadly at him. "I'm getting more of a stick vibe, or maybe a hay stalk, than a piece of straw."

"Duh." He opens one eye. "That's because I'm not in costume."

"I see. Well, in that case, three out of five stars."

"What? Only three stars?" He raises himself up onto his elbows. "Tough crowd."

"I deducted points for the speech. Last time I checked, straw didn't talk. I thought you were a method actor."

"You were talking to *me*," he argues, before gesturing at the grass next to him. "Come on, then, if you're such a professional, you give it a try. Unless you're too much of a city girl to get your clothes a bit muddy."

"Fine. Behold."

Grateful at least to have on a black coat but wishing I'd borrowed one of the old wax jackets hanging in their boot room instead of heading out in my smart one, I lie down next to him, making sure my hair is resting on a good bit of grass with as little mud as possible, then lay my hands by my sides, closing my eyes. After a few seconds of silence, I open my eyes to see him watching me, looking unimpressed.

"Terrible effort," he states, lying down again. "I wasn't persuaded in the least."

I smile and clasp my hands on my stomach, looking up at the blue sky, not one cloud in sight. "It's idyllic here," I say, closing my eyes. "I can't believe the weather. I love days like this, when it's crisp and sunny at the same time. Great holiday weather for nice country walks and cozy pubs."

"Better than *warm* and sunny holiday weather?"

"Yeah, I reckon so. I burn, so I'm not really one for beaches."

"Bet you get freckles too," he says, and I can hear by the way he says it that he's smiling.

"Loads. My face turns into one giant freckle."

"I think freckles are cute."

"When I was little, I really wanted freckles so I drew them on with a pen," I recall, giggling at the memory. "I thought it looked so real but I must have looked ridiculous because I did it with biro. I can't believe Mum and Dad let me go into school with blue spots all over my face. So embarrassing."

"I'll tell you what's embarrassing. When I was about seven, we went on holiday and I met a Welsh boy about my age. He was so cool and we got on really well, and I loved his accent. So I decided I was going to be Welsh. Apparently, I came home talking in the weirdest accent and claiming it was completely natural."

"You thought you could get away with it?"

"For two days. My family still teases me about that—even Cordelia, though I know she was much too young to remember. Doesn't stop her claiming she can."

"But you guys are close, right? Have you always been?"

"We fought a *lot* when we were younger, but we grew out of it. Yeah, we're very close. Especially since . . . Well, we've been through a lot together. I'm way too protective of her." He pauses. "Have you got any siblings?"

"No, only child. Are you two competitive?" I ask, turning my head to look at him, careful to keep the conversation away from me.

"Horribly. You can imagine the fights when Cordelia loses any kind of game. Which most of the time she does," he adds smugly. "Every Christmas we play Monopoly as a family and I always beat her."

"You play Monopoly at Christmas?" I ask, laughing.

"Yeah! Why is that so funny?"

"Because! It is! The idea of you guys in Dashwell Hall sitting down and playing Monopoly—it seems weird that you'd do something so . . . normal."

"What did you think we did at Christmas? Throw lavish masquerade balls just for the four of us? Play polo astride a herd of reindeer?"

I burst out laughing. "I wouldn't put it past you. Christmas in your house must be incredible. Now that I think about it, a winter wedding may be even more special there than a summer one. How long does it take to decorate?"

"A *long* time. Professionals do the parts of the house that the tourists see, so those bits are always amazing. I'm in charge of upstairs in the private bit. You should see me work that tinsel. I'm a master."

"I have no doubt."

"Cordelia directs the tree-decorating and it's always a very stressful affair." He turns to meet my eye with a grin. "But as I'm sure you're aware, Cordelia has a talent of taking anything and making it stressful. Even the fun stuff."

"As long as she's not too stressed about the wedding, then I'm happy."

"She's lucky to have you," he says.

And he gives me that look, the one that makes my fingers tingle and my head feel dizzy and my heart slam against my chest. Bloody hell, his eyes are nice. They're so dark and kind, framed by long eyelashes. I'm mesmerized by him.

Wait. Sophie, don't be an idiot. This is Lord Dashwell. And he's your client's brother.

Stay focused.

I jump as his finger brushes against mine on the grass. An accident, I'm sure.

But then he moves his arm purposefully, his warm hand settling over my cold fingers. His gleaming eyes are locked on mine.

He's going to kiss me. Any moment now, he's going to kiss me. And I'm going to kiss him back.

"I can't," I blurt out, sitting up suddenly. "I can't do this."

"What?" He leans on his elbows, looking baffled. "Do what?"

"I'm seeing someone."

"Oh. OK," he says, and I think there's a hint of disappointment in his voice, but I'm not sure if I'm making that up because I want there to be. "Who?"

I glance around for inspiration, my eyes coming to rest on the pub sign.

"George. A guy named George. He's very nice." I check my phone, heat rising to my cheeks. "We should get back to Dashwell."

"Yeah. Course." He gets up, brushing grass off his trousers.

On the way back, I ask him boring, simple questions about the countryside we're driving through, the history of the house, anything that distracts from the moment we just shared. Then I give up and stare out of the window in silence, watching the fields and trees blur past.

Part of me hates that I made up a stupid lie. But the sensible part of me tells me I did the right thing. What does it matter if the truth is that I'm single? That's Sophie and I'm not supposed to be Sophie.

Tom doesn't know Sophie. He *can't* know Sophie. He knows Emily. And that makes me feel utterly miserable.

Because Emily is a lie.

CHAPTER TWENTY-TWO

"Thanks so much for inviting me this weekend," I say to Cordelia, as we make our way down the twisting country lane toward the station. "It's been so wonderful to see Dashwell Hall and visualize the wedding."

She shrugs, not saying anything and keeping her eyes on the road. I take this as another step forward in our relationship. Before the weekend, she might have pointed out that technically she didn't invite me, her parents did, or she could have commented that I'd made the weekend a disaster for her, she never wanted to see me again, and why wouldn't I just quit? But she didn't.

I'll happily take an indifferent shrug.

"It's going to be spectacular," I continue, deciding to fill the silence. "And your mother mentioned that the invitations are going out this week. How exciting!"

"Yes," she says.

Even better. My heart is filled with hope. That one-word answers without a hint of malice can have such an effect on me proves how bad things were with her beforehand.

"And you're going to have your dress appointments this week. You probably just want to go with your mum, but I'm here if you want me to join in at all. You can let me know on the day."

"OK."

Oh, my God. Does this mean we're FRIENDS?

"And I penciled in a meeting with Clio Vaughn on Friday, if

you're around? But I can change it. You don't have to come. You know, only if you want to."

"Fine. I'll let you know."

Bloody hell, this is exciting. I can't believe how much difference one weekend can make. She's starting to accept me and that's all I'd hoped for.

She glances at me. "Why are you making that face?" she asks suspiciously.

"What face?"

"That one. The one you're making right now."

"I'm making a face?"

"Yes."

"I don't mean to."

"Well, you are. It's creeping me out."

"That's just my face."

"No, it's not normally like that."

"Like what?"

"Like an excitable puppet."

"What?"

"A puppet that can't move its face but is super excited. Like this." She demonstrates, widening her eyes and stretching her lips into a tight, thin smile.

I burst out laughing. "I was not making that face."

"Yes, you were," she insists. "It was just like that."

"Why would I make that face?"

"You tell me."

"I don't know!" I shrug. "We were having a nice chat, that's all."

She raises her eyebrows. "Were we?"

"Yes. We were," I state firmly.

She doesn't argue. She continues to focus on the road, looking vaguely amused. Amused. Not pissed off. Not hateful. *Amused.* How wonderful.

"You're doing the face again."

"I'm not!" I laugh, but I know I am.

I was mostly dreading the drive to the station. Lady Meade insisted in front of everyone that Cordelia give me a lift so she couldn't exactly say no when she had nothing else to do and we were supposed to be giving the impression of being the best of friends. As much as I appreciated Lady Meade attempting to give us more bonding time, I was worried that it wouldn't be a pleasant journey, but so far, so good.

Even after what had happened on the green, Tom offered me a lift back to London but I insisted I should take the train because, I explained, I already had my ticket and lots of work to do. The real reason was that I didn't trust myself around him and I really didn't like lying to him. Avoiding him as much as possible is the only answer.

Today was . . . well . . . great. He was funny and charming and kind. It was so easy to talk to him. He got my sense of humor. He was laid-back and interesting. There was a serious danger of me actually liking him. As in, *like* like. I've been desperately repeating to myself over and over and over that I *cannot* fall for this guy. It's inappropriate on so many levels. First, it would be incredibly unprofessional. Second, he doesn't even know my real name. And third, he's the future Marquess of Meade.

He's practically part of the royal family. The closest I've come to royalty is when I met a Labrador whose grandmother had been bred in the Sandringham kennels.

The whole idea is absurd. He could be with anyone he wanted. He wouldn't in a million years be interested in me if he discovered I wasn't one of Cordelia's posh friends, that I was a nobody who was paid to be there. He'd think I was pathetic.

And, anyway, he makes girls fall head over heels in love

with him all the time. I've seen the evidence. All those stories
and photos in the press of him over the years with a different
woman on his arm at every event he's ever shown up to. Who
wouldn't want to date him? He's handsome, rich, and part of
the British aristocracy. Essentially, he's a modern Mr. Darcy.
Without the grumpy, brooding persona. So, even if he did like
me a little, which he didn't, surely it would be for just a few
minutes until a better option came along. What about that
American pop star he was all over in the club the other night
or whatever?

He is not for me. He is my client's brother. That's it.

Suddenly Cordelia's voice jolts me from my thoughts. "You
look confused."

"Huh?" I shake my head as we turn onto the narrow, bumpy
lane down to the station. "Oh, I was thinking about . . . something. I was thinking about the invitations."

"What about them?"

"Just hoping they go out on time and reach everyone," I say,
making it up as I go along.

"I hope they don't reach *everyone*," she says pointedly.

"What do you mean?" I ask carefully.

I already know she means Annabel. She had another argument with her parents today about inviting the Porthouse
family—I overheard them talking about it in her father's study
earlier this afternoon. She pointed out Annabel's behavior at dinner, claiming that if she was a member of any other family, she'd
have every right not to invite someone so malicious about her
and her wedding.

But her parents held their ground, gently but firmly reminding her of the consequences should Annabel not be invited. Not
only would it be a great scandal, but it would also cause problems
with the Earl and Countess of Derrington, who would find it

greatly offensive. Cordelia needn't talk to her on the day, her mother insisted. There would be so many people, she could easily be avoided.

I didn't listen to any more as I didn't want to be accused of snooping but, judging by Cordelia's furious expression when she joined us outside afterward, I assumed she'd lost the argument.

"Nothing," she says, as we approach the station. "Forget I said anything."

But I can't. If she's brought it up like that, maybe she wants to talk about it with someone. Maybe she *needs* to talk about it.

"Do you mean Annabel?" I ask. "What happened between you two?"

"Nothing."

"I know you used to be friends and then she mentioned an incident. And when we broke into the wedding-dress studio, you said something about her betraying you and—"

"I don't want to talk about it," she snaps, her expression darkening.

"Did she say something to the press or—"

"I said it was nothing."

"I'm only wondering what exactly she did to—"

"God, what is *wrong* with you?" she yells, her voice so full of venom it makes me recoil in my seat. "Don't you ever just mind your own fucking business? I said I didn't want to talk about it!"

"OK, I was—"

"Why do you need to know every detail? Are you hoping for a juicy, scandalous story at my expense?"

"No! I know it must sometimes be hard for you to—"

"You don't know a *thing* about me."

I slam forward against my seat belt as we come to a sudden stop in front of the station. Her hands remain on the wheel, her expression thunderous, her eyes ahead, refusing to look at me.

"Cordelia, I'm sorry if you thought I was prying—"

"You can leave now."

She's so angry, there's no point in trying to reason with her. I climb out, heading round to the boot to get my bag. I've purposefully left the car door open so that I can come back and say goodbye, hoping she'll have calmed down.

"Thanks so much again for the weekend," I say, bending down to peer in at her. "I—"

"Shut the door. I have to get back."

"Cordelia—"

"I said," she begins, her voice low and quiet, much more menacing than if she was shouting, "shut the fucking door."

I step back and do as instructed. She puts her foot down, does a sharp U-turn, mud spitting out from under the spinning tires, and accelerates much too fast down the narrow lane.

Oh, well. I watch the car disappear, my heart sinking. *That was nice while it lasted.*

⌁

Over the next couple of days I feel as though I'm constantly waiting for a message from Lady Meade or Cordelia inviting me to the dress appointments, but nothing comes through. I send a WhatsApp to Cordelia reminding her of the meeting with Clio Vaughn later in the week, but she reads it and doesn't reply. I guess I'll go without her.

On reflection, I was too pushy about the whole Annabel thing. I wanted to know what had happened so I'd understand Cordelia a bit better. I thought it might bring us closer. But we don't need to be closer. We don't *need* to be friends. In the end, I was pushing her to tell me something personal that she was uncomfortable talking about.

This one is definitely on me.

When she didn't reply about the Clio meeting, I sent a follow-up message apologizing for what happened in the car. She didn't reply to that one either.

On Wednesday evening, I suddenly get a message from her out of the blue.

> Can you be at St. James's Park
> for 2 p.m. tomorrow? Meet at Duck Island

> Yes, of course. I'll be there

> Good. Do you have a colorful scarf?

> I have a red one

> Please wear that

I start typing back, asking her why I'd need to wear a red scarf, then delete my message and leave it. She won't tell me. She didn't last time. And part of me doesn't want to know. As long as we're not going to break in anywhere again, which seems unlikely, I'll do as she says.

The next day, I get to Duck Island a few minutes early, so that I'm standing right in front of it when the clock strikes two. While I wait, I imagine I'm being extremely naïve. Even knowing Cordelia as little as I do, I feel certain she's out to get revenge on me. Maybe there's a sniper lurking in the trees of St. James's Park who's been told the target will be standing in a red scarf exactly where I am now.

I shiver. It could happen.

I can't make Cordelia out at all. I've been thinking about it ever since I got back to London. Beth, the florist, really threw a spanner in the works when she described Cordelia as a hardworking, enthusiastic employee, who was loyal to her friends and threw buckets at anyone who dared disrespect them. I can barely imagine Cordelia having any friends, let alone sticking up for them.

"Emily?"

A man has approached me while I was lost in thought, puzzling over the enigma of Cordelia. He looks like he's in his late thirties, with a whiskery graying beard and heavy sideburns, and is wearing a duffel coat and a bobble hat, with a large canvas bag slung over his shoulder. "Are you Emily?" he says again, looking at me expectantly. "Cordelia's friend?"

"Yes! Yes, that's me," I say, confused, taking his outstretched hand and shaking it so as not to be rude.

Oh, my God. Has she set me up on a *date*?

"She said you'd be here with the red scarf," he explains, clearly delighted that he's found me. "I'm Jimmy, the Swan Whisperer."

The what?

"When you're ready, we'll get started," he says, rubbing his hands together. "Bit chilly today, isn't it?"

"I'm sorry, who did you say you were?"

"Jimmy, the Swan Whisperer," he repeats, frowning slightly. "I'm here to teach you to connect and communicate with swans. Cordelia said you were looking for some."

"She did," I say slowly, letting this horrifying situation sink in.

"I'm going to help you to reach out to the mute swans of St. James's Park," he explains, gesturing to the water. "They're quite stubborn, the ones here. Snobby and posh, I like to think." He chuckles. "The swans elsewhere in the country are much easier. But let's see how we get on today and whether you pick it up. I believe you don't have long to learn the ropes."

He throws down his bag and crouches to unzip it.

"Is Cordelia joining us?" I ask.

"Nope, just you and me," he says cheerily, digging around in the bag. "It's better that way, to be honest. I don't like having too many people around while I'm working. The swans don't take to crowds."

I can't *believe* this. She's set me up. Of course she has! What better punishment than complete and utter humiliation? And the worst thing is, she's not even bothered to come along to watch it.

"Look," I begin, "I don't think I have time for—"

"Here you go," he says, straightening and holding out what looks like a pair of dungarees made of Wellington-boot rubber. "Pop these on."

"Excuse me?"

"Well, you can't go into the water like that," he says, wiggling a finger at me. "Waders are a necessity."

"What do you mean, go into the water?" I say, horrified. "I'm not going into the water!"

"Sure you are!" he replies, with an amused expression. "You can't communicate with swans on the land. You need to submerge yourself in their domain. Be on a level playing field."

"We can't be allowed to walk into St. James's Park's lake!" I point out, gesturing around us. "We'll get into trouble."

"I do it all the time." He shrugs. "Nobody minds. Everyone thinks you work here or with the birds, which technically is what I'm doing. We're working with the birds."

"Can't we get some birdseed and bring them to us?"

"Oh, no," he grumbles, tutting. "That's not how you communicate with the mute swan. We're talking about a gracious, superior bird. This isn't your average mallard. Feeding them isn't going to get you anywhere. What would you do on the wedding day? Scatter food down the aisle? It would be carnage! You need to help them to accept you as one of their own. That way, they'll listen when you call."

I stare at him.

"The waders will keep you dry," he insists, holding them out again. "It's not that big a deal. You go in a little way, and then I'll teach you the call. If they come to you, it will be a wonderful start. If not, we may have our work cut out for us."

I cross my arms stubbornly. "There is no chance I'm getting in that water to call to swans. This is so stupid!"

"Ah." He lowers his arms, a smug smile that I do *not* appreciate spreading across his face. "Cordelia said this would happen. Oh, well! I tried."

"She said what would happen? That I wouldn't be stupid enough to wade into a lake in the middle of London to talk to a bird? Then she's right!"

"No, it was more something along the lines of . . . you were too much of a goody-goody, just like Graham always said."

I recoil. "She said *what*?"

"Something about Graham Slater?"

"She told you about *Graham Slater*?" I can barely get the words out, I'm so angry.

"Yeah, and how you don't take risks because you're a scaredy-cat, her words not mine," he says, waving his hand and bending down to start stuffing the waders back into the bag. "She said Graham must have been right but that you're not to feel bad about it. Her mum agreed."

"Wait. Her *mum* spoke to you? Lady Meade?"

"Yeah." He puffs out his cheeks. "She's scary, you know."

"What did she say?"

"Who?"

"Lady Meade!"

"Not much, really," he says, frowning in concentration. "She said swans were a nice touch, considering the family surname. But she didn't think you had it in you. Don't feel bad, though! She said you'd done well so far, considering. And . . ." He trails off, putting a hand over his mouth. "Never mind."

"No, what were you about to say?"

"It's nothing."

"Jimmy," I say, in my sternest voice. "What were you about to say?"

He bites his lip, looking worried. "I don't want your feelings getting hurt, but there was some talk about whether Cordelia needed a bridesmaid."

"Lady Meade said that? Or Cordelia?"

"Uh, Lady Meade. But, hey, that could be a good thing! Much more fun to enjoy the big day rather than have to trail around after the bride, right? Not that I've been to too many weddings recently, but I reckon that if there's an open bar, you'd much rather be—"

"Give me the waders, Jimmy."

He blinks. "Huh?"

"I said, give me the waders." I take off my coat and throw it onto the ground with my bag. "I'm ready to go into the water."

He pulls the waders out of the bag again and hands them over to me excitedly. "Great! I had a feeling they were wrong about you, Emily. I once knew a swan named Emily and she was as elegant as anything but could be very feisty if she got worked up. You pop those on and I'll tighten the straps for you once you're in."

I yank the waders up, rage bubbling inside me. I cannot *believe* that Cordelia has managed to get into her mother's head. That's what she's been doing all week, turning her family against me. My stomach tightens as I wonder what she might have said about me to Tom, let alone to her parents. She's managed to get Lady Meade to doubt me! After I told them about scoring a meeting with Clio Vaughn! After all the support I gave to Cordelia over the weekend! After *breaking the law* for her (not that they know that).

I hate her.

"There you go," Jimmy says, tightening the thick straps on my shoulders. "You're ready. Start heading in and I'll instruct you. Don't worry, the waders are made for this."

Having never been fishing, I'm in a pair of waders for the first time ever, and I have to say, I'm not impressed. It's like wearing a giant boot.

He points at the water. I look around to make sure there aren't many people to witness this act of craziness. Then, taking a deep breath and steeling myself, as though I do this kind of thing all the time, I walk into the water. I can feel the cold hitting the waders, but I trust them to do their job. I head in deeper and deeper until the water is at my thighs.

"Should I stop here?"

"In a bit more," Jimmy directs. "Up to your waist at least. Don't be shy! You've got your waders on, remember?"

"This is fine, this is fine, this is fine," I repeat to myself under my breath, wincing as I take more steps forward in the murky water and the cold creeps up my body. "I can do this. It's not so bad. I'm in a lake and that's fine."

"Very good!" he calls.

Slowly, I turn to face him, not wanting to splash the water too much. "There are no eels or anything gross in here, right?"

"You'll be fine! The only thing you might see is fish. Although we don't want to disturb the pelicans. I once had a run-in with one and they're not easy little blighters, let me tell you. Very large beaks. Could fit your whole head in there!"

"WHAT? Oh, my God!" I look about me, wide-eyed in panic. "You're joking, right?"

"Don't worry! I checked and they're on the other side of the lake. You're doing brilliantly. Lady Meade is going to be so impressed! Right, all you need to do now is turn so that your back is to me and call out across the lake."

"What do I call?" I ask, turning in the water.

"Repeat after me." There's a pause, and then I hear a loud "KAWWWWWWW!"

He can't be serious. *Kaw?*

"Did you hear that?" he calls.

"Um. Yes. That's really how you speak to swans?"

"Tried and tested! You get their attention, and once they're in the vicinity, the call to communicate with them is much more sophisticated. But this is how you get them to come to you. Listen carefully." There's another pause. "KAWWWWWWWWW! Now, you try!"

I can't believe I'm doing this.

This isn't happening.

This can't be happening.

Oh, God, I might as well. I'm in the bloody water, aren't I?

"KAWWWWWWWWWW!" I call, at the top of my lungs.

"Perfect! And again!"

"KAWWWWWWWWWWW!" I yell, bizarrely finding the experience a little bit enjoyable. I start laughing. I can't believe I'm doing this. It's completely ridiculous! And, surprisingly, fun. "KAWWWWWWWWWWWW!"

"I think I can see ripples in the water in the distance! I think they might be coming! You're a natural!"

"KAWWWWWWWWWWW! KAWWWWWWWWW! KAWW—" I stop. My leg feels much colder than it did. Like really cold. And wet. Oh, no.

"The waders are leaking!" I yell.

I jump around in the water so fast that I splash myself in the face, but I'm too distracted to care because I've caught Jimmy off guard by spinning round to face him. He's holding up his phone, the camera pointing at me. He guiltily drops his arm, holding the phone behind his back. "Are you . . . are you filming me?"

"No," he says, his cheeks flushing furiously. "I—I—"

"Jimmy!" I yell, wading through the water toward him.
"WERE YOU FILMING ALL THIS?"

"No! I just—uh—" He's looking around him, not sure what
to do.

"TELL ME THE TRUTH!"

"I'm sorry! She asked me to!"

And with that, he turns on his heel and runs away from the
lake, disappearing from view.

"JIMMY!"

I finally make it to the edge and clamber out of the lake,
undoing the waders and letting them drop to the ground. My
clothes are *soaked*. There must have been a hole in the waders.

"ARGH!" I scream, kicking them away from me and looking
down in despair at my jeans. It looks like I've peed myself. I throw
my hands into the air and look around for Jimmy, then hurry to
get my coat on, already shivering. "What the *hell*?"

In his hurry to get away, he's left his bag. Hoping there's
a towel in it, I pick it up to look through it. I find nothing but an
old Lucozade bottle, some indigestion tablets, and flyers for an
amateur production of Oscar Wilde's *The Importance of Being
Earnest*.

I examine the flyer closely.

Jimmy is on the flyer. He's standing with another bloke and
two women, all wearing costume. The play is opening this weekend at a pub theater in Battersea.

"He's an actor," I say aloud, closing my eyes as the cold seeps
into my skin. "He's not a swan whisperer. He's a fucking actor."

Cordelia 1—Sophie 0.

⌐━━━━━

From: customerservice@costumeheaven.co.uk

To: Sophie.Breeze@zapmail.co.uk

Subject: Thank you for your order!

Dear Miss Breeze,

Thank you for your recent order! We will let you know once your item(s) have been dispatched. You can view the status of your order by clicking here.

ORDER DETAILS

Order #5762-838

1 x STAR WARS CHEWBACCA DELUXE WOMEN'S FANCY DRESS COSTUME

Thank you for shopping at Costume Heaven, here for all your costume needs.

Have a great day!

Many thanks

Customer Service Team

CHAPTER TWENTY-THREE

I quit." I slouch further back into my sofa, pulling my dressing gown as tightly over me as possible and clutching a fluffy pink hot-water bottle to my chest.

"Now, darling, let's not be hasty," Mum says, on FaceTime, busily looking through some files as she talks to me at her desk.

My phone is propped up on my coffee table by a pile of wedding magazines. Resting the hot-water bottle on my stomach, I wrap my hands round a mug of hot chocolate, wondering if I'll ever feel warm again.

"I'm not being hasty. I've thought about it and I'm done. She wins. I quit."

"I know whoever this bride is, she's a little tricky—"

"Ha! A little tricky?" I cut in, snorting. "Mum, because of her, I was forced into St. James's Park's lake in a pair of leaking waders and shouted, 'Kaw kaw kaw,' like some kind of *moron!*"

Mum tries desperately not to laugh. I narrow my eyes at the screen. "It is *not* funny."

"No, course not, darling, and I've told your father that several times."

"Brilliant."

"Oh, Sophie, it must have been awful. I really am sorry."

"It *was* awful." I sniff, taking a sip of hot chocolate and feeling very sorry for myself. "But it was also eye-opening. I'm done taking orders from her. I'm done doing whatever she says, blindly following her . . ." I hesitate, my sentence trailing off. "She was right all along. I'm a sheep. A pathetic sheep."

"You're not a sheep, darling. You were doing your job! Everyone who works has to follow orders from someone."

"First thing in the morning, I'm going to call her mother and officially hand in my notice."

"But I thought you said this wedding was important to you."

"It was! It was very important to me." I sigh, thinking of Dashwell Hall and how magical the wedding would have been. "But I can't take a moment more. I'm done."

"Mmm."

"She can sod off. She paid an actor to pretend to be a swan whisperer. Who does that?"

"It's very cruel."

"Why did I fall for it? What is *wrong* with me? I should have known! Swans are dangerous birds! Being a swan whisperer is not a thing. You know he filmed it? I've checked online but it's not there, thank goodness. But I know he would have sent that video to her so she could have a good laugh at my expense. That would have been part of her deal when she hired him. Make sure he gets the full thing on camera so she could watch my humiliation. This is the person I'm working for." I shake my head, my heart beating fast with rage. "I've never met anyone so horrible."

Except, I think, *Annabel*. In fact, it's a wonder they're not friends. They really are as bad as each other. I have no sympathy for Cordelia anymore and the way that Annabel was speaking to her. She deserved it.

"Anyway," I continue, "she's finally got her way. I quit."

"Do *you* want that, though?" Mum asks calmly.

"Yes. I never want to see her again."

"But do you really want her to win?" Mum turns away from the camera to accept a cup of tea from Dad.

"Hello, Sophie!" Dad says cheerily, appearing on the screen. "I hear you've had a bad day."

"The worst."

"I'm sorry to hear that. It's all very unusual."

"Yes. It was."

"I wondered whether you'd mind if I use it for the book?"

Mum groans.

"I've been wanting to add a little comic relief into a recent scene," he explains, "and I thought it might perk things up to have one of the junior detectives find himself in waders in the middle of St. James's Park. Would that be all right?"

"I'm not sure now's the time to ask," Mum says, through gritted teeth.

"You can use it, Dad. You might as well. The whole world will be laughing at me once the video is up on YouTube, so the incident might as well be used for something good."

"Thank you! You're excellent inspiration, Sophie!"

"All right, off you go," Mum says, shooing him away. "Sorry about that, darling. Now, where were we? Ah, yes. I was asking you if you really wanted to let her win."

"Yes, Mum. I do," I say firmly. "If it means getting out of this toxic job, then I'm very happy to let her win."

"Has it been that bad? Last time we spoke, you were very enthusiastic about some of the ideas you'd had."

"Anything good about this wedding has been squashed by what happened today. And all the horrible things she's done before."

"All right, well, if it's making you unhappy then you must, of course, get out. You can't let someone like that make you miserable."

"Thank you."

"But there is another option you may want to consider."

"If you say anything about killing her with kindness, or however that phrase goes, I'm going to hang up."

"No, not with kindness." She smiles, knocking the phone as she moves something on the desk. "With brilliance."

I throw back my head. "Why do I get the feeling that that's going to be much the same?"

"I don't know what it is with this bride, Sophie, but you seem desperate to get her to like you. You've never been like this with anyone else."

"That's because everyone else does like me!" I wail.

"Not everyone in life will like you, darling. That's just how it is. My goodness, the number of people who don't like me . . ."

"There are hundreds!" Dad's voice calls, from another room.

"Thank you for that," she calls back sternly, then softens her voice to talk to me again. "My point is, let that go. She doesn't like you. So what?"

"She thinks I don't take risks."

"You're very sensible, darling. You always have been."

"Yes, but she thinks it's a *bad* thing," I stress. "And—and maybe it is. Maybe they're right."

Mum frowns. "What do you mean? Who's 'they'?"

I exhale. I could explain that Daniel said something very similar and that's why it's bugging me, but I know she'd go off on one if Daniel came into the conversation.

"She's mean," I say instead. "I can't work with her."

"She's not asking you to."

I frown at the phone. "I'm confused. What are you saying?"

"I'm saying that an excellent form of revenge is success. You could quit tomorrow. Or you could get out there, take pride in your amazing work, and tick all those jobs off her list. Didn't you say you got the photographer she wanted?"

"Yeah, I did."

"And how did she react to that?"

I think back on when I told her about Clio Vaughn at Dashwell. "She was speechless."

"There you are!" Mum says, so enthusiastically that her tea slops over the side of her mug. "She had nothing to say because you did what she didn't expect. *You* won, not her."

"It's a good idea, Mum, but you should hear some of the stuff on her list. I mean, think of the swans . . ."

"That's nonsense." Mum dismisses it with a wave of her hand. "And you should have told her so from the start. You were trying to please her by agreeing to things that were stupid, and she was asking you to do stupid things to make you quit. You've got to know her a little, haven't you? Do you really think she wants swans at her wedding?"

"No."

"What would she want?"

I shrug. "I don't know."

"Well, think about it. You would for your other brides. You've been trying so hard to get her to like you that you've been forgetting about the job. Remember what I told you about doctors?" She clicks her fingers. "What happened with that bride last year, the one who wanted the lanterns?"

"Eleanor? Oh, that was nothing and it was all sorted in the end."

"Tell me again?"

"She wanted guests to have those lanterns you let off into the sky when they left the venue, but she was also a big animal lover so I told her they pose a lot of danger to wildlife. I suggested she stick to sparklers instead."

"And was she happy about it?"

"Yeah, course. She had no idea about those lanterns and was pleased I'd warned her. And in the end the sparklers photo was so good, they used it on the front of their thank-you cards."

"There you have it," Mum says excitedly, as though it's all become clear even though I'm still very confused. "You carefully and respectfully told her what she shouldn't do and pointed her in the right direction. When this new bride of yours said she wanted swans, why didn't you do the same?"

"Because there was no arguing with her."

"There is always arguing with everyone," Mum retorts. "You simply need to work out how. You're much stronger than you think, Sophie."

"I don't know," I say, running a hand through my hair. "This seems like a lost cause."

"We support whatever you want to do, of course, darling. But I've never known you to quit before, and I'm not sure the person you're working for deserves to get her way. Her mum hired you for a reason. From the sound of it, they could afford a wedding planner or an assistant for her daughter. But she didn't hire anyone else. She hired *you*."

At first, I think Mum is just being Mum. In her eyes, I can do anything if I put my mind to it, and since she's a solution-finder herself, quitting is never really an option in her world.

But what she's saying makes sense. It would be easier to quit tomorrow and go back to my normal life, working for grateful, wonderful brides and grooms who are desperate for my expertise and don't go out of their way to humiliate and insult me.

It did feel good, though, when I told the Swann family that I had managed to pin down a world-famous photographer for the wedding. Cordelia looked blown away by the news, and excited by it. I felt like I really achieved something she didn't think I could do. And maybe Mum was right about me letting Cordelia get away with things because I wanted to be on her good side.

Would I feel happy about quitting? Would I feel good about myself?

That night, I lie in bed wide awake, unable to think about anything else, ideas beginning to bubble in my brain. If I push the horrible persona of Cordelia aside for a moment and think about her simply as a bride, there are some pretty amazing things I could do to add some personality to her wedding. I turn my bedroom light on and reach for a pen and paper.

The next day, Mum phones at about 10:00 A.M. I've been up since four thirty.

"Have you called the bride and her mother?"

"I haven't. No need."

"Oh?"

"I'm not quitting after all. And sorry, Mum, but I have to go. I'm in the middle of ticking off one of the jobs from her list."

"That's my girl," she says, and I can hear her smiling down the phone.

We meet at the Ritz.

I considered Lady Meade's offer to come to their Grosvenor Crescent house, but I politely suggested that a more central location would be better for me. I haven't seen her or Cordelia for a few weeks and I've been gearing up for this meeting for a while. I've never felt more nervous and powerful at the same time. This could be a *complete* disaster. But at least I can say I've tried.

They're already at the table when I arrive, ordering some drinks. They're sitting in the main gallery of the hotel, on a cluster of sofas just outside the Rivoli Bar. The hotel is in full countdown-to-Christmas mode, with elegant red and gold decorations hanging among the glittering chandeliers and in the spectacular Palm Court bustling with afternoon-tea tourists, taking selfies with their finger sandwiches and melt-in-the-mouth scones.

I remind myself of what I'm here to do—I'm a professional, not a friend—and walk toward them confidently, extending my hand as I approach them.

"Good afternoon, Lady Meade," I say, as she stands up to

greet me, looking surprised at the handshake. "Good afternoon, Lady Cordelia."

I've purposely used her formal title. There's no need to pretend we're friends with no guests or family members present.

"Good afternoon, Emily," Lady Meade says, taken aback. "How have you been?"

"Very well, thank you," I reply, sitting down opposite them.

Cordelia is watching me curiously. We haven't spoken since the swan incident. I assume she knows I realized it was all a setup. Jimmy must have told her what happened. But I decided it would be best to pretend it never took place, rather than send her a text full of expletives, cursing her until the end of time, like I wanted. I haven't messaged, asking her about the wedding and how it's getting on, and she hasn't messaged me to tell me anything willingly. I've had some updates from Lady Meade, so I've been able to keep on top of things, but there's been no other reason to be in touch.

I place my folder on the table and smooth my skirt, noticing Cordelia look me up and down as she examines my outfit. I've come dressed for a business meeting today, in a cream blouse and a black pencil skirt with heels. Cordelia is more casual, in a red roll-neck woolen jumper that's tucked into black trousers, and her black Chelsea boots. Her hair is tied in a messy ponytail and she's wearing minimal makeup.

I, on the other hand, went for full-on eyeliner today as though I was applying war paint.

"Would you like a glass of champagne?" Lady Meade offers, as the waiter reappears with a bottle and three glasses.

"No, thank you, not while I'm at work." I smile at the waiter. "Please may I have a glass of sparkling water?"

"Of course," he says, pouring champagne for the others.

I wait until he's placed the bottle in the ice bucket and left before launching straight into the conversation.

"Thank you for making the time to see me today. I won't keep you long. I'm aware we all have places to be." I open the folder on the table and start organizing the documents inside. "If you're happy, I'll go ahead and tell you everything I've done in the last week or so. You can let me know your thoughts, then tell me anything else that needs doing and I'll get onto it."

Lady Meade and Cordelia share a look.

"All right." Lady Meade nods. "Please do fill us in."

I start with Clio Vaughn. Our meeting had gone brilliantly, despite (or perhaps because of) Cordelia not being present. It turns out that renowned photographers aren't necessarily terrifying in person, as I'd been expecting. Clio was shy, smiley, and extremely modest. She explained that she was interested in being involved in Cordelia's wedding because, although she wasn't a typical event photographer, her main focus was people and this wedding was, no doubt, going to include some rather high-profile faces. She was fascinating to talk to and we ended up getting on very well.

"I told her the new date for the wedding and she says she'll move things. She is a confirmed yes, if you would like her to be your official photographer," I say to Cordelia, looking her directly in the eye. "Can you confirm yes or no now? I should be getting back to her at the latest this evening and she'd like to meet you soon if it's a yes."

Cordelia receives a sharp nod from her mother, then speaks: "Yes. I would like Clio."

"Great. I'll book in a meeting for you to chat immediately. You can send me your schedule for next week and I'll get that sorted. With regard to the nine other photographers you wanted—"

"Nine?" Lady Meade is stunned, turning to Cordelia. "You asked for *nine* more photographers?"

"It's a large wedding." Cordelia shrugs, refusing to be embarrassed by her outlandish request.

"Clio can provide three assistants. I've made a list for you of all other photographers I know or who have been recommended," I say, sliding the list across the table for her to pick up and examine. "Everyone on that list is available on the wedding day. I was sure to check. Although they're all brilliant wedding photographers in their own right, I'm sure they wouldn't mind taking instruction from Clio on the day if necessary, but we should run it past them first to be sure."

"This is wonderful, Emily, thank you, but I can't see us needing nine," Lady Meade says, frowning as she takes the piece of paper. "We can discuss this with your father, Cordelia, and then contact however many we need."

"On to the next point," I say, keeping things moving as planned. The less opportunity I give Cordelia to take control, the better. "You asked for peacocks to adorn the ceiling of the banquet hall while your guests dined."

"I beg your pardon?" Lady Meade says, but I don't let her distract me. I'm on a mission.

"I would strongly recommend that you didn't try to create something that might be cruel to animals," I explain calmly. "When I was lucky enough to visit Dashwell Hall, I noted that the ceiling of the banquet hall is richly painted with biblical scenes and, having done some further research, I've learned the paintings are from the seventeenth century. It is absolutely not my decision, but I wouldn't be doing my job if I didn't suggest you leave the ceiling as it is for guests to enjoy a magnificent piece of history."

"Cordelia, honestly, what is all this about peacocks?" Lady Meade asks her daughter wearily.

"However, if you are still keen on the peacock idea," I continue, when Cordelia purses her lips, unwilling to answer, "I've found a couple of extraordinary luxury-event companies who have assured me they will be able to create a ceiling of peacock feathers. They've sent over ideas on how they'd do it."

I pass the designs across the table.

"I'm impressed with how creative they've been, actually. So, have a look at those and tell me if you'd like me to follow up with any of them. And speaking of decorating the hall, the four thousand candles you wanted aren't a problem. I've included a list of companies I've contacted that can supply that many candles in time—" I hand Lady Meade the list. "—and I've also noted down the color of the candles next to the company details, as you'll see there. I wasn't sure if you wanted a certain color, like red as it's Christmas, or whether you wanted a white theme. The only worry I'd have, personally, is that so many candles may be a major fire hazard in Dashwell. Do correct me if I'm wrong."

"This is outrageous," Lady Meade says sternly, as Cordelia takes a sip of champagne. "We can't have that many candles, Cordelia! Do you want the house to burn down?"

"You can let me know how you want to move forward on that," I say, shuffling some papers around, preparing for the next point on my agenda. "I'd need to know fairly quickly, though, as the date really is just round the corner."

"I can tell you the decision now," Lady Meade says, looking at Cordelia with great disapproval. "No need to order any candles. I already have someone decorating the house for the wedding. She's in charge of all that."

"Perfect," I say, making a note to cross that off my list. "Now, on to flowers."

"We have a few people in mind," Lady Meade begins. "I've already contacted some of them."

"Wonderful. Well, just in case, I phoned Beth earlier this week and had a great chat with her. Beth from Paxton Flowers. I think you know her, Lady Cordelia?"

Cordelia's expression softens. "You spoke to Beth?"

"Tom introduced us when I was in Paxton and I thought she was really something. She spoke about you and I had the idea that she might just be the perfect florist for your wedding. It's amazing how, when the supplier knows the couple, they can bring their personalities into the flowers. And I find that using a local supplier is always a win for everyone involved. She's very passionate about you and your family, and Dashwell Hall."

"Beth is truly talented and a friend of the family," Lady Meade acknowledges. "But she's a very small business. I'd worry that she'd struggle with a wedding for four hundred people."

"I already thought of that and discussed it with her. She's reached out to all the other florists she knows and trusts in the area and is ready with a small army of them to help if you'd like her services. She'd be in charge creatively, once she's discussed everything you and Jonathan want, Lady Cordelia, but she'd have plenty of people ready to help." I hesitate, wondering whether to say the next bit. "I mentioned to her that you were thinking a white bouquet, then discussed black with Nicole Percy"—Cordelia shifts in her seat—"and Beth said that of course she'd be able to do whatever you wanted, but she did remember that when you worked at the shop you were very fond of big arrangements with splashes of color. Apparently you used to say those arrangements were your favorite because they were both classic and bold. A bit like you." I pause. "Her words, not mine."

Cordelia can't help but smile. "I can't believe she remembers that."

I move on swiftly, not wanting to involve any kind of emotion. "I've warned her that you'll have contacted other florists and may already have entered into a contract with them, so if you don't want to go with her, it's no problem. It was just an idea, something a bit more personal and local to Dashwell Hall."

"It's a lovely idea, Emily," Lady Meade says sincerely. "We'll discuss it with my husband, then be sure to let you and her know as soon as possible."

"Thank you. Now, the last thing on my list that I wanted to discuss with you today."

I pull out a glossy photograph from the file and place it carefully on the table facing them.

"Lady Cordelia, we'd previously discussed how you wanted Queen Alexandra's Kokoshnik Tiara to wear on the day . . ."

"Oh, for goodness' sake," Lady Meade mutters, closing her eyes in exasperation.

"I know we talked about it and you decided not to go in that direction, but I remember you saying you thought it was important that a bride wear a special piece of jewelry on their wedding day. I had an idea and thought you might be interested."

I nod to the photograph on the table. "This is known as Lucky Blue," I say, looking at the photograph proudly. "It's a spectacular sapphire and diamond horseshoe brooch. The diamonds are estimated to weigh four point six carats in total, and the sapphires are estimated at five point eight carats. The jeweler is Bentley and Skinner, just down the road from here, actually. You can go to see it in person after this meeting."

"It's beautiful," Lady Meade says, smiling at the picture.

I watch Cordelia as she looks intensely at the photograph of the brooch. She's trying not to give anything away, but her eyes can't hide it. She's already fallen in love with it.

"I've spoken to Bentley and Skinner, and they're happy to loan it to you for the day, rather than you having to buy it. That way, I thought it could be your something borrowed and your something blue. And something old," I add. "It's from the nineteen-twenties."

Cordelia lifts her eyes to meet mine. "How did you find this?"

"I thought I'd look for unique jewelry that reflected your love of horses and came across this," I explain casually. "I know animals are a big part of your life, especially Tony. You looked so happy when you were riding. It seemed important to bring horses into the wedding somehow."

"How thoughtful," Lady Meade says gently.

Having given them the documents they need, I close my file, lifting it onto my lap. "I think that's it. Was there anything else you wanted to discuss?"

Cordelia's eyes fall back on the photograph of the brooch. She doesn't say anything.

"You've covered a lot, Emily," Lady Meade says, beaming at me. "You've certainly been very busy. We can't thank you enough."

"It's a pleasure," I say, putting my file away in my bag. "Consider everything I've said and let me know any decisions when you can, so I can contact anyone you need. If you get a schedule sent across to me, I can book in meetings."

"Of course."

"Thank you for your time and I'll be in touch soon," I say, standing up. "If you could send me any other jobs by email, I'll be sure to get those done."

"You're leaving?" Lady Meade stands up, too. "You won't join us for a drink? We're in no rush. Cordelia had a fitting this morning for her wedding dress. Perhaps, Cordelia, you'd like to tell Emily about it? It really is exquisite."

"I imagine it is, but I have another client to meet," I lie. "So, unless there's anything about the dress that I can help with, or any other tasks you'd like to discuss, I should be going. But thank you very much for such a kind invitation, Lady Meade, and thank you again for your time."

"Thank *you* for everything. Really."

"Just doing my job. Thank you, Lady Cordelia," I say, nodding to her.

Cordelia looks up from the photograph and gives me a knowing smile. "Thank you, Sophie."

I leave them to it and walk back through the gallery, thanking the porter in the top hat and tails who bids me goodbye as I go through the revolving doors out into the cold air, grinning from ear to ear. Mum was right. That felt a *lot* better than quitting.

I'm on the escalator in the tube station when I realize that Cordelia called me Sophie, not Emily.

A couple of weeks ago, I'd have analyzed it, elated that it was perhaps a hint of her personally connecting with me as a friend. Today I brush it aside and forget about it almost immediately.

You are cordially invited to the wedding of

Scarlett Wilson and Emmanuel Adeyemi

27 November 2021

"Be careful!" I call to Adam. "Watch where you're going!"

Adam is one of the ushers and has enthusiastically offered to take a photo of all the bridesmaids together outside the church.

Scarlett and Emmanuel are busy with photos by the car after their lovely service, during which the flower girl shouted, "I've done a wee-wee, Auntie Scarlett!" right after the vows.

It was a beautiful moment.

They're now on their way to the reception, where they will be greeted by a surprise Nigerian band playing traditional Yoruba music. Emmanuel's mother booked them secretly as their wedding present after the couple mentioned they'd love to have one, and I helped her with the arrangements. I can't wait to see their faces, so I'm eager to get this spontaneous photo shoot out of the way and arrive at the venue.

"Get in closer," Adam instructs, waving at us as he walks backward.

"Seriously, Adam," I say, panicking. "Please watch where you're going!"

"Huddle in, everyone! And now on the count of—AAAH!"

There's a collective gasp from the bridesmaids as Adam disappears, toppling backward into an open grave. We all run forward and, gathering around the rectangular hole in the ground, peer over the edge.

Adam is sprawled on the soil, phone still in his hand. He blinks up at us. "I'm OK!" he yells, scrabbling around to get to his feet. "Didn't see that one coming!"

Now that we know he's not hurt, the giggles are uncontrollable and some of the bridesmaids are bent double, tears streaming down their faces.

"What's going on over here?" another usher asks, approaching us to see what all the fuss is about. "What the . . . Adam!" He shrieks with laughter, turning to wave at the other ushers. "Guys, you need to see this!"

"Uh . . . actually, mate," Adam coughs, "if we could keep this on the down-low—"

"EVERYONE! Everyone, come over here! Adam's fallen into a grave!"

As a horde of guests runs over, I'm glad the bride and groom have already set off in the car for the reception venue and, at least, will be blissfully unaware of such a thunder-stealing scene until later.

"Can someone give him a hand to get out?" I ask the ushers.

"Sure," one replies. "Once I've taken a few photos and up-loaded them to Instagram."

"It's not that funny," Adam grumbles, appealing to the crowd gathered on the other side of him. "It actually hurt."

"Look, everyone!" the usher next to me cries out hysterically. "Adam's turning in his grave!"

CHAPTER TWENTY-FOUR

"To be honest with you, Soph," Cara begins, topping up our glasses, "the biggest news I have right now is still the drama of one of my colleagues skipping a day's work to audition for a new ITV talent show. A singing one."

"Really? Did they get anywhere?"

"He got through to the second round, which was on a Saturday, so that was fine, but now he's through to the third, which is televised, so he must be pretty good. Downside is, he had to 'fess up and tell the boss about the first audition before she saw it on TV. She was not happy. Yelled a lot. We should be used to it by now."

"She's always yelling about something, isn't she?" I ask, recalling some of Cara's work stories in the past.

"She has a very loud voice. Sometimes I can't work out if she doesn't realize she's yelling. It's quite odd. Either way, she scares the crap out of me."

"She sounds terrifying."

"She's a brilliant lawyer but scary too. I should keep my voice down, in case she's in here," Cara says, glancing about. "If I wanted to bitch about people at work, I really should have picked a different place."

We're in a new bar that Cara suggested we try out near her office when I asked if she wanted to go for a drink and a catch-up. I know she's been so busy at work lately that she's been getting home in the early hours, so I fully expected her to postpone our drink, but fortunately she's had a quiet couple of days: now was a perfect time.

"Other than the audition drama, work is good?"

"Busy, but good. You know what I'm like," Cara says. "I whine about the hours but, secretly, I like being crazy busy. I can't believe it's already December."

"As long as you're not burning out, that's fine," I warn her. "You need to make sure you take time for yourself."

"Yeah, not really a thing for people who work in law, but thanks all the same," she says. "Nah, it's all good. I'm enjoying it. Cheer me up with one of your bridesmaid stories. There's got to be something good that's happened recently."

I lean back in my chair, swilling my wine thoughtfully. Where to begin?

"I know! Tell me how Miranda Priestly's doing? The bride who made you pick up her dry cleaning and get truffle oil from somewhere in the countryside," Cara says excitedly. "Has she got married yet? I can't *wait* to hear about her wedding. Bet there'll be some good stories from that one."

"Oh, there will. The wedding is New Year's Eve."

"Very glamorous. What's she dressing you in?"

"I don't know," I say, wincing. We have yet to discuss my outfit. "Probably something awful just to annoy me. I reckon she's leaving it to the last minute on purpose."

"I hope it's fancy dress. Remember that time a bride made you wear a Regency outfit? You in a bonnet! Mike almost had that photo you sent us framed, he found it so funny."

"I thought that bonnet was lovely," I say defensively. "And it was a really elegant wedding, with an old-fashioned ball and everything. That bride is a friend of mine. Unlike this bride, who I hope I'll never have to see again after Christmas. And the feeling is mutual, I'm sure. I almost quit, you know."

"What?" Cara looks surprised. "She must be really bad. What happened?"

"Among other things, an incident involving me walking into a lake to try to talk to swans. It turns out she doesn't even want swans at the ceremony anymore. She just thought it would be funny to have me filmed making a fool of myself."

Cara bursts out laughing. "Why did you walk into the lake voluntarily?"

"I was trying to be sassy. I didn't want her to think I was weak."

"I can't believe I'm only hearing about this now."

"All you need to know is that she's done everything in her power to make me feel shit. But instead of sacking it off, I decided I'd be awesome at the job and give her absolutely no excuse to be mean to me. And it's worked. I think she's genuinely impressed with me at the moment. I told you I could be sassy."

"That's very sassy of you." She takes a sip of wine. "Why didn't you quit, though? Sounds much easier."

"Because Mum reminded me that the best revenge is success. And she was right."

"Yeah, but there must have been something else."

"What do you mean?"

She puts her glass on the table. "If you'd *really* wanted to quit, I'm not sure your mum telling you you should work harder at the job would have done the trick. There must be something else keeping you on."

"She made me walk into a lake! I was soaked! I went, 'Kaw kaw,' in the middle of St. James's Park!"

"Yeah, exactly!" she says, through a fit of giggles. "Why would anyone stay on after that? You either think this bride has some redeeming qualities or something about her wedding has captured you. Otherwise you would in no way be working your butt off to give her wedding that special Sophie touch."

"I see very few redeeming qualities. Except," I say, with a grin, "for her brother."

"Ah, there it is!" Cara claps her hands, then tops up our glasses so enthusiastically that wine sloshes over the sides, creating a small pool in the middle of the table. "There *had* to be a hot brother! I knew it! So what's he like?" She flutters her eyelashes at me. "Does he have *dreeeeeamy* eyes?"

"They're very dreamy, actually. Oh, and here's something weird. I can't stop staring at his arms."

"Interesting. Arms can be sexy."

"I guess. But, yeah, anyway, he's nice."

"And?"

"And what?" I say shyly. "He's *nice*."

Cara gasps. "You're blushing! Sophie! You like him."

"No, he's just—"

"*Yes, you do!* This is GREAT! He likes you too, right?"

"No! I don't know," I say hurriedly, wishing I hadn't brought it up and wondering if someone's switched the heating on in here because I'm burning up. "It doesn't matter anyway. I can't like him. He doesn't know who I really am."

Cara's face falls. "Bummer. I forgot that bit. What about after the wedding? You could ask him out and explain everything? His sister wouldn't mind then because the wedding would be over."

"Yeah, OK, because people love it when you lie to them." I shake my head. "And remember his sister hates me. I doubt she's going to cheer on my love life, let alone enable it. God." I stare up at the ceiling. "I can't *wait* for this wedding to be over so I never have to see her again. Ever."

"Wow." Cara tilts her head at me. "She's really got to you. Come on, tell me what she's done that's made you make that face."

"What face?"

"The pained face you do when you're trying not to spoil things but you're really unhappy."

"People need to stop commenting on my face," I grumble, and sigh. "OK, fine. She's got to me a little. She's said a couple of things that *may* have struck a nerve."

"Go on."

"She said . . . she said that I loved being a professional brides- maid because it meant I was always hiding in someone's shadow, never in the spotlight." I take a gulp of wine. "Just like Daniel said."

"Whoa." Cara holds up her hands. "Why are we now talking about Daniel?"

"Because he said the same thing at the quiz night."

"I don't remember him saying—"

"Cara," I interrupt, "do you think I'm afraid?"

"Afraid of what?"

"I don't know." I throw my hands up. "Life. Love. Every- thing." I pause, as Cara searches my expression. "You know, I actually quite enjoyed standing in the middle of a London lake and shouting, 'Kaw,' to the swans. It was crazy and irrational and idiotic. And cold. Very, very cold." I bite my lip thoughtfully. "It wasn't like me. It was . . . out there."

"Sophie," Cara says, leaning forward and resting her arms on the table, "are you trying to say you're *grateful* to this lunatic bride for making you do something stupid?"

I stare at her. "I'm not sure."

Cara opens her mouth to reply, then stops suddenly, spotting someone over my shoulder. She looks at once shocked and irri- tated.

"Cara, what's—"

"Don't turn around, OK?" she says urgently, leaning forward and looking me dead in the eye. "Act normal."

"O-*kaaaay*."

"Daniel's just walked in."

"What? *The* Daniel?"

"Yeah. It's like he insists on being in our lives, the wanker." She glances at him again, keeping her voice low. "He's with his girlfriend."

"Fiancée," I correct instinctively. "Are you sure?"

"Yes."

"Fuck." I wish I weren't panicking. I wish I were as cool as a cucumber. But I am *freaking out*. I've never met her. She's never come along to the group events.

"OK, this is OK," I whisper, talking to Cara but really to myself. "They probably won't see us and then I won't have to talk to hi—"

"Sophie?"

That's his voice. Over my shoulder. I freeze.

"Is he talking to me?" I mouth to Cara.

She communicates "yes" by opening her eyes super wide.

I calmly turn in my seat and feign complete surprise.

"Daniel!" I say, maybe a little too high-pitched. "Hi!"

"Hey, so weird that you're here. Hi, Cara."

"Hello, Daniel," she replies, looking pointedly bored by his company.

I bite the bullet and turn to Francesca, giving her a big enough smile that she doesn't think there's any ill will, but not so big that she thinks I'm being overly friendly to compensate for secretly hating her. Without a mirror handily hanging on the wall anywhere nearby, there's no way to tell if I'm pulling it off.

"Hi, you must be Francesca. I'm Sophie."

"It's really nice to finally meet you," she says, a little too enthusiastically. She's very petite, with an oval face, big green eyes, and adorable slightly pronounced front teeth. I know her face very well. A long time ago I stared at her picture, comparing her every feature to mine. "Do you work around here?"

"No, but Cara does."

"Ah, amazing. We're here for a friend's birthday," she explains. "I think there's a private area somewhere, but I'm not sure. It's so big in here."

"It's upstairs," Cara says, pointing at the flight in the corner of the room.

"That must be it." Francesca nods.

"Congratulations on your engagement!" I exclaim, glancing down at the emerald on her left hand. It's even more sparkly in real life.

"Thank you," Francesca says, looking embarrassed. "That's so lovely of you to say."

She's nice. Really nice.

DAMN IT.

"We got your RSVP," Daniel says suddenly to me. "I was kind of shocked that you said no. You never say no to weddings. Why can't you come to ours?"

Cara's expression turns thunderous. Francesca shoots him a sharp look. Nobody likes it, but the question has been asked. It's out there, hanging in the air.

I have to answer. "It was kind of you to invite me," I begin, wondering if I should just be honest. Would it really be that bad to explain that it's much too awkward to attend the wedding of an ex-boyfriend? Surely not. I should never have been invited. I should never have been put in this position. Anyone in the world would agree that it would be inappropriate for me to go.

I should calmly explain the honest and reasonable truth.

"I'm going skydiving that day," I blurt out.

Daniel looks baffled. "What?"

"I'm skydiving," I say again, more confidently this time. "I'm so sorry to be missing out."

"Oh, my God, that's so cool!" Francesca says, impressed. "I've always wanted to do something crazy like that, but never had the guts to book it."

"You should," I encourage.

"Hold on, you can't come to the wedding because you're sky-diving," Daniel repeats, trying to get his head round it. "*You?* Skydiving?"

"That's right," I say, to myself rather than anyone else. "I will be going skydiving."

"That's amazing. I'm sorry it's on the same date but, hey, you'll probably be having more fun than if you were sitting through my dad's speech," Francesca says, rolling her eyes. "He's not the best at public speaking. He has a habit of rambling."

"Sorry," Daniel says, his forehead furrowed. "I'm confused."

"What's confusing you?" I ask, pretending not to notice Francesca giving him a sharp nudge in the ribs with her elbow. He, too, pretends not to notice.

"You don't go skydiving." He snorts.

"It doesn't have to be a hobby." I laugh, a little taken aback by his accusatory tone. "I thought I'd give it a try."

"For charity or something?"

"No. For me."

He blinks at me.

"We'd better get to this birthday party," Francesca jumps in, smiling apologetically. "We're already late. But it was really nice to meet you."

"You too," I reply sincerely. "Bye, Daniel."

"Right, yeah," Daniel says, puzzled. "Better go."

"Byeeee," Cara says, wiggling her fingers at them.

Francesca leads Daniel away toward the stairs, and when they disappear from sight, I feel like I can finally breathe again.

Cara waits a few moments before speaking. "You OK?"

"Yeah. Yeah, I am." I reach forward and pick up my glass, downing what's left. "Francesca seems nice. I like her."

"Yeah. Yet again, he's punching. He's also an arsehole to ask you why you weren't going to the wedding. Strange of him to invite you in the first place, but even stranger to bump into you and grill you about the RSVP." She takes a deep breath. "Can I say something?"

"Of course."

"What you were saying earlier," she says, glancing back at the stairs, "about you being comfortable in someone's shadow, rather than in the spotlight? Wasn't that always how it was with Daniel?"

"What do you mean?"

"He has to be the center of attention, doesn't he? And when you were together, you were always standing behind him."

"Was I?"

"Yes. Yes, you were," she says pensively, like a great sleuth. "He never let you into the spotlight. He kept it all for himself." She leans back in her seat, watching me. "And look at you now."

"Single and drinking too much with my cousin?"

"Communicating with swans and throwing yourself out of a plane instead of going to his wedding."

"I haven't actually booked to go skydiving," I admit. "It was a silly idea I had."

"Maybe it *was* just an idea, but now I think you'll do it," she says matter-of-factly. "I can feel it."

I smile at her. "Maybe."

"I hate to say it, but this Miranda Priestly bride of yours isn't a complete idiot. She may have gone about it in a weird way," she says, taking a sip of wine, "but she pushed you right into your spotlight, whether you wanted it or not."

Please leave a voicemail after the tone.

BEEEEEEEEEEEEEP

Oh! Oh, good evening, Emily, this is Victoria. Lady Meade.
Thank you so much for all your hard work recently. I can't

tell you how much it's appreciated. Not just by me, either. Anyway, I'm calling because Lord and Lady Derrington have invited us to some Christmas drinks on Saturday. They're having a gathering and I wondered whether you would be available to join us. You probably have a wedding, but if you don't, we'd really like you to be there. Our last social event before the wedding! I've cleared the diary in the run-up, of course, but we should make an appearance at this one. I've checked with Nicholas and he said he'd be delighted for you to come. He enjoyed meeting you at Dashwell. I appreciate you've already gone above and beyond, but if you were able to join us, well, I'd be grateful. Extremely grateful. Cordelia . . . finds these events hard. I'm sure she'd like to thank you in person for everything you've done for the wedding. Do call me back when you get the chance. Thank you, Emily.

CHAPTER TWENTY-FIVE

I don't buy a new dress for the Christmas party. I pick one from my wardrobe, an emerald-green, long-sleeved wrap dress that I wore to engagement drinks last year. I also don't spend hours doing my makeup or having a blow-dry. I put on some foundation, mascara, bronzer, and a nude lipstick, brush my hair and leave it exactly as it falls.

In my new *sassy* opinion, it's enough that I'm making the effort to be there with such a last-minute invitation. I won't go over and above to impress these people. I don't need to prove anything. I deliberated for a while over accepting Lady Meade's invitation but in the end I wasn't going to let my personal feelings for Cordelia get in the way of doing my job to the best of my ability. If I was required to come to these drinks as support for the bride I'm working with, then that's what I'd do in a purely professional capacity. So, I called Lady Meade back, saying I'd be there and asking her to let me know details.

"Welcome, Miss Taylor," the doorman says, checking my name against a list, while a waiter promptly steps forward with a tray of drinks and another offers to take my coat. "Enjoy the party."

The Earl and Countess of Derrington are near to the door, lurking there to welcome the guests, and they greet me warmly, telling me Annabel and Georgia are around somewhere and would *love* to see me so I *must* find them, then making conversation with much more important guests also milling about in their lavishly decorated hallway.

There's a gigantic Christmas tree by the stairs and, unable to spot anyone I know straightaway, I head over to admire it, peering at my reflection in the huge, shiny gold baubles. I linger by the tree and scan the sea of faces, hoping to see someone from the Swann family, but if they're here, they're lurking in another room. From the noise and number of guests, the party seems to be spread through the whole house.

I'm working out whether to veer to the right or left when the front door opens and Tom walks in. I beam at him and I'm about to attempt a cool-but-sexy wave to get his attention when I see that he hasn't arrived alone. A tall, slender woman has her arm linked through his and they only detach to take their coats off. She has high cheekbones, shimmering skin, and the fullest lips you can possibly imagine. She's so striking, I can't stop staring at her until I realize I'm gawping in a very undignified manner and quickly pretend to be interested in the baubles again, glancing at her and Tom as stealthily as possible.

Once she's passed her coat to the waiter—who looks as dopily mesmerized by her as I am—revealing a slinky, shimmering blue dress, she flutters her eyelashes at Tom, waiting for him to introduce her to the Earl and Countess of Derrington.

Well, isn't this mortifying? I'm *such* an idiot. These are the sort of women Tom dates. Beautiful, sophisticated models, who fit right in at a party like this one.

I grimace, thinking of how I'd felt spending that day with him in Paxton. Clearly he'd thought of it as hanging out with his little sister's friend, while I was wistfully imagining what it would be like to kiss him. *Ugh.* I'm annoyed with myself for being so unprofessional, simply because a good-looking guy with gentle eyes spends a couple of days paying me attention. What a *sap.* I have not been sassy *at all* in this area of the job.

Suddenly Tom glances in my direction.

Without thinking, I drop to the floor. I realize very quickly that this is a mistake. Just like it was at Dashwell Hall when he saw me at my bedroom window. I have got to stop falling to the floor to get out of awkward situations. *Any* other reaction would be preferable to this one: a casual wave, pretending I hadn't seen him, swiftly joining a nearby conversation, turning to survey the decorations.

Seriously, *any other reaction* would have been better than this.

"Are you all right?" someone asks me, noticing me on the floor by her diamanté heels.

"Yes, thank you," I reply, grasping for explanations before coming up with "I wanted to see the tree stand. What brand it was. I've been looking for a reliable one."

"Oh," she says, surprised. "I thought you may have dropped an earring."

"Yes," I say, slowly standing up as she turns her back on me to rejoin the conversation she'd been a part of. "That would have been a much more believable reason."

I keep my back to the door and use the reflection in the baubles to try to work out if Tom and his date are still standing by the door. Unfortunately, all the guests seem to be blurred blobs and I can't work out who is who. Ignoring the strange looks of the woman who'd spoken to me and the rest of her group, I stop peering closely at the baubles and slowly turn to glance at the door. I breathe a sigh of relief that they've gone, ushered into another room.

Spotting the back of Tom's head going through the door to my right, I duck through the crowd and scurry into the sitting room to my left, only to walk straight into Cordelia and Jonathan, who are standing by the door.

"Emily!" Jonathan cries, greeting me with a kiss on each cheek. "We were wondering if you were here yet."

Cordelia reluctantly follows suit, giving me two air kisses and an attempt at an enthusiastic hello.

"I'm glad I found you," I say, not sure if I'm telling the truth or not. "I don't really know anyone here."

"That's a good thing," Cordelia mutters, while Jonathan rolls his eyes at her. "Annabel and Georgia are here somewhere. Annabel's already told me three times that her wedding is better than mine."

"That's not quite what she said, darling," Jonathan corrects. "Although she does have a way of putting things. She was going on about Nicole Percy."

"Whatever," Cordelia says, twisting a lock of hair. "Beth is much better. And we're going for the personal touch. Anyone could hire Nicole, but Beth is a more exclusive florist."

"You booked Beth?"

Cordelia nods. "Thanks for the idea. I think she'll do a really good job."

"Was Beth your idea, Emily?" Jonathan asks, surprised.

"Not really. Cordelia's being nice. I met her that weekend at Dashwell and thought she was cool. I don't know much about florists, though," I say breezily.

I catch Cordelia smiling into her drink.

"I hope Tom gets here soon." Jonathan sighs, craning his neck to scan the room. "I need to ask his opinion on the ushers' waistcoats."

"Jonathan wants them to wear patterned ones," Cordelia explains to me. "But he's worried that it won't be traditional enough for my parents."

"I think you should have your ushers wearing whatever waistcoats you like," I say firmly, not that he's asked me. "It's your wedding."

"That's what I said," Cordelia says, looking up at him.

It's weird having such a normal conversation with Cordelia.

She hasn't said anything snarky or rude, or turned her back on me or anything. She's acting . . . strangely. Nice, almost.

"I'll ask Tom," Jonathan tells us. "Since he'll have to wear one, it'll be handy to know his thoughts."

"He said he'd be here by now," Cordelia comments.

"He is, I think," I say casually, as though I've only just remembered. "I saw him come in with . . . uh . . . someone."

Cordelia raises her eyebrows in surprise. "He came with someone?"

"Yeah." I shrug. "I think so. Not sure. His girlfriend maybe?"

"He doesn't have a girlfriend."

"Well, they looked friendly. Very friendly." I sip my drink, looking around the room, wanting to change the subject. "So, what else is going on with you two?"

"Actually," Cordelia says suddenly, "Emily, would you mind coming for a chat? I wanted to talk to you about something, but"—she smiles sweetly up at Jonathan—"you can't hear it."

"Oh! Is this about the dress? How exciting!" he replies, kissing her head. "No worries! I'll go and find Tom and this mystery woman."

"Come on," she says to me, as Jonathan disappears into the next room.

I follow her warily through the house, dodging the busy caterers buzzing around the kitchen, and out through the patio doors to the garden at the back. I'm grateful that a couple of people are smoking and chatting out here, as you can never be too sure with Cordelia. She might have been leading me here to murder me, then heading back inside, and my body would be found and it would be like an amazing whodunit story with all the high-society, champagne-guzzling guests as suspects.

But she can't murder me in front of these witnesses, so I'm probably safe.

"Do you want one?"

She's offering me a cigarette. "No, thanks."

She takes one out of the packet for herself and lights up, hovering around a garden table where ashtrays have been laid out. It's cold outside and I'm rubbing my arms, waiting for her to strike up the conversation. I wish she'd told me we were coming here so I could have grabbed my coat, but hopefully this won't take long.

"Thanks for coming today," she says, looking out at the garden. There's a huge, out-of-place fountain with a Greek goddess statue slap-bang in the middle of it.

"No problem," I say neutrally. "It's my job."

She nods, taking a drag. "It was my idea to invite you."

"Really?"

"Yep. I asked Mum to call you."

"Oh. OK."

There's a long pause.

"You've done some good work for the wedding the last few weeks. The brooch and everything. And the photographer and Beth. It's all good."

"Great."

"I shouldn't have hired that actor. The whole Swan Lake episode," she says, waving her hands about, a trail of smoke zipping around her, "it wasn't cool."

"We don't need to talk about it."

"I know, but I want to." She bows her head, eyes to the ground. "I feel bad about it. It wasn't . . . it wasn't the right thing to do."

I stare at her. "Cordelia, are you *apologizing* to me?"

"What? No. No, I just . . ." She trails off.

"You are! You're apologizing!"

"Oh, my God, do you have to make it *such* a big deal?" she hisses, checking the other smokers aren't listening.

"But it is a big deal! You're apologizing!"

"Who is stupid enough to walk into a lake?" she asks, rolling her eyes. "Why didn't you question it?"

"I did question it! He was very convincing."

"He's a terrible actor."

"No, he was good. He really looked the part and then he brought your mother into it."

"Ah, I'd told him to do that. I said you'd hate her being disappointed." She hesitates. "I wasn't sure if you'd go in just because *I'd* said you had to."

"Yeah, well," I say, shifting my weight from one leg to the other. "Did Jimmy show you the video, then?"

"Yes." She tries and fails to stifle a laugh.

I scowl at her. "Are you going to put it on YouTube?"

"No!" She looks irritated that I'd ask. "Don't flatter yourself, it wasn't *that* funny."

"Jimmy called me a goody-goody. You used that personal information against me."

"Yeah, well, you gave away your weakness telling me about Graham Slater."

"You gave away your weakness telling me about Annabel."

"I haven't told you a thing about her. That's why you asked all those questions and started the fight."

"I did not start the fight!"

"You kept pushing when I asked you not to." She exhales thoughtfully. "But I overreacted."

"Is that another apology?"

"Absolutely not."

"I can't believe you've apologized," I say, still in shock at this conversation. "But I'm glad you have. I know I pissed you off, but you went way too far with your retaliation."

"Always been my problem," she admits. "I'm not very good at controlling my temper."

"I've noticed."

"*You* care too much about what people think."

"You know, this doesn't have to be a competition. You don't have to point out all your flaws and then start listing mine."

"You have too many," she says, with a sly smile. "We'd be here all night."

WHAT IS GOING ON?

Who is this person and where is the real Cordelia? Is she seriously making *jokes* with me now? I need to pull back. I need to rein it in. I need to stop responding to her. I need to stop being so friendly. I am not her friend: I'm a professional bridesmaid who has been hired by her mother to—

"I'm sorry," she says suddenly, tapping the end of her cigarette into an ashtray but looking up at me.

"Huh?" I reply intelligently.

"I'm sorry," she repeats, "for the way I've treated you."

I don't know what to say. I'm still unsure as to whether this is real or whether it's a huge prank and some actor is standing nearby ready to throw a vat of custard over my head.

"I mean it," she continues. "You've made the wedding a lot better and I'm grateful."

I stare at her, stunned.

She laughs. "I'm being serious. I really don't like apologizing, either. But you're right, you deserve an apology. You've worked hard and been really thoughtful about certain things when you could have walked away. I really appreciate everything that you've—"

"Are you about to fire me?" I blurt out.

"What?" She frowns at me.

"It sounds like you're about to fire me."

"No, it doesn't."

"Yeah, it does. You're making things right by apologizing, going on about how I've helped so much . . . It feels like you're tying up loose ends."

"Jesus," she says, exhaling a plume of smoke. "Why is your brain so busy overthinking everything all the time?"

"I don't overthink things . . . I don't think. OK, maybe I do."

"Look, are you going to accept my apology or not?"

I cross my arms, still trying to rub away the goose bumps. I consider telling her that I don't accept her apology, but she can rest assured that it won't affect my work ethic. She really has put me through a lot, *but* I can tell she means it. I can tell she's sorry.

"Yeah," I say eventually. "OK."

"Good." She puts her cigarette out in the ashtray. "Now, let's go inside before you freeze to death."

"Why are you apologizing here? Today, I mean," I ask, stopping her as she heads back toward the door.

She turns to face me. "I wanted to apologize in person so you'd know I mean it. And it took me a few days to get over my pride."

"Oh." I hesitate, taken aback by her honesty. "OK."

"You really don't have to overthink this," she says, giving me a knowing look. "I wanted to say sorry to you. That's it."

"And what's going to happen now?"

"Right now? We'll go back into the party and have to put up with all these dreadful people telling us about their Christmas plans in Barbados. The canapés are good, though."

"No, I mean what's going to happen with the bridesmaid stuff? Are you still going to try to make me quit?"

"No. I'm over it."

"Really? Promise?"

She lets out a sigh and then holds up her little finger. "Yes."

"What are you doing?"

"What do you think?" She wiggles her finger. "I'm doing a pinky promise."

"I'd have thought you'd think pinky promises are lame. Are you doing this because you think I—"

She groans, reaching out and hooking her little finger with mine. "I pinky promise I won't try to make you quit from now on. OK?"

"Wow." I beam at her as we drop our hands. "I feel like that was such a big moment."

"Oh, my God, you're annoying."

She swings open the door and lets me pass through, then follows me in. I apologize to the caterers again for getting in the way and head back into the sitting room to find Jonathan with Lord and Lady Meade, while Cordelia joins the queue for the bathroom.

"How was your chat?" Jonathan asks, after I've joined him and said hello again to Lord and Lady Meade.

"It was good, thanks," I say, catching Lady Meade's eye and smiling. "Really good. What were you talking about before I rudely interrupted?"

"We were saying how lovely the party is," Lord Meade explains. "Ned has really gone all out for it. It should be a wonderful evening."

"Cheers to that," Lady Meade says, raising her glass. "Let's just hope there's no drama."

CHAPTER TWENTY-SIX

"Y_{ou} look lost."

I spin round to see Tom grinning at me by the bottom of the stairs, holding two glasses of champagne. I've just emerged from the loo, and had been looking round the party trying to find any of the Swanns, so I had someone to talk to.

Of course, the one member of the family I've been trying my best to avoid all night is the one I stumble across.

"I was looking for Cordelia," I explain, trying not to be flustered at just the sight of him. "Have you seen her?"

"Afraid not," he says, before offering me one of the drinks he's holding.

"Don't worry. I can get my own. I don't want to steal a drink from your date. She's lovely, by the way." I mean that, too. I ended up having a chat with Mona about ten minutes ago when I found her standing on her own, looking out of place, while she waited for Tom to get back from topping up her drink—unfortunately, he'd been cornered by the Earl of Derrington on the other side of the crowded room. She isn't a model, as I had assumed, but actually works for an auction house and told me in great detail about the recent sale of some ceramics that were, in her opinion, priceless. I was hoping she would be horrible or boring, but she was neither and, annoyingly, I enjoyed her company.

Luckily, so did some guy named Frazer, who wandered over to introduce himself as one of Annabel's old friends. They fell naturally into a flirtatious conversation and I sneaked off to the loo without either of them taking any notice.

"Mona already has a drink." Tom holds out the glass insistently. "This one has your name on it."

"Thanks," I say, taking it. "Please don't feel you have to stand here and chat with me. You should be with Mona."

"Honestly, I think she'd rather chat to Frazer," he says, giving me a knowing smile. "A definite spark there."

"Ah."

"I wouldn't feel too bad for me. We only met last night at the Chanel event."

"Wow. You've only just met her and already invited her to a big Christmas party where your family would be among the guests? She must be a really good kisser."

Tom raises his eyebrows, smiling in surprise. To be honest, I'm slightly taken back by my own sassiness, but I'll go with it.

"Actually, she was already coming to this party," he corrects. "We got chatting last night, the party came up, and we thought we might as well go together. And we didn't kiss."

"Oh. OK. I mean, it's none of my business." I take a large gulp of champagne.

"So, where's George?"

"Who?"

He frowns. "Your boyfriend. You know, the guy you were seeing?"

Oh, yes. George.

That guy I cleverly made up to stop myself getting too close to Tom, which would be unprofessional and would lead to a world of trouble. It would be smart and sensible to keep up with this pretense, and make sure absolutely nothing can happen between me and my client's brother, who doesn't even know my real name.

Under no circumstances should I change this imperative story.

"I'm not seeing anyone," I blurt out.

DAMN IT.

Look, I blame the champagne and Tom's cologne. There's really nothing I can do.

"Really? I hope you're OK," he says, watching me carefully.

"I'm great. Anyway, how amazing are these decorations?" I say hurriedly, desperate to change the conversation. "The baubles on the tree are the size of my head!"

Way to go, Sophie. Very sexy chat.

"Yeah, well, Lord and Lady Derrington never do anything by half." He sighs.

A waiter stops next to us and holds out a silver tray of canapés.

"May I tempt either of you with a delicious red-wine-braised and deep-fried oxtail with horseradish cream?" he says, with pride.

We politely decline and he waltzes off to another group.

"What are your feelings on canapés?" Tom asks, as he watches the waiter go.

"I'm sorry?"

"How do you feel about them?" he asks. "Because I'm not a fan."

"What? How can you not be a fan of canapés? They're delicious mini portions of food."

"They're completely useless," he argues, moving closer to let another guest pass. "What's the point? They don't fill you up, they're awkward to eat. Why don't people serve sandwiches at events?"

I blink at him. "Because then you'd be serving sandwiches before a meal! Canapés are like little tasters of what's to come. Or, at an event like this one, which doesn't include a sit-down meal, they keep guests content. They keep hunger at bay."

"You know what else keeps hunger at bay? Sandwiches."

"This is ridiculous. You can't seriously be arguing that people should serve full-on *sandwiches* at a Christmas party like this one. It wouldn't make any sense! I couldn't stand here eating a sandwich while talking to other guests!"

"Why not? Are you embarrassed about how you eat a sandwich?"

"No! I just wouldn't want to be stuffing my face with one while I ask the Countess of Derrington about her holiday plans."

"So, you'd rather have a teeny-tiny barely existent bite of oxtail that does absolutely nothing to fill you up and is so small you can't really taste it anyway."

"You cannot say that canapés don't taste of anything. Many wonderful chefs and caterers can create a tiny morsel of full flavor," I argue, wondering when I became so passionate about canapés. "It's an *art*."

"The truth is that no one at this party wants any of these bizarre, posh bites that are as satisfying as air," he says, gesturing at the other guests. "What they really want is proper food. I mean, look at these." He points at a tray of food passing us as another waiter works the room.

"What can you *possibly* have against mini burgers?"

"Nobody in their right mind has ever eaten a burger and said, 'You know what? I wish this was an eighth of its size,' " Tom says, throwing his eyes to the ceiling. "Just bring me a normal-sized burger!"

"You're wrong," I say, leaning against the banister. "Canapés are designed for elegant events. If we asked these guests, they'd agree that this is neither the time nor the place to dig into a burger."

"They'd all say that, but they wouldn't mean it," he retorts smugly.

"I'm not going to stand here and argue all evening about canapés with you." I sigh.

"Why not? I'm happy to stand here and argue with *you* all evening."

I'm so taken aback that I can't think of anything to say or do. As if what he said wasn't enough, he then reaches over and tucks a lock of my hair that has fallen over my eye back behind my ear.

Yeah. I know.

The closest thing I've had to sex in *months*.

"Emily," he says softly, as my heart rate speeds up and my cheeks grow hot under his intense eye contact.

Oh, God, he's so close. And he's moving closer. Uh-oh. Break the eye contact, Sophie.

BREAK THE EYE CONTACT BEFORE IT'S TOO LATE.

Suddenly we hear heightened voices from upstairs. He lifts his head away from mine and looks up in concern. I follow suit. It sounds like an argument and it's coming from one of the bedrooms. Since we're standing next to the banister, we hear them first but it isn't long before others around us are glancing up curiously.

"What do you think is going on?" I ask Tom.

Part of me hopes he'll reply by stripping off his shirt, going "*Who cares?*," and then kissing me passionately.

That doesn't happen.

Instead he looks panicked and says, "Uh-oh. That sounds like Cordelia."

"And Annabel," I add, grimacing.

We leap into action, leaving our drinks on a table and marching upstairs to see what's happening before anything can get out of hand. We follow the sound of the argument to a closed door at the end of the landing. I raise my hand, glance at Tom, who nods in solidarity, and knock.

The door flies open and we're greeted by Annabel in an eye-catching yellow sequin dress, apparently about to explode with anger.

"Thank goodness," she says dramatically, before pointing at Cordelia. "Someone needs to control her."

"Hi, Annabel! Wow, you look amazing," I begin, hoping to lighten the mood of the room. "Like a bauble!"

She wrinkles her nose. *"Excuse me?"*

"A very pretty, sparkling bauble. Never mind. Everything OK in here?" I ask chirpily.

"Everything is *not* OK," Annabel replies, so loudly that I usher Tom in quickly and shut the door behind us, desperate for the rest of the guests not to hear and to go on enjoying the party.

"What's going on?" Tom asks, giving Cordelia a weary look as though he's been put in this position many times before.

"Nothing," she says. "Annabel accused me of something and I was defending myself, that's all."

"I came up here and found her snooping around in my room with the door shut." Annabel bristles.

"I got lost. I was looking for the bathroom."

"Please!" Annabel snorts. "You've been to this house before. You know where the bathroom is."

"I think I came here once, years ago," Cordelia says, bored. "We always hung out at your flat, not your parents' house."

"That is such a lie! You are such a liar!" Annabel cries. "You came here all the time!"

"I'd forgotten which room was which," Cordelia answers.

"You came in here to do drugs at my party," Annabel spits.

Tom tenses next to me. Cordelia's jaw clenches at the accusation.

"As I've already told you," Cordelia says sharply, "that's not true."

"People never change," Annabel says, flicking her hair back in a superior fashion. "You can't help it, can you, Cordy? You couldn't fight that urge."

Cordelia's hands clench into fists before she looks directly at Tom to reply. "I haven't been doing drugs. I came up here to get some peace."

"I'm sure this is a misunderstanding," I say, sensing something dangerous bubbling beneath the surface of this conversation. "We should all go back downstairs. Annabel, you can't be missing at your own party. Everyone will be wondering where you are."

"Yeah, come on," Tom says, taking a step forward. "Let's drop this and enjoy the rest of the night."

"Tell her to stay away from my room," Annabel remarks coldly.

"She will," Tom assures her. "Right, Cordelia?"

Cordelia nods, snatching up her bag and her glass of champagne from Annabel's dressing table. Tom opens the door and I lead the way out onto the landing.

"Thank goodness I walked in here before anything got out of hand," Annabel mutters, as we all file past her out of the room.

"From what I remember, you were the one making sure things always got out of hand, Annabel," Cordelia retorts, over her shoulder, with Tom shaking his head behind her and whispering at her to "shut up and walk away."

Annabel's jaw drops and she stomps across the landing, stopping us as we make our way down to the party.

"You're the one who overdosed, Cordelia," Annabel hisses. "Not me."

Cordelia stops dead on the stairs, the color draining from her face. Tom looks as though someone has slapped him. He reaches out to clutch Cordelia's arm protectively. She shakes him off and turns to walk back up the steps to the landing.

"Cordelia," Tom pleads quietly, but she ignores him.

Annabel stands tall, wearing a triumphant smile. She doesn't flinch when Cordelia gets to the top, clearly thinking she's won.

"Fuck you, Annabel," Cordelia says, before she throws the contents of her glass straight into Annabel's face.

Annabel yelps loudly. The guests' faces swivel upward,

causing a ripple of gasps through the party as they see what's happened.

"You *bitch!*" Annabel cries, champagne dripping through her hair and down her face. She spins round and runs into the bathroom, slamming the door.

Cordelia, seeming unaffected by what she's done, glides down to the party while everyone watches, whispering to one another. Tom and I have little choice but to follow her.

Georgia appears, tackling the stairs in a ridiculous pair of heels, looking full of concern. "Was that Annabel yelling? What's going on? Oh, hey, Tom, how are you? I've been looking for you! Talk in a min, babe. I'll come and find you—Annabel, are you OK?"

The crowd parts in the hallway as Cordelia makes her way to the door.

"Cordelia, wait," Tom says, smiling awkwardly at guests as they recoil from us, pretending everything is completely under control. "We need to get our coats."

But she's already asked the doorman to let her out, and as the door opens, there's a rush of noise from a crowd outside and a host of camera flashes.

"Great. The press is here." Tom groans. "Cordelia, wait!"

I grab Tom's arm and say, "I'll go, it's OK," then hastily follow her outside.

I shield my face with my hands and, head bowed, make my way down the steps. Most of the photographers are, thankfully, crowded round Cordelia as she hails a taxi at the side of the road, and none pays any attention to me.

"Cordelia, wait for me!" I yell at the top of my lungs, hoping she'll hear me over all the questions being fired at her from reporters.

"Hurry up!" she calls, stepping into the cab.

The paparazzi reluctantly let me through, and Cordelia leans across to shut the door behind me as I jump in. I launch myself across the floor of the car, yelling at the top of my lungs, "Go! Go! Go!"

The driver puts his foot down and we speed away, leaving behind all the drama.

CHAPTER TWENTY-SEVEN

Cordelia laughs, nudging me with her shoe. "All right, James Bond, what are you doing lying flat on the floor?"

"I was hiding my face from the reporters," I explain, lifting my head. "Are we safely away?"

She nods. I clamber onto the seat next to her and lean back, brushing my hair off my face and brushing dust off my dress. The taxi driver asks us where we want to go and Cordelia shrugs. "Is there a pub around here?" she asks him.

"A few."

"We're after a low-key one," she instructs. "A shitty old-man pub."

"No problem." He chuckles.

"Thank you. No one will think to look for us in a place like that."

"Are you OK?" I ask her.

"I will be."

"Thanks for letting me come with you. I didn't think you would."

"I need a drink," she replies, looking out of the window. "No fun on your own."

I sense she doesn't want to go into it right now, so we sit in silence for the remainder of the journey, getting out at a pub that perfectly fits Cordelia's request. The sign declaring it to be named the Duck is grubby, and so wonky it might fall off at any second and take out some poor unsuspecting passerby. You can't see in through the windows from the outside thanks to them last being cleaned in the eighteenth century, and as soon as you push open the heavy, creaky door, you're struck by a waft of lager mixed with stale smoke, even though no one's supposed to have smoked in here since 2007. To make it worse, there's an added smell of bleach in the mix, not too potent but as though someone started to clean and gave up after the first swipe. A few people are dotted around the small tables but the place is so dimly lit you can barely see their faces. The barman looks up from his phone when we walk in, his eyebrows shooting up his forehead in surprise.

"This is great," Cordelia says, making a beeline for the bar. "I haven't been in a place like this for years."

"Yeah," I say, less enthusiastically. "This is great."

She hops up onto a stool at the bar and asks the barman to see the wine list.

"We have white wine or red wine," he replies, frowning. "That's your choice."

"Oh. In that case, I'll have white wine. Sophie?"

"*Emily*," I correct. "I'll have red."

I'm confident in my selection as the barman reaches for two wineglasses and sets them in front of us, heading to the fridge for the white. I'm by no means expecting a delightful red wine, but at least it won't have the horrible tangy aftertaste a bad white produces that makes your face scrunch up like you've eaten a sour sweet.

"This is much better than a stuffy party," Cordelia declares. "It was getting a bit too busy in there. I needed some space."

"I should probably text your mum and let her know I'm with you and you're all right," I say, getting out my phone but waiting for her permission before I start typing.

"Go ahead." She smiles at the barman as he announces that will be £9.45. "For both? Are you sure?"

He nods while I send a quick message to Lady Meade. She replies immediately, thanking me.

"What a bargain," Cordelia exclaims, beeping her card on the reader. "I'm going to come here again. Thank you!"

With a furrowed brow, he moves away from us, repositioning himself on a stool behind the end of the bar and getting out his phone again. I can't imagine he meets such enthusiasm on a daily basis, or a promise of a repeat customer.

"Do you want to talk about what happened?" I ask carefully, having learned my lesson from the weekend at Dashwell.

"Not really." She sighs. "But I'm thankful you're here and not Jonathan. I love him, but he'd be so mortified about how I behaved that he'd make me feel even guiltier than I do. He's such a good person. Too good, almost."

"She provoked you," I reason.

"Mm." She takes a sip of wine and recoils. "Eugh. That tastes like . . . petrol."

"It was a bargain, though."

"True." She laughs, placing the glass back on the sticky-topped bar. "OK, I have a question I've wanted to ask you ever since you strolled into my parents' kitchen that day and introduced yourself. I haven't asked because . . ."

"Because you hated me," I offer, when she trails off.

"I never hated you." She frowns. "I didn't like what you represented. You were being paid to hang out with me."

I roll my eyes. "I've already told you that that's not—"

"Blah, blah, blah, I know," she says, waving my sentence away impatiently. "I'm saying that's how I felt."

"What was the question you wanted to ask?"

She takes a deep breath. "Why do you like being a bridesmaid? I can't understand it at all! I can see why people might *want* a bridesmaid, but who would want to be one all the time?"

"I love it!"

"I don't believe you," she says firmly. "You have to spend all your time around brides, who all think their day is the most important one. You have to put up with their whining and whinging and demands, and once the big day arrives, you can't enjoy it because you're too busy making sure they're happy. I don't get it! You're dedicating your life to a load of nonsense."

"Don't hold back, Cordelia! Bloody hell!" I burst out laughing at her tirade. "And you're missing the point."

"All right, then." She winces, taking another sip of wine. "Tell me the point."

"Weddings are fun," I say. "At a wedding, everyone in the room is important to the couple and they've made the effort to be there to celebrate and support them, to get merry together, to dance stupidly and have a *laugh*. That's really for me the best thing about a wedding. Life is one big mess and the world can be really shit. But at a wedding everyone is happy. Everyone is given a few hours of escape from the everyday. How many events can claim that?"

She looks at me thoughtfully. "So you enjoy your job? You like babysitting all these brides?"

"I'm not babysitting them, I'm helping them. And, yeah, I do," I say, before adding, "although not the parts where the brides throw their smoothies over me and ask me to write to the Queen demanding the loan of her tiara."

She closes her eyes, nodding slowly. "Yeah. Sorry about all that."

"Two apologies in one day," I point out. "I'm not sure what I've done to deserve this, but keep 'em coming."

"I wanted you to quit." She sighs.

"No kidding."

She holds up her hands. "I've said I was wrong. I'm not . . . used to having friends. I don't like having friends, I mean. I like being on my own. Or I'm used to being on my own. Jonathan is one of those people who has hundreds of friends. He's always busy, being sociable. He makes time for everyone and they all love him. When we first met, I never thought he'd be interested in someone like me. I wasn't exactly his type. But, inexplicably, we clicked."

"Sometimes that's the way it is. You can't explain it."

She rolls her eyes. "Gross."

"Why is that gross?" I laugh. "You're so uncomfortable with emotion."

"I'm not! You're just cheesy."

"Well, I am a professional bridesmaid."

She takes a large gulp of wine, nearly finishing her glass, and waves the barman over. I take a few swigs of mine to catch up, realizing that it's easier to drink if I get it down fast without really tasting it. "I'll get this round," I say.

"No, I shall get this round," she insists, waggling her card at the barman, who looks bored with us already. "Two more glasses of your fine wine, good sir."

He plods back to the fridge and returns to fill her glass, before seeing to mine.

"Do you know what?" she says, once we've clinked. "This could be my hen do."

"What? Don't be silly."

"Come on, I'm not having a hen do, am I?"

"You haven't requested one."

"Then this can be it!" She holds her glass up at the barman, who has wandered back to his stool and is watching her with an unimpressed expression. "This is my hen do!"

"Congratulations," he says to his phone screen.

"You should count yourself lucky, Sophie—"

"*Emily.*"

"Many people would be very honored to be the only person in the whole world invited to Lady Cordelia Swann's hen do. Come on, then, what do you do at a hen do?"

"Normally, I'd have been given a little more preparation time," I tell her.

"Time to get creative."

"OK. Well, we'd do some drinking games, bring up some embarrassing moments from the past, and probably tease the bride about ex-boyfriends."

"Oh, God." She grimaces. "Who do you want to hear about?"

"All the famous ones."

"Course." She sighs. "I bet you lap up all that celeb stuff."

"I won't deny it. Is it true you dated Prince Harry?"

"No. We really were just friends."

"What about Justin Timberlake? Oooh, and the guy from Westlife."

"Do you believe everything you read?"

"No smoke without fire," I say as she laughs, burying her head in her hands. "You can't be embarrassed already, we've only just started. Once we've run through all your ex-boyfriends and some hilarious tales, we move on to your fiancé."

"What about him?"

"You have to spill the beans."

"On what?" she asks, aghast.

"On your sex life—normally we'd do it via a game like Mr. and Mrs., but unfortunately we don't have such tools, so I'm just going to have to ask you a load of quick-fire questions and you can answer them."

"So, your version of a last-minute hen do is purely to embarrass me? How is this fair? Aren't you supposed to be celebrating the bride, not humiliating her?" She smiles mischievously. "And on a hen do, isn't there supposed to be a stripper?"

"Usually, but I'm not sure who'd be available at such late notice."

We pause and crane our necks to look at the barman. He glances up and then, blushing furiously, shuffles round on his stool to face away from us. We giggle uncontrollably, and once we've wiped the tears from our eyes, I get back to grilling Cordelia about her love life.

After our third large glass of wine in the pub, combined with the champagne at the party, I'm pretty tipsy and ask the barman to provide us with pints of water. I'm also having a great time. Cordelia is *finally* opening up. I wish she was like this all the time—relaxed, funny, feisty, and excellent company. I'm seeing the side to her that I'd heard about from Jonathan, Tom, and Beth.

I thank the barman for our water and take some large gulps. He's warming to us and, every so often, I notice him chuckling at something we say.

Cordelia ignores her water, and takes a deep breath, as though she's about to let me in on an important story. "Have I ever told you about the time I—"

"Let me stop you there, Cordelia." I laugh, putting my glass down. "You haven't told me about *any* of the times."

"Fine," she says, rolling her eyes. "Let me tell you about the time I founded my school's origami club."

"You *what*?"

"I was eight and my mum had taught me how to do a swan, because, well, the name, right? I thought it was the coolest thing ever. I bought a book and everything. So, I spoke to my teacher and asked if I could start an origami club, and she said yes. I put the word out and arranged the first meeting for a Tuesday lunchtime. Do you know how many people showed up for the inauguration of the origami club?"

"No one?"

"Wrong!" she cries, wagging her finger at me. "It was actually one! One person turned up."

"Was that one person, by any chance, you?"

She narrows her eyes at me. "So what if it was?"

I laugh. "How long did this crowd-pleasing origami club last?"

"An entire term," she says triumphantly. "I persevered and made many works of art. Paper swans, rabbits, pigeons, dinosaurs. All sorts! I got a special badge."

"You got a *badge* for founding a club that no one went to?"

"I got a badge for being an excellent origami-club captain," she protests. "Sadly, the club folded before it had a chance to spread its wings."

"What might have been."

She nods solemnly.

"But it's cool that your mum taught you how to do origami. Not really something I see Lady Meade doing in her spare time."

"She's very artistic. We used to paint a lot together. Mostly horses and dogs and stuff, but she's really good. We'd sit outside on that small patio bit—you know, where I had that cigarette after Annabel pissed me off?—and she'd set up a little canvas, one for me and one for her, and we'd paint next to each other and chat. I used to love it."

She hesitates, reaching for her water and taking a few gulps.

"You and your mum clash a lot, huh?" I say gently.

"How could you tell?" She gives me a knowing smile. "The wedding has put extra tension on our relationship."

"That's normal. Most brides go through the same thing."

"I don't know, maybe it's all part of growing up," Cordelia says, sighing heavily. "We had a lot of fallouts when I was a teenager. I disappointed her a lot then. But, recently, I've had to work at not being disappointed by *her*."

"In what way?"

"I wish she wasn't so caught up in the things that don't matter." She runs a hand through her hair. "The society stuff, the society people. Sometimes I wonder if she even cares about what I want for the wedding. It's all about how things *should* be. Does that make sense? I want her to be happy. I know how much work she's put into it, but I also don't want any of it to be a farce. I don't want it to be the spectacle that all those people expect from us. You know?"

"Yeah." I nod. "I can see why you'd be worried about that. But if you want proof of what really matters to your mum, just look at me."

She frowns. "You?"

"She hired *me*, Cordelia. She knew you'd be furious with her about it, she knew you'd argue and rail against it, but she did it anyway. She wanted someone to be there for you and she made sure that was the case, whether you thought you'd need it or not. She wasn't going to let you do any of this alone."

She stares at me, my words sinking in.

"I've never thought about it like that," she says eventually. "I figured it was because she didn't think I'd be very good at any of the wedding planning. And that maybe she was embarrassed I didn't have any friends to parade in front of the guests."

"I think she cares less about that society stuff than you think she does. I mean, I've seen her with all those people at your engagement party and I've seen her among her chickens, and let me tell you, she is *way* more animated with the chickens."

Cordelia bursts out laughing. "She loves those chickens more than anything. Did she tell you about Lord Cluck?"

"I met him!"

"Lord Cluck is the light of her life, not me or Tom. He really is her pride and joy."

"He's *magnificent!*"

She giggles, shaking her head, then slides off her stool announcing she's going for a cigarette. I wait for her, scrolling through Instagram. When she gets back, she looks determined, sitting down and leaning toward me.

"About tonight," she begins. "About what Annabel said. The reason I threw the drink over her."

I can tell this is serious, and I put my phone away. "You don't have to talk about it."

"I want to," she says slowly. "I want to explain. It's quite tiring to keep it all a secret. I shouldn't have thrown the drink at her. And I shouldn't have been in her room. I wasn't snooping, I promise. Everyone was asking about the wedding and I got a bit overwhelmed and wanted a time-out. I knew Annabel's bedroom best from when we were friends, so I ducked in there without thinking about it. Stupid of me to think she wouldn't mind. I'm going to have to apologize and there's nothing worse than apologizing to Annabel Porthouse."

"I was there, Cordelia. She was nasty to you, too."

She nods appreciatively, before launching into her story. "Annabel and I used to be best friends. There was a group of us. We went to the same school from the age of eleven and were with each other all the way up to the sixth form, so we were super close. We did everything together, told each other everything. Annabel and I were inseparable. I couldn't live without her. Like sisters. Do you have a mate like that?"

"My cousin and I are very close."

"You know, then. We partied a lot together. We were both in the public eye, so were invited to all the same events, the nightclub openings, the premieres, the dinners, all that stuff." She waves away her glamorous past. "It was fun, especially when we left school. At first, I wasn't interested in drugs." She looks up at me, her eyes gleaming. "I knew my parents would kill me if they ever found out. But Annabel and Georgia, along with my group of girls, were always big on that scene and, eventually, I started doing them with Annabel. A lot."

She pauses, taking a drink of water. I don't say anything, waiting for her to continue, concerned about where this story is going.

"One night, I was out with Annabel. I overdosed."

I blink back tears, having guessed that it was coming but still finding it hard to hear. "I'm so sorry."

"It was a long time ago. My own stupid fault. I was taken to hospital, almost died." She starts to chew her thumbnail. "My poor parents. And Tom. I'll never forgive myself for putting them through that night."

I swallow the lump in my throat, desperate to reach out and put a comforting hand on hers. She drops them to her lap, clasping them together, as though she knows what I'm thinking.

"When I came round, they were there. But no one else was. Not one of those friends visited me in hospital. Not even Annabel." Lines form on her forehead, as though she's deep in thought, still not understanding an event that happened years ago. "She was embarrassed. She dropped me. Just like that."

"But why?"

"I was a social pariah," she explains. "Annabel wouldn't go near me. The rumors were all flying. The only reason the press never found out was thanks to Mum and Dad, who spoke to Annabel's parents and begged them to make sure she never told a soul. They were like my second parents so were just as protective. We were at least safe in the knowledge that Annabel wouldn't tell the press. Her dad would have killed her." She gives me a sad smile. "So that was something."

"And you and Annabel?"

"Were never friends again. I tried talking to her about it, desperate to salvage our relationship." She hesitates. "It turns out that the night it all happened, her boyfriend at the time tried it on with me. I would never have done that to her, but he had a very different story. Apparently, Annabel and I had argued about it, but I can't remember."

"And she believed him?"

"Yes, she did. And, in the end, they broke up a few months later because he cheated on her with one of her friends. Twice. But by then his lie about what happened with me didn't matter. She hated me. And I felt betrayed by her."

"I don't understand why your friends weren't there for you. It must have been so horrible going through that."

"Because they weren't really my friends. They liked my title and my fame, but they didn't like me. It was all a lie." She reaches for the water, gulping it down. "That was when I decided friends were a waste of time. I could only rely on my family and myself. I dropped out of the public eye and focused on the real things in life. I pushed everyone away. I figured if everyone hated me, I wouldn't have to like them." She smiles to herself. "Then, years later, when I thought I was happy by myself, Jonathan came along, and as much as I tried not to fall for him, I couldn't help it. I had no choice in the matter."

"He's crazy about you."

"Who knows why? I think he finds my outlandish comments funny."

"He has a great sense of humor."

"So, there you have it, the full story." She's spinning a beer mat around absentmindedly. "The truth is, Annabel broke my heart. And it hurt much more than the breakdown of any romantic love."

"No wonder you don't want her at the wedding. Now I want to throw a drink in her face."

Cordelia laughs. "I'm going to be in so much trouble. I'm sorry for bringing the tone down with that sad story. Not really hen-do material."

"I'm glad you told me."

"I know I don't need to say this, but you won't tell anyone, will you? Not even Jonathan knows about that episode. I need to tell him, but I haven't found the right time. I'm so embarrassed about it."

"You don't need to say it. Mainly because I signed an NDA." I grin. "And it's nothing to be embarrassed about. I'm just glad you're OK now. You should be proud that you got through it all. But your secret is safe with me. I promise I won't say a word."

She holds up her little finger and I laugh, linking it with mine.

"Pinky promise."

CHAPTER TWENTY-EIGHT

I get it now. I get why Cordelia is so difficult, why she never wanted me to be close to her. I can see the full picture of her and Annabel's twisted, messed-up relationship.

After Cordelia told me her story, we talked for a bit longer and then it was time to go home and face the music. She thanked me for a fun night and then, when Joe arrived to pick her up, she gave me a hug.

A *hug*.

It was admittedly very awkward. She's obviously not a very huggy person and I didn't want to overstep the mark and embrace her, like an old friend, so we sort of laughed nervously at first, then did a quick pat on the back before springing apart.

I went home overwhelmed with emotion, thanks to the cheap red wine. Cordelia had confided an extremely painful part of her life that she hadn't even shared with her fiancé. I felt a huge sense of duty toward her now, on top of what I'd already felt as her hired bridesmaid. She finally trusted me.

I thought about it as I got ready for bed, putting the kettle on for some peppermint tea. I hoped she hadn't felt as though she'd *had* to tell me, simply because I'd overheard Annabel's comment on the stairs and witnessed the drama. But Cordelia didn't seem the type of person who would feel she had to do anything for anyone.

I considered that maybe it had been a relief for her to tell someone who hadn't known her for very long. She'd been carrying this sad secret around with her for all those years, having lost all her friends, and unable to make new ones because she was too worried about what they'd think if they knew—or, worse, that they might leak it to the press. She must have assumed everyone would react like Annabel had, repulsed by her actions.

I now hate Annabel as much as I hate Graham Slater.

I climbed into bed with my peppermint tea, wondering what Cordelia was like before the incident. I created a picture of her in my head—fun, carefree, spoiled, headstrong. That was how Beth had known her, enthusing about her love for colorful wildflowers one minute and her penchant for throwing buckets at people who dissed her friends the next. But everything had changed because of a stupid mistake—and instead of the same friends she'd once defended showing up for her, they dropped her the minute she went out of fashion.

By the time I turned off my bedroom light and snuggled down into my duvet, I decided to forgive Lady Cordelia Swann for what she'd put me through and vowed to be the friend she'd been missing. Even if the friendship had a deadline.

Hello, hope you got home all right.
Thanks for this evening, it was a great
spontaneous hen. And thanks for
listening. Means a lot.

"Oh, my God, look at you," Cara says the next day, when I give her an edited version of what happened. "You're so pleased with yourself. It's like you've been on an amazing first-friendship date."

"Is that a thing?" I ask, tying my hair into a messy bun on top of my head.

"Maybe it should be when you get to our age." Cara shrugs. "You could see if you click and whether the friendship is worth pursuing. We don't have time for new friends, what with all the weddings and baby showers crowding our weekends, so people need to be worth it."

"Either way, I think things will be a lot smoother moving forward." I finish sorting my hair, then put my hands on my hips, glancing round at the other women in the room laying out their yoga mats. "Tell me about this class you signed us up to, then. Everyone else in here looks very sporty and like they know what they're doing."

"This is a beginners' yoga and meditation class. You said you wanted to try new things, so I thought this might be fun. Two hours of peace and calm, focusing on you."

"Two hours. Isn't that a bit long for a beginners' class?"

"Not when meditation's involved." Cara breathes in and exhales loudly. "I'm so ready to feel calm on the inside. I've always wanted to get into yoga. You know, be one of those people."

"Are you sure this is a beginners' class?" I ask, watching the woman in front of me stretch up and bend down to touch her toes with ease. "We're the only ones in T-shirts and leggings. Everyone else is in a fancy sports bra."

"Honestly, Sophie, you're so shallow!" She shakes her head at me disapprovingly. "Look past what people are wearing."

"They're all talking as well," I point out, as a couple of them greet each other. "It's like they come here a lot."

"Or they could be friends? Stop worrying," she says, looking a little unsure. "Don't you trust me? This is a beginners' class. I checked. Have a little faith."

The instructor enters the room and everyone spaces their mats, sitting on them cross-legged to face her.

"Welcome to the advanced yoga and meditation course today," the instructor says, in a calming voice. "Let us begin."

"Oh," Cara breathes. "Fuck it."

⌐━━━━━┚

"Are you almost ready?" Carolyn calls from her sitting room. "Sorry, I don't mean to rush you, I'm so excited!"

"Just a minute!" I reply, placing the long-haired mask over my head.

I stand in front of the mirror in the bedroom of her Holland Park flat. I laugh, tipping my head back and steadying the mask before it goes flying off. This may be the best I've ever looked.

"Coming out now!" I announce, swinging open the door and flouncing into the sitting room.

Carolyn squeals with delight, clapping eagerly.

"You look *amazing!*" she claims, her eyes tearing up. "The best Chewbacca *ever!*"

"Do you think?" I ask, giving her a twirl, my voice muffled by the mask. "This costume is very realistic."

"I can't tell you how much I love it," she says, fanning her eyes with her hands. "You look perfect. Just perfect. How does it feel? It's not too heavy or anything?"

"It's surprisingly comfortable," I confirm, moving about in the hairy bodysuit, swinging my hips to show her the flexibility of the costume.

Carolyn gives her high-pitched, slightly irritating giggle, and I realize I must look ridiculous, Chewbacca wiggling about in her sitting room.

"Shall I practice holding a bouquet?" I ask, holding up my Wookiee-gloved hands. "The fingers are slightly too long, so it might be tricky. I can sort that, though, before the big day."

"Good idea!" she says, scurrying across the room and disappearing from my vision. The eyeholes of the mask are quite restrictive, especially since they're surrounded by tufts of hair.

"Here you go!" she says, suddenly in front of me and making me jump. She's clutching a bunch of pens held together with a thin elastic hair tie. "Sorry, I don't have any flowers in the house, but these are sort of like stems."

She transfers them into my giant hands and I hold them tightly, moving slowly around the room as though I'm walking down the aisle.

"How does it feel?" she asks.

"Fabulous," I enthuse, handing the pens back to her. "Holding the flowers won't be a problem."

"Now, no pressure at all," she begins gingerly, "but how are you getting on with the famous Chewbacca roar? As I say, no pressure. You've got loads of time to practice. But we've been talking about it, and we think it would be so great if when we're pronounced husband and wife you do the roar."

"Sounds great! Gosh, better make sure it's perfect."

"I'm sure you'll do a fabulous job."

"I've been practicing a little at home. There's a Chewbacca Sound Tutorial on YouTube, so I've been learning from that and having a try every now and then. But it's very early days and I've got a long way to go."

She looks at me expectantly. "Any chance I can hear what you've got so far?"

"Oh, I don't know," I say, shuffling my hairy feet. "It's probably not very good."

"I'm sure it's great," she encourages.

"OK. Well, the first step is to get the tongue roll," I explain, enjoying the opportunity to fill her in on what I've been learning. "And then you push the back of your tongue to the roof of your mouth, relax the jaw, and then you get the right note, and the trick is to make the sound clear at first, then lead into the tongue roll, so it has that kind of trill at the end."

"Wow," she says, wide-eyed. "You've done your research."

"Are you ready?" I clear my throat and then, feeling weirdly nervous in front of a diehard *Star Wars* fan, I tip my head back and give it my best shot. "*RWWWAGGGGHHHHH!*"

Carolyn gasps and then screams in my face, but thankfully it's a really happy scream and not a you're-going-to-ruin-my-wedding-dream scream.

"*That was awesome!*" she yells, giving me a high-five. "How can I ever thank you? I feel so emotional! You're really capturing the spirit of Chewie!"

I steady the mask on my head as it tilts. "Really?"

"Yes! And you know what?"

"What?"

She takes one of my Wookiee paws and clasps it with both her hands. "You have so many Chewbacca qualities, Sophie. You really do."

"Oh, cool. Thanks!"

My phone, sitting on her coffee table, starts vibrating with a message. Then another. And another. A stream of messages comes through.

"Hang on," I say, shuffling across the floor to the table. "Let me check these."

I try picking up my phone, but it's hard in the costume, so Carolyn kindly picks it up for me. I tell her the passcode so she can unlock it and then she clicks on the conversation and places the phone in my hand.

"I'm going to call Darren," she says excitedly, rushing to the other side of the room. "He's going to *die* when I tell him how amazing you are."

But I'm hardly listening, because I'm reading the stream of messages from Cordelia.

EMERGENCY!!
Where are you?
Can you come here now?
[Location pin drop]
Hello?
Hello?!
Sophie
Sophie, can you come now
NOW SOPHIE!!!
This is important!
I need you!!
EMERGENCY!!!!!!
Please come!!!

"Carolyn, I've got to go," I say, my breath catching in my throat. Thank goodness I'm in West London: she's in Notting Hill, not far at all. "There's been an emergency!"

Carolyn pauses her conversation with Darren, looking over, stunned. "Everything OK?"

"I'm sorry, I have to run!"

Rushing into the bedroom, I shove my clothes into my bag and sling it over my shoulder.

"I hope everything's OK!" Carolyn says, full of concern as I race out of the front door. "Careful with the costume!"

Ignoring the strange looks, the pointing, the laughing, and someone yelling, "Run, Chewie, run!," I leg it down Holland Park Avenue toward Notting Hill.

Pausing to catch my breath at a street corner, I pull off the mask and take the turn according to the map, Chewie's head now tucked under my arm. I reach Cordelia's pin location, huffing and puffing, with a whole new respect for those who choose to run marathons in costume. Without looking up to see what establishment I'm entering, I push open the door and step into a posh boutique.

Cordelia is sitting in a plush velvet chair holding a floral china cup and saucer while a shop assistant holds up what looks like a blush pink satin bridesmaid dress. They turn their heads to look at me as I burst through the door.

"Oh, my God!" Cordelia gasps, her mouth dropping open.

The shop assistant looks horrified and begins apologizing to her, "I'm so sorry, Lady Cordelia, how embarrassing," and starts shooing me out. "This is a private appointment!"

"Wait!" Cordelia says, before she can kick me out onto the street. "That's my bridesmaid!"

The assistant freezes, staring at me, unsure what to do. She's at risk now of having insulted Lady Cordelia's friend, but I'm not sure she can quite bring herself to welcome a Wookiee into the shop.

Cordelia is cackling loudly now. She stands up, walking over and pointing at my costume. "W-what are you *wearing?*" she manages, between bursts of uncontrollable laughter. "You look like Bigfoot!"

"You said it was an emergency!" I cry, my cheeks burning, sweaty strands of hair plastered across my forehead.

She shrieks with laughter, bent double, having the time of her bloody life. "Why are you dressing up as a yeti?"

"I'm not a yeti. I'm Chewbacca," I explain, holding up the head for her to see properly.

"What's a Chew-barka?" she asks, sniggering.

"It's not Chewbarka," I correct grumpily, exaggerating her posh pronunciation. "Chewbacca!"

"From *Star Wars*," the shop assistant notes.

"Correct. Thank you," I say politely, and round furiously on Cordelia. "You sent me those messages saying it was an emergency and you needed me straightaway! I was in the middle of trying on a bridesmaid outfit in Holland Park for a *Star Wars*–themed wedding! Hence my current state."

"Did you run here? Wearing that?" Cordelia wipes the tears from her cheeks. "So many people must have seen you! This is *hilarious!*"

"Cordelia!" I practically yell. "You said it was an emergency! I thought there was a crisis!"

"There is a crisis," she says defensively, the shop assistant nodding in agreement. "Show her, Beryl."

Beryl clacks away from us across the wooden flooring and selects two gowns from the rail, one in navy blue and the other in blush pink, the one I saw when I rushed in. She returns, holding them up, one in each hand.

"I love this style," Cordelia explains, stroking the satin material. "I think it would suit your figure nicely. But they only have it in these two colors and it doesn't go with the theme. The navy isn't quite right and you know I'm not one for blush pink. I'm thinking a deep, rich red, you know, to go with the flowers and the time of year. What do you think?"

I stare at her. "This was the *emergency*?"

"I didn't expect you to run here dressed as Bigfoot," she says. "Although I have to say I'm very impressed with your dedication to me as a bridesmaid."

"Yes," Beryl says, nodding, still holding the dresses. "It's very sweet. Would you like me to fetch you a glass of water?"

"Thank you, Beryl." I wheeze, clutching the stitch in my side. "That would be lovely."

She places the dresses back on the rail and scampers through a door at the back of the shop.

Cordelia starts giggling again.

"It's not funny," I tell her. "I was really worried! I thought something bad might have happened!"

"Why didn't you call?"

"I didn't have time! I was too busy running here! To you! Because you said it was an emergency!"

"I admit my messages were a bit over-the-top, but I really was panicking," she argues. "The wedding is less than two weeks away and I remembered I hadn't chosen a dress for you."

"Here we are," Beryl says, coming over with a glass of water. "Why don't you sit down? Cool off a bit."

"Would you mind if I change my clothes, Beryl?" I ask, nodding toward the changing cubicle in the corner. "I'm feeling a little overheated in all this fur."

"Of course," she says brightly. "And I have good news for you both! I've just had an email from a customer canceling her reservation of *this* dress." She runs to the office at the back again, and reappears moments later holding up a similar satin dress to the others, but in a deep, rich red.

"After all that," Beryl says, as I glare at Cordelia. "Emergency over!"

Are you free to join us for dinner tonight?
It's an emergency!
JOKING!
Too soon?

        Hilarious

It was funny
Everyone is so annoyed I didn't film it or take any pictures

        What do you mean "everyone"?
        Who did you tell???

Just Jonathan!
And also Mum

And Dad

Then Tom

And my yoga instructor

And my masseuse

But that's it!

Oh, wait, also my hairdresser

They think it's funny!

Dad actually snorted

He said you remind him more of R2-D2

Whatever that is

So are you free for dinner?

No

Tom's cooking

He's TERRIBLE at cooking

The worst

Usually it's completely inedible

It will be fun

I have dinner plans

With your fellow yetis?

WOOKIEES.

Chewbacca is a WOOKIEE

Invite the Wookiees, too, then

It will be quite the party

OK, fine, I'm asking you to join us for dinner as my

bridesmaid

It's my request as the bride

This is like a pre-wedding dinner before we go to

Dashwell

It's going to be crazy busy there

So, this is like a nice, chilled, family get-together

You can't say no to a request like that, can you?
Isn't part of your pitch that you ALWAYS put the
bride first?
Isn't it your job to come to pre-wedding dinners if the
bride asks?

> You are very sly

I know
I'm a manipulative bitch
Thought you already knew that
Sooooo, is that a yes?

> All right
> But no Wookiee banter

Pinky promise

> What time do I have to be where?

At Mum and Dad's for 7 p.m.
Make sure you eat before you come

CHAPTER TWENTY-NINE

I would like to give a toast," Lord Meade announces, standing up and raising his glass.

Cordelia and Tom groan, while Lady Meade smiles graciously at her husband. Jonathan gives an enthusiastic "Hear, hear" even though Lord Meade hasn't said anything yet.

"First, to the cook, Thomas," he begins, as there's a ripple of laughter across the table at Tom's expense. "What a success! We were all worried, but the starter of mozzarella and tomato was well presented, the mushroom risotto was edible, and the pudding, a shop-bought lemon tart, was the best of the lot. A lovely evening, thank you, Tom."

Tom bows his head as we all cheer. He catches my eye across the table and smiles bashfully. At least, I think it's bashfully. It seems bashful.

Whatever. He's adorable.

"Next, to my beautiful wife, for all the hard work she's done for the wedding, not to mention Christmas at Dashwell. I've never been so terrified of her in my life! She's bulldozing through that job list, taking no prisoners! Well done, darling. And, of course, to Jonathan and Cordelia. The big day approaches. Don't panic! I've been working on the speech and I promise I won't embarrass you. Too much. In all seriousness, Jonathan, you're already part of the family but we're looking forward to making it official."

"Still time to back out," Tom mumbles, earning him a glare from Cordelia.

"And, last, to Emily," Lord Meade says, everyone's eyes on me.

I blush, hating the attention. Normally, when a bride's parent mentions me by whatever name and character I'm playing, I hold my chin up, smile, and accept the thank-yous graciously, no hint of guilt, simply part of the performance.

But it's different with this family. This mad, complex, dramatic, ridiculous, wonderful family.

"Emily, I don't know why Cordelia's been hiding you away, but I'm delighted that the wedding has forced her to share you with us, too."

Jonathan interrupts with another hearty "Hear, hear!"

"It's been a busy time with all this wedding nonsense—"

"Thanks, Dad!"

"Sorry, Cordelia, not 'nonsense,' you know what I mean. It's been a busy time and I know that Cordelia has been able to lean on you, and that is the sign of a true friend. Not many people would run through Notting Hill dressed as Chewbacca to make it to a bridesmaid-dress appointment on time." He pauses for laughter, while I bury my head in my hands. "You weren't here last night, Emily, but your ears must have been burning. Cordelia was saying how lucky she was to have you."

I look up at her in shock, unable to hide my true reaction.

"I know." Lord Meade chortles. "I think that's the nicest thing she's ever said about anyone. Including Jonathan."

"All right, wrap it up, Dad," Cordelia instructs, before pointing at him and motioning a drinking action to Lady Meade.

"To conclude, I would like to toast to us, to family. Exciting times ahead! Cheers!"

Chair legs scrape backward as we all stand up, clinking glasses. The formality of dinner over, Lord Meade directs us all into the

312 ••• KATY BIRCHALL

sitting room but, as much as I want to, I feel I can't stay. While the others drift from the kitchen, I find my coat in the hall cupboard, reaching into the pocket for my phone to order an Uber.

"You all right?" Cordelia says, behind me, making me jump.

"Yes, thanks. I should be getting home. Lots of work to be getting on with. Thanks, though," I add, getting the app up on my phone and requesting a car. "It's been a really lovely evening."

"Dad's always enjoyed giving a speech," she says, leaning on the banister. "Even when it's just the two of us, he likes to round off the meal with a toast."

"It's sweet. It was really nice what he said. And, you know, what he said you said."

"It wasn't as smushy in the original context."

"Did you say 'smushy'?"

"You know what I mean."

"You said 'smushy'!"

"Why is that a big deal?"

"Because you got annoyed when I used the word 'magical.' 'Smushy' is even worse. It's such a non-Cordelia thing to say."

"How would you know? Maybe I say 'smushy' all the time."

"Do you say 'smushy' all the time?"

"Is your Uber here yet?"

I smile, checking my phone. "A few minutes away. I should say goodbye."

She nods, gesturing for me to go ahead of her back down the hall and into the sitting room to announce my departure. There's a big rumpus about my going so soon and Jonathan tries to persuade me to stay, with the promise of a night of silly board games ahead, while Lord Meade suggests I stay at least for coffee, but I stand my ground.

"See you at Dashwell, Emily." Cordelia grins. "Merry Christmas and all that."

"Merry Christmas!"

"I'll show you out," Tom says suddenly. "Make sure you're not waiting around in the cold for your Uber."

"Thanks," I say, my heart fluttering as he hands me my coat.

He leaves the door on the latch, then comes down the front steps with me, his hands in his trouser pockets.

"You should go back in," I say, wrapping my coat around me. "The Uber is just around the corner and you're not wearing a jacket! It's freezing."

"I wanted to ask you something," he begins, shifting his weight from one foot to the other. "I wondered whether you'd like to go for a drink. With me, I mean. After Christmas. And the wedding. Basically, in the new year. Yeah. Sorry."

I'm so taken aback, I don't say anything straightaway, staring up at him, a rabbit caught in headlights.

"Look," he continues, "I only asked Mona to the Christmas party because Mum told me you were coming and I thought you might be there with George. But I felt like such an idiot because I didn't want to spend time with anyone else."

"Oh."

"Don't feel awkward if you don't want to go for a drink. I get it. It's quite soon after George and stuff. But it's just been really nice getting to know you. I like being with you. So, yeah, thought I'd ask."

No. I'm sorry, Tom, but I can't go for a drink with you, because you think my name is Emily Taylor and that I've known Cordelia for a few years. You have no idea who I am. And it really sucks because I like you. A lot. But I can't go for a drink with you because that would be unfair. It would be a lie.

I'm so sorry, Tom, but as your sister's friend and with so much going on with the wedding, I think it would be inappropriate.

I'm so sorry, Tom, but it's too soon after George. I hope we can still be friends.

That's the answer. He gave you the perfect out. *That's the answer.*

Say it. Say no.

"Yeah. I'd love to. That sounds fun."

His face lights up. "Great!"

I blush, my eyes searching his.

He's not sure at first, faltering slightly as he brings his hand up to brush his fingers so gently along my cheekbone that I can barely feel them, but a jolt goes through me all the same. As his eyes flicker across my face, trying to read my expression, I lift my chin purposefully and glance down at his lips before meeting his eyes again. We kiss, soft at first and then harder as he pulls me closer, his hands sliding down my back, until I pull away slightly, coming up for air, unable to stop smiling.

"I . . . I have to go," I say quietly.

"Merry Christmas, Emily," he says, our foreheads touching, the crinkles forming around his eyes from his wide grin.

"Merry Christmas."

He steps back and I turn in a mad daze, walking toward the waiting Uber in the middle of the road, its hazard lights flashing, the driver yawning at the wheel. Tom stands on the pavement, watching the car pull away before he heads up the steps and goes back into the house.

I slump back in my seat and close my eyes.

Things just got a lot more complicated.

The adrenaline from the kiss keeps me lying awake. I can't stop thinking about him. How he smelled. His eyes. His warm body pressed against mine in the cold. I feel excited and stupidly giddy, rolling over in bed from one side to the other, fluffing my pillow, tucking my duvet under my chin, as though that will make the slightest difference. But then a wave of fear hits me. The sound of his voice as he called me *Emily*, so affectionate.

How could I let this happen? I stare at the ceiling, the back of my hand resting on my forehead, like an actress from the Shakespearean stage showing despair.

After the wedding, I'll have to tell him. I can't go on a date with him as Emily. I'll have to sit him down and explain everything, tell him who I really am, hope he understands. And I can only do that if I get permission from Cordelia and Lady Meade. They didn't want him to know—they didn't want anyone to know. I signed an NDA, for goodness' sake.

Why did I agree to a date? All I had to do was say no.

Thanks to my busy, agitated brain and unbearably fast-thudding heart, it takes me ages to get to sleep, and when my alarm goes off in the morning, I'm sure I've only managed a couple of hours. I drag myself groggily to the bathroom and huff at my reflection, my eyes puffy, my hair tangled from the restless night.

Once I'm showered and dressed, I try to push Tom from my mind and focus on work, going through my emails and checking I'm on schedule for my other weddings. Every now and then I catch myself smiling, lost in the memory of the night before.

I've been standing in the kitchen dreamily stirring my coffee for about five minutes when my phone rings, Lady Meade's name flashing up.

"Good morning, Lady Meade," I say brightly, picking up. "How is the journey to Dashwell? Hope the traffic hasn't been too bad so far."

"We're still in London," she says matter-of-factly. "We need you to come round to talk. There's been an emergency."

Something in her voice is off. Her words are sharp, no hint of warmth.

"Everything all right?"

"Please get here as soon as possible. And I would bring a scarf or sunglasses, something to cover your face."

She hangs up. No goodbye, no thank-you, no sense of acquaintance. Formal, cutting, cold. I'm rattled by the swift conversation and its execution. Why on earth would she want me to cover my face? As I scramble around the flat, gathering my things, dread seeps through me that maybe someone in their circle has worked out who I really am. Maybe Annabel, looking for revenge on Cordelia after the Christmas party, has discovered the truth and is threatening to tell.

I swallow the bile that's risen into my throat, and my fingers tremble as I pick up my keys from the coffee table, head out of the door, and lock it behind me.

Am I about to be fired?

I've never been fired before. I've barely been in trouble before. I'm not the sort of person who breaks rules and gets fired. I take a lot of pride in doing a job well. This is unfamiliar territory for me.

I consider ordering an Uber, but start walking toward the tube. With London traffic, it will be quicker. The platform is busy, and when the train arrives, it's packed. I hate rush hour. I find myself pressed up against someone's backpack, trying not to shudder too obviously every time the person squished in behind me breathes on my neck. I'm so distracted, sick with worry about what I'm heading toward, that I don't notice when we get to a popular stop and everyone shuffles around the carriage as people jostle each other to get off. I'm in the way, and as a woman barges past me to get off, she tuts loudly, muttering something under her breath about "selfish passengers."

"Sorry," I say hurriedly, when what I want to say is *Give me a fucking break, lady! I'm about to be fired.*

I keep telling myself it's going to be OK. People have been fired before: I'm not the only one. If they can handle it, so can I.

Everyone fails sometimes. I've covered my tracks as best I could, and if Annabel has worked out who I am, it's not entirely my fault.

By the time I get to Grosvenor Crescent, it feels like it's taken hours. And I understand now why Lady Meade warned me to cover my face. Reporters are *everywhere*. Oh, shit. Were paparazzi lurking around the house last night?

Did someone get a photo of *me and Tom*?

I think I'm about to be sick. How could I be so *stupid*? We kissed out in the open! Right here in the street! Anyone could have seen us! This is all my fault. *Why* didn't I check the celeb news on my way here? Then I'd have some idea of how much they know! I've been so worried about being fired that I was too distracted for even a cursory google.

I tentatively approach the crowd buzzing around their front door, careful not to draw attention to myself. I'm wearing an old Wimbledon cap that Mum bought me as a souvenir when we got Centre Court tickets a few years ago, and I've got a long, heavy scarf wrapped around my neck and mouth. I slip on sunglasses as I nudge my way toward the door, deciding that anyone wearing sunglasses in winter might be a bit suspect so best to leave it to the last minute.

If the scenario weren't so serious, my getup would be hilarious.

As soon as I start making my way up the steps, the reporters leap into action. Flashes go off, microphones are shoved into my face, and everyone starts yelling at me, asking who I am, why I'm there. I clutch my scarf around my face to make sure it doesn't fall even a tiny bit, and as I lift my hand to knock on the door, it swings open. I hurry in, tripping over the doorstep because I can't really see anything, and the door slams behind me. I turn to see Lady Meade standing behind the door, stern creases on her forehead. The house is jarringly silent in comparison with the chaos outside the door.

"Good morning, Lady Meade," I say, taking off my hat and sunglasses, then unraveling my scarf.

She nods curtly in acknowledgment, holding out her hand for my coat. I undo the buttons, let it slide off and give it to her. As she hangs it in the cupboard, I swallow the saliva that's built up in my mouth from nerves.

"Come through to the sitting room, please," she instructs, leading the way, her Jimmy Choo heels clip-clopping across the polished floor.

I come into the room behind her and start. We're not alone. Lord Meade, Cordelia, and Tom are in there. Lord Meade is leaning against the mantelpiece above the extravagant fireplace, one hand massaging his temples. Tom is standing by the window, arms folded, eyes to the floor. Cordelia is sitting in the middle of the sofa.

Her skin is splodged, her eyes are red and swollen. She's been crying. She's hugging her knees to her chest. She looks so small and vulnerable, like a child.

"Cordelia," I say quietly, upset by her state, not sure what to do.

"I assume you've seen the news," Lady Meade says, turning to face me. Lord Meade won't even look at me.

"No," I say truthfully. "What's happened?"

In response, she types something into her phone, waiting for the search results to appear. The room remains silent. My eyes flicker to Tom, but his are empty, fixed on the floor.

I close my eyes in resignation. A journalist must have seen us. There must have been a photographer lurking somewhere, behind the parked cars on the other side of the road maybe, waiting patiently for a money shot, for one of the famous Meade family to make a mistake. And they got it, all right. They got the bridesmaid making out with the brother.

Lady Meade approaches me, the phone held out so I can see the headlines up on the screen.

THE SWANN SCANDAL!

How a family covered up the mistakes of drug-obsessed wild child, Lady Cordelia

ARISTOCAT-FIGHT!

New claims that former best friends Lady Cordelia and Lady Annabel fell out over Lady Cordelia's alleged drug addiction and the night she took it too far

LADY CORDELIA DRUG DRAMA!

The truth behind the socialite's disappearance from the limelight

My stomach drops. I'm so horrified, I can't speak. I stare at the phone, reading the headlines over and over. And then it dawns on me why they wanted me to come over. Why they won't look me in the eye. I know what they're thinking before Lady Meade says it.

"We need to know who you told," she says calmly.

"I didn't tell anyone," I say softly at first, then raise my voice, angry and hurt that they can possibly think this of me. "I didn't tell *anyone*."

"It had to be you," Cordelia says weakly. "It had to be."

"Cordelia, I didn't tell a soul! I would never do that to you! I don't know how they found out but, I swear, I did not tell anyone. It must say who they got this information from," I reason, my voice shaking at the injustice of it all. "It has to say in the articles who—"

"It says a source close to Lady Cordelia," Lady Meade informs me.

"It wasn't me!"

"It can't have been anyone else!" Cordelia cries, standing up to face me, her eyes bloodshot, a tear rolling down her face as the betrayal clouds her brain. "No one else knows!"

"Annabel knows," I croak, desperately trying to think. "Maybe one of her family—"

"Why would they tell now? After all this time of keeping it a secret?"

"Ned would never allow it," Lord Meade growls, shaking his head. "It wasn't them."

"I did not tell anyone," I say firmly, clenching my fists. "Cordelia, you can't think that I—"

"Funny how I tell you and then a few days later it's splashed everywhere across the press." She runs a hand through her hair, her eyes wild with chaos. "God, I'm so stupid! I'm so stupid to have trusted you! I knew this would happen! It always does."

"Cordelia!" I plead, stepping toward her, prompting her to recoil from me. "I swear I didn't tell anyone! This wasn't me! You have to believe me!"

"Why should I? Why should I believe *you*?"

"Because you know I would never do that!"

"I thought we were friends," she says quietly, and for a second her temper's vanished and all that's left is her hurt.

"We are. We are friends."

She shakes her head. "Jonathan won't talk to me. He's walked out and I don't know where he is. He won't pick up the phone. He told me he couldn't even look at me right now."

"Please—"

"He said that if I'd kept such a big secret from him so easily, how could he trust me? How could he claim to know me when he had no idea about such a momentous event in my life?" She looks up at me, her lip quivering. "He was so angry."

"He'll understand," I say gently, attempting to comfort her. "He'll need time, but he'll understand. Once he's calmed down—"

"It's all your fault," she spits, her words full of venom. "I've lost him and it's all because of you." She looks me up and down, repulsed. "There I was, thinking you were a timid wallflower who never put a foot out of place. Who knew you had it in you, eh?"

"You have to listen—you have to believe me," I say desperately, appealing now to the other members of the family. "I wouldn't do this to you! I didn't tell anyone."

"I don't think you did it," Tom says, offering me some hope, and I'm so grateful I could run over and kiss him (although that would definitely make everything worse). "I believe you."

"Oh, Tom!" Cordelia laughs, throwing her head back. "You're so *stupid*. Love really is blind."

"I know you're upset, Cordelia," he says, blushing and holding up his hands as if surrendering to the truth, "but we know Emily. Do you really think she's capable of this? She's your bridesmaid!"

"Her name's not Emily," Cordelia says coldly, her eyes meeting mine. "Her name is Sophie."

No. Please don't do this. Please, not now. Not like this.

"Cordelia," I warn, but it's too late.

"She's not my friend," Cordelia states. "She's a professional bridesmaid. Mum hired her to help me organize the wedding. Her name isn't Emily Taylor, it's Sophie Breeze. She makes a living pretending to be the best friend of brides who think they need one. Everything you think you know about her is a lie. It's all completely made up." She turns to Tom, and twists the knife in as far as possible. "You don't know her at all. You don't know anything about her."

Stunned silence descends upon the sitting room. Tom looks bewildered, and his eyebrows knit in confusion and shock. I'm too scared to speak, frantically seeking the words that will make this better somehow, but coming up with nothing.

Lord Meade straightens. "What? You're not Emily?"

His wife exhales, her shoulders slumping for the first time ever as she sinks into a chair. I look to her for guidance, but she seems lost, too, a hand placed over her mouth.

"Go on," Cordelia pushes angrily. "Tell them the truth. Your NDA is void now."

"No, I'm not Emily," I eventually manage to say. "My name is Sophie."

"You were *hired* to be a bridesmaid?" Lord Meade asks, aghast at this revelation.

I nod.

"So, you were lying," Tom says, his voice hollow. "About everything."

"No, not everything," I reply, not sure who to direct my justification to.

I want to tell him that the feelings were all real, the great, easy conversation was all real, it was my name and career that wasn't. But at the same time, I need to get Cordelia to understand that I would never spill her secrets because the friendship wasn't a lie, either.

"Don't you think I should have been consulted on this?" Lord Meade asks his wife, looking more puzzled than angry. "I genuinely thought she was a friend of Cordelia's, and now it turns out it was a complete stranger that I invited to my house."

"I thought Cordelia needed the support, Nicholas," Lady Meade replies wearily, waving her hand, not prepared to go into detail. "Sophie is a professional—she does this sort of thing all the time. We did a full background check and she signed an NDA."

Bloody hell. That's the first time I've heard about the background check. I'm not sure why I'm surprised: of course a family as prominent as this one would need to check up on someone before they let them into their inner circle, but still, I feel irritated by it. Annoyed that they didn't trust me right from the off. I could have told them anything they needed to know. I think I give off the vibe of a very sensible, trustworthy person.

Although, from the current situation, clearly I'm wrong.

"I appreciate that this is all a lot to take in," I begin, glancing to Tom, who has gone from shocked to furious, his jaw clenched as he stares at the carpet as though he's trying to burn a hole right through it. "But the most important thing for you all to know is that I did not leak this story. Cordelia, *I didn't leak this story.* I haven't told a soul. No one. Whoever did this, it wasn't me."

I look her right in the eye, willing her to believe me. And it's there, I can see it in her face: she *wants* to believe me. There's a flash of doubt, a tiny flicker of puzzlement as she wonders who else it could have been. But the timing fits and her previous experience of an untrustworthy friend wins out.

"I never want to see you again," she concludes.

She storms past me through the door and runs up the stairs, before we hear her bedroom door slam. Lady Meade sighs, defeated.

"I think you should leave, Emily or Sophie, or whatever your name is," Lord Meade says gravely. "If you are the leak, I suggest you own up sooner rather than later."

"Lord Meade, please! You can't think it was me! If you don't trust my character, then at least think about the logic. What would I possibly have gained from it?"

"Money," he replies, his brow furrowed. "It's always down to money."

"I would never do that."

"We don't know what you would do," Tom speaks up. "We don't know you."

"Tom—"

"Sophie, it's time for you to leave," Lady Meade says, pushing herself up from the chair and gesturing to the door. "I'm sure this won't come as a shock, but I'm afraid we're going to have to let you go. Your contract to us and to Cordelia is over. We can sort final details another time. If you want to go to the press and tell them your story, you can, I suppose, although I hope you will have some compassion and decide against it."

"I would never go to the press, NDA or no NDA," I argue, through gritted teeth. "I wouldn't do that to anyone."

"You can show yourself out," Lord Meade instructs, putting an end to the conversation.

I'm too numb to find the words to protest. I can't do anything else. I have no evidence to prove I did not tell. And, in their eyes, I'm the only person capable of this crime. I get my coat, my hands shaking, and wrap my scarf back round my face, before shoving on my cap and sunglasses. I open the door and am immediately blinded by all the camera flashes.

It slams behind me. I'm on my own.

CHAPTER THIRTY

I push my way through the reporters, my brain whirring as I try to make sense of what just happened. They think I leaked the story to the press. *Me.* How could anyone possibly think that I could do something so cruel?

And Tom's face. He was so disappointed, so furious with me. What must he think of me now? I'm such an idiot for considering it might somehow work out between us.

I manage to flag down a taxi at the end of the road, shaking off the few reporters who stuck with me that long, and ask the driver to drop me at the tube station.

This is a disaster. A HUGE disaster.

And not just for me. For Cordelia, for Jonathan, for the whole family. The wedding will be overshadowed by these headlines, dredging up the past, splashing about these horrible memories as though no one involved has any feelings at all. I feel sick for them, for what they'll be coping with over the next few days, wishing I could make it go away.

But there's nothing I can do. I can't stop the journalists writing the stories. I have no idea who the source is because, let's face it, the most viable suspect is me. And I can't change the past. I can't protect Cordelia from what's already happened.

The only thing I could do was be there for her as her friend, and now I can't even do that.

I've never felt so helpless. My whole life revolves around

finding solutions. When a bride or groom needs help, I'm there to sort it. That's *what I do*.

But this time I have simply to fade away, leave them to cope alone. In their minds, after all, I'm the one who created the problem.

I pay the taxi and walk into the tube station glumly, trying to find my card to get through the ticket barrier. Rummaging in my bag, I think about Jonathan and how he must be feeling. Betrayed and humiliated, confused as to why Cordelia didn't tell him something so important. I wish I could remind him of how much he means to her—in times of crisis, sometimes you need to hear that from someone else. I hope he comes out of hiding and goes home to her soon. It must be horrible for him to be alone, trying to make sense of this—and worse for her, desperate to comfort him and not knowing where he is.

Hang on. He's *hiding*.

"Excuse me!" a man says gruffly behind me, and I realize I've stopped right at the barrier.

"Sorry, sorry," I mumble, stepping aside and letting him through, too focused on the idea that just popped into my head to worry about the irritable mutters and glares I receive from the queue now filing past.

It's a long shot. He's probably gone to a friend's house, maybe even decided to go back to Norfolk. But if he wanted to be on his own and have a good think over a proper pint . . .

I start running, trying to work out the quickest way to get to Chancery Lane as I race onto the platform.

When I emerge from the tube station at the other end, I jostle past Christmas shoppers and tourists in my haste to get to Ye Olde Mitre. By the time I push through the doors, I'm completely out of breath, wheezing as I burst in from the bitter cold to the cozy warmth of the tiny pub.

He's at the bar, on a stool, hunched over his pint.

I take a moment to sort myself out, wiping the sweat from my forehead and shrugging off my coat. He does a double take as I appear next to him.

"Emily!" he says, looking baffled as I pull over another stool to plonk myself next to him. "What are you doing here?"

"I thought I might find you somewhere you feel hidden," I explain. "And don't worry, I'm alone. I haven't told any of the family where you are."

He nods and waits while I assure the barman I don't want anything.

"How are you doing?" I ask, watching him pick at the corner of a beer mat. "You OK?"

He shrugs. "I've been better."

"Me too."

He looks up at me. "You didn't know either?"

"Actually, I found out a few days ago. And there's a few things I need to tell you, Jonathan. I haven't been honest."

"Apparently you're not the only one." He sighs.

"My name isn't Emily."

"Sorry?"

"My name isn't Emily," I repeat matter-of-factly. "I'm Sophie Breeze. I'm a professional bridesmaid who was hired by Lady Meade to help Cordelia cope with the stress of the wedding. That's why you hadn't heard of or met me before the engagement party."

He blinks at me. When he doesn't say anything, I continue, "I appreciate that it's a lot to—"

"What's a professional bridesmaid?" he interrupts, frowning.

"I'm hired by brides, sometimes couples, in this case the bride's mother, to help them with certain tasks and make sure they can enjoy the process of organizing a wedding. Most of the time I'm hired secretly—the bride doesn't tell anyone that I'm a professional, and together we come up with a believable story and a fake name so that I can play a role, pretend to be a friend or a distant relation."

"You're . . . you're not Emily?"

"No. I'm Sophie."

"A professional bridesmaid," he says slowly.

"That's right."

"Cordelia hired you."

"Technically, her mother hired me. Cordelia didn't love the idea, but she warmed to it eventually. Well, she warmed to me. Anyway, I'm telling you this because the rest of the family know now, so I thought you should, too."

"They didn't know?"

"Just Lady Meade and Cordelia. Her father and Tom knew nothing about it."

"Right. OK." He exhales, swiftly finishing the rest of his pint and gesturing to the barman for another. "That's a lot of new information. It would seem I'm learning quite a bit about my fiancée today."

"Most of my brides don't tell their other halves they've hired me," I say firmly. "It's important to the process. The majority also don't tell their parents. It's preferable that only the bride and I are in on the secret. The fewer people who know, the better I can do my job. It isn't anything to do with trust between the couple."

He snorts, reaching for his fresh pint and taking a large swig before slamming it back down on the bar. "Yeah, well, I'm not sure how much trust exists between me and Cordelia anyway."

"I'm not going to apologize for lying to you, Jonathan," I tell him. "I was doing my job. It's just how it is."

He shrugs, focusing on the beer. "OK."

"OK." I lean forward, forcing him to look at me. "Now, I want to talk to you about Cordelia, and what you've read in the news."

"What's there to talk about? I'm the only one who was kept

in the dark about it. The person marrying her. I'm hardly important."

"You're the most important person in the world to her. And that's why she didn't tell you."

"That doesn't make any sense," he says sadly, shaking his head.

"You know her better than anyone else. I can imagine you're feeling hurt right now, upset that she didn't share this big part of her life. But you have to find a way to step into her shoes for a moment and ask why she would do that."

He doesn't say anything.

"It's never easy to admit something you're ashamed of to someone you love," I say quietly, aware that I'm telling him something he already knows. "You persuade yourself that you'd be disappointing them, and if you don't feel good enough anyway, it's difficult to tell them something you're afraid will break the spell. I don't know about you, but I've definitely been there. It's easy to get caught up in pushing off the truth until the right moment, but the right moment doesn't really exist. Usually, you don't realize that until it's too late."

"Yeah," he says glumly. "I suppose I know what you mean."

"Jonathan, in my line of work, I've honestly come to learn that the cheesiest rubbish people say about love tends to be true. That's why it's been repeated over and over, for centuries, in every song, film, and book. And an absolute classic is that love really is the most important thing we have. Ugh." I make a face and he can't help but smile.

"My point is," I continue, smiling back, "I understand you're hurt she didn't tell you and I'm so sorry you found out in such a horrible way. But she loves how you look at her, what you see in her, and she didn't want that to change. I think that's why she didn't tell you."

He sighs, his shoulders drooping, giving in. "I know."

We sit in silence for a bit.

"Thanks, Sophie," he says eventually, "for coming to find me. I'll go home and talk to her."

"Thanks for talking to *me*." I slide off my stool. "I should go."

"If you don't mind hanging around for a bit while I finish my drink, we could head back to the Meades' house together? We may need your help to . . ." He searches for the right word. ". . . navigate everything over the next few days for the wedding."

"I think it's best I leave you to it." I hesitate, wondering if I should tell him what's going on. He's going to hear about it anyway. It might as well be from me. "Truth be told, I'm the last person they want to see right now."

"Why? Are the others angry that Victoria hired you?"

"Well, that, and they think I leaked the story to the press." Jonathan looks shocked. "Did you?"

"No, I didn't."

"You've told them that?"

"Yes."

"And they don't believe you?"

"The timing doesn't exactly work in my favor. Cordelia told me because she was beginning to trust me, and days later the story comes out. I'm not sure *I* would believe me."

"But you really didn't tell anyone?"

I shake my head. "Not a soul."

"Discretion must be part of your job description."

"It is."

"Nothing in it for you to leak that story to the press."

"Nothing at all. And also . . ." I trail off.

"Yes?"

I look him straight in the eye. "I wouldn't do that to a friend."

He nods in understanding. "I believe you. She didn't tell anyone else when she told you?"

"No. I was the only one there. It was just the two of us sitting at the bar, no one else could . . . Oh, my God."

I gasp as it dawns on me.

I *wasn't* the only one who heard her story that night. We weren't alone.

"What?" Jonathan asks anxiously, reading my shocked expression. "What is it?"

"I have to go," I tell him, grabbing my handbag. "Good luck with everything!"

"Wait, Sophie! Where are you going? Is everything all right?"

But I don't have time to stop and explain. I'm already out of the door and running back toward the tube.

~~~

I push open the heavy door of the Duck with such force that it bangs loudly against the wall, causing the few customers in there to jump and look up at me in confusion.

I march across the pub, more determined than I've ever been in my life.

The same guy is lounging around behind the bar. As soon as he looks up and sees my thunderous expression, his eyes grow wide in fear. Good. He should be afraid.

"*You!*" I yell, jabbing my finger at him, leaning over the bar. "You overheard everything she told me that night. You leaked the story to the press! Didn't you? *Didn't you?*"

He holds up his hands, backing into the bottles lined on the shelf behind him. I'm surprised I have the power to intimidate him in any way, but I go with it.

"I—I—"

"*How could you?*" I hiss, my cheeks hot with fury. "Do you have *any* idea what you've done? Do you know how much hurt and pain you've caused?"

I stomp around to flip up the entrance to the bar top, so there's no barrier between us.

"Now, y-you look here. It's not my f-fault!" he stutters, his eyes darting around to the customers, who are curiously watching the drama play out. "She should be more careful! Coming in here and going on about drugs and her ex-boyfriends. Anyone here that night could have told anyone!"

"You are *despicable*," I say, with such venom that he flinches. "If I read one more story in the press about my friend—"

"You can't threaten me," he interrupts, putting his hands on his hips in an attempt to look more confident than he feels. A prominent swallow gives him away. "That family can't touch me. The paper told me so."

"That family wouldn't go near you. They're better than that. And they know you're not worth it." I narrow my eyes at him. *"But I'm not a Swann."*

He gulps again.

"I know who you are now," I remind him. "I know the source of these stories. And if one more story about Cordelia Swann— *one more story*—appears in the media, I'll know *exactly* who's to blame."

To be honest, I'm not sure there's anything I can actually *do* with the knowledge that he's the source—but he appears to be worried, which is as much as I can hope for.

"So," I continue, standing up straight and lifting my chin, "unless you want me to become a very regular customer here at the Duck, I would strongly recommend that you reconsider any future grand plans you may have to spill any other secrets you overhear at this establishment."

I pause, letting my words sink in. He opens his mouth to speak, then thinks better of it.

"What sort of person sells that kind of story to the press?" I ask accusingly, keeping my volume up to make sure the rest of the pub can hear everything. "You have no idea of the damage you've caused, just so you can make a bit of money. Imagine if someone did this to someone you love. You seemed like a nice guy. I am *extremely* disappointed in you."

His eyes fall to the floor.

"You know," I say, in a softer tone, hoping a gentler delivery will really hit home, "Cordelia is a good person, a strong person. She'll move on. She'll forgive herself for what she did. I wonder if you ever will."

With that, I turn on my heel and walk confidently toward the door, all eyes on me as I go, leaving him red-faced and staring at the floor.

Dear Sophie,
These flowers are just a little something to say THANK YOU! Our wedding day was the best day of my life. So much of that was down to you! Thank you for being there every step of the way. I hope it's OK that I now consider you a true friend.
Lots of love, Scarlett xx

PS Let's meet for drinks soon so you can tell me what really happened at the church. Apparently Adam fell into a grave???

CHAPTER THIRTY-ONE

I try to enjoy Christmas. I do everything you're supposed to do at this joyful time of year. I ask Alexa to play Christmas songs while I do the washing-up. I buy cinnamon-spiced coffees any time I leave the house to go anywhere, even though they're too sweet and ridiculously expensive. And I spend the evenings working in front of *Love Actually* and *The Holiday* and some annoyingly enjoyable Netflix Christmas film about an underpaid waitress who, by a strange twist of fate, looks identical to the first female American president, who could really use a few days off, so they secretly switch places and fall in love with each other's colleagues.

I send all my clients a Merry Christmas email and receive a flurry of excited replies about the big year ahead as they prepare for their 2022 weddings. I make a list of everyone I need to contact in the first week of the New Year, people I need to chase, and companies that still need to confirm.

I drink prosecco and buy a box of Quality Street, telling myself I'll take it to Mum and Dad's. It remains unopened for a few hours before I dip in to help myself to all the toffee sticks.

Cara and I visit Jen and the baby, Harry, who has made his grand arrival. I hold him while Jen fills us in on the birth details, Ollie chipping in with his side of events every now and then, but I'm not really listening, because I'm mesmerized by this tiny person. He has such tiny fingernails and a tiny little nose. How is he so small? And he makes little squeaks when he moves and I love holding him but I'm also terrified because he's so small and delicate. Jen affectionately points out that I'm being very quiet today. I tell her it's because I'm in awe of Harry. I leave out the part about feeling sad.

Cara can tell something's up but doesn't push it until we're walking to the tube. We've already gone over how adorable Harry is, how Jen and Ollie are taking to it so well, and how it kind of sucks that he was born around this time because lots of people will give him only one present to cover his birthday and Christmas.

"How is everything?" she asks lightly, pretending it's a casual question.

"Fine, thanks. You?" I reply, pretending to have a casual answer.

"I rang your mum the other day to ask her what she needed us to bring on Christmas Day. She told me you've been avoiding her calls."

"Really? I haven't meant to. I've been busy."

"You look drained."

I smile. "Is that another way of saying I look shit?"

"No, if you looked shit, I'd tell you," she points out, and I have to agree. "You've been working too hard. Are you looking after yourself?"

"Hey, if anyone's working too hard, it's you. Your hours have been nuts recently."

"I'm not the one who's avoiding my mother's phone calls," she says, keeping to the point. "What's going on?"

"Fine. I'll tell you but I don't want you to make it a big deal, OK?"

"OK."

"I got fired by the Miranda Priestly bride."

She tries to hide her shock. "What happened?"

"I won't bore you with details," I say, too tired and hurt to tell her everything just yet, "but they think I did something. I didn't. But they didn't believe me. So, I got fired."

She blows out a stream of air, doing her best not to get riled on my behalf. "After everything you did for her."

I pull down the sides of my beanie so that it covers the tops of my ears. My nose has started running from the cold. "I'm fine," I say. "I'll tell Mum tomorrow when I go home. I've just been a bit out of it."

"All right," Cara says, studying my expression. "I'm here if you need to talk."

"Thanks, but I really am OK."

"What about the brother? You liked the brother. Now that you don't work for Miranda, can you at least ask him out on a date? Silver lining, perhaps?" she says hopefully.

I shake my head, pulling my scarf up over my mouth so when I speak my lips graze against the wool. "He thinks I did the bad thing, too. He hates me. That's over."

I blink back tears, hating myself for getting emotional. Tom and I didn't even go on a date. We kissed once. There's nothing I really lost.

But it feels like I have. It feels like I've lost a lot.

"Your mum thinks it's something to do with Daniel," Cara says, amused.

"What? Why would she think that?" I find myself pleasantly surprised that I haven't thought much about Daniel recently. Maybe bumping into him and meeting Francesca was a strange type of closure. A wake-up call that he'd found someone special, and I couldn't dwell on the past.

"She thinks you're coming to the end of the year and you're

musing over everything that's happened. Him inviting you to his wedding and stuff."

"I hadn't even thought about that. I'm happy for him."

"Yeah. That's what I told her." Cara grins. "And you'll be busy skydiving that day, anyway, so who cares?"

"You shouldn't tease people who just told you they got fired."

"I can see you rocking a parachute. Just saying."

When I get home that night, I put the TV on in the background as I pack some clothes for Mum and Dad's. I ponder over my feelings, miserably acknowledging that, although I'm sad about what might have been with Tom, I'm more cut up about losing Cordelia.

I feel like I'm back at school and the popular girl, whom I've spent all term winning over, doesn't want to sit at my table anymore. I wish I didn't care so much, but I'd put a lot of time and effort into gaining her trust. We'd formed a strange, reluctant friendship that had ended up meaning something to me, whether I wanted it to or not.

As the days go by, I realize how angry I am with her for not trusting me. We haven't known each other very long, but it hurts that she thinks I could betray her like that.

Nothing about my life has really changed. That's how I've been comforting myself. I've still got all my real friends, I've still got my wonderful brides and grooms who do trust me, and it's unlikely this will damage my career. Lady Meade won't splash about what went down because, as long as I don't go to the press with my story, they'll want to keep my role in the wedding a secret outside family ranks.

She won't be recommending me for any other high-society weddings any time soon, like I'd hoped, but that's OK. I don't *need* the kind of money she'd been paying me. I was absolutely fine doing more weddings and earning the same amount. I might hate that the Marquess and Marchioness of Meade, Cordelia and Tom think I'm somebody I'm not, but does that really affect my day-to-day? Does it really matter? Cordelia said I cared too much about what people think. So, I won't care.

I'm fine.

On Christmas Eve, I get myself home to my parents' house in the mindset that I will not let this work hiccup ruin my Christmas. I arrive with a big smile, dump my bags in my old bedroom, and go into full holiday mode, placing my bag of presents under the tree, fishing the board games out from the broom cupboard, where they're stowed for the rest of the year, and declaring I'll make some mulled wine if anyone else would like some. I don't want to give myself any time to wallow.

"It's so lovely to see you, darling," Mum says, throwing her arm round me as I stir the wine in the saucepan. She smells so comforting that I almost start crying there and then. I can't bear to tell her about being fired quite yet. She'll be so lovely about it and tell me that it's their loss, and I know that will set me off. I'll tell her after Christmas, when things are quieter.

"I'm really happy to be home," I manage. I mean it.

She squeezes my shoulders, giving me a kiss on the side of my head, then hurries off to ask Dad to do something or other in preparation for Cara's family coming to lunch tomorrow. He grumbles about having to spend his holiday being ordered around like a servant, then winks at me when Mum's back is turned. He makes me laugh.

You see? I tell myself. *You're fine. Nothing's changed. Why are you letting this affect you so much?*

Christmas Day is a blur of noise and chaos as various members of the family arrive. The morning starts well when we're treated to the wonderful entertainment of Uncle Fred attempting the harmonies of all the hymns at church, and by the end of the service Dad and I are shaking with silent laughter, tears streaming down our cheeks as he belts out "Hark! The Herald Angels Sing" an octave or so too high. No one gets into an argument all day, which is a wonderful surprise, and we listen to the Queen's speech in respectful silence, Dad nodding to everything she says, while Cara makes the annual comment of how amazing she is at her age.

I think I'm being perfectly normal, trying to be helpful and smiling whenever I can, but mums always know.

"You're being very quiet," Mum says, when she catches me alone in the kitchen.

"Am I?"

"You seem sad."

"I'm not sad. I'm great!"

She doesn't buy it, but she leaves it. During the afternoon lull, I check my phone and am disappointed there are no messages. I don't know why I would expect Cordelia or Tom to contact me, but I guess I was hoping the season of goodwill and forgiveness might have seeped in and grabbed hold of their subconscious. As I watch Cara snuggle up to Mike to watch *Paddington 2*, it's hard not to feel so . . . single.

I make the decision to date more next year. I'll put myself out there. I'll be bold and unafraid, go on dates and feel that spark. The one I had with Tom. I'll get that with someone else.

"Count yourself lucky you don't have the fights about where to spend Christmas every year," Cara told me once, when she was preparing to go to Mike's. "His family have the weirdest traditions. You know, they don't do smoked salmon and champagne. What's wrong with them? Everyone knows it's a Christmas-morning thing! Do you know what they do? Olives. What sort of fucked-up person eats olives on Christmas morning?"

But the idea of arguing over whose family to spend time with sounds nice to me. I let myself have a fleeting thought of Tom and me bickering over whether to spend Christmas here or go up to Dashwell, and smile to myself at the notion. Christmas at Dashwell Hall. That would have been something.

The wedding will be something, too.

There's been a lot of noise surrounding Cordelia in the press since that story leaked, and I feel protective of her, uneasy at the idea of her being hounded by photographers asking her questions about that night all those years ago. But their interest has been helpful in some ways—a photo popped up on Twitter of Cordelia and Jonathan laughing together while walking down the Paxton high street yesterday, taken by a nosy local.

They've made up. The wedding is still on. They're happy. That's all that matters.

That's not all that matters, though, is it? You want to be happy. You want to be there for the wedding. You want to be there for your friend.

I tell myself to shut up.

I sleep badly that night, and the next morning I try to give myself a bit of a lie-in, snuggled warmly under my childhood duvet that's much better quality than my current one in London, but I'm too stressed to sleep, so, after ten minutes of trying to clear my mind, I get up.

As well as dating next year, I will also get into meditation and yoga, so that I learn how to make my crazy anxious brain Shut. The. Fuck. Up.

It's just Mum, Dad, and me for the day until I go back, but while I'm brushing my teeth, I text Cara asking if she'd mind popping back here alone for a cup of tea.

"Is everything all right, Sophie?" Mum asks, when Cara pads into the room, having driven here in her slippers.

My growing up so close to Cara's family has meant that we're all completely at home in each other's houses. I always remind Mum of that when she spruces up the house for Christmas, acting as though the Queen herself will be dropping in, but she ignores me.

"Yeah, fine," I say, watching Cara make a beeline for the fridge and have a good rummage to check what's on offer. "Tea, anyone? I'll put the kettle on."

Once we're sitting in the living room, lightly discussing how much fun yesterday was, I decide I might as well get this over with.

"Mum, Dad, you know how I had that super-high-maintenance bride? The one I wanted to quit from, but then decided to work really hard for? She ended up firing me."

Dad lowers his cup of tea, his forehead creased with concern.

"That's awful. How could anyone possibly fire you?" Mum says, and I sense her brain whirring as she works out the best thing to say next. "What happened?"

"They thought I sold a story to the press about her."

"What?" Cara sits up, intrigued. "You didn't tell me what the bad thing you were supposed to have done was."

I shrug. "I've been thinking about it and, to be honest, there's no reason I can't tell you. I'm fired now. The contract has been terminated and I'm under no obligation to keep her identity secret."

"You're going to tell us who she is?" Cara asks.

"Only you three. No one else needs to know, so please keep it to yourselves," I say firmly. "But I've been struggling with this whole . . . thing. And if you know who it is, it would help you to understand why I've been a little more upset about it than I might have been. I know I can trust you."

"Who was it?" Cara asks eagerly, and I don't blame her. The nugget of information about the story in the press means it's someone famous.

"Don't freak out."

"We won't."

"Lady Cordelia Swann."

They stare at me. Mum's mouth has dropped open. Cara is shaking her head in disbelief. Dad is thoughtful, and I smile, knowing he's trying to remember who she is and why he's heard the name.

"You're shitting me," Cara says, receiving a sharp look of disapproval from Mum for swearing. "*Lady Cordelia Swann.*"

"Yep."

"That's who you were bridesmaid for. Miranda Priestly is, in fact, Lady Cordelia Swann?"

"Yes."

"Oh, my God! That's amazing!" Cara shrieks, but then must remember that the reason I'm telling her is because I've been fired, and she goes back to being solemn.

"The story about her doing drugs," Mum says. "They think you leaked that to the press?"

"Yeah, they do."

"That's ridiculous."

"Not in their minds."

"Lady Cordelia Swann," Cara mutters, under her breath. "Holy crap."

"Don't they own that big estate up in Derbyshire? Dashwell Hall?" Dad asks, clicking his fingers.

I confirm that they do and he seems pleased with himself for working out the puzzle all on his own.

"I can't believe that all this time you've been hanging out with Lady Cordelia Swann. And her brother! Lord Dashwell . . ." Her eyes widen. "Ooooh."

"So that's that," I say, exhaling. "I was given the opportunity to be a part of the wedding of the decade and it's over."

"Oh, Sophie," Mum says, with so much feeling that hot tears prickle behind my eyes.

"None of that is your fault," Dad points out. "It's a misunderstanding. They think you did something you didn't."

"I tried to explain that when it all happened but they wouldn't listen. I can sort of see why they would point the finger at me. I was the only new person in their circle who learned anything about Cordelia and her past," I say vaguely, not wanting to confirm whether what the press had said was true. "It couldn't have been worse timing. But I thought . . . I thought Cordelia, at least, knew me better than that. I was wrong. I guess none of it matters now. They're all in Derbyshire. The wedding is New Year's Eve."

"You know what? Good riddance," Mum says, sitting up straight with a fresh batch of energy. "If they think you could do something like that and they're not prepared to see reason, that's their own fault."

"Yeah!" Cara says enthusiastically. "And you hated working for her anyway. She was the biggest Bridezilla *ever*. Remember what she put you through? You don't want to support her on her wedding day. She doesn't deserve you."

"I don't know. All that stuff was a stupid defense mechanism on her part. She was trying to force me to quit because she's afraid to let new people in. Her old friends deserted her, so she didn't think it was safe getting close to anyone. But once she decided to trust me, she was really great to hang out with. She's got a brilliant sense of humor—she'd get on well with you, Cara. She forced me out of my comfort zone, too." I pause, and add quietly, "I'll miss her."

Mum and Cara exchange a look. Dad sits back in the armchair, sipping his tea.

"Anyway," I say, brightening, "I wanted to tell you to get it off my chest. Now, I'm going to move on. I'm snapping out of this horrible mood. Plenty of weddings to keep me busy next year and lots to get excited about."

Cara smiles encouragingly. "You're right. It's going to be a wonderful year. I can sense it. You're much better off. Who needs Cordelia Swann's family?"

"Exactly," I say. "Who needs them?"

CHAPTER THIRTY-TWO

Mum tries to persuade me to stay until after New Year's, but I'm keen to get back to my flat and kick-start my exciting new plans. I'm going to sign up for yoga. I'm going to set up my dating profile. I want to feel positive and fresh and happy.

I'm living my absolute best cliché life, right now.

I head back on the thirtieth and, since I've completely lost track of what day it is, I'm surprised to check my phone and find it's Thursday. Unfortunately, I've also forgotten to delete "Cordelia and Jonathan's wedding" from my calendar. Tomorrow's notification glares up at me.

I let myself have a moment of wondering what they're up to right now. I smile, picturing Dashwell Hall awash with Christmas decorations, no expense spared. I imagine all the lights they must be putting up, the staging for the band in the ballroom, the long dining tables in the banqueting hall. I can hear Lady Mcade's heels echoing across the wooden floorboards as she marches around the house, making sure everything's in order. Tom will have been roped in to help with something and he'll be making dry comments about Cordelia and her regal demands, secretly very proud of his little sister. Jonathan will be in a panic—what still needs to be done? Am I supposed to be doing anything? Goodness, who could have thought there'd be so much to do? I'd better practice my speech for the twenty-eighth time today! I picture Lord Meade hiding in the library, going over documents, pretending he knows what's going on when really his wife is in charge.

Cordelia will be up at the stables. She'll be away from all the madness, having a moment of peace with her horse, the only companion she can really rely on.

I scroll through Cordelia's and my WhatsApp thread. The last messages were her persuading me to come to dinner. It was a "family get-together," she said, and I should be there.

Maybe I could message her. I could tell her the truth. I could tell her I found the real source of the story. Maybe then she'd apologize profusely, beg me to forgive her for accusing me, ask me to get on a train to Derbyshire.

I start typing a message. I delete it. I start typing again. I delete it. I start typing again . . .

FUCK'S SAKE. What's the point? I message Cara instead.

> I need your help

> Is this about the party tomorrow? Because the answer is yes, Mike's hot single colleague is coming and I'm putting strategic mistletoe up everywhere

> What party tomorrow?

> The New Year's Eve party

> What New Year's Eve party?

> Oh bollocks
> I forgot to invite you
> Hey, are you free tomorrow?
> Because we're having a party and you're invited!

> Oh, thanks, I feel really special

In my defense, you were supposed to be at a
wedding

> That's true. I'll forgive you if you help me.
> I need you to tell me I shouldn't message
> Cordelia

OK. You shouldn't message her

> I had wanted to say
> good luck, hope it goes OK, stuff like that.
> It's going to be really overwhelming for
> her and I feel bad that she doesn't have
> a friend there.
> There will be all those fake people at
> her wedding she doesn't like and she
> needs an ally.
> But I shouldn't message her
> Should I?

NO
Obviously don't message her, you crazy person!!
SHE FIRED YOU!
You don't send nice messages to people who fire
you!
THIS IS THE TIME TO BE SASSY

> Right. You're right
> I am sassy
> I should be focusing on myself

Exactly
She's a crazy, horrible person

> She's actually not horrible,
> she's just insecure and doesn't like
> people getting too close

She made you pick up her dry cleaning

        Yeah, but to be fair that wasn't personal

OK, Sophie? You're making this hard.
Stop defending her

        Sorry. Go on

You don't need her, you have enough friends

        Yes! True

And so what her brother was hot?
Loads of guys are hot
And smart and funny
And into you
And own estates in Derbyshire
It's not a big deal that that's finished

        Exactly

Don't message her and don't message him

        You're right. I won't

You didn't do anything wrong, remember?
They're the ones who betrayed YOU

        Yes. They did

So, you won't message her?

        I promise I won't

And we'll see you at the New Year's Eve
party tomorrow night?

        I will bring pink gin

I put my phone down, feeling much better. Cara is *right*. I must stop feeling guilty and worried for Cordelia. I should be livid instead. Technically, they accused me of libel. Technically, I could sue. Maybe I will. Maybe I'll sue.

I start googling "how to sue people who accuse you of selling a story to the press" and then I realize I'm losing my mind.

I close my eyes, throwing my phone away from me across the sofa.

It's a mistake to be on my own today. I should have stayed at home with Mum and Dad. At least I'd have had some company. The flat is so quiet. I can't bring myself to go into the office (CUPBOARD) and do any work. I'm not in the right headspace yet.

I'm cheered by the thought of Cara's party tomorrow. That's something. It'll be fun. Maybe I'll meet someone. Maybe we'll kiss at midnight. I wonder if Tom will kiss anyone at midnight. Oh, my God, he will, won't he? He'll be at a WEDDING on NEW YEAR'S EVE. Everyone kisses at midnight at a wedding on New Year's Eve. It's the most romantic setting to be in. Georgia will be there! She'll be looking to kiss him. He'll be drunk and happy after his little sister's nuptials. She'll look beautiful in her designer dress and towering heels! Why wouldn't he kiss her? I mean, look at her! She's gorgeous! Anyone would kiss her!

I bury my head in my hands, begging my brain to SHUT UP. I'm better than this. I'm not going to sit around feeling sorry for myself and torturing myself with scenarios that I'm making up in my head.

I push myself up off the sofa and decide that the best thing to do right now is to get into my gym gear. I don't know what I'll do once I'm in it, but it's a start.

I pull on my leggings and a baggy T-shirt, tie up my hair, and, amusing myself, put on a neon-green headband that I find flitting about my sock drawer, purchased back at university when

I went to an eighties disco fancy-dress night. I look in the mirror and start pretending to box the air.

"Boom!" I say, hopping from foot to foot, punching forward. "Boom! Boom!"

Yes. I'm feeling it now. I'm feeling ready for a fresh start. New clients, new boyfriends. This year is going to be fantastic! And I'm going to be so healthy, too. I'm going to get fit! I'm going to eat better! I'm going to be positive and happy for people. I'm happy for my ex-boyfriend who's getting married to the perfect woman. I'm happy for Tom and Georgia . . . I'm happy not to hang out with Cordelia . . . I'm happy . . .

I stop boxing the air.

No! Don't let those thoughts come creeping in. Go away!

I get YouTube up on my TV and use the controller to type in "fun workout." Loads of videos come up and I scroll down until I see one in which the instructor is wearing neon clothes. It's a sign, I think, catching the reflection of my bright headband in the window. This is the video for me. I click on it and my flat is filled with a strong beat and funky music.

It turns out it's a dance workout. It couldn't be more perfect.

I turn the volume up super high, for once not caring what the neighbors think. I always care what everyone thinks. This coming year, I'm going to care what *I* think. I start bopping to the music, greatly enjoying the instructor's enthusiasm and his bright getup.

"We're going to have so much fun!" he yells, from the dance studio he appears to be in.

"Yes, we are!" I shout back at the screen.

"I'm going to show you how exercise doesn't have to be boring!"

"Great!"

"Are you ready to feel the burn?"

"I'm ready for the burn!"

"LET'S GO!"

"OMG, LET'S GO!"

He starts off with a simple walking-on-the-spot to warm up. I can do that. It's not a problem. This is fun. I walk on the spot, wiggling my hips, to "Jump (For My Love)." Absolute classic. We move into the side step. Easy. I'm smashing this workout. We're getting the arms involved now, reaching over the opposite side as we step.

"This is great!" I yell at the instructor, but he's too busy going "And arms! And arms! And reach! And reach!" to care.

And also he's on TV and can't hear me.

The track changes to "Flashdance . . . What a Feeling."

"A *classic!*" I cheer.

The instructor starts with some lunges to match the slow buildup at the beginning of the song, and when the chorus kicks in, we're star-jumping like no tomorrow. I decide to go a bit freestyle and let the music take over, dancing around, waving my arms in the air, shaking my bum to show that I am well and truly *sassy* (thank you very much, Cara), and then jumping round in a circle.

That's when I notice the person watching me in the doorway.

"AAAAH!" I scream, stumbling backward and clutching my heart.

"It's me!" Cordelia yells, getting a bit of a fright herself from my scream. "It's only me!"

"WHAT THE FUCK!" I wheeze, my heart thudding so hard against my rib cage I can hear it in my ears. I grab the controller and turn off the TV. "*What are you doing?*"

Cordelia bursts out laughing. "More to the point, what are *you* doing?"

"You're in my flat!"

"That really does look like a fun workout. I might quit that gym of mine and start coming here. Do you do classes?"

"Cordelia!"

"The headband is a nice touch. You were really getting into that song."

"How long have you been there?"

"Since toward the end of 'Jump.' And, by the way, you were right, 'Flashdance' really is a classic."

She folds her arms, leaning on the doorframe. She should be in her stately home in Derbyshire getting ready for her big pre-wedding dinner right now, being professionally made-up and preparing to get into her evening gown. Instead, she's in my poky little flat, wearing her old school hoodie and tracksuit bottoms.

I catch my breath, hands on my hips, staring at her. "How did you get in?" I ask eventually.

"I tried buzzing for a while. I knew you were in because I rang your mum and she told me—"

"You rang my mum?"

"I thought you weren't letting me up, but then one of your neighbors came out and let me in. And your door was open. It's a nice flat," she says, glancing around. "The office is a bit small. Was it a cupboard?"

"What are you doing here?"

"I came to say sorry," she says, as though it's the most obvious thing in the world. "You know I like to apologize in person."

"But . . . you shouldn't be here. You're supposed to be in Derbyshire!"

"I was in Derbyshire. Popped back here to do the apology."

I go to run a hand through my hair, forgetting I'm wearing a headband. I catch it in my fingers and pull it off, pretending I was going to do that anyway.

"I don't . . . I'm not . . ." I try to work out what I want to ask her first but it's all a jumble in my head. "I'm confused."

"I found out about the barman at the Duck."

"You—you did? How?"

She holds up her phone. "The magic of social media. He sent me a DM apologizing."

"Oh."

"Apparently, a friend of mine laid into him recently and whatever she said got through. He felt bad for causing any pain and suffering." She watches me carefully. "Why didn't you tell me?"

I shrug. "I wasn't sure you'd believe me. And the damage had already been done. It didn't matter."

"It matters to me."

I feel fidgety and unsettled, rubbing my forehead as I think about what this means. My name has been cleared. They know I didn't do it.

But so much has happened now.

"What are you doing here, Cordelia?" I ask tiredly.

"I told you, I came to apologize," she replies, stepping forward. "I'm sorry, Sophie. I'm sorry for not trusting you and I'm sorry for outing your secret and fucking up all the work you'd done for the wedding. I was hurt and stupid. I should have looked into it before making any accusations."

She chews her thumbnail nervously, then realizes she's doing it and drops her hand. When I don't say anything, she continues: "Jonathan told me about you finding him after he'd stormed out. We'd accused you of something you didn't do, fired you, thrown you out of the house, and the first thing you did was to find Jonathan so that the two of us would be OK. I don't even know what to say about that, Sophie, except that you might be the best person I've ever known."

I cross my arms stubbornly. It's a good apology. Really good. And she did drive for several hours just to say it.

But it's been a tough few days. I tried to be there for her, time and time again, and she pushed me away.

I know I'm being selfish. If anything, it's been much worse for her, having to suffer the pain of the worst experience of her life being brought up again, with the guy she's about to marry finding out about it through online gossip. On top of that, the whole world has discovered her secret and has been watching her every move.

"OK," I say coolly. "Thanks for the apology, I guess."

"The whole family are really upset about it," she continues. "Especially Mum. She feels terrible about the way we all spoke to you and making you leave like that. She wanted to come with me, but I told her I'd rather speak to you alone. And Dad, he's mortified. He said to pass on his apology as well."

I give her a sharp nod in acknowledgment. "How are you and Jonathan?" I ask, because I genuinely want to know and because I feel for him. His world was turned upside down over the last few days, too.

"We're good," she says, unable to stop a smile. "It was tough at first, but it's a relief that he knows. I always worried about him finding out and what he'd think of me. But the only thing he was angry about was that I'd kept it a secret from him."

"That makes sense. I'm glad he's OK."

"He thinks the world of you." She hesitates. "I'm sorry for telling Tom about you. You know, in the way I did."

I've only started to cool down from my workout, but the heat comes rushing back to my face. I pull at the neck of my T-shirt as though it's too tight, even though it's from a hen do I went on a year or so ago, and it only came in one gigantic size. It has "BRIDESMAIDS KNOW HOW TO BOOGIE" on the front. I delegated the job of getting T-shirts for the hens to the other bridesmaid.

She had *one* job.

Anyway. A story for another time.

"It's fine," I say hurriedly.

"I feel bad for blowing your cover. He was pretty upset."

"I can't be angry with you about that," I admit reluctantly. "I couldn't be Emily forever."

She nods and we both fall silent. I'm not sure how much

she knows about me and Tom. I can't imagine he's said much, especially after finding out that I'd been lying to him since we met.

I rub my forehead, starting to get a headache. "Cordelia, I appreciate the apology, I really do. It's good of you to come all the way here to say it in person, but you should go."

She frowns. "Why?"

"*Why?* Because you're getting married tomorrow! In Derbyshire! In front of four hundred people! It's your wedding!" I throw my hands into the air in exasperation. "Trust me, I know how much there is to do. You should be there preparing for the biggest day of your life."

"That's why I'm here!"

"What?"

"I'm here in your flat because I'm preparing for the biggest day of my life."

She waits for me to respond, and when I just stare at her blankly, she rolls her eyes and speaks again: "Oh, my God, you're so annoying! You *have* to make me explain the cringe stuff—you can't just get it without me having to spell it all out." She sighs, exasperated. "I want you to be at my wedding, Sophie. I'm here to pick you up. Hopefully. I want you to be my bridesmaid. Not a professional one. A real one." She's fiddling with her car keys. "We're friends. I think. If you still want to be. Oh, my God, I hate this."

"Wait." I hold my hands up. "You're asking me to be . . . your *bridesmaid?*"

"Yes, Sherlock. I literally just said that."

"Your real bridesmaid. Not a professional one."

"Those were my exact words."

"Seriously?"

"YES! If you think you can forgive me." She bites her lip, waiting for my answer. "So? Will you be my bridesmaid?"

I can't believe it. Cordelia wants me to be there for her. She means it, too. She's looking at me anxiously, as though she's unsure what I'll say. I keep her waiting an extra moment.

The truth is, I knew what I was going to say as soon as she asked.

"Wow," I begin, smiling as the sadness that's been hanging over me begins to ebb and excitement takes over, "that was a very *smushy* proposal. Thank you. Really lovely words, Cordelia. Telling me how much I mean to you. Very mature. Very emotional."

"What?" She recoils. "It wasn't that smushy. And what do you mean 'proposal'? Don't make this weird. It's not a big deal."

"It's a *huge* deal. You're asking me to be your bridesmaid! You should be down on one knee! Make it feel official."

"I knew you were going to make this weird," she mutters.

"Lady Cordelia Swann, I will! I accept your smushy proposal to be your bridesmaid."

"Now I'm considering taking it back."

"No take-backs once it's been accepted. Those are the rules."

"There are no rules. You're ridiculous."

"We're going to be very happy together." I give her a meaningful look and we burst out laughing.

"Wait!" I say suddenly. "I never picked up my dress! How am I going to get another before tomorrow?"

"It's been delivered to Dashwell. All you need to do is grab some shoes and we can get going."

"OK." I grin at her. "We can spend the entire road trip talking about our feelings and how we're BEST FRIENDS."

"Oh, my God. This journey is going to be unbearable. Speaking of which . . ." She checks the time on her phone. ". . . we really should go. I'm going to be several hours late for dinner. And I should probably get an early night. Big day tomorrow."

"Yeah. Big day." I walk over to her and put my hands out, grabbing her shoulders. I can tell she's thankful I didn't go for a hug. "Are you ready?"

"Yeah." She gives me a nervous smile. "I am now."

———

Do you think a punch bowl is weird?
Mike thinks it's weird
He says people in their thirties don't have punch
bowls at parties

> I don't think they're weird
> I enjoy a punch
> It's quite fun using a ladle to pour drinks

Exactly!
OK, cool, I've told him we're having one
He says you can be in charge of the ladle
That sounds a bit sexual when I type it out
Is my husband flirting with my cousin?
Gross

> Wait, Cara, I forgot to tell you that I can't
> come tomorrow!
> I'm so sorry, but thanks so much for the
> invite
> Also the ladle thing did sound sexual

WHAT?
I already texted several guys saying they need to
look good because my hot cousin will be there
I even made you a hat with some mistletoe glued to
the top!
What are you doing instead?
You're not going to be sitting alone doing those
weird Chewbacca Sound Tutorials, are you?
I've told you, it's not healthy

Nope, I won't be doing that
I'm going to be at a wedding

Which wedding?

Guess

You're not . . .

I am!!

Leonardo DiCaprio's?????

What?
What are you even talking about?
WHY would you think I'd be
going to Leonardo DiCaprio's
wedding?!?!

I heard a rumor he might be getting married
in London

Is he even engaged??

I honestly don't know
I think someone tweeted something

Sounds like a reliable source

What wedding are you going to????
Wait
Not Lady Cordelia's??

YES

AAAAAAH!!!
What happened??

They found out who really leaked the story
She's apologized

AND asked me to be her bridesmaid
Her REAL bridesmaid

THIS IS THE BEST NEWS
JUSTICE IS SERVED
OMG
WHAT ABOUT THE HOT BROTHER???

Oh, God.

WHAT??

No, nothing
Cordelia glanced over just then
She's driving
She could read the caps lock
About her hot brother
She's now laughing
I'm SO EMBARRASSED

WHO CARES??
YOUR BROTHER IS HOT, CORDELIA, IF YOU CAN
READ THIS
IS HE GOING TO BE THERE??

It would be weird if he wasn't

HOW CAN YOU BE SO CALM?

I'm not calm!
I'm bricking it
I ruined my chance with him

No, you didn't!!
It's not over until I SAY SO!

I have to play it cool
Maybe we can still be friends

BE MORE THAN FRIENDS
BE SEXY FRIENDS

> What do I say?
> When I see him, I mean

Say something SEXY

> Like what?

Like . . .
Hey, Mr. Lord
I've missed you

> OH, MY GOD, CARA
> That's not sexy!

Imagine it in a sexy voice

> You give terrible advice

A sexy growl

> I'm going to go now

I missed you babyyyyy
Say it like that
All sexy
Mike says "Don't say baby"
Sophie?
Fine, you've gone. Off with your new famous friend.
Whatever. I don't care.
OMG DON'T FORGET TO KISS HIM AT MIDNIGHT

CHAPTER THIRTY-THREE

I skip the dinner. We arrive much too late anyway and, while it's important that Cordelia goes to see everyone to salvage what's left of the evening, I'd rather not face the family for the first time during such an intimate event. I don't want Lord and Lady Meade to feel awkward in front of their guests about everything that's happened, and I still feel terrified at the idea of seeing Tom. It's best for everyone if I have a quiet night hiding in my bedroom.

On the drive, Cordelia and I talked about how we were going to handle the Emily/Sophie situation and she put forward the solution of only telling those who needed to know. She wasn't particularly embarrassed about explaining my job to certain people. Hopefully, she said, most of the guests won't remember my name.

"We can introduce you again as Sophie and they'll feel embarrassed that they thought your name was Emily."

"I suppose most of them know me simply as the bridesmaid/escort."

"Quite a cool alter ego, if you ask me. Very mysterious. You're welcome."

"Thanks so much. What about Annabel? And her family?"

"You don't need to worry about that," she said, moving lanes as we sped down the motorway. "I've already told them."

"You have?"

"Yeah. They've been up in Derbyshire for Christmas, so we had them over for dinner the other night and I explained the whole saga. They've already kept one secret for me so I hoped they wouldn't mind keeping another. It made Annabel's year. You should have heard some of her catty remarks. They were inspired."

"Aren't you worried she's going to tell?"

"I guess I'm secretly holding on to the fact that she wouldn't go that far." She shrugged, then shot me a sly grin. "That, and the fact that I know *plenty* of her secrets. She knows that if she spills mine, I might spill hers."

I know Cordelia would never do that. But I guess it's a good thing that Annabel might think differently.

It's both weird and wonderful to be back at Dashwell. Going up the drive toward the imposing house, passing all the trees decorated with thousands of fairy lights, I got a shiver down my spine at how grand it all was and how nervous I felt to be there. But as soon as I got to the bedroom where I stayed last time, ushered Cordelia out of the door to her dinner, and plonked my case on the bed, I felt strangely at home.

I'm in the middle of steaming my bridesmaid dress when there's a knock on the door.

I immediately panic. I'm in my winter pajamas! They're neon-green flannel with bright orange carrots all over them! Cara and I bought a pair each because we thought they were hilarious! *What was I thinking getting into these so early?* Have I got time to change?

There's more impatient knocking on the door and I reluctantly put down the steamer and walk over to open it.

Please don't be Tom, please don't be Tom, please don't be Tom . . .

"Jonathan!"

"Hey, Sophie." He grins, as I breathe a sigh of relief.

He steps forward and gives me a giant hug. He pulls back to step past me into the room, revealing Lady Meade right behind him.

"Hello, Sophie," she says. Her eyes flicker to my pajamas and she does her best to cover her alarmed expression. You need to understand that they're *very* loud pajamas.

"Hi, Lady Meade."

"May I come in?"

"Of course!" I step back so she can walk into the room, joining Jonathan, who is standing by the full-length mirror, busy checking his reflection from various angles, sucking his stomach in and prodding it.

"I ate too much at dinner." He sighs. "Probably shouldn't have had Cordelia's sticky toffee pudding as well as mine."

"How was your journey, Sophie?" Lady Meade asks politely, giving Jonathan a stern look that immediately makes him break from his reflection and turn his attention to me. "I hope the traffic wasn't too bad."

"It was fine. We got here in good time. How was the dinner?"

"Great fun," Jonathan declares. "Nicholas has so far done five speeches. I think he has at least one more in him."

"You should join us," Lady Meade says. "You'd be very welcome."

"Thank you, that's really kind, but I have lots to do for tomorrow," I tell her, gesturing to the steamer.

"Sophie," she says, clasping her hands together and looking me in the eye. "I want to apologize to you most sincerely. I should never have accused you of leaking the story to the press. I'm embarrassed by my behavior and I hope you can find some way of forgiving me."

"Uh . . . sure," I say, taken aback by her serious tone, and wishing I weren't in stupid carrot pajamas. "Water under the bridge."

She smiles warmly at me. "Thank you. You've done so much for Cordelia. I'll never forget it."

"Oh, well"—I wave my hand about, brushing her compliments aside—"I'm just pleased that it all worked out in the end. The most important thing is that you and Cordelia are happy, Jonathan."

"We both owe you a lot," Jonathan says, beaming at me. "Thank you for being here."

"Wouldn't miss it."

"While I remember, can I give you this?" He pulls an envelope out from the inside pocket of his jacket and hands it to me. "It's for Cordelia. If you wouldn't mind giving it to her tomorrow morning. It's her gift."

I gasp excitedly. "You managed to get what we discussed?"

"I did. I hope she'll be pleased."

"Are you kidding? She's going to *love* it."

"Thanks, Sophie. Really. For everything."

Pretending to notice the time from the clock on the mantelpiece, but secretly wanting them to leave because I can't bear another second of standing in front of the *Marchioness of Meade* dressed in *carrot pajamas*, I feign surprise.

"Is that the time? Goodness, you should really be with your guests," I say, gliding toward the door. "They'll be missing you. But thank you for coming up here. It means a lot."

"Have you had any supper?" Lady Meade asks, following Jonathan out of the room and stopping in the doorway to look at me with a concerned expression. "You need to make sure you have something to eat."

"I'm honestly fine, I don't need—"

"You know where the kitchen is—the smaller one in the private wing? Not the main one, the caterers are using it—there's plenty of food in the fridge. You can sneak down and help yourself. You don't need to worry about bumping into anyone there."

She gives me a mischievous smile and I know she's referring to the pajamas.

That's it. I now officially *hate* carrots.

"See you tomorrow, Sophie!" Jonathan calls, as he dances away down the corridor. "On my wedding day!"

I laugh and wait for them to disappear down the stairs before closing the door and getting back to my steaming. My stomach gives a loud rumble as I finish. Lady Meade was right: I probably should eat something. I didn't realize how hungry I was.

Must have been all that vigorous "Flashdance" exercise earlier.

Lady Meade said I wouldn't bump into anyone, but I'm not taking any chances. Pulling the fluffy white dressing gown provided over the carrot pajamas, I leave the bedroom and make my way to the kitchen, trying to remember which turning leads where. I'd forgotten how much of a maze this place is. I finally get to a corridor I know and, relieved that I recognize the door to the kitchen, I hurry down it, ready to grab something and get back to the sanctuary of my room.

As I reach the door, which is ajar, I hear voices. I jump back against the wall, hidden from view, confused as to what the caterers are doing in this kitchen, too.

"That is so *gross*, Tom! Don't drink from the carton, you pig."

"Chill out, Bridezilla. I'm going to finish it. I'm not putting it back in the fridge."

I freeze at hearing Tom's voice. What are they *doing* here? They should be in the dining room with their guests! Why does Tom have to track down cheap sugary drinks during a *dinner*? Oh, God, I shouldn't have left my bedroom. I need to get back there *immediately* without him seeing me. If I tiptoe back down the corridor, I might be all right. As long as he doesn't stand anywhere near the door, he won't see me from inside the kitchen.

I'm about to take the first step when he speaks again. "So, she came back with you, then?"

My breath catches.

"Yeah, she did," Cordelia says. "Can you pass me a Twix? On the top shelf of the fridge, at the back."

"The sticky toffee pudding not to your liking, Your Highness?"

"Jonathan ate mine while I was busy saying hi to everyone," she replies grumpily. "At least I'm not sneaking away to drink juice from the carton like a child."

"At least I'm not sneaking away to hide from my guests."

"Shut up."

"You shut up."

Oh, my God, *siblings are the worst*. They're in their thirties!

I hear the fridge door open and close, then the sound of a chocolate wrapper crackling.

"How is she?" Tom says casually.

"Who?"

He sighs, irritated. "*Sophie*."

"She's good. I'm glad she's here."

There's a long pause.

"It was all my fault, you know," Cordelia says, cutting through the silence. "She was just doing her job. She couldn't tell anyone her real name. She signed a contract."

"Yeah."

"If it means anything, she's a terrible actress."

HOW DARE SHE? I'll have her know that I am *extremely* convincing at playing a variety of roles for my bridesmaid profession. Not to mention I once got cast as the understudy for the part of Knuckles for my school's performance of *Bugsy Malone*.

I didn't make it onstage, but I might have done.

"She wasn't playing anyone but herself," Cordelia continues. "She had a different name and she pretended we met in an art gallery, but everything else is exactly who she is. I don't want to boss you around—"

"Right, because you've never done that before."

"—but you should really forgive her. Come on, Tom, don't be an idiot. You're finally *you* around someone. You're relaxed and goofy when she's in the room. It's nice to see. And don't think I haven't noticed you trying to impress her. You offered her a lift from London to Dashwell, and you'd only met her a couple of times."

"I was being nice to your friend."

"You were being all *smushy*. You loser. And what about the special tour around Paxton? You've never done that before."

"I've taken people into Paxton!"

"Yeah, but not like that! Maybe to grab something from a shop, but you've never given them *a tour* of where you grew up! You wanted to show her around and tell her things. You were basically bringing her into your life. You don't need to blush— Mum and I think it's adorable," she teases.

"You're very annoying."

"All I'm saying is, your dopey, loser face lights up when you see her. So, don't let her go. Trust me, you won't find anyone else like her."

I hear Cordelia crush her empty chocolate wrapper in her hand and it suddenly comes flying toward the bin, which is next to the doorway. The wrapper lands short.

"Terrible throw," Tom declares.

His arm appears as he bends down to pick it up and put it into the bin. I hold my breath and flatten myself against the wall, breathing in as much as possible, as though that might somehow help to make me invisible.

He moves away and I quietly exhale, my heart thudding against my ribs.

"We should go back to the dinner," he says.

"Yeah. Who are you sitting next to?"

"Great-Uncle Edward, who keeps mistaking me for Dad and

calling me a punk," Tom grumbles. "It's all my fault—I made a joke this morning about Lord Cluck being unnaturally stupid and Mum hadn't finished the seating plan. She's well and truly punishing me."

Cordelia bursts out laughing. "At least you can sit there and chat to a couple of people. I've been working the room from the moment I got here. I don't know how Jonathan's managed it all night. My jaw is already aching from smiling at everyone. And it's not even the wedding day yet. I'm not sure I'll last."

"Yeah, you will," Tom says, and I can hear he's smiling. "Tomorrow is going to be brilliant. I know you know this, but I'm proud of you, sis."

"Shut up."

"You shut up."

I hear their footsteps fading as, thankfully, they leave through the door on the other side of the room, heading back to the dinner party.

I smile to myself, listening to them go, teasing each other the whole way.

I take it all back. Siblings are the best.

You are cordially invited to the wedding of

Lady Cordelia Swann and Jonathan Farlow

31 December 2021

I try not to cry when she steps out in her dress. I know she'll hate it if I'm crying.

"Are you crying?"

"No!" I squeak.

"You're doing that weird puppet face again."

"No, I'm not."

"It's creepy."

"I'm not doing it. This is my normal face."

She smiles. "Well? What do you think?"

It really is true, you know, that every bride looks beautiful on her wedding day. All those overused words to describe brides are overused for a reason. Radiant. Stunning. Gorgeous. I think it's because they know they're allowed to be unabashedly happy that day.

"Beautiful," I say, grabbing a tissue from the hairstylist and dabbing the corner of my eye. "You look beautiful."

Lady Meade lets out an "eep" sound next to me. The hairstylist offers her a tissue, too. Clio Vaughn moves so gracefully and quietly around the room taking pictures that she's almost invisible to the rest of us.

It's an exquisite dress, designed (very quickly) by the team at Alexander McQueen. A halter neck, fitted at the top, showing off her delicate shoulders, then a gentle, sloping A-line skirt with an overlayer of hand-embroidered floral lace with a train. It's elegant, sophisticated, and romantic. It's perfect.

She turns round to show me the giant bow at the back, in the middle of which is pinned Lucky Blue, the sapphire horseshoe brooch I found.

Beth steps forward holding out our bouquets for us. Her hands are full so she can't dab her cheeks, tears flowing freely down her face. There was an awkward moment this morning when we were having our hair done and Beth came bustling in, saw me, and went, "Emily! Hi!" But Cordelia explained the story with such flair that Beth not only thought my job sounded fabulous but got tears in her eyes when Cordelia reached the bit about asking me to be her bridesmaid for real.

"What a lovely story of friendship." Beth sniffed. "It's like . . . fate!"

"Oh, God." Cordelia sighed, nodding toward me. "Don't get her started."

Beth hands me my bouquet and, unable to stop blubbing, passes Cordelia hers. Through great sniffs, she tells Cordelia how wonderful she looks and how she can't believe that she's so grown-up and sophisticated. "It feels like just yesterday you got your foot stuck in that toilet," she says, blowing her nose.

"Umm, I'm sorry," I say, holding up the hand that isn't holding the bouquet. "What's this about the toilet?"

"Oh, it was when Cordelia was working in the shop and—"

"It's a story for another time," Cordelia interrupts Beth, giving me a warning look as I stifle a laugh. "Now that I'm ready, shall we get Dad in here? We should be setting out soon."

"Actually, before we do," I say, picking up the card from a dressing table, "this is for you. It's from Jonathan."

Her eyes light up. "He wrote me a card?"

I nod, passing it to her. We all wait patiently as she opens the envelope. She reads it, a smile spreading across her face, and then, I assume when she gets to the bit about her gift, her jaw drops, and she clasps her hand around her mouth. She looks up at me. "Is this *true*? My wedding present . . ."

"Yes, it is."

"Oh, my God!"

"What is it?" Lady Meade asks curiously.

"He's got me a puppy!" she cries, waving the card around in the air. "A Labrador puppy! This is the best present *ever*!"

I burst out laughing at how happy she is, already excited for the day when Clio's pictures come through and Jonathan is able to see her reaction. When he and I were sitting in the pub that day, it seemed obvious what she was missing. Jonathan's story about her relationship with his family dog, Gus, revealed that in a moment of nerves—going to his parents' house for the first time—she found comfort in getting on the floor and cuddling the Labrador. Just like her mum, she was at her best around animals. They don't have a clue about titles or fame or status—they just love you back.

"I can't believe it, I'm so excited," she says, rereading the card. "I've wanted a dog for so long. Jonathan writes that we can pick him up when we get back from our honeymoon!"

"He'll be waiting for you," I say. She beams at me, gripping the card. But eventually I manage to prize it from her fingers, reminding her that we're on a fairly tight schedule.

Lord Meade is ushered in and his eyes widen when he sees his daughter. His lip quivers as he tries not to get emotional, and he gives her a kiss on the cheek, saying, "Very good, very good," repeatedly.

Lord Meade and I had the big conversation featuring apologies and explanations this morning. I told him to forget about it, that I was happy it was all resolved. I apologized for having to lie to him, but he brushed it aside, telling me it was nothing. He tried to make a few jokes about Emily being very nice but he'd have to wait and see about Sophie, before Lady Meade told him affectionately that it was only funny the first time, and even then, at a push.

As Lord Meade admires his daughter in as few words as possible, Lady Meade and I are informed that our car is waiting. We tell Cordelia that we'll see her at the church, then make our way carefully down the sweeping staircase of Dashwell Hall in our heels.

I get into the car first, ready to help Lady Meade, who has to hold her head at an awkward angle to get through the door, thanks to her *ginormous* blue hat. She really has gone down the route of go big or go home, and I am *loving* it.

We fill the short few minutes to the church with small talk about how wonderful everything looks and how lucky we are with the weather. It's cold, of course, but sunny, meaning guests will not only be able to enjoy the splendor of the interiors of Dashwell Hall, but also the views from the windows of the fields stretching into the distance. I tell her I don't think I've ever seen a more magical wedding venue. There are twinkling lights everywhere you look, and the house is filled with the most magnificent flower arrangements, full of vibrant colors—dark reds, burnt oranges, and, every now and then, a pop of dark blue or pink. Beth has truly outdone herself.

Lady Meade agrees that it does look good, joking about whether they should consider decorating the house like this all year-round. I say maybe they should.

The car pulls up at the church and I feel a flutter of nerves.

I'm not that worried about walking down the aisle in front of all those fancy people, although obviously that's a bit daunting. I'm largely worried about seeing Tom. Listening to his conversation with Cordelia in the kitchen last night, I found it hard to tell how he was feeling. He didn't say much. Which probably means he's over it, but didn't want to say so out of respect for his sister's friend. If that's the case, then it's OK. I'm fine. I was hoping to catch him this morning, to smooth things over and work out where I stood. But he was nowhere to be seen and I realized that, of course, he was an usher and staying at the same hotel as Jonathan.

Lady Meade goes into the church, while I wait nervously outside on my own with the vicar. Clio and her army of photography assistants get some candid shots of me smoothing my dress and trying to stop the styled hair tendrils moving out of place.

The bridal car arrives just as Clio's getting a very arty shot of my bouquet, and the photographers move into position. Some of the Paxton locals have crowded onto the banks outside the church, desperate to catch a glimpse of the bride. They all cheer and wave as Lord Meade helps Cordelia out of the car, and it feels a bit like a royal wedding as she waves back.

The vicar welcomes her and asks if she's ready for him to signal her arrival to the organist.

"Yes, I'm ready," she says, as I make a few tweaks to her veil so that it's hanging evenly on each side, while Lord Meade picks a bit of fluff off his morning suit. "Thanks, Sophie."

"You're welcome."

"I'm nervous."

"Just focus on Jonathan."

"What happens if I mess up the speaking bit? If I say the wrong bit of the vow?"

"Take your time, the vicar will guide you. And it doesn't matter if you do mess it up. It's endearing when that happens. I'll laugh very loudly at you."

"As long as you don't snort." She smiles mischievously. "You're the type that might if you were really going for it."

"How exactly did you get your foot stuck in a toilet?"

"All right," the vicar says cheerily, coming back over. "Shall we get into position?"

After a last-minute check of Cordelia's train, I line up behind the vicar, trying not to laugh as I hear him give himself a little pep talk about the sermon under his breath, while Lord Meade and Cordelia move to stand behind me.

The organ starts, the congregation rise to their feet, and, just like that, it's time to go.

CHAPTER THIRTY-FOUR

We're never talking about this again."

"I don't know why you're being so uptight about it."
I sigh, keeping my eyes on the ceiling and Cordelia's train off
the floor. "I've done this a million times. Every bride needs help
peeing in her dress. Think about brides with those really big
skirts, how do you think they pee? And you're lucky to have this
big bathroom. Imagine being in a portaloo and attempting it. It
takes a lot of skill."

"Stop talking," Cordelia snaps. "You're giving me stage
fright."

I clam up and wait patiently for the tinkle.

"Do you remember our chat in the loos at the engagement
party?" I ask her, when she's started going. "I was in the cubicle
and you came bursting in."

"Oh, yeah. I was so angry that you hadn't quit already."

"You made me stop mid-pee."

"Seriously?"

"You gave me such a fright, the pee literally stopped."

"I had no idea I had so much power." I hear her tear off the
loo paper.

"All done," she announces, standing up and flushing, then
gliding over to the bathroom mirror while I sort out her train.
"So, how do they do it, then?"

"Do what?"

"Brides in big skirts," she says, washing her hands.

"You can approach the loo frontway on, so your back is to the cubicle door if you get me. It's more of a straddle," I inform her, opening and holding out my clutch, which has all her makeup inside. "Or there's an extremely neat trick with those big blue Ikea bags."

"You're joking," she says, selecting her eyeliner from my bag.

"You cut a large hole in the bottom of the bag and step into it, pulling it up by the handles. The bag neatly contains the skirt, lifting it off the floor."

"You're telling me that brides are supposed to bring an Ikea bag to the wedding?"

"No, I make sure there's a prepared one stowed away in the loo."

"That's so . . . *smart*."

"I know."

She finishes reapplying her makeup and I snap the clutch shut, holding open the door for her to lead the way back downstairs to the reception.

"What did you think of the food?" she asks, taking my hand for balance on the stairs because the banister is covered with opulent flowers entwined all the way round.

"Potentially the most delicious meal I've ever eaten."

"And do you think everyone liked the speeches?"

"They were brilliant! Went down a storm. All of them were the perfect balance of funny and emotional. Yours was obviously the best, but don't tell the others. I loved the story about Jonathan's pants in Tuscany. And I got a bit emotional when you thanked me."

"Of course you did. Your tear ducts are very overactive."

"Are you happy with everything?"

She smiles at me. "I've never been happier."

And I believe her. All day she's been radiant and relaxed, and no one could possibly watch her and Jonathan and believe they shouldn't be together. I always look out for the almost unnoticeable, seemingly insignificant moments on a wedding day—the way Jonathan's fingertips lightly brushed hers when the vicar was welcoming the congregation; how he proudly held out his hand to help her down the steps for some photos in the grounds of Dashwell; her giving him a kiss on the cheek before they went into the wedding breakfast together when she thought no one was looking, then gently wiping the lipstick off his skin.

Cordelia told me that she feels closer than ever to him, now that he knows about everything that happened. They'd talked about it for hours. His insistence that she must have been very brave to overcome that when she was just a teenager is making her start to believe it, too.

These two really are going to look after each other for the rest of their lives.

Cordelia stops at the bottom of the stairs. "Teeth check," she announces, making sure no one's around, then curling her lips back so I can inspect.

"You're all good."

"What's happening now?"

I check the time. "First dance in six minutes. Stand still while I sort your bustle."

While I crouch down to sort the ribbons and shorten her train, a guest spots us hidden round the corner on her search for the bathroom and takes the opportunity of Cordelia being on her own to come and tell her how wonderful the wedding is. As Cordelia's dress swishes this way and that when she reacts and gestures, I move like a red satin crab around the hem, concentrating on matching each ribbon on the train with its fellow on the inside skirt of the dress.

"Now, ladies and gentlemen, let's welcome the happy couple

to the floor for their first dance!" the master of ceremonies announces.

Cordelia forgets what I'm doing and happily floats off toward the dance floor, leaving me in an odd squat, which is hard to get out of in a fitted satin dress on my own. At least I'd just managed to tie the knot in the last ribbon of her dress. I only hope it holds.

A venomous voice floats down. "I know who you are."

I look up to see Annabel towering over me, her hands on her hips, her eyes flashing victoriously.

"Annabel, always a pleasure." I grimace, straightening and praying that my dress doesn't rip. Thankfully, it doesn't.

"You and Cordelia are pathetic," she declares, once I'm at her eye level.

"Would you mind if we discussed this outside?" I ask, with a winning smile, leading her away from the reception. "I'd rather no one else heard our conversation."

"Fine." She sighs, letting me guide her away, eager to offer her opinion on the matter. "Yet another cover-up I'm selflessly aiding."

I take her out through the same doors onto the patio to which I'd followed Cordelia on my last visit to Dashwell, when Annabel had invited herself round for dinner just to taunt her. This isn't one of the designated smoking areas, so we have it all to ourselves.

"All right, Annabel," I begin, ready for whatever she's about to throw my way. "You can say your piece now."

"This family is full of secrets and lies. And you are no better than any of them. A professional bridesmaid? It's so embarrassing! She had to *hire* a friend! My God, I think I'd leave the country if anyone thought I'd do any such thing."

"It's not embarrassing, Annabel. It's my job. And hiring a bridesmaid isn't the same as hiring a friend."

"Why should I keep this secret for Cordelia?" She smirks, relishing the moment. "Maybe people deserve to know the truth about her."

"What truth is that?" I ask, irritated. "Anyone planning a wedding for four hundred people would need a little bit of help."

"The press would *love* this. Lady Cordelia Swann is so pathetic that she had to hire someone just to spend time in her company." She shrieks with laughter. "It's too hilarious!"

"Cordelia is not pathetic," I argue, ruffled on Cordelia's behalf. "If anyone is pathetic, it's you."

She recoils. "Excuse me?"

"You heard me," I say confidently, the rage bubbling inside me, brushing any fear of her aside. "You're the one who's pathetic, Annabel. You were friends with Cordelia once, and she'd have done anything for you—in fact, I think part of her reluctantly always will because of whatever bond you once had—but you don't deserve her. You care more about status and how the world sees you than the character of the people you choose to keep close. It's a bad mistake."

She looks furious, riled at the audacity of my allegations. "How dare you? I'm not the bad friend! I'm not the one who kissed her boyfriend!"

"Oh, for fuck's sake," I say, exasperated. "Annabel, do you really believe that the boyfriend who cheated on you several times with your mates didn't also try to cheat on you with Cordelia? Do you really think *she* instigated it? I've only known her for a few months and I'd be willing to bet a lot of money on the fact that there is no way in hell she'd do that to you or anyone else. She's fiercely loyal, to the point where she's scared now to let anyone else in, because she doesn't have the energy to be so heartbroken again."

She looks frazzled and suddenly unsure, her eyes darting around us, searching for a solid argument to throw in my face.

"She was . . . she was stupid. She was a bad influence. She over-dosed, not me."

"Do you know what I think, Annabel? I think the reason you're still angry with Cordelia is because you're angry with your-self. She's a good person and a good friend."

"Oh, really?" She snorts. "If she's such a good friend, then why does she have to pay you to be one?"

"She doesn't," I say simply. "She fired me a while ago. I'm here as a genuine bridesmaid, not a professional one. Do you have any genuine bridesmaids, Annabel?"

"I beg your pardon?"

"I saw that you'd announced your bridesmaids on social media. Your sister Georgia obviously makes sense, but I was surprised to see you'd asked . . . What were their names? Oh, yeah, Ella and Madison. You met them a few months ago, in the summer, right? At Ella's dad's restaurant opening. Madison is a model based in New York, yes?"

"So?" she asks haughtily.

"So, did I hear a rumor that Madison has dropped out of the wedding because she's launching her acting career and has been cast in a movie that's filming soon?"

"She has other commitments in May," she explains, sniffing. "I completely understand. It doesn't matter anyway."

I nod. "I'm sorry to hear that. Genuinely. It's hard when a friend lets you down, especially on such an important day."

She narrows her eyes at me. "Why are you saying any of this? None of this professional-bridesmaid nonsense has anything to do with me. This is about Cordelia."

"As someone who's been to a lot of weddings, trust me when I say this, Annabel." I take a step toward her, speaking in a sincere and kind tone so she knows that I mean it—I'm not being pa-tronizing. "You deserve people around you on your wedding day whom you trust. You're going to need them. Go ahead and spend the rest of your time surrounding yourself with people who bring you more status and fame, but when it comes to a day that really means something, make sure you have people at your side you can rely on, people who genuinely care about you." I offer her a smile. "People who would have your back on your wedding day, should someone accuse you of being pathetic when you're not in the room. That's all there is to being a bridesmaid."

She stares at me, baffled.

"Anyway," I say brightly, stepping back to give her some space, "it's been great talking to you. We should go and enjoy the party. We'll have missed the first dance, but the band is meant to be really good. Also, it's definitely time for a Jägerbomb, don't you think?"

She collects herself, flicking her hair behind her shoulder and giving me a look of disgust, sneering, "I have to go."

She turns on her heel and marches back into the house, slamming the patio doors behind her. Oh, well. I tried. I take the opportunity of a moment to myself, looking out over the view, listening to the muffled music.

"That was intense."

I yelp, jumping out of my skin at the sound of Tom's voice as he appears from the shadows, behind a pillar. "*What the* . . . Have you been there the whole time?"

He holds up his hands. "Sorry. I didn't mean to eavesdrop."

"What are you doing out here?" I ask, my heart thumping so loudly from the fright he's given me that I can hear it ringing in my ears.

"I was having a cigarette."

"You don't smoke!"

"I used to. I thought I might allow myself one, as it's a wedding and I'm letting my hair down. Always tempting when I've had a few drinks."

"Well. This isn't a designated smoking area."

"Yeah, but it's quieter out here and I thought I might be able to get away with it, you know, because it's my house and everything."

I nod, chagrined, and then we stand awkwardly in silence, listening to the thud of the bass from the speakers reverberating through the house and out across the grounds. I've spent the majority of the day avoiding eye contact with Tom, glancing away and pretending I'm not staring at the back of his head whenever he turns in my direction. Earlier his hair was neatly styled—I was impressed in the church when I stole a look—but by now it's sticking up in all directions. He's taken off the jacket of his morning suit but, sadly, his wonderful arms are covered with his shirtsleeves. I hope he rolls them up later if he gets hot on the dance floor.

He steps forward with his hand outstretched, a grin spreading across his face. "Sophie, is it?"

I take his hand and shake it, laughing at how cheesy the gesture is. "Yeah, Sophie. Nice to meet you properly."

"You too. Those were lovely things you said about my sister. Thanks for protecting her. I'm sorry about the way Annabel spoke to you."

"It's fine. I can handle it."

"Yeah, I know," he says, looking impressed. "I thought I might have to step in but you seemed to have it covered. I can't help but think after that showdown you might have earned yourself a new client."

"Why?" I frown at him. "Are you in need of a bridesmaid?"

"After what I just heard, I actually feel that, yeah, everyone needs a bridesmaid." He grins. "But I was talking about Annabel. She should have taken your card."

"There's no chance Annabel would ever consider hiring me.

And now I've probably given her even more reason to blab about who I really am. No doubt it'll be all over the press in the morning."

"I wouldn't be so sure. When Cordelia told them the truth about you, Annabel's parents seemed to think it was a very good idea. Apparently, she's been under a lot of pressure and they're worried about how she's handling it. I wouldn't be surprised if you wake up to a phone call from Lord or Lady Derrington. You may have locked in your next gig." He grimaces. "Although that would mean you'd have to put up with Annabel and her demands for months."

"After Cordelia, I'm sure I can handle anything," I point out, to which he nods in agreement. "I'll worry about Annabel tomorrow. Tonight, we should enjoy the wedding."

"Good thinking."

"Tom," I say, turning the conversation serious for a moment, "I'm sorry about . . . everything. I feel really bad about it."

"It's OK," he says, looking at the floor. "I understand. You were doing your job, and you'd signed contracts. And you've become an amazing friend to Cordelia—you've really been there for her. You don't have to be sorry about anything."

"Well, I am. I'm really sorry for lying to you." I hesitate, trying to read his expression. "Not that *everything* was a lie."

"Is that right?"

He lifts his eyes to meet mine, allowing himself a small smile. Cordelia might have got through to him last night. I let myself hope again.

"Yeah. Like when you asked me if I'd like to go for a drink with you and I said I would. That wasn't a lie."

OMG! I'M BEING SO SASSY RIGHT NOW.

"Really. That's interesting."

"So, if you'd still be game, then we should go on a date. Would you like to go on a date with me?"

UNBELIEVABLY SASSY.

"Yeah, that sounds good. I'd like that," he says, making my heart soar and my smile break so wide, my jaw hurts.

"Cool! Great," I say, in a very non-sassy, gushing manner. "What do you want to do? Is there somewhere you'd particularly like to go?"

"With you, Sophie?" He grins. "Anywhere."

"You have very sexy arms!"

"What?" Tom shouts back over the band.

"Your arms!"

"What about them?"

Wait. Oh, God, what am I saying? Why have I blurted out how I feel about his arms while we're on the dance floor with hundreds of other guests, dancing wildly to the Proclaimers? All those Jägerbombs have made me completely delirious.

Or maybe it's Tom.

"What about my arms?" he asks again, pausing his wild array of dance moves to lean in close to be sure he can hear my next answer.

I panic.

"You have them!" I yell.

He gives me a strange look. "Yeah."

"Cool!"

He starts laughing. "Sophie is weirder than Emily."

"Your dad made a very similar joke this morning."

"Dad and I have the same jokes? Uh-oh. That's not good."

I smile as he gets back to his dancing, wondering if it might be possible to ask the band how much extra they'd charge never to stop playing, so we never have to end this evening. Since our chat outside, we've had to mingle with other guests (him) or help the bride to pee again (me) or wrestle the microphone from Lord Meade before he proposes yet another toast (both of us), but somehow we've found ourselves drifting back to each other between our tasks, and now it's finally late enough that everyone is merry and dancing, and we have an excuse to be together without any duties calling.

The song comes to an end and we belt out the last line, laughing and clapping along with everyone else. As he looks to the stage, I take the chance to gaze at him. He has a very nice neck.

Uh-oh. A new obsession.

"Ladies and gentlemen," Cordelia announces into the microphone, slurring her words as Jonathan stands with an arm around her shoulders, steadying her even though he looks mightily unsteady himself. "It's just a few minutes until midnight, so the countdown to the New Year will soon commence!"

The crowd cheers. She wobbles down the steps from the stage and then, grabbing Jonathan's hand, she makes a beeline for me and Tom, waving and going, "Yoo-hoo!"

"Are you aware you were saying 'yoo-hoo' as you came toward us?" I laugh, as she falls into my arms, the countless glasses of champagne transforming her from an awkward hugger to a normal one.

"Yeah, I really don't know where that came from. Anyway, I got you a gift. Jonathan!" She whacks his arm, interrupting his conversation with Tom. "Jonathan! Focus! Give Sophie her gift!"

"All right, just a minute." He laughs, reaching into his pocket and pulling out a small black box.

She takes it and excitedly passes it to me. "I read that it's nice to give your bridesmaid a token of your appreciation. I should have given it to you this morning, but I was too distracted with the puppy news. Open it."

"You didn't have to do this."

"*Open* it," she insists.

Embarrassed by her generosity, I shyly push open the lid of the Swann & Co. box and stare down at its contents. It's a necklace from her jewelry line, but I haven't seen this one before. It's a silver pendant in the shape of a swan.

"What do you think?" she asks, anxious for my reaction.

I clutch the box. "It's beautiful. Thank you."

"I know you like people to spell things out, so let me tell you exactly what this is," she says theatrically.

"It's . . . it's a swan."

"All right, smart-arse, yes, I know you know it's a swan, but let me tell you what it *means*," she says, rolling her eyes. "You're my best mate. That makes you family. So it represents my family."

"Cordelia," I croak, blinking back tears.

"And also, you are a swan whisperer. I have video proof if anyone should doubt it." She grins. "You inspired me. It's going to be part of my next collection. It's called the Sophie Swan. Cute, right?"

I burst out laughing, pulling the delicate chain out of the box.

"Here," Tom says, taking it from me as I hold up my hair. "Let me."

He clips it on at the nape of my neck and I let my hair fall loose again, admiring the pendant resting on top of my dress. Cordelia gives me another hug, then pulls back, smiling at me. She doesn't say anything. She doesn't need to.

"So, now you've made sure the bride is happy," Tom begins, when Cordelia and Jonathan move away to the middle of the dance floor ready for midnight, "what's next for a professional bridesmaid?"

"Ladies and gentlemen," the band's singer announces into the microphone, "prepare for the countdown to the New Year!"

The crowd cheers again. A spotlight falls on Cordelia and Jonathan in the middle of the guests. I smile over Tom's shoulder as Cordelia gazes at Jonathan, her hands around his waist.

"Bridesmaid rules . . . ," I begin.

"TEN!" the singer's voice booms around the ballroom.

". . . if the bride is happy . . ."

"NINE!" the guests all join in.

". . . then I'm happy."

"EIGHT!"

"And if you're happy . . ." He smiles, putting a hand on the small of my back and pulling me close to him . . .

"SEVEN!"

". . . then I'm happy." He gently brushes a loose tendril of hair behind my ear.

"SIX!"

I wrap my arms around his neck.

"FIVE!"

I stand on tiptoe and kiss him. He kisses me back.

"FOUR!"

I know you're supposed to wait until midnight.

"THREE!"

But, right now, I don't care.

"TWO!"

It's like Cordelia says.

"ONE!"

Sometimes it's fun to break the rules.

<hr />

From: Dwayne@extremeskydiveuk.com

To: Sophie.Breeze@zapmail.co.uk

Subject: Booking Confirmation

Dear Sophie,

Congratulations, your booking is confirmed for your
TANDEM SKYDIVE ADVENTURE on Saturday, 12 February
2022!

Please find details of your booking attached and don't
hesitate to contact us if you have any questions. We look
forward to seeing you soon!

Best wishes,

Dwayne

Extreme Skydive UK . . . ARE YOU READY TO TAKE THE JUMP?

ACKNOWLEDGMENTS

I am so grateful for the ridiculously talented team at Hodder & Stoughton for bringing this story to life. Special thanks to my genius UK editor, Kim, for believing in Sophie right from the start, and to the fabulous Amy, Hazel, and Jo. Huge thanks to my wonderful U.S. editor, Sarah, and the fantastic team at St. Martin's Press. I feel so lucky and honored to work with you all.

To my friend and agent, Lauren G., thank you, thank you, thank you. I couldn't do any of this without your guidance and support. To Lauren F., my Scholastic children's editor, thank you for all your encouragement. I'll never forget that lunchtime where, over some delicious sushi, you both listened to my brewing idea for an adult novel and told me I *had* to write it. It is thanks to my two wonderful Laurens that Sophie's story exists!

To my family and friends, thank you for supporting me through the exciting and terrifying process of writing my first adult fiction novel. Special thanks to those of you who gave me the great honor of asking me to be your bridesmaid. Thanks to you, I fell in love with weddings and found the inspiration to write this book. Particular thanks to Mekhla and John for answering all my many queries and guiding me through the wonderful details of your wedding.

To my bridesmaids—Chloe, Lizzie, Alex, Abi, Katie, Susie, Liv, and Annie—you guys are the best. Thank you for all you do.

Mum, Dad, Rob, Nat, Charlie, Jess, Sam, Lukey, Thomas,

Lily, and Ted—thank you for cheering me on, making me constantly laugh, and for always being there. What a corker of a clan. Big thanks go to my loyal canine companions, Dougie, Archie, Lara, West, and my little rescue, Bono, my perfect sidekick.

Finally, special thanks to Ben. 2020 may have put a small spanner in the works, but I can't wait for our big day whenever it comes along.

ABOUT THE AUTHOR

Imogen Forte

KATY BIRCHALL is the author of numerous books for young readers and a former editor for *Country Life* magazine. *The Secret Bridesmaid* is her first adult novel and her American debut. She studied English literature and linguistics at the University of Manchester and currently lives in London.

KatyBirchallAuthor.com

 @KatyBirchall

 @katybirchallauthor